TROPICAL BLUES

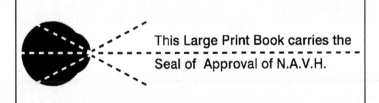

This Large Print Book carries the
Seal of Approval of N.A.V.H.

MOLLY DEWITT MYSTERIES

TROPICAL BLUES

SHERRYL WOODS

THORNDIKE PRESS
A part of Gale, a Cengage Company

GALE
A Cengage Company

Farmington Hills, Mich • San Francisco • New York • Waterville, Maine
Meriden, Conn • Mason, Ohio • Chicago

Copyright © 2018 by Harlequin Books S. A.
Hot Property © 1992 by Sherryl Woods.
Hot Secret © 1992 by Sherryl Woods.
Molly Dewitt Mysteries.
First published as Hot Property and Hot Secret by Dell Publishing, 1992.
Thorndike Press, a part of Gale, a Cengage Company.

LIBRARY OF CONGRESS CIP DATA ON FILE.
CATALOGUING IN PUBLICATION FOR THIS BOOK
IS AVAILABLE FROM THE LIBRARY OF CONGRESS

ISBN-13: 978-1-4328-5833-9 (hardcover)

Published in 2019 by arrangement with Harlequin Books S.A.

Printed in Mexico
2 3 4 5 6 7 23 22 21 20 19

CONTENTS

Dear Friends,

It's been many, many years since I first wrote the four-book Molly DeWitt Mysteries series. I was in love with the sort of bantering, romantic dynamic found back then on TV shows like *Moonlighting.* Even more, I wanted to write about the Miami area, from Key Biscayne, where I live now, to South Beach, where I lived when I first moved to South Florida.

I'm absolutely delighted to have these lighthearted romantic mysteries back in stores after so many years, especially in two-in-one volumes that will give you an opportunity to savor two stories at a time.

In this book you'll meet Molly, a single mom, and the very sexy detective Michael O'Hara in *Hot Property* as they work together — often at cross-purposes — to solve a murder in Molly's condominium complex. And in *Hot Secret,* they'll be at it again on South Beach to solve the murder of a Hollywood film director.

Hopefully you'll love getting to know Molly and Michael and be looking for two more stories in *Rough Seas.* Welcome to one of my favorite places in the world — sunny, tropical Miami.

All best,

Sherryl Woods

■ ■ ■ ■

HOT PROPERTY

■ ■ ■ ■

1

Key Biscayne, Florida
1992

Discovering a corpse first thing in the morning shot the hell out of Molly DeWitt's plans for getting to the office early. Outside the condominium's wall-to-wall sliding glass doors, wispy clouds scudded across a near-perfect spring sky. Faced with death, Molly had the irrational feeling that those clouds should have had the decency to shade the sun. Instead the unrelenting light streamed into the Ocean Manor cardroom, illuminating the murdered man in a macabre spotlight. She stood frozen in the doorway, her gaze fastened on the glistening serrated knife sticking out of Allan Winecroft's back. The bloodstain surrounding it had absolutely ruined his designer polo shirt, which had once been the golden color of melted butter. It now looked as if it had been tie-dyed.

11

Swallowing hard and staring at the mess, Molly thought about all those new condominium rules legislating absolute tidiness in all of the public areas. Allan Winecroft had drafted every one of them. Little had he known that he was about to become the rules' worst offender. The irony of that didn't escape her. In fact, that little glimmer of gallows humor was about the only thing keeping her from screaming her head off, not so much in fear as in frustration. She was really getting tired of murders, especially in her own backyard.

Less than six months earlier Molly had sold her lovely Spanish-style house in an older bayside section of Miami because of the burglaries and because a Colombian drug dealer had been shot to death under the corner streetlamp just outside her door. She'd been watching the news at the time.

It had been a fairly routine news night, actually. There had been another home invasion robbery in Fort Lauderdale and another record haul of cocaine discov ered on a decrepit fishing boat in the Miami River. More AIDS-infected needles had been found near a school playground. The sound of shots had sent Molly diving for the floor. When her knees hit the tile, she'd spent about ten seconds cursing at the pain, then reached for the phone and called a real estate agent. She'd figured someone else could summon the police.

The minute a deal for the house had been struck she'd begun looking for someplace safe for herself and her eight-year-old son. The thought of leaving South Florida had never once occurred to her, only getting away from that jinxed house where even her marriage at the end had been almost criminal in its polite emptiness. Beyond that, though, she loved Miami's ethnic diversity, its vibrancy, even its conflicts. There was a passionate undercurrent here that either invaded the soul or robbed you blind. She wanted the passion, but was determined to minimize the danger. How many TVs and stereos and VCRs could she be expected to replace in one lifetime anyway?

In practically no time at all, she had chosen Key Biscayne. Not only was the island beautiful, but more important it was a relatively safe haven compared to Miami. Bumper stickers, faded navy blue with yellow lettering, proclaimed it PARADISE FOUND. Like all bumper sticker philosophy, the phrase held more than a grain of truth.

Only a fifteen-minute drive from downtown Miami, Key Biscayne was a world apart in attitude. The old-timers on the island, in fact, were still bemoaning the loss of the drawbridge. That bridge had intimidated most criminals. They had stayed away for fear of being caught on the wrong side with police on their heels and a yawning emptiness over Biscayne Bay ahead of them. Now an almost blinding white span climbed into the sky and curved down again, providing three lanes of clear sailing back to the mainland. The new bridge had provided easier access for developers, beachgoers, and criminals alike.

It also made Key Biscayne convenient to Molly's job. The Miami/Dade Film Commission office, which had inexplicably been made part of the parks department, was housed in the old gatehouse of the famed Vizcaya estate, practically at the end of the Rickenbacker Causeway. She could be there in exactly twelve minutes, ten if she ignored the forty-five-mile-an-hour speed limit the way everyone else did.

Having decided on Key Biscayne, Molly chose Ocean Manor partly because of its view of the Atlantic and mostly because it had beepers and Medco security keys for every entrance, plus guards at the gate, guards at the door, and a security chief who was a former Nicaraguan freedom fighter with a nasty, intimidating scar on his cheek.

Too bad one of those guards hadn't been on duty in the cardroom last night.

Although Molly was tempted to sneak right back into the elevator and pretend she'd never left her apartment, her conscience wouldn't let her. Perhaps it had something to do with the fact that the murder weapon happened to have come from her own kitchen. She recalled the last time she'd seen the knife. Drucilla Winecroft, the dead man's wife, had been using it to slice the frosted double fudge cake served following last night's heated bridge competition. The couple had lost.

Molly felt it was probably important to point out that the Winecrofts were avid bridge players. She wasn't. In fact, she was barely adequate, with bidding skills more suited to an auction than a bridge table. She had agreed at the last minute to substitute for an ailing neighbor. Within minutes she had vowed never again to be trapped into playing opposite the competitive pair. Their constant bickering over strategy throughout the evening had set her nerves on edge. If the game had gone on much longer, Molly might have been tempted to kill both of them herself. Even so, it was impossible to imagine that Drucilla had

15

been so irate after the defeat that she'd stabbed her husband in retribution for the crummy bid he'd made in the final hand.

Attuned to the crackling tension between the couple, Molly had been very careful not to gloat as she'd laid her winning trump card — a paltry deuce — on the table. She hadn't stuck around for the debate over who the real dummy had been or for her serving of cake.

Perhaps she should have stayed, she thought as she stared at the dead man. Perhaps if she'd lingered long enough, the murder weapon would have been washed and dried and back in her kitchen where it belonged instead of stuck between the shoulder blades of the controversial president of the Ocean Manor condominium association. She didn't envy the person who had to come up with a list of suspects. Allan was hated equally by everyone except the tight coalition of residents who'd maneuvered him into office. Some suggested the election had been about as valid and free of ballot-box stuffing as those held in many reluctantly democratic Third World countries.

Without moving an inch farther into the room, Molly glanced around. There was no sign of a struggle. Not so much as a rattan chair or a chintz-covered cushion was out of place at any of the half-dozen card tables. Someone had wiped off the Formica-topped bar, clearing away the remnants of the bridge game refreshments. Even the trash can had been emptied of paper plates and cups. She had to assume the players had done all that before leaving the previous night, probably at Allan's insistence. If it had been left to the cleaning staff, and they had been in this morning to tidy up, surely they would have mentioned the body. The manager was a stickler for discretion, but even he would expect them to acknowledge a dead man. Besides, there were a few cashews ground into the pale-peach carpet, which meant no one had been in to vacuum.

Molly wished she'd paid more attention to those college lessons in deductive reasoning. Since he was still wearing the same clothes he'd had on the previous night, the only conclusion she could reach was that Allan Winecroft had been killed after the games ended and all the card players except the killer had gone back to their own apartments. Unless they'd all stood around and watched, which she doubted. Most of them liked to be in bed by midnight, so they could make their 8:00 a.m. tennis games or tee times. In fact, someone was probably pacing the marble-floored lobby in pricey sneakers right this minute waiting for Allan to show up.

Molly knew enough about crime scenes and murder investigations — mostly from TV and film scripts — to guess that this was going to be a very long morning. Steadying herself, she walked to the security desk in the lobby and announced . . . nothing. She couldn't seem to squeak out so much as a single word. *Dead* or *murder* would have been sufficient, but she had to settle for pointing down the hall. Apparently she looked convincingly desperate. Security Chief Nestor Perez hefted his dark-green pants over his pot belly and ambled off in the right direction. Within minutes she heard the excited babble of Spanish over his walkie-talkie. Guards suddenly appeared from every which way, running now. Lord knew who was left to open the gate for the police, who she devoutly hoped would be arriving at any minute.

When Nestor returned, he spewed what sounded like a barrage of questions at her. Molly stared at him blankly. It wasn't that she was still speechless. It was simply that her understanding of Spanish failed her when the words came at her too fast.

"Despacio, por favor," she pleaded, sinking

onto the bright chintz cushions of the lobby sofa. "Slowly."

"*Sí, sí,*" he promised, his head bobbing. "*¿Qué pasa?*" He gestured wildly toward the cardroom.

Molly shook her head. "I have no idea what happened. When I left last night, everyone was eating cake. My cake, as a matter of fact. It was double fudge, from some Junior League cookbook my mother gave me as a wedding present. I baked it after work. I promised Brian a slice to take to school, but I forgot to take the leftovers upstairs. I ran down this morning to get them to put in his lunch box, but it was too late. I guess it was too late. Actually I forgot all about looking for the cake, once I saw the body. Allan is dead, isn't he?"

Nestor's expression grew increasingly puzzled as she babbled on and on, uncharacteristically unable to form a simple declarative sentence.

"*¿Qué?*" he said finally. The scar on his face was drawn tight.

Molly sighed and shortened her response. "I don't know what happened."

He patted her hand, the gesture awkward but sympathetic. The scar curved with his smile like an elongated dimple. "Is okay, Mrs. DeWitt. Police come soon."

He sounded almost as relieved by the prospect as she was. "God, I hope so," she said fervently.

Nestor left her to her prayers and headed back to the action down the hall.

"Hey, Mom! Are you down here?"

Molly recognized her son's voice and jumped up, racing toward the cardroom. The thought of Brian stumbling across Allan Winecroft's body panicked her. He'd probably be traumatized for life. She'd spent days thanking God that he'd been with his father the night of the murder outside their former home. She drew in a deep breath now, preparing herself to deal with his shock. He saw her coming and ran to meet her. He skidded to a halt on the marble floor, a freckle-faced kid with a gap-toothed smile and blue eyes sparkling with excitement. He looked anything but traumatized.

"Hey, Mom, did you know there's a dead man in the cardroom? Who is it? Can I see? Juan and Nestor said I had to ask you. So can I? I never saw a dead guy before."

Molly winced. When had her child become so bloodthirsty? Was it cartoons or the evening news tht had done it? Or maybe Nestor's endless reminiscences about the violence of the revolution back home? He was particularly proud of a couple of bloody ambushes he'd led.

"No, you may not see," she said firmly.

Brian obviously took the denial as nothing more than a minor setback. "What happened? Did he have a heart attack? There are a lot of old guys around here. I'll bet that's it. He had a heart attack, right?"

"No." Molly wondered exactly what the psychology textbooks had to say about explaining murdered neighbors to an eight-year-old. The textbooks probably couldn't help with a kid like Brian. He was precocious and wise beyond his years, his IQ in a range that intimidated the daylights out of her. Witness the fact that at the moment he was far more curious than scared. Maybe you had to be thirty to be shaken. Not that she was that old, but she'd been trying the age on for size ever since her twenty-ninth birthday. It still didn't fit. Fortunately, she had another four months to get used to it. God, she was still rambling.

"Why don't you meet Kevin and walk to school this morning," she suggested. When textbook answers eluded her, she'd grown into the habit of relying on evasive tactics. "I'm probably going to be tied up here awhile."

"Heck, no," Brian said. He peered at her

intently. "You don't look so good, Mom. You aren't gonna be sick, are you? Was it really gross in there?"

"Gross enough," she muttered under her breath.

Brian followed her back to the sofa. He sat next to her and slid his hand into hers. "It's going to be okay, Mom."

She hugged him. "Yes, it is. Now, please, won't you go on to school?" As soon as the words were out of her mouth, she knew she should have made them sound more like an order. The truth of the matter was she didn't want him to go. Brian kept her grounded in reality. There was a lot to be thankful for in her life, but this feisty, independent kid of hers was at the top of the list.

He shook his head. "You can take me later. I'll write a note and you can sign it."

Molly glanced at him ruefully. How had she managed to raise a child who thought he was the parent? "Thank you."

Suddenly his expression grew worried. "Mom, we're not going to have to move again, are we?"

Since she had no idea where they would go next if all these guards couldn't protect them from murder, she shook her head. "No. We're not moving."

A relieved smile spread across his face. "Good. I finally figured out how to ace the tests in this school. I'd hate to have to start all over with some other teacher."

Just then two green-and-white Metro-Dade police cars roared into the circular driveway, followed by the bright yellow Fire-Rescue ambulance. Local Key Biscayne officers arrived, though they'd followed Miami-Dade's lead. It was, indeed, a homicide. At the sound of all the sirens, Nestor rushed back.

Practically delirious with self-importance, he led the police and the paramedics through the fancy lobby toward the crime scene at a clip that had him puffing before they hit the turn in the corridor. Molly briefly considered following them but decided they'd find her when they needed her. She had no particular desire to take one last look at Allan Winecroft's body, much less to get into a sparring match with Brian over why he couldn't go with her.

As she waited, two couples left for the tennis courts and one man, briefcase in hand, left for the office. All of them smiled politely. None of them bothered to question the presence of all the police. It had been Molly's observation since moving in that apartment dwellers tended to avoid overtly poking their noses into their neighbors' business. Condo and island politics gave them more than enough to gossip about over breakfast at the packed Doughnut Gallery counter.

Thirty minutes later, a muddy Jeep van turned in to the crowded drive. After an instant's hesitation while he considered the limited options, the driver wedged the oversize vehicle into the too small space between the last police car and the garage entrance. The next person hoping to get into the garage was going to have a conniption. Either the Jeep's driver didn't know Miami driving conditions or he had a death wish. Maybe he just had good car insurance.

The man who emerged was drop-dead-gorgeous, an unfortunate turn of phrase this morning, she realized, but accurate. Molly considered warning him about the parking risk he'd taken, just to save his handsome neck.

He had dark hair, dark eyes, a dark suit, and a dark expression. Actually she wasn't all that sure about the eyes. They were hidden behind a pair of silvery sunglasses that reflected everything but the wearer's emotions. Molly pegged him as a cop.

After a muffled conversation with the nervous guard Nestor had posted at the door, he headed straight for the cardroom.

Thirty minutes later he was back again. This time he came straight toward Molly. His tie wasn't quite as neat as it had been, but beyond that he was as unruffled and businesslike as a banker about to conduct an interview for a loan. He'd removed the sunglasses, but he held them as if he couldn't wait to shove them back into place.

"You're Mrs. DeWitt?"

"Yes."

"Michael O'Hara. I'm with the Metro homicide division. I'd like to ask you a few questions."

"O'Hara?" She tested the Irish name and tried to reconcile it with the distinctly Latin appearance and faint Spanish accent. She couldn't.

"It's a long story," he said, apparently guessing her confusion.

Since Molly really wanted something to take her mind off Allan Winecroft's murder, she considered asking him to indulge her by telling the story now. In detail. She decided against it.

"Brian, why don't you go get your things ready for school," she said instead. "We'll leave as soon as I'm finished here."

"But, Mom . . ."

"Go. Be back in fifteen minutes and bring

my purse."

"Couldn't I just ask one question?" he pleaded.

"One," she agreed.

He cast a suspicious look at the policeman. To the detective's credit, he withstood the scrutiny patiently. "If you're really a cop," Brian said, "where's your gun?"

It was an apt question, since Michael O'Hara's attire was considerably more stylish than the beige-and-brown Metro-Dade uniforms. If he had his gun in the standard blank patent leather holster, it certainly wasn't visible underneath the tailored jacket of his black pin-striped suit. This man was dressed for dinner at Les Violins and, except for the slightly askew tie, far too fastidious to be packing the bulge of an automatic weapon.

Detective O'Hara's smile was every bit as devastating as Molly had anticipated. "Don't worry, son. I can get to it, when I need it. Want to check my badge, instead?"

"Heck, no. Timmy Rogers brought his dad's to school once. It was no big deal. But I've never seen a gun up close before."

Molly nearly groaned aloud. She wondered if she ought to consult a shrink about this fascination with guns and dead men. Definitely, she decided, but later. Right now, she just wanted to get this interrogation over with and get to work where she could deal with men who just wanted locations for fictional TV murders.

"Enough, Brian. I said one question. You've asked it. Now move it."

He cast one last, longing look at the detective, but Molly's stern tone discouraged argument . . . for a change. "Yeah, okay," he grumbled and left, feet dragging in protest.

When Brian had gone, Detective O'Hara claimed the seat he'd vacated next to her. She couldn't help noticing that the man had great thighs, the thick, muscled kind ballplayers got from hunkering down behind home plate. The observation startled her, not because he did, but because she'd noticed. She hadn't had much time or inclination to think about sex lately, but suddenly it was almost impossible to think about anything else, even the murder.

Why was it that some men could turn up the female thermostat just by walking into a room? Worse, why did it always seem to happen under impossible circumstances? This man was here to investigate a murder, for God's sakes. *His* mind certainly wasn't on sex. She glanced just to be sure. He was scrutinizing his notes, not her thighs. Just as she'd thought, businesslike.

"So," he said. "Tell me what happened." His tone was as casual as a first date's inquiring about a movie plot. His eyes missed nothing. Humorless, relentless, those eyes made her very nervous. She was accustomed to flirting glances, even cool dismissals, but not this cold assessment. She almost wished he'd put those sunglasses of his back on.

"What happened when?" she asked, rattled by the distrust she sensed. She was used to being viewed as one of the good guys, an upstanding citizen.

"You choose."

If she hadn't been the target, Molly would have congratulated him on his interrogation technique. He'd left her all sorts of room to hang herself. Since she wasn't guilty, she took a deep breath, started with the bridge game, and brought him up to date. "And that's all I know," she concluded ten minutes later. Apparently he didn't think so. He still had questions.

"Was he still fighting with his wife when you left?"

"Yes."

"About the bridge game?"

"Yes," she said slowly.

He was all over the hesitation. "What else?"

"Well, if he weren't in there on the floor with a knife in his back, I might never have thought of this, but in retrospect it seems as if their argument wasn't really about bridge at all. I mean the words were, but . . ."

He pinned her with skeptical brown eyes. "Is this one of those women's intuition things or something concrete?"

"Don't dismiss women's intuition. I read a script just the other night . . ."

"A script? You're an actress?"

"You don't have to say it as if it's only one step up from working the streets," she retorted. "No. I am not an actress. I work for the Film Commission. We read scripts in advance sometimes so we can help the production company find locations. Anyway, in this script if the stupid policeman had paid attention to the star witness's intuition . . ." She caught the expression on his face. "No offense."

"None taken," he said, though it didn't sound as if he meant it.

"Anyway, do you want to hear this or not?"

"By all means, guess away."

She ignored the patronizing tone, though it was dimming his attractiveness considerably. "I can't say what it was. It was just this undercurrent. If you're married, you must know what I mean."

"Divorced," he said tersely, but his tone was suddenly less skeptical. "I think I see. Keep going."

"Okay. Nobody gets that upset about bridge unless they've been fighting about something more serious, something they don't dare fight about in public."

"But you have no idea what this other argument might have been about?"

"No. I could ask around, though. Some of the other bridge players probably know them better than I do."

He was shaking his head before she finished the offer. "Let me ask the questions, okay? This is a murder investigation, not some TV script. You stay out of it," he ordered Molly in the tone of a man instructing the little woman to remain dutifully in the kitchen. It was his first serious mistake. Molly did not take kindly to orders, even those intended to be in her own best interests. It was a knee-jerk reaction, she supposed. It wasn't as if the man were challenging her civil rights, after all. Even so, she responded to the arrogance with her finest sarcasm. She figured he'd get the idea that she wasn't pleased.

"Much to my regret I found the body," she reminded him. "To my further regret the murder weapon matches the set of knives in my kitchen. I'd say I'm already in the middle of it."

"You said you left early last night and that the knife was still there. You dutifully called the police when you found the body and waited around to be questioned. Unless you have some motive you haven't mentioned, you're probably not a prime suspect. Unless you have a license, you're not an investigator. That puts you in a league with Nancy Drew. I don't need amateurs meddling with this case. Forget you ever stumbled on the body this morning."

"A fat lot of good that'll do you when I have to testify in court." She didn't bother to mention that she wasn't in the habit of discovering dead men first thing in the morning and that, therefore, she couldn't be quite as cavalier about it as he seemed to be. She was likely to recall Allan Winecroft's untimely demise for some time to come. She would not be able to forget it until the killer had been revealed and safely stashed behind bars.

"Back-burner it, then," Detective O'Hara advised. "Go bake some cookies or something."

Already at the end of her patience, Molly bristled. He hadn't suggested that she go on to work. No. Just *go bake cookies*. His

31

whole demeanor screamed of generations of machismo. Hal DeWitt at his worst before the divorce couldn't have matched the implied put-down. Molly's chin automatically rose a defiant notch.

"Fine. This evening, when I get home from work, I will bake chocolate chip cookies. Then I will invite the neighbors in and serve them *café cubano* and these freshly baked cookies. If the name Allan Winecroft happens to creep into the conversation, I will ignore it. If one of them confesses, I won't hear it. Will that make you happy?"

He ran his fingers through already unruly black hair, in a gesture she'd begun to recognize about three seconds into the interrogation. "No, Mrs. DeWitt, that will irritate the hell out of me."

She smiled. "Perfect. Oh, and you may call me Molly."

"I'm not going to call you at all." He was gritting his teeth.

"We'll see."

As she stalked off, head held high, her waiting son observed, "Mom, I'm not real sure it's such a good idea to tick off a cop."

"The man investigates murders, Brian. He doesn't commit them."

"Yeah, right. You must not have seen the way he looked at you."

She had, actually. She'd been hoping it was lust. It would improve her mood considerably to see that such lust went unrequited.

2

The more Molly thought about the marital rift theory she'd suggested to Detective O'Hara, the more she wanted to check it out herself. There had been a definitely hostile undercurrent to the tension between her bridge opponents. She'd had enough battles with her own ex-husband in public to recognize the symptoms of a volatile relationship gone sour and the wasted attempts to camouflage it. Maybe she was afflicted with the same bloodthirsty curiosity as her son, after all. She would give almost anything to be there when the police interviewed Drucilla Winecroft about her husband's murder. She considered racing the detective to the woman's apartment, but decided that would only increase his displeasure with her. Besides, what would she say to the widow?

I'm so sorry that Allan's dead. Could I get my knife back?

Or perhaps, *Drucilla, dear, did the knife slip when you were cutting the cake?*

Neither seemed quite right. Nor was she able to muster up the sincere sympathy of a close friend. She'd known the couple only casually before last night. She doubted that her winning hand had endeared her to them. En route to the car, she considered what she did know.

Though he was short and overweight, Allan Winecroft had always managed to create a distinguished impression. He dressed elegantly. Even his sports clothes looked as if they'd been ordered from a British tailor with understated taste. Only a single strand or two of gray had dared to thread its way through his impeccably styled, sun-bleached hair. Molly had heard that he'd been some sort of hotshot broker, maybe stocks, maybe land. For all she knew, it could have been frozen foods, brokered to grocery chains, that had made him rich and allowed him to retire comfortably before his sixtieth birthday. He had turned sixty-two several weeks earlier. Drucilla had thrown a lavish celebration.

As for Drucilla, she spent her days playing tennis, her evenings playing bridge, and any leftover time writing checks to local charities. Word was that Allan's money had bought her seats on several cultural organization boards since they'd taken up residence in Florida from October through April three years earlier. They spent summers on Long Island — Bridgehampton, East Hampton, one of those places where the rich summered and continued their games of tennis and bridge. In her spare time during those months, she had various body parts lifted until her skin was taut as a twenty-year-old's and her eyebrows were almost up to her carefully tended hairline. Personally, Molly found the attempts to defy age and gravity a little pathetic.

She still wanted to talk to her.

"Wait here," she told Brian, impulsiveness winning out over discretion.

"Where are you going?"

"I forgot something."

"What?"

"My briefcase."

"I could get it, while you get the car."

She glared at Brian, which he didn't deserve. "I'll do it. Here, take the keys and wait in the car. It won't take a minute." If it took any longer than that, she was likely to come face-to-face with the detective in the corridor. As attractive as he was, it was not an encounter she cared to have. She had a feeling he'd have a temper to go along with

36

that hot-blooded Latin machismo of his.

After casting a quick glance in the direction of the cardroom to make sure that Detective O'Hara was still occupied, Molly raced to the elevator. For once it was on the lobby level. It whisked her to the eighth floor before she could fully formulate her questions for Drucilla.

The Winecrofts had bought two apartments facing the ocean and combined them into what Molly had heard described as a showcase of excess. No one had ever explained to her satisfaction what they did with two full kitchens, especially since they never seemed to eat at home. At any rate, she approached the special double doors they'd had installed and rang the chiming bell, also their own touch. Most people in the condominium had settled for the brass knockers installed by the builder ten years earlier.

Molly braced herself to deal with the weeping widow. When a petite Salvadoran housekeeper with a perfectly placid expression opened the door instead, she momentarily was taken aback.

"Is Mrs. Winecroft in? I'm a neighbor, Molly DeWitt. We played bridge together last night. I just wanted to express my condolences."

Round brown eyes stared at her in confusion. *"Sí,"* the woman said finally, but without apparent comprehension. She struggled for words. "She asleep." She folded her hands together and rested her head against them in case her meaning wasn't clear. "Asleep, *sí?*"

"Asleep," Molly repeated. "You mean she doesn't know?"

"¿Qué?"

She didn't know, Molly surmised. Neither of them knew, not the housekeeper and definitely not the sleeping widow, unless she was a cold-hearted bitch. Since Molly did not have the least desire to be the one who broke the news, she waved politely. "I'll see her later."

She stepped straight back into the waiting arms of Detective O'Hara. She knew they were his because she recognized the suit. To her disgust, she realized she wouldn't mind lingering longer so that she could recognize his embrace. In case it happened again. Under other circumstances, that is. It wasn't men who betrayed women, she decided in disgust. It was women's own undiscriminating female hormones that lured them into relationships with the wrong men.

"Imagine meeting you here," he said. He didn't sound overjoyed.

"She doesn't know," Molly whispered with a certain amount of urgency as the house-keeper cast shy, appreciative glances at the detective. Molly felt a little less guilty knowing that his appeal was universal.

Not the least bit sidetracked by his hormones he said, "Unless she did it and took a sedative."

Molly grimaced at the cynicism, even as she admired the astuteness behind it. "I never thought of that."

"That's why I'm a policeman and you're a whatever it is you are."

He still didn't sound especially interested in being more informed about her career. She supposed it was extraneous. However, since she was proud of it and irritated by his attitude, she told him anyway. "An administrative assistant."

"Does that pay better than secretary?"

"Are you intentionally trying to provoke me or does it just come naturally?"

"I'm trying to conduct a murder investigation."

"Then maybe you shouldn't be so quick to insult a witness."

Amusement dashed across his lips so quickly, she almost missed it. Fortunately, since she'd been considering slugging him in the teeth at the time, her gaze had been

39

fastened on her target. "Unless I missed something earlier, you didn't actually see the murder, right?" he said.

He had her there. "Well, no," she admitted with great reluctance. She could see where this was headed. It was not going in her favor.

"Then as a witness, you're of limited value to the case. I can spare you."

"The state attorney might not see it that way."

"Then let that office deal with you."

The housekeeper's round, dark eyes were following this exchange with evident fascination. "Look," Molly said finally. "This isn't getting us anywhere. You don't want me here. My son needs to get to school. I'm off." She meant to appear gracious about it. She sounded miffed. Which she was. A savvy detective wouldn't miss it. From the amused expression back on Michael O'Hara's face, he hadn't.

Before she could take the first step, she heard Drucilla inquire sleepily, "Conchita, who's out there at this ungodly hour?"

Ungodly? Ten o'clock? Molly hadn't slept that late since college, when she'd scheduled all of her classes after noon to accommodate her need for rest after waiting tables until midnight. She delayed her departure to catch a glimpse of the woman who thought their mid-morning arrival so ill timed.

Pulling a bright orange silk wrapper around her, Drucilla swept into place at the housekeeper's side. Though she appeared only half awake, her makeup was flawless and not one strand of her auburn hair was mussed. Unless her hairdresser lacquered it with acrylic, she'd worked to achieve that perfection.

"Molly, what on earth?" Her gaze traveled from Michael O'Hara's polished loafers to his rumpled hair . . . approvingly. Another casualty, Molly thought. The man probably had an ego the size of Texas.

"Who are you?" Drucilla inquired.

Her eyes flared slightly when he introduced himself and flashed his badge for her inspection. "A policeman? How fascinating. Come in, won't you? *Café, por favor,* Conchita."

Molly hesitated, uncertain of her own welcome. Drucilla waved her inside. "Come, Molly. I assume you're together. Did someone steal a deck of cards last night?"

As she stepped inside, Molly cast a triumphant look at the detective. She wasn't actually thrilled at the prospect of being there when Drucilla came unglued at the news of her husband's death, but the idea of being a

41

thorn in Michael O'Hara's side made her morning. For an instant she thought he was going to dismiss her, but instead he motioned her toward the living room, graciously, as a matter of fact. Molly took it as a deliberate comment on her own surly manners.

In the huge, sunny room, which offered sweeping views of the ocean, Molly had to control the desire to wander. She felt as if she'd stumbled into an art exhibit. Competing with the Atlantic on the east was an entire wall filled with a single modern painting in splashes of sea green, sky blue and sunset orange. It lacked subtlety. It did, however, provide the room with its color scheme, all shades of blue, green and orange designed to enhance Drucilla's own vibrant coloring. Lush plants decorated the balcony. Inside, more plants provided the backdrop to pedestals topped with sculpture. Every surface was crammed with jade carvings, twists of copper, and hammered tin. Though she couldn't identify the abstract designs, Molly suspected none were ashtrays. She stared at an ivory piece that appeared to be . . . intimate. She blushed when Michael O'Hara caught the direction of her fascinated gaze. It was the second time that morning she caught the faint twitch of stubborn lips as he fought a smile. It was the second time she considered assaulting a police officer.

He turned back to their hostess. Or his chief suspect, to be more precise. "Mrs. Winecroft, I understand you were playing bridge with Mrs. DeWitt and several others last night."

"Yes."

"What time did you leave the cardroom?"

"Shortly before midnight, I would say. Why?"

"And what did you do then?"

"I came upstairs and went to bed. Why?"

"Was your husband with you?"

"No. He stayed behind to talk business."

Molly noticed that Drucilla didn't bother to ask why. Apparently she'd finally realized this was going to be a one-sided interrogation. The parameters had been set. She'd been assigned to give the answers. The detective was the only one who got to ask questions.

"With whom was he talking?" O'Hara continued.

"I don't recall. Henry Davison, I suppose. Juan Gonzalez stopped by for coffee. He doesn't play bridge." She glanced at Molly. "Who were the other men there last night?"

"Tyler Jenkins and Roy Meeks," Molly

responded, then wondered why Drucilla was being so deliberately vague about a group of people who obviously played together regularly.

"Yes, of course." Her dismissive tone indicated the two were of little importance. Since Roy Meeks had been Molly's winning partner, she could understand the reluctance to acknowledge him. As for the others, her forgetfulness made little sense.

"And did your husband have business with those men?"

"No, I don't believe so. They were just chatting about the stock market, the new hotel here on the island, things like that. General conversation. Really, Detective, I don't understand what you're getting at here."

"Did you and your husband argue last night?"

This time Drucilla cast an anxious look at Molly. Long, smooth, ageless fingers, tipped with bright-red nails and adorned with impressive chunky diamonds, worried the sash of her dressing gown into a knot. "No more than usual. After thirty-five years of marriage, we have our ups and downs."

"Which are you having now?"

Drucilla calmly picked up her cup of coffee, but couldn't disguise the shaking of her hand. The hot liquid splashed on her silk gown, staining it in a way that reminded Molly all too vividly of the brown stain soaking Allan's shirt. Drucilla bit back an oath, waved off the detective's offer of a handkerchief, and with supreme effort gathered her composure around her as if it were a mink stole. There was barely a tinkle of china against china as cup met saucer.

"Detective, I have a luncheon to go to today. If you're finished."

"Not quite yet. What time did your husband return to the apartment?"

"I have no idea. As I said, I went to bed. Now, really, I must get ready."

"You may want to change your plans."

Drucilla stared at him in astonishment. "Why would I want to do that?"

"I'm very sorry to have to tell you this, Mrs. Winecroft, but your husband is dead."

The blurted announcement, coming during questions that under other circumstances might have been no more than polite chitchat, took even Molly by surprise. The man's timing sucked. She stared at Drucilla, expecting hysterics. When none came, she decided maybe O'Hara had accomplished exactly what he'd set out to do: get a completely honest reaction.

Drucilla appeared to have been stunned

into silence. Time stood still for a heartbeat. Then confusion flickered in her green eyes. The announcement was either news or she was a better actress than the celebrity model currently starring in the television pilot being shot on Miami Beach.

"Allan? Dead? That can't be." Her voice was barely above a murmur. There was a distinct catch in it. "His heart is fine. He just had his physical. I'm sure, absolutely certain the doctor said he was okay. Where . . . ?"

She stared helplessly at Molly, as if looking for confirmation. At this hint of vulnerability, contrived or not, Molly was suddenly overcome with more compassion than she'd expected to feel. She moved to Drucilla's side and clasped her fidgeting hands. They were icy cold. There were still no tears.

Though his voice had softened, Michael O'Hara was relentless now, imparting information faster than the just-bereaved widow could accept it. "It wasn't a heart attack. Your husband was murdered, Mrs. Winecroft. He was stabbed, right here at Ocean Manor. I really need you to help me discover who did it."

Drucilla trembled as his words hit home. Any help she was likely to offer was going to be delayed. With one quiet gasp, she proceeded to faint in Molly's arms.

"Well, that was certainly tactful," Molly said, as she patted the woman's wrists.

He shrugged off her indignation. "I've learned it's better just to get the bad news over with."

"Then why didn't you tell her the minute you walked in the door. 'Hello, your husband's dead.' That sort of thing?"

"I wanted a couple of uncensored answers first."

"Is that legal?"

"Legal enough."

Molly cast a skeptical glance at him and wondered what the Supreme Court had to say about that. She decided — wisely, probably — to keep her inexpert legal opinions to herself.

"Get Conchita. Maybe she has some smelling salts or something. Unless, of course, you have time for her to languish like this until she comes to on her own."

He started to argue, then shook his head and headed in the direction of the kitchen. Molly heard him and the housekeeper conversing in fluent Spanish. When he reappeared, he was carrying a damp cloth and smelling salts. Conchita was trailing along behind, wringing her hands and muttering what sounded like prayers in rapid-fire

Spanish that eluded Molly's comprehension.

As much as she wanted to stay and see the scene played out, Molly knew if she didn't get to work in the next half hour, she was very likely to end up every bit as dead as Allan Winecroft. She didn't want to look that bad the next time Michael O'Hara saw her.

Before she could go, though, Drucilla began to come to. She blinked once, then impatiently pushed away the smelling salts.

"Damn Tyler Jenkins," she said. She said it fervently enough that there was little doubt about who she thought had murdered her husband.

3

Michael O'Hara didn't have the smug look of a man who'd just wrapped up a murder case in less time than it usually took to get a car emission system inspected in Dade County. Molly could practically see him mentally ticking off the evidence and comparing it to his own gut instincts. She certainly was.

Tyler Jenkins had access to the murder weapon. He had the opportunity. The only thing missing was a motive powerful enough to incite a sixty-eight-year-old man who'd once marched for peace to commit a cold-blooded murder. Personally, Molly was also struggling with the concept that a man just recovering from bypass surgery had enough strength to wield that knife in a deadly manner. The detective seemed equally skeptical without ever having met the man. Experience had apparently taught him to beware of quick, tidy solutions.

"Tell me why you think Tyler Jenkins is responsible for your husband's death," he suggested to Drucilla.

Drucilla appeared startled. "Oh, I doubt that Tyler killed him," she said. "The old goat wouldn't have the gumption."

Not by so much as the flicker of an eyelash did O'Hara indicate that he was disappointed or even surprised. Molly, however, had been hoping to have this whole thing wrapped up before she left for work.

"What then?" he said to Drucilla.

"Tyler was responsible for getting Allan to run for the presidency of the condominium association," Drucilla explained. "We haven't had a peaceful moment since that awful election. Just last week someone called in the middle of the night and threatened Allan."

Molly was stunned. She couldn't imagine any of her neighbors stooping to late-night threats. The residents of Ocean Manor were all relatively well-to-do, well educated, and presumably civilized. Her own modest income was probably pocket change to a majority of the owners. Many of them owned two residences, this one and an old family home up north or a summer place in a resort area such as Aspen or Vail or Newport. Many were South American or

European. Most seemed too busy perfecting their tans to indulge in such skulduggery.

Of course, she admitted, the election had been every bit as nasty as some hotly contested senatorial race. Campaign diatribe had been slipped under the doors on an almost nightly basis. And the contentious annual meeting had proved beyond a doubt that possessing money did not always imply an understanding of social niceties. Her good neighbors had fought like hellions over everything from wall sconces to cable TV. On second thought, perhaps Drucilla's claim wasn't so farfetched after all.

"Did he recognize the caller?" Molly asked. "Was he certain it was another resident?"

"That's what he said, but he didn't explain how he knew. He didn't want me worrying. He dismissed it as a childish prank by someone old enough to know better."

"And he didn't state the nature of the threat," Michael O'Hara said.

"No."

"Did he say whether it was specific, like a threat to slash his tires, or just a vague threat to get him in some way?"

"He didn't say, but it must have been a death threat. Isn't that obvious now?"

Molly certainly thought it was. The detective looked less convinced. The department must issue skepticism along with the badge, or maybe the fact that it was ingrained was what had made him choose to be a cop.

"Any other enemies?" he asked. "Old business rivals? Maybe he clashed with someone over a debt or gave someone bad business advice."

"I can't think of anyone. Allan was capable of irritating people. He had an abrasive personality, but I can't imagine him making anyone angry enough to drive them to murder."

The detective nodded. "If you think of anyone, you'll let me know."

"Certainly."

At the door, he paused for just an instant. "I really am very sorry, Mrs. Winecroft." There was a warmth in his eyes that hadn't been there before, a hint of genuine compassion. Molly had to revise her opinion of him all over again. He might be suspicious and cynical, but that was what he was paid for. Underneath the official act, he was not without sympathy.

He was, however, all business when he turned back to Molly. "Coming, Mrs. De-Witt?"

It sounded more like an order than a question. Because she had to get to work anyway — and only because of that — Molly dutifully followed him into the corridor. There was no point in lingering. Within the next hour there would be an endless parade of curious people along to console Drucilla. No doubt she'd want to change into more subdued attire before they arrived. Her scanty tears had barely streaked her makeup, and every coat of mascara was still right where she'd put it before greeting them, but that orange wrapper was a jarring note. Molly wondered if the killer would be among those offering condolences. The very thought made her shiver.

When the door had closed behind them, Michael stuffed his hands in his pockets and turned to Molly. "So, what'd you think?"

"You're asking me?" She was torn between shock and the heady sort of pleasure she always felt when some producer asked her opinion about his million-dollar script.

"You know her better than I do. Was it all an act?"

"If it was, it was a good one."

"Good, not perfect," he corrected. "She was supposedly asleep when you arrived, right?"

"That's what the housekeeper said."

"Then is it only the women I know who

take forever putting on their makeup?"

Molly shot him a look of grudging admiration. She saw exactly what he was getting at. "You think she was actually awake and expecting company. The police?"

"I was thinking more in terms of a lover."

Once again Molly understood why he'd reached detective status and she was an amateur. Her mind wasn't nearly devious enough.

"Have you heard any rumor to that effect?" he asked.

"No, but I've lived here only a short time. With my hours at work, I try to spend most of my evenings with my son. I know only a few neighbors really well and they're mostly the year-round folks." Once again it occurred to her to invite them all over for tea and an informal chat. That was what Nero Wolfe might have done, though he usually waited until he had the evidence to pin the murder on one of his guests.

As if he'd read her mind, Michael O'Hara said, "Don't go snooping around on your own. What were you doing at Mrs. Winecroft's apartment anyway?"

"I explained that. I wanted to pay my respects."

He regarded her skeptically. "So you said. At least you're consistent. You intrigue me, though, Mrs. DeWitt. For a woman who stumbled on a body this morning, you're awfully calm."

Calm? She was quaking inside, but years of practice had taught her to hide her fears. Since he seemed to find her self-control damaging, she admitted, "It's all a facade, Detective."

His intent, curious gaze locked with hers. "Really? It might be interesting to see what happens when that facade is stripped away."

Molly wasn't one bit sure, as he sauntered away, if he was interested as a man or as a cop. Then she wondered if it was even possible for a man like Michael O'Hara to separate the two.

Brian had a thousand questions about why Molly had been delayed. She forestalled them by stopping for breakfast and buying him French toast with powdered sugar sprinkled on it. It was his favorite and a rare treat. She sipped a cup of coffee while he ate. The place was still busy, but the islanders had gone, leaving the drugstore's three U-shaped counters to tourists. None of them had heard yet about the murder or Molly's connection to it, which left her with ten peaceful minutes to think about everything that had happened.

"Mom," Brian said, powdered sugar on his cheeks and milk on his upper lip, "who do you think killed Mr. Winecroft?"

She whirled around so fast, she almost spun off the stool. "Why do you think someone killed him? You didn't go back there, did you?"

Brian wiped the powdered sugar away with the back of his hand, ignoring the napkins in front of him. "Come on, Mom. With all the cops and everything, it doesn't exactly take a genius to figure it out. Why else would they come? Do you think we'll get fingerprinted?"

She'd wondered about that herself. Not Brian, of course. But there was every reason to anticipate that she would be, if only to eliminate which prints were hers on the murder weapon. "I suppose I might be," she admitted.

"But not me?"

"You weren't in there."

"Maybe Detective O'Hara would let me be, if he's not still mad at you. You could ask him."

Molly sighed. "Brian, I am not going to drag you off and have you fingerprinted just to add a little excitement to your life."

"It'd be great for show-and-tell. I'd probably get an A."

"If it takes being fingerprinted to earn a top grade, you just may have to settle for a B."

"I'll never get into some fancy school with lousy grades. Isn't that what you and Dad are always telling me?"

"Your father tells you that. I just want you to do your best."

"Maybe I could talk to Detective O'Hara myself."

"You do and I'll ground you for a year with no Saturday morning cartoons or video games."

Brian's eyes were wide as saucers by the time she'd finished the threat. "You really don't like that guy, do you?"

"He's just doing his job," she said, deciding a little circumspection was called for, especially since her feelings were oddly contradictory. Her son had been known to innocently blab her opinions far and wide. The prospect of his sharing his astonishing insights with the detective did not please her. In fact, before he shared any more with her, she hurried him off to school, a written excuse in hand. He'd drafted it himself, printing it neatly on lined notebook paper.

She should have had him jot one down for her as well. Her boss scowled ferociously when she finally walked in. Molly scowled right back at him. She was in no mood for one of his snits this morning.

"You're late," Vincent Gates announced unnecessarily. He glanced pointedly at the clock that hung on the wall opposite her desk in the cramped film office. It was twenty-five after eleven.

"I can tell time, Vince. Don't start on me. I've had an awful morning."

His management duty taken care of, he settled into his more familiar sulking posture. He reminded her of a pouting star, upset over an unflattering camera angle. "You've had an awful morning? If you'd been here, you'd know the real meaning of awful. The mayor's furious because he got caught in a traffic jam on the Rickenbacker Causeway."

"Which mayor and how is that our fault?"

"The county mayor. He's blaming us because it was caused by gawkers watching the filming of that new soft drink commercial."

Molly hadn't expected sympathy from Vince. The man had the sensitivity of a coconut shell. She had accepted that within a week after taking the job with the Miami/Dade Film Commission. He had one agenda in life, his own. Unless she'd been personally murdered in her sleep, he didn't think it should interfere with her work. It was pointless to belabor her own lousy morning.

"The sexist ad with all the women in bikinis?" she asked dutifully.

Vince glared at her. His own opinion of all the bouncing boobs was much more liberal. She was surprised he hadn't been out there gawking himself. Then, again, the producer had left a copy of the storyboards with him so he could indulge his fantasies at his leisure.

"That's the one," he confirmed. "I'm not sure if he was more upset about the slowdown on the causeway or because his view was blocked. On top of that Larry Milsap called. He needs the permits to shoot in Crandon Park no later than three. He's running over budget and they want him to finish up by the weekend. I can't find the damned things on your desk. I told him you'd run them over the minute you got in. I expected you hours ago," he added accusingly.

Molly lost patience. It rarely took longer than five minutes with Vince to accomplish that. "And I expected to be here hours ago. I was detained by a murder. I would have called, but they wouldn't let me near a phone. I guess it's only the accused who gets to make a phone call." Okay, so she was stretching the truth a little. Without missing a beat, she added, "I sent those permits to Larry last week. He's lost them again. I'll get him a new set."

Vince's irritated expression faltered. "Forget the permits for a minute. What's all this about a murder? Run it by me again."

The only thing Vince loved more than seducing women was gossip and intrigue. For the next minute or two, she had him right where she wanted him. "Only if you'll get me a very large cup of very strong coffee."

He didn't waste time protesting that serving coffee was beneath him. He grabbed the mug from her desk and filled it from the pot sitting on the credenza at the back of the conference room. "Drink. Then talk. Fast. We don't have all morning."

"Your concern is touching."

"Okay. Okay. I'm concerned. That goes without saying."

"Vince, almost every kind, compassionate thought you ever have, assuming you have any, goes without saying. Some of us would occasionally prefer to hear the words spoken aloud."

He blinked. "You're upset." He seemed startled by the concept. Since flashes of such insight were rare with him, she could understand why.

"Bingo," she confirmed.

"At me?"

"Among others."

"Why?"

"Vince, I started my day by discovering that our condo president had been stabbed in the back."

"So what? I thought you said he was a pompous ass. Isn't he the one who dug up all the rare tropical plants and replaced them with impatiens?"

"Please don't share what I thought of his gardening taste. At this point, it might be considered a motive."

"They don't know who did it?"

"They don't know who. They don't know why. The only thing they seem to know for sure is that I found the body and that he was killed with one of my knives."

"Holy shit!"

"That about sums it up."

"You want to go home?"

This time it was Molly's turn to gape in astonishment. Vincent was not in the habit of doling out leave time. "No, thanks," she said, wondering if she should have taken it just to establish a precedent.

"Oh." He hesitated. "Then I guess you

might as well take care of those permits."

She sighed. "Right away. By the way, if you'd get Jeannette to do the filing she was hired to do, you'd be able to find the permits yourself."

"I refuse to tangle with that woman."

Molly barely suppressed a grin. The Haitian clerk absolutely adored muttering imprecations that could be interpreted as curses. Vincent was convinced if she aimed one at him it would forever limit his prowess as a stud. He hadn't issued a direct order to Jeannette since her first week. When it suited him, he claimed it was Molly's job to run the office. It did not suit him, however, to pay her accordingly. Therefore, it frequently didn't suit her to run the office. Meanwhile the filing was stacking up.

Molly found the permits for Larry Milsap's Palm Productions and grabbed her purse. She stuck her head in Vince's office. "I'm off to see Milsap. If he calls, tell him . . ."

Guessing the snippy comment that was to come, Vince substituted his own more politically sound version. "I'll tell him we're absolutely thrilled to be of service. The man spends three hundred fifty thousand dollars a year on production in the county. Even if he wastes a small portion of our time, it's worth it."

"Then let him waste your time." She held out the permits.

"I have meetings all afternoon."

"You mean you're playing golf with some Hollywood producer again, hoping he'll let you on his set to ogle his starlets."

"I don't ogle."

"Like hell," she muttered, turning away to grab the ringing phone. "Yes."

"Molly, what the hell's going on?" her ex-husband demanded.

Molly had to swallow a groan. The day had just gone from bad to worse. When Hal DeWitt had that tone in his voice, it meant nothing but trouble.

"Could you be more specific?" she replied cautiously.

"I just heard about the murder. It's all over the goddamned radio. I told you moving there was a mistake, but would you listen? No, you had to prove yourself. Well, I'm telling you now, I want my son out of there."

"*Our* son," she reminded him furiously. "Brian is *our* son, though frankly, there are times when I regret your role in that more than I can tell you."

"I'm picking him up today."

"You do and I'll slap you with a court

order so fast it'll make your head spin." Her own head was pounding. There hadn't been one conversation since she and Hal divorced that he hadn't found some way to let her know how inept he thought she was, how unfit a mother. He'd threatened her with a custody battle so often, she should be used to it by now, but she wasn't. Even though she knew rationally that he didn't have a shred of evidence on his side and that the accusations were the unjustified slurs of a sick, pitiful man who thrived on demeaning her, it didn't stop her from trembling with fear.

"I have to go. We'll discuss this sometime when you can be more rational about it," she said. Her voice was calm and deliberate, but inside she quaked as she replaced the phone in its cradle.

"You okay?" Vince asked.

"Just fine," she snapped, turning away and straight into the arms of Detective O'Hara. Again. She took a deep breath before meeting his eyes.

"Running away?" he inquired.

At the moment, the idea of fleeing held tremendous appeal. "No," she said with a sigh. "Just doing my job."

"Which is?"

"At the moment it's delivering permits to

an irresponsible producer."

"Mind if I tag along?"

"I thought you had a murderer to catch."

"I do. I told you I'd be in touch."

"I wasn't expecting you to show up quite this soon. I'm flattered that you're willing to take time out of your busy investigation schedule to be with me. Wasn't it just a couple of hours ago that you told me to stay far, far away from this case?"

"Something's come up. Could we do this someplace private?" he suggested, apparently catching sight of the fascinated gleam in Vince's eyes.

"Your car or mine? I have to get these permits out to Crandon Park before Vince ruptures a blood vessel."

"Before we lose thousands of dollars in revenue in this county," Vince corrected, not bothering to hide his
eavesdropping.

"You tell me where else Larry Milsap is likely to shoot a commercial on Miami tourist attractions," she snapped back. "Never mind. Come on, Detective."

"I had someone drop me off. You drive," he said. "Maybe I'll catch you speeding."

"Don't tell me homicide detectives give out tickets in their spare time."

"Don't test me. Actually, I was thinking of

65

it more as a test of your moral character."

Molly glared at him, but led the way to her prized white convertible, one of her rare indulgences. When she'd turned onto Miami Avenue, she asked, "Since when did my morals come into question?"

"Since I found out that the knife used to kill Mr. Winecroft is covered with just one set of fingerprints. Since you admit owning the knife and bringing it last night, I think we can assume for the moment that they're probably yours."

There was a sudden sinking sensation in the pit of Molly's stomach. The implications were not heartening. "Just one set? You're sure? Maybe the murderer's are blurred."

"One set. We're going to need yours to match them up in the lab, of course."

"But his wife used that knife to cut the cake last night."

"No prints, unless you'd washed that knife clean and carried it downstairs wrapped in a towel. Did you?"

"Of course not. Dammit, I watched Drucilla cut that cake."

"Did she wear gloves?"

"Look," she said impatiently, "I know society types tend to dress up for all occasions, but I can assure you that little white gloves would have been out of place at the bridge table. Someone would have noticed. Besides, how would she have handled the cards?"

"How about those clear plastic throwaway gloves used by kitchen help?"

"I didn't see any. You don't seriously think I killed him, do you?" She was not proud of the little catch in her voice. She really did not want to be a serious suspect in this case — or any other, for that matter.

"Let's just say I'm confused. I have a theory I'd like to throw out." He glanced at the speedometer as she approached the Rickenbacker toll booths. Molly automatically lifted her foot off the accelerator as she guided the car into the emblem lane that provided access for residents who paid an annual fee. Then she noted that she was going only five miles an hour anyway. He grinned. "Guilt is a fascinating emotion, don't you think?"

"I am not guilty, either of speeding or murder." She crept through the lane to make her point.

"Just listen to my theory. What if Mrs. Winecroft used the knife to cut the cake, then wiped it clean. Her prints would be gone."

"But so would mine."

"Not if you came back later and used the knife to stab her husband."

The words landed as if they'd been dropped from the top of a thirty-story high rise. Inane individually, together they packed quite a punch, the sort of punch that could send her to prison. She was still reeling as she pulled to the edge of the road and hit the brakes. She whirled on him furiously.

"That's a really crummy theory. Why the hell would I do that? I don't have a motive. I even won the damned bridge game."

"That is a problem," he admitted.

"Why couldn't she have wiped it clean and then used the knife?"

"Why would she bother to wipe off your fingerprints and leave her own?"

"Hell, I don't know. You're so great at coming up with theories, you figure it out."

"I'm working on a couple of ideas."

"How lovely. Would you care to share them with me?"

"Not yet."

She scowled at him. "We are talking about my motives here, aren't we? Don't you think I have a right to hear your speculations on the subject?"

"Sure. Later, after I've tested them on a few other people and we have those fingerprints ID'd positively as yours."

Molly glanced at the stunningly blue water on either side of the causeway and tried to grasp some of the serenity the sight always brought her. Instead, this gnawing sensation seemed to be eating a hole in the pit of her stomach. "You really know how to ruin a perfectly beautiful day, don't you?"

"Most people would have considered the day ruined the minute they found the body. Unless, of course, you were glad to see the man dead." He fixed her with a penetrating gaze that could have drawn a confession from the most professional criminal. She wasn't even amateur. It rattled the dickens out of her.

"How did you feel about Mr. Winecroft?" he asked.

Molly recalled her very recent conversation with Vince and decided Michael O'Hara would not have to use thumbscrews to get her boss to share her views. "I was not overly fond of some of his decisions," she said cautiously.

"Such as?"

"I hated the impatiens."

"The what?"

"All those little pink and white flowers."

His lips twitched. Apparently he didn't view that as a motive for murder any more than she did. "And?" he prodded.

"You don't think those crummy little flowers provide a powerful motive? They wilt in the heat. They look thoroughly bedraggled by noon."

"I'm sure that's distressing, but there must be something more."

"Okay, there are the assessments. They keep going up. I know the cost of living is going up, too, but there's been a lot of talk of mismanagement. The owners will end up paying, no matter who's at fault. That's tough for the people on fixed incomes."

"Even if they're fixed in the millionaire range?"

"Not everyone in that building is filthy rich. Just as an example, if I hadn't sold my house, in which I had a fair amount of equity, I couldn't have made enough of a down payment to whittle the mortgage down to a size I can manage."

"So if the assessments go up, your apartment's at risk?"

Oh, hell. Nice work, Molly. She had just provided herself with a motive. "I really shouldn't have said that, right?"

He grinned. "An attorney would have advised against it. However, the fact that you did suggests to me that you're not a hardened killer."

"And the person who did this is?"

"A killer has to be pretty motivated, either by anger or a long-standing and deep-seated grudge to stab someone. It's not a clean method of killing. Women generally prefer poison or even a dainty but deadly shot."

"So I'm off the hook?"

He grinned. "Not entirely. I wouldn't leave town, if I were you."

"You will let me know when you're convinced, I'm sure."

"Absolutely. Until then I think you can expect to be seeing a lot of me."

If almost any other drop-dead-gorgeous man had said that to her, she might have been thrilled. Knowing that this man considered her capable of murder more or less took the edge off her anticipation.

4

Molly DeWitt, onetime debutante, a murder suspect? All her life she had fought against being categorized as some frivolous airhead just because her parents had insisted on putting her through the tortures of a debutante ball. Compared to being a murder suspect, however, those days had been heavenly.

Reluctantly, she tried the suspect label on for size. It was ludicrous, but there was no denying that the evidence could be interpreted that way if another candidate didn't turn up. Even though Michael O'Hara seemed competent and she'd been taught — naively, perhaps — that the police were friends of the innocent, she wasn't about to take any chances. She'd better find the real murderer herself. The alternatives, including turning her son over to Hal DeWitt to raise while she went to jail, were unacceptable.

Highly motivated by the time she dropped Detective O'Hara at the Key Biscayne police station and undaunted by his repeated warnings to stay out of it, she planned her own informal investigation. She would interrogate every one of those present last night, starting this afternoon.

She made a U-turn on Crandon, heading toward home. With the car phone tucked on her shoulder, she punched in Vince's beeper number. She reached him on the third green at the Biltmore golf course. Obviously he wasn't worried about things back at the office. He figured carrying his cellular phone in his golf bag constituted working.

"What is it? I'm about to birdie this hole, Molly. Make it fast."

"I need to take the rest of the day off after all."

"Sure. Whatever," he muttered distractedly. He was probably on his knees sighting the curve of the green.

Molly started to hang up, when her words apparently registered.

"Hey, wait a second. Molly!"

She took her time responding, while he bellowed her name a few more times. "What?" she said finally.

"You'll be in tomorrow, though, right? We

have that meeting at ten with the producer from Paramount. You have all the details."

She *always* had all the details. Vince's idea of being prepared consisted of putting the appointments on her calendar. "I could bring you up to speed just in case I can't make it," she suggested generously. "It wouldn't take more than a half hour or so." She enjoyed envisioning the ashen hue beneath Vince's tan as he measured the distance from ball to cup and saw the chance to play it out evaporating.

"No, no, I want you there. Gotta go, Molly." He hung up quickly, obviously afraid she might start briefing him right then and there.

As she turned into the palm-lined Ocean Manor entrance, she saw that police cars still filled the circular driveway in front of the gleaming white-and-glass building. Architecturally undistinctive, it was typical of dozens of beachfront condos along the Florida coast. Clean lines, light colors, classy if unimaginative decor.

Though she could have avoided the lobby, Molly took the main entrance just to see who was hanging around the murder scene. A small cluster of residents hovered near the security desk, as if being close to Nestor would protect them. The sight of the desk reminded Molly of something she should have considered much earlier. If anyone had come into the building last night, the name would be on the log, either at the desk or at the front gate. If the latter, a license tag number would have been recorded as well. She hoped the police hadn't already taken them as evidence.

While everyone was chatting, she inched closer to the desk and peered at the register. Tuesday's page was still on top. The last person to sign in had arrived at 10:00 p.m., a Sylvia Machado, visiting Hector Alonso in 1020. There were no names after that. Anyone who'd arrived in the midst of this morning's confusion had slipped in unnoticed. Not even Nestor would have dared to make the police log in.

She was about to move away, when she realized that the gate log was also on the security desk. Obviously the guard had dropped it off before going off duty at seven. Again, Sylvia Machado was the last person registered, logged in at 9:55 p.m. It was possible that she was the killer and had lingered in the building until after the bridge game participants had gone to bed, but it seemed unlikely. It would be easy enough to check with Alonso to be sure that she'd been there as his guest.

Disappointed, Molly edged away from the desk. Jack Kingsley, the building manager, separated himself from another group near the bend in the corridor and met her in front of a scraggly potted palm that didn't appear to be in much better shape than Allan Winecroft.

Kingsley was a tall man, at least six-two, with a jovial round face and shrewd eyes. He looked to be about fifty. Bushy eyebrows sprinkled with gray tried to compensate for the thinning sandy hair on his head. Partial to the informal, open-necked guayabera shirts favored in the Latin community, he wore them with khaki trousers and boat shoes.

But while Kingsley's attire contributed to the impression that he was just about to head for a *café cubano* on Calle Ocho in the heart of Little Havana, word was that he ran a tight, businesslike ship. Molly had met him only twice, when she'd applied to the board for approval to buy her condo, and later when she'd gone to the office to make a maintenance payment. She'd been impressed, even a little intimidated by his odd balance of informal dress and militaristic regimentation. There was a lot of *yes, sir* and *no, sir* going on in that office. She'd been surprised that the secretaries hadn't snapped salutes.

"Mrs. DeWitt, could we talk a minute?" he asked her now. Without waiting for an answer, he steered her away from the crowd and toward the elevators. His pace was brisk. They were on their way to her apartment before she realized it. "I'm terribly sorry you've had to go through all of this," he said as he punched the button for the fifth floor. "I assume the police questioned you this morning."

"Some. They're going to want a formal statement later, I'm told."

"This is a terrible thing. Terrible. Do you have any idea what might have happened? Did you see anything at all?"

"Actually, no," she said, though she thought finding the body was quite enough. "Allan was fine when I left the cardroom last night."

"What time did you discover his body?"

"It must have been about eight."

"Had he been dead long?"

The question was natural enough, she supposed, but why ask her? She was no expert. The place was swarming with people likely to be better informed than she was. "I couldn't say. I'm sure the medical examiner will have to pin down the time of death. Is Allan . . . have they taken him away yet?"

"Yes. A few minutes ago. They've sealed off the cardroom for the time being. There are technicians all over the place in there and the detective in charge, Mr. O'Hara, I believe, said they'd want to speak with everyone."

"You mean those there last night?"

"No, he said everyone. I assured him we would make whatever arrangements he required. I've made up a list and set up a timetable, subject to his approval, of course. I'm expecting him back shortly."

Molly suddenly remembered something she'd wondered about earlier as she'd surveyed the exceptionally tidy cardroom. "Mr. Kingsley, what time does the cleaning staff get here?"

"Eight."

"So, there's no way they could have been in there this morning?"

"You mean prior to your arrival?"

She nodded.

"It's not impossible. Occasionally the director of housekeeping makes her rounds early before her staff arrives. Why?"

"Because the room was spotless, except for Allan. I wondered if they'd had time to pick up from last night's bridge game."

"I doubt it. Even if Mrs. Rodriguez had been in, she wouldn't have done the cleaning herself."

So, Molly thought, it was likely that the other players had cleaned up before leaving last night. Which of them had remained behind to do it? Allan himself, concerned about sticking to his own stringent rules? Had he lingered, then been attacked by the killer, perhaps not a member of their own group, but a late arrival he'd never even seen? He had been stabbed in the back, after all. Or was it possible that the killer himself had tidied up, worried about leaving behind any evidence linking him to the crime? For that matter, was it possible that Allan had gone down this morning to pick up something he'd left behind? Aside from his clothes, she had no confirmation that he'd been killed last night. Drucilla certainly hadn't noticed that he'd been missing all night.

"Is there something more?" Mr. Kingsley asked, regarding her curiously.

"No. I suppose not."

"Well, if there is anything I can do for you, you will let me know, won't you?" he said as they reached her door. "I remember what you told me about your reasons for leaving your house. I would hate to have you regret buying here. Ocean Manor needs more young, year-round owners."

Molly wondered if he feared a rush of sales. Were condos seriously affected by such signs of instability? For that matter, wouldn't a murder intimidate a lot of prospective buyers? Whatever his concerns, she sought to reassure him about her own plans. "I can't say I wasn't rattled when I discovered the body this morning, but I have no intention of being chased away, Mr. Kingsley." She paused. "You know, on second thought, you could tell me something else about Allan. Was he fully retired or did he still have business interests? Is there anything listed on the office records?"

"Why on earth would you ask something like that?" His expression was thoroughly puzzled.

"His wife mentioned that he'd stayed on last night to discuss business. I wondered if perhaps a deal had gone sour on him. Then, again, maybe it was just general financial chitchat."

"I'm sure that must have been it. Once you've been a CEO, the tendency to stay on top of things must always be there."

"Was Allan on top of what was happening here? I would think a man like that would make an excellent condominium president."

"He was very savvy."

Though the manager responded quickly,

Molly couldn't help thinking that there was more he wasn't saying. She recalled all those troubling rumors she'd heard and risked asking him about them. "I've heard there was some mismanagement by the old board. Is there any truth to that?"

"None at all," he said, again without hesitation. This time, though, he elaborated. "Condominiums are complex businesses. Not everyone understands all the intricacies. I'm sure that's why there was some confusion over decisions made in the past. Allan was brought up to speed on everything by the accountants. I think he was satisfied that everything was in order in the reports we showed him."

Molly nodded politely, but made a mental note to ask the accountants about that. "Good. I know how nervous people get when their money is at risk, and how rumors can take on a life of their own."

"Tell me about it. I've been managing condominiums in this state for the past twenty years. There's not a one of them that hasn't had its problems," he told her in confidence. "It's bound to happen when you get a few hundred owners with very different backgrounds all mixed together. We've got Cubans and South Americans, a few Germans, some Brits, plus all the retirees from up north and a handful of young professionals like yourself. No two of them has the same likes or the same expectations. Just try redecorating the corridors and you can end up with World War Three on your hands."

Molly could just imagine trying to get them all to agree on a color scheme, much less style or architectural alterations. "I'm sure," she said sympathetically.

"You just let Nestor or me know if you have any problems," he said. "That's what we're here for. You get the shakes or anything from all this, give Dr. Meeks a call. I hear he's a pretty decent shrink."

"I'll do that," she said, though Roy Meeks was on her list of suspects and likely to be every bit as shaky as she was herself.

Comforted somewhat by the manager's solicitude, she made herself a tuna salad sandwich and took it onto her balcony overlooking a garden of sea grapes and beyond that the beach and ocean. The temperature had climbed into the low eighties and the humidity was high. Only a breeze kept it from being unbearable. It was still the perfect place to collect her thoughts. It reminded her of carefree summer days on her front porch overlooking the Rappahannock in Virginia. She'd spent endless hours on that porch daydreaming and making plans.

Today, though, there was no time for daydreams. If anything, she was in the middle of a nightmare. Leaving the sandwich untouched, she began making a list of those she wanted to see: the Davisons, Tyler Jenkins and his wife, Roy Meeks. She'd have to ask them to identify some of the others who'd been there last night. She considered asking them all over for tea despite O'Hara's objections. Tapping her pen against the table, she tried to imagine anyone making incriminating revelations under those conditions. It wouldn't happen. She'd have to approach them one by one. Divide and conquer. The phrase suddenly held new meaning.

Before she could pick her first target, though, the phone rang. She ran inside, but when she picked up the phone, there was no answer on the other end.

"Hello," she repeated. "Is someone there? Hello!"

The only response was a soft click.

"A wrong number," she murmured, walking slowly back to the balcony. Something deep in her gut, however, told her she was wrong. She couldn't help remembering what Drucilla had said earlier. Allan had been receiving threatening phone calls before he was killed. As dark clouds rolled in, warning of the impending onset of the typical afternoon thunderstorms, she shivered in the sudden gloom. She picked up her notes and sandwich and took them inside.

In the kitchen, she glanced at her list and decided the place to start would be with the man who'd championed Allan's election to the board, the man Drucilla so clearly resented: Tyler Jenkins.

Despite the threatening weather, she found Tyler walking laps around the perimeter of the pool, looking dapper in a crisp short-sleeved cotton shirt and shorts that displayed his knobby knees. His leather sneakers still looked brand-new. Apparently this was a recent regimen, probably prescribed after his bypass.

Molly smiled a greeting, which drew only a cursory nod and a terse, "Mrs. DeWitt."

"Mind if I join you?"

He stopped and studied her, his suspicious blue eyes intent. "Why?"

"I'd like to talk to you a little about Allan, if I could."

"The man's dead," he said, resuming his pace. "No point in talking about him."

"He was a friend of yours. I'm sure this

has been a terrible shock."

"Damned fool," he muttered.

Molly wasn't sure if he was referring to Allan or to her. "Why would you say that?" she asked.

He waved aside the question. "Don't mind me. You're right. This has been a shock."

"Drucilla says you worked very hard to get Allan on the board."

"Thought he'd be good. Not like all those others who were greedy and power hungry. Man had business sense. Ran a huge corporation. This should have been a piece of cake for him."

"Should have been? Wasn't it?"

"Different kettle of fish altogether, he told me. Might have been president, but he wasn't really in charge. Board outvoted him at every turn. Should have thought of that," he said, stepping up his pace until Molly practically had to run to keep up with him. For a man still recuperating from surgery, he seemed awfully fit to her.

Molly was also having some difficulty in reconciling the image of Allan as kindly businessman out to do good with the petty tyrant he'd appeared to be to others. The sheet of rules, circulated less than a week ago, came to mind as did a few incidents she'd heard about.

"Wasn't there a suit of some sort?" she asked. "Something about a cat?"

Faded blue eyes snapping with indignation glowered at her. "A lot of damned nonsense," Tyler decreed. "Can't have animals roving all over the place. The rules are clear. No pets. Allan was just enforcing them."

"But as I understand it, Mrs. Jenko had owned that cat for nearly fourteen years. She brought it with her when she moved in. No one told her she couldn't. Besides, it never left her apartment. What possible difference could it make if she kept it?"

"A rule's a rule. Can't have exceptions. Leads to chaos."

Molly was beginning to get an idea of where Allan had gotten his notions about condo law and order. Tyler Jenkins was a crotchety old man. He'd probably instigated the incident over the Firths' child being barefoot in the lobby. Liza Hastings, who lived across the hall from Molly, had told her all about it. Four adults — the Firths, Allan, and Tyler — had stood in the middle of the lobby shouting, while two-year-old Hettie Firth screamed, probably in a rage over being singled out for her tiny bare feet. It had taken Nestor and another guard to calm things down.

"Mr. Jenkins, Drucilla seems to think that Allan was being threatened because of something he'd done as condo president. Is that possible?"

"World's a terrible place when a man's condemned for just doing his job."

"Does that mean yes?"

"Wouldn't surprise me. That guard threatened him. He's probably the one. That policeman won't go after one of his own, though."

It took Molly several minutes to figure out what Tyler meant. The guard in question, Enrique Valdez, had been fired over some incident at the front gate. He'd admitted someone without noting it in the log. The guest happened to be visiting Allan. Allan had fired Enrique, setting off a barrage of criticism from those who thought he should have been given a second chance.

"Have you told Detective O'Hara about the incident?"

"Haven't seen him. Doubt he'll listen, though. Those Cubans protect each other. That's a fact."

Molly refrained from offering her own observation about the detective's impartiality. He liked her — at least she thought he did — and that wasn't keeping him from putting her on his list of suspects.

"Did Allan suggest that Enrique was making those calls?"

"No."

"Did he mention what the calls were about?"

"Said they were a damned nuisance, no more than that."

"So he wasn't frightened?"

"Take more than an anonymous call or two to scare a man like Allan."

Molly wasn't so sure about that. It had taken only one hang-up to make her jittery. She was about to comment on that when Michael O'Hara himself fell into stride beside them. She doubted he was there for the exercise.

"Is this a private conversation or can anyone join in?" he inquired. His expression indicated that any hint of exclusivity would not be appreciated.

The old man's eyes narrowed. "You that cop?"

"Michael O'Hara."

Tyler looked as if he'd been offered a dose of castor oil. "Time for my nap."

"I'm afraid your nap will have to wait for a few more minutes," Michael said, following him as he headed toward the building. Molly stayed in stride partly out of habit, but mostly out of curiosity. Why was Tyler

Jenkins so afraid of talking to the police?

"Doctor says I have to rest. Can't change the schedule."

This from a man who'd just done twenty laps around a very large pool at a pace just under a trot. Molly had her doubts. Apparently Michael did as well. His determination never faltered. "Perhaps if we sit here in the shade," he suggested.

Still grumbling under his breath, Mr. Jenkins sat. Michael sat opposite him. Molly lingered hopefully.

"Sit," Michael said finally. She pulled up a chair before he could change his mind.

"Mr. Jenkins, tell me about your relationship with Allan Winecroft. Was he a protégé of yours?"

"Got him to run for the board, if that's what you mean. Saw that he got elected."

"You must have a lot of influence in the building then."

"Some."

"Why didn't you run yourself?"

"Bad heart. Doc said I couldn't take it."

That hadn't kept him from running a vitriolic campaign, however. Molly had read some of his campaign letters on Allan's behalf. The Republican National Committee couldn't have taken nastier potshots at the Democrats.

"Once he was elected, was he panning out the way you'd hoped he would?" Michael asked.

"He was tough. Given the chance, he would have made a damned fine president."

"Any idea who might not have wanted him to have that chance?"

"Always a few malcontents. Doubt they'd have killed him, though."

"Why not let me be the judge of that? I'd like their names anyway."

"Talk to Manuel Mendoza."

"Who is he?"

"He's the man Allan beat in the last election. Thought he had a lock on the position. Damned Latin coalition. Always talking Spanish in the elevators. Wouldn't know we're still in America, if they had their way."

Even though there was no sign of a reaction on Michael's face, Molly winced. She'd heard Tyler Jenkins's frustration from an increasing number of Anglos as the Hispanic population began to dominate the county. Apparently Tyler didn't care that the man he was talking to was also Hispanic. Nor was he worried about sharing the depth of his bitterness over the community's changes.

No doubt Michael had heard similar complaints before. Ignoring the prejudiced comment with admirable restraint, he asked, "Mr. Jenkins, where were you between midnight and eight this morning?"

The old man didn't even blink. "In my apartment."

"Anyone with you?"

"My wife. She'll tell you I never left."

Michael closed his notebook. "Yes. I'm sure she will. And she was at the bridge game as well, is that right?"

"Yes. We play every Tuesday. Won last year."

"Congratulations and thank you for your time, sir." He stood up and gestured to Molly. From the stern expression on his face again, she decided it wouldn't be wise to argue.

Before he could launch into a tirade, she said, "I got a call this afternoon. I wasn't going to say anything, but maybe you should know about it."

"What sort of call?"

"A hang-up, but I could tell someone was there at first. I'm sure it was nothing, probably just a wrong number. I mean no one would expect me to be home this time of day, right?"

"Did anyone see you come in?"

"Yes," she admitted. "There were at least a dozen people in the lobby."

"Any of the people who were playing cards last night?"

She tried to recall if she'd seen anyone she recognized. "No," she said finally. "Other than the guards and the manager, they weren't people I knew."

He nodded. "Did the call upset you for some particular reason?"

"No. Not really. It's just that I went through something like this a few years ago. It gave me a start to have it happen again."

"It was probably nothing, but let me know if you get another call, okay?" He took a card out of his shirt pocket and jotted a number on the back. "Call anytime. My home number's on the back."

"Why was I less nervous before I told you?"

"Because I'm taking it seriously?" he suggested. "I have to. In situations like this it's never smart to overlook anything. I tend not to believe in coincidence. You have a cute kid to worry about, too. It might have been nothing more than a wrong number, but don't take any foolish chances if it happens again. Call."

Molly nodded.

"And one more thing," he said, his tone light. It contradicted the cold look back in his eyes. "Stay away from the other suspects.

Finding you with them is really getting on my nerves."

"Maybe you ought to be quicker," she said, then wished she hadn't. Michael O'Hara was definitely not in any mood for jokes. If anything, he looked like someone who was only a frayed strand of self-control away from throttling her.

5

For all of Tyler's obvious bias in bringing up Enrique Valdez as a suspect in the first place, Molly couldn't help wondering if the security guard had harbored a grudge against Allan. It would have been natural under the circumstances. For that matter, what about Violet Jenko? Since the elderly resident was essentially housebound, Molly decided to stop by her apartment en route to her own. A social call, in case Detective O'Hara asked.

Molly tapped loudly on the door of the first-floor apartment and waited patiently. Mrs. Jenko was both hard of hearing and required the use of a walker to get around. The combination slowed her down. Finally Molly heard the soft thud of rubber against tile as Mrs. Jenko neared the door.

"Who's there?" she said, her voice clear and sharp.

"It's Molly DeWitt, Mrs. Jenko, from

upstairs." She spoke loudly enough to be heard over the argument on *Geraldo.*

The door opened a cautious crack, revealing a frail, bent woman with flyaway wisps of white hair. She was wearing a flowered housecoat and fuzzy pink slippers. Assured that it was indeed Molly, she removed the chain and opened the door wide. She waved Molly inside, then replaced the deadbolt and the chain.

"Would you like some tea?" she offered, obviously glad of the unexpected company.

"I would love some," Molly said, adapting her steps to Mrs. Jenko's slow progress into the kitchen. "Could I help?"

"What's that?"

Molly raised her voice. "Do you need any help?"

"No need. Just sit there at the table. This won't take a minute."

The walker thumped across the tiles as she moved from sink to stove to cupboards. The room had been painted a bright sunshine-yellow once, but the color had dimmed with grease and time. Maybe Mrs. Jenko couldn't see all that well to clean.

The elderly woman carefully placed two English bone china teacups on the table. Next she brought over a plate with wedges of Scottish shortbread, the kind made with enough butter to clog the heartiest arteries. Molly loved it. She was just sorry there were only four pieces on the plate. When the tea had been poured and she'd taken her first sip, Molly said, "How are you doing, Mrs. Jenko? Have you been getting out at all?"

"What's that?"

"Have you been out?"

"Just to the mailbox. That takes most of the afternoon," she said wearily. "Can't move the way I used to. Why, when I was a girl . . ."

Sensing the start of a long session of reminiscences, Molly interrupted. "You haven't been too upset over Mr. Winecroft's murder, have you? Are you nervous being here alone?"

"Doesn't have a thing in the world to do with me," she said adamantly, thumping her walker for emphasis. "The man deserved to die."

"Because of that suit you had over your cat?"

Her nut-brown eyes misted over. "It was a cruel thing, what he did. Prissy was all I had in this world. She barely made a sound, never even left the apartment."

"How did he know about her then?"

"That hateful Tyler Jenkins told him. Tyler used to come nosing around, pretending to be concerned about how I was doing. He knew what that cat meant to me, but he told Allan about her anyway. Next thing I knew I was told Prissy had to go. I fought it as long as I could, but my son finally insisted I stop. Said it wasn't good for my blood pressure. Wish I had dropped dead. Then we really would have had a claim against the old coot."

"You don't mean that."

"Course I do. You think it's any fun living like this? Might as well be dead. Only thing worth staying alive for was seeing Allan Winecroft with that knife sticking out of him."

"You saw him?"

"You bet. The minute I heard the news. Went right over there to see for myself that someone had done him in."

"Any idea who?"

"No, but if I did, I'd surely thank them."

Molly finally excused herself and left, after seeing Mrs. Jenko settled in the living room again, her television tuned to the early evening news. The sound followed her all the way down the hall. Her talk with the old woman had confirmed the depth of the bitter feud she'd had with Allan, but it also had proved, to Molly at least, that she wasn't capable of plunging that knife herself. She wouldn't have had the strength for it.

Enrique, on the other hand, was a powerfully built man. Molly spent an hour trying to track him down, to no avail. His wife claimed he was working somewhere as a painter. She had no idea where. Her grasp of English conveniently faded in and out. Molly left a message, but she wasn't surprised that Enrique never returned the call. She went to bed every bit as confused as she had been when she'd discovered Allan's body that morning.

Once Molly dropped Brian off at school in the morning, she turned automatically into Harbor Plaza Shopping Center. Down at the end, an *R* missing from its restaurant sign on the overhang, was the Doughnut Gallery, or the DG, as it was fondly known by the regulars. Long and narrow, the place was an island institution, its back wall decorated with snapshots of customers. Even the *Miami Herald* knew to send its reporters here when it wanted the latest word on Key Biscayne happenings.

Naturally, this morning the talk at the crowded counter centered on the Allan Winecroft murder. As she waited for a seat to open up, Molly listened as two other condo presidents worried aloud. They were less concerned with Allan's fate than with the possibility that their own lives might be at stake.

"You should have heard that guy last week, when the board turned down his renters," Jacob Gelbman said as the waitress set his daily breakfast of juice, cereal and a banana in front of him. He was so nervous he nearly poured his juice on his corn flakes. "He threatened to get us all for depriving him of his livelihood. I sympathized with the guy, but I couldn't vote to let the prospective tenant in. He had too many kids for a two-bedroom apartment. The owner was furious, practically turned purple, said we were ruining him."

"That's just talk," George Calhoun retorted, going against medical guidelines to douse his scrambled eggs with salt. He picked up a piece of crisp bacon in his fingers and waved it between bites. "If I had a nickel for all the threats made against our condo board, I'd be a rich man."

"You are a rich man," Gelbman reminded him. "Maybe you and I can afford to take a few knocks. What if this guy in our building couldn't? What if he goes berserk like that guy up in Broward County last year? He allegedly shot the condo president, then went home and had a drink. That's where they found him, out by his pool, a drink in his hand, calm as you please. Desperation makes people do crazy things. Now this thing with Winecroft. Who knows what's behind that? I tell you, I'm thinking of getting off the board. Let somebody else take the heat. What do you get for doing it? A lot of aggravation. That's it. Nothing but aggravation."

A stool opened up next to Gelbman. Molly squeezed onto it, nodding to the men. She knew them the way she knew all of the regulars, by name and condo. She knew very little about their backgrounds, though both appeared to be retirement age. Gelbman had thinning white hair and nervous mannerisms even when he wasn't contemplating a murder. Calhoun had the tanned, leathery skin of a man who couldn't stay away from the beach or the golf course. They were always together and always here when she arrived.

Before she could blink, her cup of coffee was in front of her, along with the skim milk for her high-fiber cereal. If she ever wanted to change her order, she'd have to shout it from the doorway. Once she was seated, her usual breakfast materialized automatically. There was something especially comforting about that routine this morning.

"What do you think, Molly?" Jacob Gelbman asked. "You live in the building. Was it one of the owners who stabbed Winecroft? There's always some brouhaha going on over there. Maybe one of 'em turned nasty."

"I have no idea who did it," she said honestly. Nothing she'd done so far had narrowed down her initial list of suspects, much less added anyone to it. Despite her desire to dig for more clues, she'd spent the previous evening helping Brian with his homework after her visit to Violet Jenko. Though on the surface Brian was nonchalant about the murder, she'd sensed a vague tension in him that she attributed to unspoken fears. She hadn't tried to force him to talk, but she had remained available to listen. He'd spent most of the evening talking about snakes and what terrific pets they made. She'd shuddered at the very idea. Thank goodness the rules forbade it.

"But the paper says you discovered the body," Gelbman protested. "Surely you have some theories about what happened."

"I found Allan's body, but unfortunately the killer didn't linger with it. Your guess is as good as mine." She patted herself on the back for remaining dutifully neutral. Detective O'Hara would be proud of her. Just to be sure she kept her opinions to herself, she stuffed a spoonful of bran flakes into her mouth.

"I heard there were a lot of bitter feelings after the last election, though. Who was that guy who ran against Winecroft and lost?"

"Manuel Mendoza," Molly said, recalling that Tyler Jenkins had raised the same possibility.

"Right. That's it. Mendoza. Maybe he's still holding a grudge."

"The election was eight months ago," she reminded them. "If you ask me, he ought to be relieved he lost. The board has been catching flak from the owners from the minute they took office. They're fighting over the assessments. They're fighting over cable TV. They're fighting over the decorating. When those cheap lighting fixtures went up in the halls, I thought Miriam Powell was going to have a fit of apoplexy. She said the property value was going to be ruined. I don't think that makes her a murderer."

"But you can't say that for sure. You've got three hundred apartments, right? Every owner's taste is different. You try pleasing them all. It can't be done. Not a day goes by that someone's not mad at you. If the police are on top of this, that's where they'll start looking, at the board minutes. See who was griping about what. Maybe somebody tried to sell and the deal wasn't approved by the board. Could be the seller was real anxious. Or maybe the buyer resented being turned down. That's the place to start, in the minutes."

"Good idea." The approving comment came from behind the newspaper to Molly's right. Already it was a familiar voice.

She nabbed a corner of the paper and folded it down until she could peer straight into Detective O'Hara's eyes. "It is not polite to eavesdrop."

"It's worse than that to defy a direct police order."

"I'm not defying anything. I'm eating my breakfast." She waved a spoonful of now soggy flakes in his direction.

"But the name Allan Winecroft did cross your lips, did it not?"

"Not mine, theirs."

"A technicality."

Both men on her left suddenly seemed totally absorbed with stirring their coffee. Molly recognized an evasion tactic when she saw one. Neither man used sugar. Or cream. Unless one of them had switched to tea and was trying to change his fortune in the leaves, they were trying to avoid the detective's attention. Since they'd dragged her into this conversation, she saw no reason to hang alone.

"Gentlemen, I'd like you to meet Detective O'Hara. He's in charge of the Winecroft investigation. Perhaps he can answer your questions. I have to go to work." She slid off the stool and grabbed for her check in one fluid motion. Even if it hadn't been there, she knew the amount by heart. It never changed.

"Oh, no, you don't," the detective said, snagging her wrist and holding her in place. "I heard something last night that might interest you."

The entire restaurant was not much bigger than her living room, just the right size for spreading gossip. A definite stillness fell over the row of diners. The only sounds were the sizzle of eggs on the grill and toast popping up. Michael was quick enough to pick up on the sudden fascination with their conversation.

"Not here," he said, snatching his own check off the counter and steering her down the narrow aisle toward the door. He barely paused at the cashier to hand over a fistful of bills. "Hers, too," he said.

"I'll pay for my own breakfast."

"It's already done," he muttered, nudging her toward the door. Molly barely had time to grab the cup of coffee she always ordered to go. It was thrust into her hand just as she scooted out the door.

When they were outside, Molly jerked her arm out of his grip and demanded, "Were you in there spying on me?"

"I was in there for toast and coffee."

"Right." She wondered exactly how long he'd lingered over refills of the coffee. The place had been open since five thirty. Unless he drank decaf, by now he ought to be wired for the day. She wasn't about to risk tangling with a man whose nerves were jittery and who carried a gun. She kept a lid on any further sarcastic observations. She couldn't help it, though, if her expression remained skeptical.

"Okay," he muttered finally. "Maybe I thought I could pick up on a little local gossip, see if Allan was beloved or hated. I'm well aware that half the movers and shakers on the island stop in there for breakfast." He slammed his fist against the roof of his Jeep. "Damn! Why am I explaining myself to you?"

"Guilt," she suggested.

"Not a word you should be throwing around under the circumstances."

"What is that supposed to mean?"

"Word has it that Allan recently had a

set-to with your son. The person who mentioned this suggested that you are a very protective mother."

Molly regarded him incredulously. "What exactly was this set-to supposed to be about?"

"The informant seemed a little vague on that."

"I'm sure. It never happened, Detective. Brian would never argue with an adult."

This time the detective looked skeptical. Obviously interrogating witnesses gave him a lot of practice.

"Okay," she agreed. "He can be a little sassy, but that's with me. He's been taught to respect his elders. Besides, he would have told me if Allan had been on his case over something."

"That's the point. He told you. You got huffy and stabbed the man. At least that's the theory."

"Yours or the informant's?"

"The informant's."

"Good, because I'd hate to think you were that stupid."

"Not stupid, just thorough. I have to check out everything."

Maybe he was just being cautious. Or maybe he'd been taken for a ride once and vowed never to trust his own judgment again. Molly preferred those theories to the one giving him one more item to add to her own list of motives. "Did some sweet-talking person fool you once? Did she mess up a case for you?"

"Nope, and that's not going happen if I can help it. When it comes to a case, I don't trust my parish priest. Now that we're clear this isn't personal, let's stick to the specifics of this case. You're saying the incident between Allan and Brian never happened?"

"That's right. It never happened."

"Could we talk to your son about that?"

"Why? I've told you."

"And I'm trying to cover all the bases."

She glared at him. His gaze met hers evenly, unfazed by the scowl. There was enough chemistry in the air to blow up a lab. For once it didn't have much to do with physical attraction. She was furious, resentful of the fact he wouldn't take her at her word. He was patient, which only magnified her irritation.

"He's at school," she said finally.

"Later, then. I'll stop by this evening."

"Whatever," she said stiffly.

"Thank you," he said formally, a glimmer of amusement in his eyes.

She relented. He was just trying to do his job. "By the way, what was the consensus in there this morning?" she asked. "Was Allan loved or hated?"

"Actually, it was odd. Everyone had something to say about the murder, but very little about Allan. Except for the condo, did he pretty much keep to himself?"

"He played tennis, but those guys are already on the courts by now. Other than that I have no idea if he'd involved himself in any of the other island activities. Try the Yacht Club or check with *The Islander.* Someone at the paper might know if he was active."

"Maybe I'll just drop in on his wife, instead."

There was an unmistakable spark of anticipation in his voice. "You're hoping she'll have company, right?"

"I must admit to a certain curiosity about who was expected yesterday. A lover, especially one interested in her husband's estate, might have a particularly good motive for stabbing Allan."

If Molly hadn't had that damned meeting with Paramount, she might very well have begged to tag along. Instead, she drove to work at a daring ten miles an hour above the speed limit. Despite her defiance of the traffic laws, she still had to stay in the slow lane to avoid being run down by everyone else. Where the hell was a cop when you really needed one?

6

When Molly arrived at the office, Vince and Jeannette were in the midst of a standoff. For the second time that morning she was grateful that the world around her was still so normal.

"What are you two bickering about now?" she asked as she inched between two floor-to-tabletop stacks of *Variety,* the *Hollywood Reporter,* tourism brochures, and magazines to reach her desk.

Jeannette, a tall, stately black woman with close-cropped hair, rolled her expressive eyes and launched into a soft but eloquent tirade in Creole. There was just enough English to give Molly the idea that Vince had been behaving in character. Apparently he recognized the phrase that meant son of a bitch as well. He dragged Molly into his office and slammed the door, leaving an indignant Jeannette on the other side.

"I can't deal with this," he said. "I've had it."

"What's the problem?"

"She refuses to do the filing."

"Did she say that?"

"Well, not in so many words," he admitted, "but do you see any sign of her doing it? She's just muttering all that voodoo stuff again."

"What on earth makes you think she's invoking some curse?"

"It's the way she looks at me. Gives me the chills."

"Perhaps she looks like that because you're behaving like a jerk. I've occasionally felt a need to regard you that way myself. Look, I'll talk to her. We'll get caught up on the filing. Maybe if the phone didn't ring off the hook around here, she'd have time to do it."

"It's not my fault that they eliminated a secretarial position."

"Nobody said it was. We just have to do the best we can. Have a cup of coffee. Go over your notes for the Paramount meeting. Daydream about your golf game. Did you make that birdie, by the way?"

"Now that," he said with a satisfied sigh, all thoughts of Jeannette banished in a wave of pure nostalgia, "that was perfection. You

111

should have been there, Molly. A fifteen-footer, straight into the cup."

"Did you win?"

"Naw, but who cares? Came in six over par, the best I've played in months. I'm telling you, if I could hit the course every day I could turn pro."

"Vince, by the time you're ready for that you'll have to go on the seniors tour. Stick with the amateur stuff. Now let me go see if I can calm Jeannette down."

She found the clerk diligently filing. Jeannette glanced up, a twinkle in her dark-brown eyes.

"Okay, tell the truth, what'd you say to him?" Molly asked.

"I wished him many children," she said innocently.

Molly chuckled. "So he was right. You did put a curse on him."

A grin spread slowly across Jeannette's flat features, her white teeth gleaming against a mahogany complexion. "He would see it that way, yes."

"Jeannette, one of these days he's going to fire you. Why can't you just talk to him in plain English? You speak it every bit as well as I do."

"But what would be the fun in that? Vincent, he has an idea of who I am. Why should I distress him by confusing the matter?"

"I have a pretty good idea of who you are, too, my friend, and you are a fraud. You have more business and political savvy than Vince would if he got an MBA. Don't let him sell you short."

"This is a clerk's job, Molly. If he sees I am overqualified, it will make him very nervous. I watch the county listings. When a better job comes along, I will apply. Until then I will do this one well, even the filing." Her grin was back. "And have a little fun, yes?"

Molly chuckled. "Okay, yes."

Jeannette's expression sobered. "Now we talk about you. You are okay? I saw in the paper about the murder in your building."

"I'm okay. I just wish I could figure out who was behind it. It makes me very nervous to think that someone in Ocean Manor is capable of murder. That means they have access to all the apartments."

As Jeannette went back to her filing, Molly considered the suspects who had surfaced thus far: Drucilla, Manuel Mendoza, perhaps Tyler Jenkins, the fired Enrique Valdez, some unidentified and possibly nonexistent lover of Drucilla's, some of the others who'd been there last night. She excluded herself for obvious reasons. She knew she hadn't done it. If the police had a more solid list, weeding out the unlikeliest prospects, she wasn't aware of it.

She glanced at her watch. She had about ten minutes before the meeting with the Paramount producer. That ought to be just about long enough for a chat with Mendoza. She looked up the number of his development company in Coral Gables.

To reach him she had to convince a receptionist and then a secretary that her business with him was important. Fortunately, dealing with Hollywood office help had given her the necessary skills to bluff her way past the most protective executive secretaries.

"Mr. Mendoza, this is Molly DeWitt. I live at Ocean Manor."

"Right. Right. You're the one who discovered Allan's body, right?"

"Yes. I was wondering if you might tell me a little bit about condo politics. I'm new to the building and I'm wondering how Allan got elected."

Although Mendoza had been speaking perfectly fluent, unaccented English, her question brought on a barrage of Spanish.

"You didn't like him, I take it."

"He was an interloper."

"What an odd choice of words. Hadn't he lived in the building for many years?"

"A few, but only recently did he become interested in power."

"Perhaps that was because of some of the concerns about mismanagement I've heard."

"You have been misinformed. The building has been run very well," he said coldly. "I have seen to that. Now, if you'll excuse me, I am very busy."

"Wait," Molly said, anxious for a more definitive explanation.

"Good-bye, Mrs. DeWitt."

Manuel Mendoza's abrupt end to their conversation stayed with her throughout the meeting with the producers from Los Angeles. Had the ex–condo president interpreted her comment as an accusation? Had guilt made him anxious to be rid of her? Mendoza had been president of the board for three terms, and it was during that time that suggestions of impropriety had been raised. If someone had been offering sweetheart deals to contractors, who better to do it than a developer? Allan's election would have brought an unwanted close to a lucrative side business. Was there enough at stake to justify killing him to pave the way for a new election? And how did Jack Kingsley fit in? Wouldn't the manager have to know what was going on?

When she got home that afternoon she went straight to the office and asked to see copies of the most recent budgets. Mr. Kingsley emerged from his office just as the reports were being handed to her.

"What brings you in?" he asked, taking the papers from Celia before Molly could get her hands on them. He glanced through them, then passed them on. Reluctantly? Molly couldn't be sure.

"I thought I'd try to catch up on what goes on around here," she said, tucking the papers into her briefcase before he could change his mind. "I wasn't here when the budget was approved. I have no idea how a place like this operates. If I'm going to pay a thousand dollars every quarter for maintenance, I want to see how it's spent."

"Very prudent," he agreed. "Celia, get her the proposed budget as well as last year's actuals."

The petite blonde bobbed her head. "Should I get the report that just came in from . . ."

"No, that won't be necessary."

"Which report is that?" Molly asked. "Everything is a matter of public record, isn't it?"

"Once it's been presented to the board, naturally."

"I see. Then this report Celia mentioned hasn't gone to the board yet?"

"It's on the agenda for next week. Of course, with all that's happened, the timetable could be shifted. I imagine most of the meeting will be devoted to replacing Allan."

"The bylaws call for another election, isn't that right?"

"Yes. He had most of his term remaining, so there will need to be a new election, rather than an appointment."

"Any idea who might run?"

"Mendoza's the most likely candidate. Has all sorts of experience from before. He could move right in and know what needs to be done."

She nodded. "Yes. I'm sure that's important." She stepped to the door. "Well, thanks for these, Celia. Good-bye, Mr. Kingsley."

He nodded. Before she'd taken two steps down the hall, however, she could hear his raised voice. She got the distinct impression he wasn't happy with Celia's generosity with the building's budget figures.

When Michael showed up a half hour later, she was still going over the two reports. Although in some areas the costs seemed high, she couldn't find any obvious discrepancies. Not that she knew what to look for. Obviously the figures were going to add up. The only way to find really lousy deals would be to see comparative bids on everything.

"What do you have there?" Michael asked, glancing at the papers she'd spread out on the coffee table. "You bring some work home?"

"No. Actually, it's the condo budget."

He groaned. "I don't suppose it just happened to be in the mail today."

"No. I asked for it. It seems to me that . . ."

"Dammit, woman, haven't you heard a single thing I've said to you?"

She gazed at him innocently. "Which things were those?"

"Let me narrow it down to one." He leaned in close. "Stay out of this case."

"Hey, you're the one who put me on the list of suspects."

"But we both know you don't belong there."

Surprised to hear him actually say it, she said, "Thank you. When did you decide that?"

"I've never believed you are capable of murder. However, someone is taking great pains to make me believe you are, starting with using your knife, making sure only your prints were on it, and then telling me about a set-to between you and Allan over your boy. Hasn't it occurred to you that someone, possibly the killer, is very anxious to see you behind bars? If it is the killer and if he or she decides that the tactic isn't working, it may seem to him or her that more drastic measures are called for."

With all those *hims* and *hers* and *some-ones* scattered around, it was tricky, but Molly was relatively certain she understood what he was getting at. In fact, the picture he was painting made her blood run cold. Just in case she'd got it wrong, she asked, "Meaning?"

"Meaning, dammit, that you could be in danger. Now will you just stay the hell out of my way!"

She was ninety-nine percent certain that it wasn't a question. "Okay, yes. I'll back off. I still think there might be information I could get for you . . ."

"As a detective I have access to more information than you could possibly imagine."

"But people might be more open with me."

Wiping his hand wearily across his face, he sat down. "Okay, let's just suppose for a minute that you do get someone to spill his guts. Then you'd have exactly the information the killer is trying to keep us from getting. Talk about a motive for murder."

"Okay, okay, I get your point."

"Is Brian home?"

"Yes. He's in his room."

"Get him, please."

His temper appeared to be on a very short leash. Molly went to get Brian. Naturally, he wasn't in his room. He was standing in the shadows just beyond the living room. He'd obviously heard every word. For the first time since the murder, he looked scared. When she gestured for him to come, he hung back.

"What did he mean, Mom? Is somebody going to hurt you?"

"No, Brian. You and I are going to look out for each other, and we'll be just fine."

"Maybe Detective O'Hara ought to look out for us. He has a gun."

"We're not going to need a gun. Come on, kiddo. The detective has a couple of questions for you."

For once the prospect of being a part of the investigation didn't seem to appeal to him. He stayed right where he was.

"Brian, what on earth is wrong? He just needs to ask you a couple of questions."

"I don't know anything, not really."

The *not really* worried her. That generally meant he knew something but didn't deem it important according to his own value system. His system quite often varied considerably from those of such authority figures as his mother and his teachers.

"I want you in the living room right now, and I want you to answer every question Detective O'Hara asks with the truth. Do you understand me?"

"Yes, ma'am," he said dutifully, but he didn't look happy about it. She recognized that stubborn set of his mouth and wondered how the detective would do at getting past it.

Michael looked up from the budget papers and smiled at Brian. "Hey, *amigo,* how's it going?"

"Okay, I guess," Brian said, leaning against Molly's knee.

"I need your help."

"My help?" he said, straightening a little. "What can I do? I'm just a kid."

"I need to know if you ever saw Mr. Winecroft around the building."

Apparently Brian thought the question was innocuous enough. He responded readily. "Sure. He was always around."

"Did you ever talk to him?"

"Not much. I don't think he liked kids

very much."

"What made you think that?"

"He was always yelling at us."

"Us? You and who else?"

"Timmy and Kevin. We'd swim every afternoon. Sometimes we'd go to the beach and forget to wash the sand off our feet before we went into the pool or we'd sit on one of the chairs without a towel."

"Did he yell at you recently?"

Brian glanced at Molly uneasily. "Yeah, I guess."

"How recently?"

"Day before yesterday."

"What were you doing then?"

"Nothing, not really. We were in the garage, see, just messing around. We weren't hurting anything. And he caught us. He said he was going to call the police if he saw us near there again." His lower lip quivered and Molly could see the sheen of tears welling up in his eyes.

"Near where?"

"I don't know. That was the really weird part. I mean we were just sort of hiding and stuff."

"Was he alone or was someone with him?"

"I didn't see anybody."

"Could you show me where you were?"

Sensing finally that he wasn't in any real

trouble, Brian's expression brightened. "Sure."

Michael nodded. "Let's go take a look."

The building's garage was on a single level, beneath the structure but aboveground. Outside light filtered in, but it was the overhead fluorescent lights that kept it from being gloomy. Unlike some dark, shadowy parking garages that scared Molly to death, she'd never felt anything but safe in this one. Until now. There was something about Brian's story that suggested that something had been happening in the garage that Allan Winecroft hadn't wanted anyone to know about.

Brian led them to the area near the greenhouse along the outside perimeter of the garage. The building's plants were brought here to recuperate. The area was filled now with a few small potted palms and trays of impatiens and two or three plastic sacks of potting soil. As far as Molly could see there was nothing sinister going on.

"Was this the way it looked when you saw Mr. Winecroft here?" Michael asked.

"I guess," Brian said slowly. "We weren't even in the greenhouse part."

Molly noticed the nearby hoses, kept there both to water the plants and for resident use in washing their cars. "You weren't spraying each other with the hoses, were you?"

"Not exactly."

"Either you were or you weren't."

Brian scuffed the toe of his sneaker along the cement. "Maybe just a little. It was really hot that day."

"You had an entire ocean and a pool, if you wanted to cool off."

Brian looked subdued.

"Were you getting water on the cars?"

"Maybe some of them," he admitted.

"Is that why Mr. Winecroft got mad?"

"Maybe. I guess."

Molly and Michael exchanged a look. "So much for that," she said.

Michael nodded. "Maybe."

"You think it was something else?"

"I'm not sure. I just can't imagine him getting all worked up over a couple of cars getting sprayed."

"Maybe one of them was his."

"So what? All he had to do was ask the kids to dry it off. Remember what I was told, that he'd been so furious with Brian that you'd gotten even by stabbing him to death."

"How mad was he, Brian?"

"Pretty mad. He was really yelling and stuff. He turned real red. He even said he'd have us all kicked out. I was gonna tell you, Mom, but I forgot."

"More likely you figured I'd punish you."

"Not really, because we didn't *do* anything. Not anything bad."

Allan Winecroft apparently hadn't seen it that way. Was it possible that Brian had seen something and just hadn't realized it? She could tell from the speculative gleam in Michael's eyes that he was thinking the same thing.

"Did I help?" Brian asked.

"Yes," Michael said slowly. "Yes, I think you did."

As they started back toward the building, Molly heard a faint scrambling sound, a slight rustling. Michael and Brian apparently heard it too. They all looked back toward the greenhouse.

"Probably just a raccoon," she said.

"Probably," Michael agreed.

He didn't look as though he believed that any more than she did. Someone had been lurking in the shadows, possibly listening to discover just exactly how much they knew.

7

Years ago, when she was still single and living alone, Molly had endured a series of harassing phone calls. They began benignly enough, just like the calls she'd been receiving the last couple of days. But the hang-ups escalated into obscenities, and eventually the nature and frequency of the calls went from the realm of nuisances into very real threats. The caller turned out to be a stranger, a man who'd stumbled on her number by accident and liked the sound of her voice. Even so, she was left with an odd sense of being watched. More than once, she had caught herself looking back over her shoulder, filled with a vague sense of unease.

Since the first hang-up call she'd received after the murder, all of those old nervous feelings had resurfaced, leaving her thoroughly jittery at the sound of the phone. The incident in the shadowy garage tonight didn't help a bit. She left the light on when she went to sleep.

When the phone rang at 1:00 a.m., she sat bolt upright in bed. Instantly wide awake, she grabbed the phone and waited, saying nothing herself. She hung up, only to have it ring again at once. This time she said, "Hello." She wasn't surprised when no one responded to her greeting. Remembering everything she'd been told before about not challenging the caller, about not feeding the desire for a reaction, she quietly hung up. She did make a note of the time, and then she tried to go back to sleep.

The next call came an hour later. Again no one spoke. Again she hung up, but she was losing her patience and her anxiety was mounting. When the fourth call came, though she was quaking inside, she said quietly, "I'm recording these calls for the police. I'd suggest you stop making them."

"You bitch!" The voice was a low, menacing growl. She couldn't even make out whether it was a man or a woman. She considered trying to goad the caller into saying something more, but the line clicked dead.

Her death grip on the phone had tensed the muscles across her shoulders. Anxiety sent perspiration trailing down her back.

Every nerve on edge now, Molly pulled the pillows into a stack behind her, turned the radio on to the soothing sounds of WLYF, and sat up, waiting. As the minutes ticked by and then the hours, she realized there would be no more calls, not tonight. At dawn she finally fell into a fitful sleep.

It was less than twenty minutes later when she was jarred awake again. Before she could grab the phone, the ringing stopped. She heard the faint murmur of a voice in the living room, then a crash as the phone clattered to the floor.

"Mom!" Brian yelled, barreling through the door and throwing himself onto the bed, his expression panicky.

His whole body shook as she clutched him to her and tried to soothe him. "Sssh. It's okay. What happened? Who was on the phone?"

"I don't know," he said and again his body shuddered in her arms.

"Did he say something?"

"He said . . . he said you'd wind up like Mr. Winecroft, if you didn't stay away from the cops." His arms clung even more tightly around her neck and his lower lip quivered. "Mom, I don't like this. I'm scared. Maybe we should move. It wouldn't be so bad changing schools again."

Molly could barely control her own trembling, but now hers was less fear than gut-deep fury. How dare someone terrorize her son like this! Instinctively, she thought of Michael. She picked up the card he'd given her, reached for the phone, and dialed his home number.

A soft, musical, feminine voice answered, the accent distinctly Hispanic. So the detective was *involved.* It shouldn't matter, but to her surprise it did. She didn't like the shaft of pure jealousy that shot through her as she waited for him to take the call.

"What is it?" he said seconds later, about the time it would take to pass the phone across a bed. There was no sleepy sensuality to his tone. It was fully alert and all business.

"I think you'd better get over here," she said. Her voice tripped in mid-sentence, then caught on a sob.

"Calm down," he said quietly, using the same soothing tone she'd used with Brian only moments earlier. "What's happened?"

She swallowed hard. "I'll explain when you get here. I think it might be a good idea if you put a tap on my phone, while you're at it."

After that he didn't ask questions. "I'll take care of it. You just sit tight."

Molly managed a faint smile as she ran her fingers through her son's hair. "I wouldn't budge out of this apartment right now if you paid me," she said.

She did, however, persuade Brian to take a bath so that she could shower, untangle her shoulder-length hair, and change. She had too much pride to compete, even just mentally, with that sultry-voiced woman while wearing a faded one-size-fits-all T-shirt with a tiger on the front.

As soon as she'd dressed, she put on a pot of coffee and sat on the sofa to wait, Brian right beside her. They talked about everything except the call that had scared him so.

Michael arrived in far less time than she would have anticipated. It was the first time she'd seen him in anything other than his impeccably tailored suits. He'd obviously grabbed the first thing at hand, jeans and a dress shirt with the sleeves rolled up. He'd combed his hair with his fingers, a sure sign of his rush and his nervousness. Worried lines furrowed his brow. There was an ashen hue beneath his olive complexion and dark stubble lined his jaw. Under other circumstances, she might have indulged in several fantasies about the sexy masculinity of his slightly disheveled look.

The scrutiny he subjected both of them to

was thorough. He sat opposite them, legs spread, elbows on knees as he leaned forward to study them intently.

"Are you okay? What the hell happened?"

Molly's response was succinct. "There were more calls during the night."

"How many?"

"Five."

"Hang-ups?"

"At first."

"At first? Why didn't you call right away?"

"I thought he'd give up."

He bit back a lecture, but not a low, heartfelt curse. "But he didn't, right? What happened next?"

"I said I was recording the calls for the police and the caller got nasty."

"You said the caller. Male? Female?"

"I couldn't tell. Maybe Brian could."

"Jesus, you let him answer the phone?" he muttered accusingly. "What were you thinking of?"

"I was asleep," she said defensively. "He got to it before I could pick up."

His gaze shifted to Brian and his tone immediately became gentler, more soothing. "Okay, so you took one of the calls?"

Brian nodded, still clinging to Molly's hand. "Like Mom said, she was still asleep."

"What did the caller say?"

"That Mom would end up like Mr. Winecroft, if she didn't stay away from the cops."

Michael held out his hand and Brian moved to him. "That must have been pretty scary. I know you'd probably rather not think about it, but could you try real hard to remember if it sounded like a man's voice or a woman's?"

Brian bit his lower lip the way he always did when he was really concentrating on something. "It was real soft, like a whisper, but I think it was a man."

"Had you ever heard the voice before?"

Brian shook his head with certainty. "Never. You won't let anything happen to Mom, will you?"

"Absolutely not, I promise. Now, how about giving your mom and me a couple of minutes alone?"

Brian looked at her uncertainly. Molly said, "It's okay, Brian. Go on and fix yourself some cereal and a glass of juice. It'll be time to leave for school soon."

Alarmed blue eyes met hers. "I can't go to school, Mom. Who'll protect you?"

"I will," Michael reassured him. "I think going to school is a very good idea. I'll drive you over myself."

Brian looked torn. "Do you have a police car with a siren and everything?"

"Nope. Sorry. Just a Jeep. I do have a siren, but it's only for emergencies."

"Maybe this is an emergency," Brian said hopefully.

Michael considered the suggestion seriously. "Maybe it does qualify at that," he said. "Now get moving, so we won't be late."

"Are you sure it's okay to send him to school?" Molly asked as soon as Brian had left the room.

"That's the best place for him. I'll speak with his teacher and the principal, just so they're on the lookout in case anyone hangs around the building who shouldn't be there. The thing to remember is that the caller threatened you, not him. Exactly how much snooping around did you do on your own yesterday? More than I know about?"

"None after you left." At his skeptical expression, she said, "I swear it."

"Then let this serve as a warning. You've already made somebody very nervous. No more conversations with the neighbors, no more secret trips to the scene of the crime."

She shot a startled gaze at him. She'd only walked by to see if the crime scene tape had been removed. It hadn't been. "How did you know about that?"

"They pay me for my astute observations."

"You weren't anywhere near here."

He shrugged. "Astute observation. Lucky guess. In my business they pretty much add up to the same thing. Remember, sweetheart, I have years of experience at this. You have none. It's no contest. I'll outguess you every time."

"Dammit, we're not playing guessing games. The killer is threatening me."

"Because you're an easy target. Let me be the target. It's what I get paid for." He leaned forward, his gaze intent. "Please, Molly, let it alone. If not for me, then do it for your son. I know what it's like to be a scared kid, to be terrified that you'll never see your mother again."

She heard the surprisingly ragged emotion in his voice and knew that he was telling her the truth. Maybe she just needed to keep him talking. Maybe she needed to understand him, needed to understand this pull that had been there between them despite all the superficial differences and whatever his current involvement was with the woman on the phone. Mostly she needed to trust him.

"How do you know something like that?" she asked. "Did something happen to your mother?"

"Not exactly."

For a minute she thought he wasn't going

to say anything more. Something about the memories hurt him deeply. She could see the pain in the depths of his eyes, the hint of vulnerability that after all these years hadn't gone away.

"Thirty years ago I was just a kid in Cuba," he began slowly, his voice quiet. "I lived with my mother and her family. We had no idea where my father was. He was an American GI stationed at Guantánamo. My mother wasn't even sure of his name. She just remembered it was something Irish, so I wound up being Michael O'Hara, instead of Miguel Javier."

Suddenly Molly understood why there were so many incongruities in his personality. The flawless Spanish and unaccented English. The swaggering Latin persona, modified by an intriguing sensitivity. Though he'd never known his father, still he was caught between the cultures.

"I don't remember much about that time," he said, a haunted, faraway expression in his eyes, "except that I was part of a big family and that I was loved. Then one day in 1962 my mother took me to the airport and put me on a plane for Miami. You've probably read about those flights, Operation Pedro Pan, organized by the Catholic Church in Miami and two people inside

Cuba. Families packed up their kids and sent them away to save them from Castro, to give them a better life. Some of us were sent to relatives we'd never even met. Some went to live with strangers. Fourteen thousand in all, mostly young boys. I was barely five."

Molly tried to imagine what it would have been like for a small boy to be separated from everyone he knew and loved. It was impossible. She had grown up with a warm and loving family of her own. Though she sometimes felt her parents' emphasis on high society had been misguided, she'd never known the kind of loneliness or fear that Michael was describing.

"It was three years before I saw my mother again, before she was able to leave Cuba on one of the freedom flights," Michael said. "For most of those three endless years I hated her for what she'd done. I was scared and lonely, even though *Tía* Pilar was good to me. It wasn't until the day my mother arrived in Miami, until I saw how she had been aged by the pain of letting me go, that I realized she had done it because she loved me. You see, for the longest time I thought she'd sent me away just to be rid of me, because she didn't want me anymore."

There was a telltale sheen in the brown

eyes that clashed with hers. "Don't ever intentionally do anything that could separate you from Brian. Okay?"

Molly couldn't seem to swallow past the lump in her throat. She simply nodded. "I'll do whatever you say," she said finally.

"Go to work. Follow your normal routine. Avoid discussing the murder with anyone. Most of all, don't speculate about what might have happened. Do you have a friend you two could stay with for a few days?"

"Yes, but I'd rather not. It hasn't been that long since the divorce. The move out of our house shook Brian's life up enough. I don't want to disrupt things for him again unless it's absolutely necessary."

"Where's his father? Could he stay with him for a few days?"

"Not a good idea," she said tersely.

"But feasible?"

"Things would have to be a lot worse than they are right now for me to turn Brian over to my ex-husband."

"Is there a problem there?"

"Not really. He's just looking for an excuse to say I'm an unfit mother. He has this idea that a boy should be raised by his father so he won't turn out to be a sissy. Real macho stuff. I mean, maybe he does have a point about a boy needing a male influence. I'm not denying him visitation rights. I'm going to make sure Brian gets involved in Scouts and Little League and all that sort of thing."

"Maybe Brian would like to play soccer," Michael suggested. "I coach a team. Should I ask him?"

As soon as the impulsive words were out of his mouth, he looked as though he wanted to take them back. For her own part, Molly considered the wisdom of allowing her life to become any more entangled with Michael's. Then she thought of Brian and how thrilled he would be to be asked to play on a team. Whatever second thoughts either of them had, her son's happiness had to come first.

"I think it's a wonderful idea," she said.

He nodded briskly. "I'll take care of it, then. The boys seem to have a good time. A lot of them don't have fathers around. I know what that's like. This gives me a way to pay back a little of what I've been given."

"Given?" she said. "It sounds to me as though you've earned whatever you have."

"I'm living in this country. That was my mother's gift. Knowing what I do now about life in Cuba, how could I not be grateful? I'll talk to Brian and see how he feels about it."

Now that Molly had approved, it was between him and Brian. That was what he was telling her. It had nothing to do with her. Okay, she got the message. She could be as generous and understanding as any mother when it came to her son. If Michael asked her to bake cookies for the team, though, she was going to cram them down his throat.

"Do you still live with your family?" she asked, thinking again of that sweet, musical voice on the phone.

"No," he said tersely, his face closed again. Despite the morning's revelations, he was shutting her out, distancing himself from any hint that what was growing between the two of them might be personal. Though she could tell he knew exactly what she was asking, there would be no elaboration, no explanation. She supposed he didn't owe her one, but a little clarification would have set the record straight once and for all.

Then again, maybe she didn't want to know. Things between them were complicated enough. Michael O'Hara's secrets were none of her business.

Naturally, however, the fact that he had secrets at all made her more curious about him than ever. Perversity, thy name is woman! Whoever'd said that had summed up her life fairly accurately.

8

Molly did her best to forget all about Michael and the murder. She didn't succeed worth a damn in either case. As a result her temper was frayed. When a producer called at midmorning with some petty annoyance about a location for his TV movie, she uncharacteristically bit his head off.

"I have a murder of my own to worry about. I don't have time to deal with yours. Leave the body in the Everglades for all I care."

Vince overheard her and grabbed his own extension. "Sorry, Greg. Molly's under a lot of stress just now. Let me help. What do you need?"

She knew she ought to be grateful. Instead, she was merely irritated that Vince, of all people, was suddenly the voice of reason in the office. When he'd soothed Greg's ruffled feathers, he hung up and stepped into her office. He lingered near the door, probably so he could flee if things got too tense.

"You okay?" he inquired cautiously.

"No. I feel so darned helpless. I ought to be doing something, but Michael . . ."

His brows rose suggestively. "Michael, is it?"

"Get your mind out of the gutter, Vince."

"Hey, I saw the way the man looked at you the other day. What's the story? Is he single? Go for it, Molly. You're not getting any younger."

She groaned. "Twenty-nine is hardly ancient and I don't need you as my social life guru."

"Who better to give you advice than a man-about-town such as myself?"

"Vince, the kind of relationships you have I'm better off without. Has the word commitment ever crossed your lips?"

"Heaven forbid," he said, looking horrified. "That doesn't mean it's not okay for some people. Boring people. Dead people."

Despite herself, Molly smiled, albeit weakly. "You're incorrigible."

"But cute, right? Now about your cop, you have to send him the right signals." He began to warm to his subject. "I mean, it does get a little complicated since he's investigating this murder and all, but once that's wrapped up, it should be clear sailing."

"He has a live-in girl friend."

"That could be tricky," he said as if it were no more than a minor inconvenience. "Are you sure? Did he tell you that?"

"No, as a matter of fact, he didn't. I called at dawn. Never mind why," she said, when Vince started to interrupt. "She answered."

"Could have been a housekeeper. Could have been a one-night stand. Did you ask?"

"More or less."

"And?"

"In essence, he said to mind my own business."

"In essence," he mimicked. "What does that mean? You women are all alike. You get bent out of shape over something instead of just asking straight out. You gotta clarify things. The look I saw in that man's eyes the other day was not the look of a man who is committed elsewhere."

"So his attention wanders. Do I need that in my life? No." She said it adamantly, but she wondered. Did she really want anything more than a casual flirtation? Not really. However, there was no need for Vince to know that. It might give *him* ideas.

"But . . ." he said.

"No *but*s. Attraction isn't love. Chemistry

isn't commitment. And I'd like to drop this matter now. Go play golf or something."

Vince sighed heavily, his expression one of disappointment. "Think it over, Molly. You want the advice of an expert, all you have to do is ask."

That afternoon after going home early again Molly couldn't shake Vince's observation about Michael's interest in her. She kept telling herself he'd been mistaken, that Michael had made it clear he would open his heart to her son, but not to her. Even so, with Brian in his room doing homework she had plenty of time to stew over the ambiguities. Wasted effort, she knew. She'd be better off trying to figure out the killer. She found her list and added a few notes. There wasn't much.

She was still at the dining room table an hour later, lingering over a second cup of coffee, her tuna salad untouched. She was going over the list of suspects for the fourth time, when the front door burst open. Before Molly could panic, Liza Hastings breezed in, key in hand, an indignant expression on her face and her red hair standing up in a trendy flattop that had been moussed into place. Fortunately she had the perfect gamine face to carry off the style and the friendly, fearless personality to carry off barging in unannounced.

"Why didn't you wake me?" she demanded, flopping into the chair across from Molly and putting her bare feet onto the seat of another chair. Her toenails today had been painted a deep bloodred, perhaps in honor of the murder. Liza tended toward dramatic statements.

"I didn't even know you were back in town," Molly said. "The last I knew you were on a mountaintop in Tibet."

"That was last month. I've been in Brazil since then. I wanted to see the rain forest before it all vanished. I got back late yesterday afternoon. I've been asleep ever since."

"I'm not surprised," Molly said. Just the recounting of Liza's frequent adventures exhausted her, even as they fascinated her. In another life, devoid of parental expectations and coming-out parties, she would have enjoyed such an impetuous, daring existence. "I'm glad you're back. I really need your advice."

"Not until you tell me everything that happened Tuesday night, and I do mean everything. I ran into Rhea Wilson downstairs. She said Allan Winecroft was stabbed to death and that you're a prime witness."

As Liza listened, she grabbed Molly's untouched mound of tuna salad and wolfed it down. Her expression reflected her increasing astonishment as Molly concluded, "Which makes me a possible suspect."

"You can't be serious," Liza said finally. "It's ridiculous. Anyone who knows you knows you're incapable of murder."

"Detective O'Hara doesn't know me. Besides, he doesn't seriously consider me a suspect even though my fingerprints are all over the weapon. At least, he says he doesn't. I'm sure he's just trying to keep an open mind. I guess if you're a policeman you can't afford to dismiss anyone too early in an investigation."

"He's wasting his time on you," Liza declared loyally. "But you do have a point. If no one else turns up, it would be just like them to take the easy way out and arrest you. I guess we'd better come up with an alternative. Tell me again exactly who was there for the bridge game?"

"Here, I've made a list." She shoved the paper across the table, grateful to have an ally. "Allan and Drucilla. They played against Roy Meeks and me. Tyler Jenkins and his wife played the Davisons. I didn't know the two couples at the third table. I think one of the women owns a boutique in the Square, the one with all the Italian designs that can only be worn if you're under twenty-five and weigh less than a hundred pounds. Just looking in the window depresses me."

"How do you know she owns it, if you've never been inside?"

"I heard somebody asking her about the shop at the pool one day. You must know who I mean. You bought that denim outfit in that store."

"Three fourths of my clothes are denim. It travels well. Weighs a ton, though. Maybe I should switch to linen. That would be the environmentally correct thing to do, wouldn't it?"

Molly was undaunted by Liza's conversational diversions. Eventually she always came back to the topic at hand. "I'm afraid I'm not up on environmentally correct attire," Molly said. "I just know you have to iron linen."

Liza wrinkled her nose. "That is a problem. So, which outfit?"

"The one with the skirt the size of a postage stamp. How do you have the nerve to wear that out in public?" Molly wondered, then decided that digression must be catching.

"It doesn't take nerve. It takes dieting."

Molly glanced pointedly at the scattered crumbs on a now empty plate.

"There are no calories in tuna fish. Every dieter knows that." Liza plucked up a wayward bit of celery and popped it into her mouth. "Okay, now, let's get serious. We'll never figure out the murderer, if we don't concentrate."

"I'm supposed to stay out of it," Molly reported dutifully.

"Who says?"

"The police."

Liza was unimpressed. "Well, you can't just sit back and let them send you to jail, can you? Besides, we're just having a private conversation. It's not as if we're out knocking on doors or something."

"I suppose," Molly said, doubting that Michael would see it that way. Of course, it was a private conversation. He'd never even have to know. If she picked up any tips from Liza, she could dutifully pass them along.

"Okay," she said, suddenly more cheerful, "what do you know about Roy Meeks?"

"Isn't he the one who walks the beach every morning at precisely seven fifteen, rain or shine, no matter what the tide is? Compulsive, if you ask me. Write that down. It could be important. How did you get roped into playing with him anyway? He's too old for you."

"It was hardly a date. Claire Bates came

down with the flu the morning of the game. She called me at work and asked me to take her place."

"How did she pick you?"

"I ran into her at the mailboxes the other night. She mentioned the bridge games. I said I'd played in college, not well, but endlessly. I guess she remembered."

"But there must be others who usually substitute. Did she try them first?"

"I don't know. What's your point?"

"Maybe she wanted you to be there to take the rap."

"Oh, for heaven's sakes, Claire Bates is a sixty-four-year-old widow who sings in the church choir. Does that sound like someone who'd stab a man in cold blood and pin the rap on someone she barely knows?"

"You make her sound like some dowdy frump without a brain in her head. May I remind you that she's head of some high-tech personnel search firm. She spends at least two hours every morning downstairs in the workout room and four weeks every year at an exorbitantly expensive California health spa. She's gorgeous enough to appear on the cover of *Lear's,* and she could probably run circles around the two of us."

"Maybe me. Not you. You climb mountains. I don't even use the steps."

"You're missing the point again. What makes you think she didn't have the hots for Allan?"

"Liza!"

"Don't look at me like that. Face it, most things do come down to sex. They don't refer to it as the war between the sexes without good reason. When couples aren't in bed, they're usually battling."

"Let's leave Claire Bates and your twisted philosophy about relationships out of this for the moment and concentrate on the people who were playing bridge the other night. You must know more about Roy Meeks than I do. He seemed like a pleasant enough man. He never once looked as though he wanted to throttle the Winecrofts, despite their nonstop bickering."

"If he's the one I'm thinking of, he's a retired psychiatrist."

"That's what Mr. Kingsley said."

"I knew it," Liza said triumphantly. "Freudian, I'll bet. Don't you think he looks the type?"

"Because he has a beard?"

"No. It's those dingy sweaters. I can just see him in some dark, musty room listening to people's secrets. He's probably one of those psychiatrists who attribute all emotional problems to deep-seated hatred of the mother or to premature separation from a pacifier. Listening to the Winecrofts probably made him feel nostalgic."

"What about the Davisons? Do you know them?"

Liza's expression brightened. "Sure. He teaches political science at the University of Miami. She teaches creative writing at Miami-Dade Community College. He's the real academician. Publish or perish and all that. She just wants to get kids excited about writing. They've been married for thirty years. They had a house in Coral Gables in the early seventies. When the kids went away to college, they moved here. They're depressingly normal. No skeletons in the closet that I've ever heard of. Nobody even complains about their grandkids when they come to visit. Actually, for kids, they're pretty cute."

"Capable of murder, either of them?"

Liza shook her head slowly. "I can't picture it."

"Do all these couples socialize outside the bridge games?"

"Dinners occasionally. I think I saw them lined up by the pool one day. Tyler and Allan play . . . *played* . . . tennis together. They might have been doubles partners, in fact."

"Any rifts you've ever heard about?"

"None. Couldn't you tell that night if everyone got along okay?"

"After the initial greetings, the only people who spoke above a whisper were the Winecrofts. These people take their bridge very seriously. They can't wait to turn the results in to *The Islander* for publication. Maybe the mood changes once the final hand is played, but I didn't stick around that long. All that bickering made me uncomfortable. I couldn't wait to escape."

"Which brings us back to Drucilla. Why aren't the police concentrating on her? Isn't the soon-to-be-wealthy widow always the most likely suspect?"

"I know she hates losing, but blowing a bridge game is hardly grounds for homicide. Besides, she says she went home right after I did. Allan was alive when she left."

"She says," Liza mocked. "And you believed her? As for a motive, how about divorce?"

"She wouldn't divorce him over his lousy bridge bid either."

Liza scowled at her. "No, forget the bridge game," she said impatiently. "Molly, you really need to spend more time at the pool. That's where you really find out what's going on around here."

"When would you suggest? By the time I

get home from work, the only people out there are as exhausted from working all day as I am. The only thing they're interested in is cooling off. They swim. They leave. They don't hang around to gossip."

"Don't say it like that," Liza said, scowling.

"Like what?"

"That judgmental tone. I'm not a gossip. I can't help it if sound carries out there and I'm naturally curious about human nature."

"Fine. We won't get into a discussion of the ethics of eavesdropping or the admissibility of hearsay evidence. If you know something relevant, just spit it out."

"Okay, don't get testy." Liza paused dramatically. "Picture this. Allan Winecroft was about to divorce his lovely wife of thirty-five years for Ingrid Nielsen, the beautiful bimbette in eight-twenty-six."

Molly stared at her, sure her mouth must be hanging open. "That's just two doors down the hall."

"I know. Tacky, huh? Installing his mistress right under his wife's nose takes a certain amount of nerve."

"Are you sure about this? Surely even Allan had better taste than that."

"Check the deed on the apartment. The buyer's name was printed in the paper, when the apartment was sold two years ago. I saw it myself: Allan Winecroft. I don't know if he bought it as an investment or for Ingrid, but she's in there now."

"Maybe he was just renting to her."

Liza rolled her eyes. "Molly, you are so middle-class."

"Well, she could be renting," Molly said defensively.

"Right. And he was over there at midnight fixing the plumbing."

"How do you know he was over there at midnight?"

"The Loefflers, the couple across the hall, told me. I saw him myself, after that. I wangled an invitation to their apartment for dinner."

"You spied on him?"

Liza shot her a look of disgust. "I did not spy. I spent the evening with a perfectly lovely couple. Mr. Loeffler told me all about dry cleaning."

"Dry cleaning?"

"He owned a whole chain of dry cleaners in Ohio before they sold out and moved here. He even told me how to get that raspberry stain out of my cream silk blouse. It was fascinating."

"I'm sure," Molly said. "But not nearly as fascinating as the comings and goings in the hall, I'm sure."

Liza just grinned, refusing to be insulted.

Molly ignored her smug demeanor. Refusing even to consider what Michael would have to say, she picked up the dishes, carried them into the kitchen, and headed for the door. When Liza didn't follow, she said, "Don't just sit there. Let's go."

"Where?" Liza said, but she was already on her feet, ready for action.

"You don't think I'm going to see Ingrid Nielsen by myself, do you? The police would never forgive me if I got myself murdered."

9

Molly had been around enough movie sets to understand the charisma of power. Producers and directors exuded it, though some of them had to work harder than others to accomplish it. Even so, she couldn't quite imagine Ingrid Nielsen with Allan Winecroft. Not even in the same room, much less in the same bed.

Talk about odd couples. She was tall. He was short. She was young. He had been heading into his golden years at a downhill clip. She was a statuesque beauty of Miss Universe caliber. He, to put it politely, probably hadn't seen the inside of a gym since high school required him to be there. Tennis had done nothing to reduce his flabby stomach. She spent her days languishing at the pool, fascinated with the latest tabloids. He spent his engaged in high finance. The only possible ground for mutual attraction was money. She wanted it. He had it.

Unless he had to fork it all out to an irate ex-wife.

"Okay, assuming for a minute that you're right about an impending divorce," Molly said thoughtfully as she and Liza waited to take the elevator to the eighth floor. "If Drucilla was about to take her husband to the cleaners, wouldn't she be more likely to wind up with a knife in her back? Both Allan and Ingrid would have pretty powerful motives for knocking her off."

"Your divorce really must have gone more smoothly than most," Liza countered. "Drucilla couldn't afford to take the risk of a nasty divorce. The way I figure it, she probably had some skeleton hidden in the closet. By the time Allan Winecroft finished airing the family scandals, whatever they were, Drucilla would have been publicly humiliated. Worse, she would have lost access to his — by all reports — very deep pockets. With him dead, she gets it all and keeps her pure reputation. She'll be married again by the end of the year, probably to some enterprising businessman half her age."

Molly recalled Michael O'Hara's assumption that Drucilla had been awaiting the arrival of a lover when they arrived to question her. Could that have been the skeleton

Drucilla would have killed to hide? "Was she having an affair?" she asked Liza as they took the elevator up.

"If I knew that, so would everyone else. Then there wouldn't have been much risk involved in exposure, would there? If she is, unlike Allan, she is very discreet. There's never been so much as a whisper of scandal that could be substantiated."

"Then what makes you think Allan had any ammunition to take into court, especially if he was having an affair himself? Sounds awfully messy on both sides to me. Or maybe if there was no whispering, it's because there was no scandal. Drucilla's alimony would have been safe enough."

"No. More likely the old double standard. If he could prove she'd been playing around, his own tawdry little affair would be viewed sympathetically. Male privilege or something."

"So, who should we see first? I thought Ingrid, but maybe we should go straight to Drucilla instead."

"You've already seen Drucilla. She's probably surrounded by her friends now or under sedation or something. I doubt if anyone's in there weeping with Ingrid. She could probably use a sympathetic ear."

As the elevator doors slid open, Detective

O'Hara started to step inside. He took one look at Molly, who'd gotten out without thinking. If she'd been smart, she'd have stayed right where she was and gone to some other floor. Any other floor. He gave her one of his *I-don't-believe-this* looks and let the elevator leave without him.

"Explain," he said succinctly as her only route of escape vanished.

Since Molly knew he wouldn't like the explanation, she introduced Liza instead. It was an ideal diversionary tactic. His eyes lit up with an interest Molly found herself envying. She knew better than to think it had anything to do with the murder. Liza always had that mesmerizing effect on men. She radiated the kind of energy that attracted them, though their efforts to evoke a response from her were usually wasted. Liza's trail of broken hearts was legendary, and those were just the ones on the island. She didn't have time for romance, or so she claimed. Molly suspected that her own heart had taken a beating years before and she'd adopted a self-protective shell as a result. Whatever the real story, she'd never shared a word of it with Molly despite their immediate and confiding friendship that began when Molly and Brian moved in across the hall.

The detective's attention wandered only briefly. All too quickly, he focused on Molly again. Under other circumstances, she might have found that satisfying. "Your apartment's on five," he said.

"Yes. And you don't have one. Why are you here?"

"Police business." He glanced at Liza. "And your apartment?"

"Right across the hall from Molly," Liza informed him cheerfully. "Want to drop by and see my collection of African masks? They're quite extraordinary."

"I'll bet they are. Perhaps we should all go take a look." He regarded Molly quizzically. "Unless you had other plans."

"Well, I was going . . ." Her voice trailed off.

"Yes?"

"Never mind. It can wait."

"Actually, we were on our way to visit a friend," Liza said. "Ingrid Nielsen. Do you know her?"

The detective gritted his teeth. "No, but I have the distinct impression I should. Why?"

"Well, for one thing she is absolutely beautiful," Molly said hurriedly before Liza could give them away. She'd only made that promise to Michael hours before. He was not going to be thrilled that she'd forgotten it already.

"And?" he said.

"And what?"

"I'm sure you weren't going to see her because she's beautiful. What's her connection to the case?"

"Who said there was a connection?"

"You did."

"I never . . ."

"Your face gave you away. Unless my detecting skills are rusty, which they rarely have time to get, you're still worried about being considered a suspect despite my reassurances just this morning. That means you're probably ignoring my advice to leave the investigating to me . . . again. Are you following me so far?"

She nodded reluctantly.

"How am I doing?"

"You're on the money," she conceded grumpily.

He beamed. "Swell. Then the only thing left to figure out is what this Ingrid Nielsen has to do with Allan Winecroft's murder. Suppose we all drop in together?" He turned back down the hall. "Which apartment?"

"Oh, what the hell," Liza said, leading the way. "The more the merrier."

Molly wasn't so sure about that. Michael

didn't look very merry.

His mood improved considerably when Ingrid Nielsen opened the door, her blond hair pulled back from a face so stunning that any agency in New York would have hired her as a model in an instant. Thick lashes rimmed eyes of navy-blue velvet. She was wearing an oversized hot-pink T-shirt that barely reached her knees and clung to every lush curve of her young, tanned body. What he couldn't seem to pull his gaze from, however, were the tears tracking down her cheeks. She swiped at them with a fistful of crumpled Kleenex.

Liza didn't waste time being coy. She drew the girl into a hug. "I'm sorry. You must be feeling absolutely lousy."

Ingrid didn't even spare her a glance. Her frightened eyes were riveted on Michael.

"This is Detective O'Hara," Liza said briskly, ushering them all back into the living room. "He's going to find Allan's killer."

The announcement brought on a fresh onslaught of sobs, all the more devastating because the young girl made not so much as a whimper of sound. Michael stared at her with the bemused expression of a man totally at a loss. Molly almost felt sorry for him, until she realized that his attention had already moved on.

His gaze went to the silver-framed photograph of Allan sitting in the middle of the huge marble coffee table and froze there. She could see the pieces click into place. A fresh arrangement of long-stemmed apricot roses sat beside the photo. The florist's card had been crumpled, then smoothed out. Molly edged closer for a better look. She wasn't surprised to see that the flowers had been sent by Allan. Posthumously, though? Maybe the man had placed a standing order and no one had thought to cancel it. At forty bucks or more a dozen, a greedy florist might be reluctant to cancel the order himself until he was told to.

"Ms. Nielsen," Michael said quietly, "what was your relationship with Allan Winecroft?"

"He was . . ." she began, but her voice choked up on her. She cleared her throat and looked him straight in the eye. "We were going to be married as soon as he divorced that bitch down the hall."

Molly winced at the blunt description of Drucilla. Michael's face remained stoically impassive. "Did he have any immediate plans to do that?"

"He told me it had to be handled carefully."

Which meant, Molly thought, that Allan had been dragging his heels. Why? She voiced the question aloud.

"Because the old witch controlled all the money."

If the others were as stunned as Molly, they did a better job of hiding it. If all their suppositions about the source of the Winecroft money had been wrong, it played havoc with any motive Drucilla might have had for murder. She could have dumped Allan in a heartbeat. "I thought he had been CEO of a big corporation in New York," Molly said.

"That's true, but it was her company originally. He took it from a nothing little business started by her father and turned it into a conglomerate. He deserved all the credit and she knew it, but she still controlled the purse strings. He told me all about it. If she'd cut him loose, he would have lost everything."

"Then where was he getting the money to pay for this apartment?" Liza blurted, not fearing to rush in where Molly wasn't about to tread.

Ingrid shrugged, obviously not one to question a gift horse. "He had a few things going on the side, I guess. I never asked. Or maybe he took the payments out of petty cash. It's not much of an apartment, compared to what they own. I asked him to get a bigger place, but he said he couldn't afford it, all because of that awful wife of his. I hope you arrest her," she said to Michael. "She probably killed him just for spite. She didn't want me to have him."

Molly glanced around at the expensive furnishings, the decorator touches. There had been one brief moment when they'd first walked in when she had felt sorry for Ingrid. She'd seemed like a girl who'd innocently gotten caught up in something sordid and was now paying the price. Now Molly wondered if she wasn't just a grasping, spoiled brat, perhaps even more of a manipulator than the woman she sought to replace. It dismayed her how often ugliness turned up when the veneer of beauty was scraped away.

Having surmised Ingrid's true colors, Molly wondered if Allan had provided for her in his will. If so, perhaps Ingrid had tired of waiting to share wedded bliss with him and gone for the payoff. She decided against asking straight out about the contents of any will. The girl would only lie. She seemed more than capable of protecting her own hide.

"What will you do now?" Molly asked, managing to sound sympathetic.

"Do?"

Getting a job was clearly a concept with which Ingrid wasn't familiar. "Will you be able to stay on here?" Molly persisted. "Or will you need to go back to modeling?"

Michael O'Hara shot her an approving glance.

"I'm getting too old to model," Ingrid said, too quickly. "Besides, I'm sure Allan arranged for me to keep this place in case anything ever happened to him."

"Your name was on the deed?"

Ingrid managed to look demure. "He was a very considerate man."

"And very generous," Molly observed. "I'm sure you're right. He must have worried, though, at his age, that something could happen to him and you would be left with nothing. An apartment like this is expensive to maintain. Did you ever talk about that?"

Ingrid's eyes suddenly narrowed. "You mean a will, right? Well, of course he had one. Any man in his position would. We never discussed the contents, though, not specifically."

"So you don't know that he left you anything besides the apartment?"

A fresh batch of tears appeared, as if on cue. "What does any of that matter now?"

she whimpered. "All that matters is that he's dead."

By this time, though, Molly doubted if anyone in the room believed the performance, except possibly Ingrid herself.

"Fascinating," Liza said, the minute the door had closed behind them. "Molly, I had no idea you could cross-examine anyone like that."

"Me, either," Michael admitted. It wasn't said with the sort of admiration Molly would have preferred. "Was I wasting my breath this morning? What the hell possessed you to go traipsing up here on your own without telling me what you were up to?"

"You'd have told me to stay out of it."

"Damn right, I would. After last night, you should know better."

Liza stared from one to the other, obviously confused by the crackling tension arcing between them. "What happened last night?"

"It was nothing," Molly murmured.

"Then why did you wake me from a dead sleep to tell me about it?" Michael demanded. "You were practically incoherent."

"I had an attack of nerves, okay? That's all it was. That's hardly incoherent. By the time you got over here I was just fine."

"Fine? I don't think so. Let me remind you one more time that amateur snooping is the fastest way I know to go from witness to victim."

Molly shivered but remained defiant. She wasn't going to allow this whole awful situation to make her run and hide or stop looking out for her own interests. "Look, I got Ingrid to admit that she's probably better off with Allan dead than she was with him alive. That makes her a suspect, right?"

"Yes," he said grudgingly. "But you've also warned her that we're on to her. Any evidence we were likely to get could wind up buried so deep now that we'll never find it."

Liza patted his cheek consolingly. "Don't look so glum, Detective. I'm sure you'll be able to find whatever you put your mind to. Now, come along and tell us what else you've discovered today. I'm sure if we all put our heads together we can have this solved in no time."

"I have lots of help from my fellow officers, thanks."

"Ah, but they don't know the cast of characters the way we do, do they?"

"No," he said, barely controlling a sigh of regret.

"Then come along. Molly makes a great

café cubano. While she's doing that, we can all get better acquainted."

Molly had a feeling things were spinning out of control. Liza had a way of taking charge that wasn't always appreciated. "I'm not sure getting better acquainted goes along with police procedure," she said, offering the detective an out she was sure he'd grab. He'd obviously seen more of her in the past few days than he'd cared to.

"That's your trouble, Mrs. DeWitt. You don't understand a damn thing about police procedure. I think getting acquainted is definitely in order."

He even led the way to her apartment. When he walked through the door, Brian took one look at him and said, "Oh, wow, you haven't arrested Mom, have you?"

"Not yet," he said with a pointed glance in her direction.

Molly took the hint and practically ran into the kitchen. To her dismay, the detective was only one step behind her. When she toppled the can of Cuban coffee onto the floor, he picked it up and took over. His movements were efficient and practiced. When the powerful coffee was brewing, he turned toward her again.

"Why won't you leave this investigation in my hands?"

"Because I've learned through the years not to count on anyone but myself. There are fewer disappointments that way. If things get screwed up, I have no one to blame but myself."

"In this instance, there is more at risk that way. Assuming that you're not the killer, which I do assume, by the way, then the real murderer could get very nervous at all your snooping. For all we know, he or she could already think you know too much. We've been over this before. If you insist on pursuing this, the only way I'll be able to protect you is by putting you under guard. Frankly, I don't have the manpower to waste on a meddlesome woman who insists on jumping into the path of danger."

"Thanks," she muttered, thoroughly miffed. *Meddlesome woman,* indeed.

"You know what I mean. You work for the county and know every bit as much as I do about the budget crunch, I'm sure." A wicked gleam put sparks in his dark-brown eyes. He took a step closer. "Unless, of course, you're hoping I'll move in, just to protect you."

"Detective O'Hara," she protested.

"Michael, please," he reminded her, inching closer still. She could smell his aftershave. It was a spicy scent she particularly liked. If he'd meant to intimidate her, it wasn't working. On the contrary, she was likely to throw herself into his arms in another humiliating second.

"It appears we're going to be better acquainted than I ever dreamed," he murmured, deliberately provoking her.

Reacting on cue, Molly gritted her teeth. "I do not want you — or anyone else — to move in here to protect me."

"Actually, it could be convenient," he said thoughtfully, his gaze locked with hers. "It's a long drive from Little Havana. It would save me time if I just bunked on your sofa."

"I'm sure the county can still afford to pay for your mileage."

"I was talking time, not money. Just think what clues I could pick up if I lurked about the halls at all hours."

"And your roommate? What will she think?"

"Bianca does not interfere in my work."

Naturally, Molly thought sourly. The *little woman* wouldn't. Chauvinist pig. Reminding herself that she absolutely hated his sort of macho superiority helped to slow the pace of her pulse, but not by much.

"Well, I for one think it's the perfect solution," Liza said from the doorway, where she'd once again been indulging in her favorite form of entertainment, eavesdropping. "I know that I would feel much safer having you close by."

"Then invite him to your apartment," Molly suggested.

He shook his head. "You're the one more likely to be in danger."

"Liza is every bit as nosy as I am."

"But she wasn't around when the murder occurred. You were." He nodded decisively. "The more I think about it, the better I like it."

"Well, I don't." She shot Liza a frantic plea for help. Liza was studiously watching the coffee perk and humming.

Michael ignored the objection. "I'll get my things and be back in time for dinner. My treat."

"This is not orthodox police procedure," Molly said desperately. "The director will hate it."

He winked at her as he headed for the door. "And I've already reminded you that you don't know beans about procedure. Call my boss and complain, if you object. He'll only tell you I'm here for your own protection, which is what I intend to tell him myself."

"Well, who the hell is going to protect me from you?" she demanded before she could stop herself.

Unexpectedly flirtatious brown eyes raked her up and down. "You don't have a thing to worry about on that count," he said insultingly. "You're too skinny. You know us Latin types like our women to have hips. It bodes well for breeding."

"Breeding!" Molly's voice climbed an octave as she repeated the offensive word.

He was chuckling as the door closed behind him. She glared at Liza. "This is all your fault. You had to go and encourage him to stay. I'm sure I could have talked him out of it."

"Why on earth would you want to talk a hunk like that out of staying in your apartment? I don't think your Detective O'Hara is easily swayed once he's made up his mind."

"He is not *my* anything."

"You could do worse."

"Right at the moment, I can't think of how."

"You could wind up with someone like Allan Winecroft."

"Bite your tongue."

Liza grinned. "I wonder where he'll take you to dinner. That Thai restaurant in is good. Maybe Italian, you like Italian."

"He'll probably bring back a couple of

pizzas from Sir Pizza. Why are we talking about this? How am I going to explain him to Brian? It'll scare him to death, if he thinks we're in danger. The calls last night have already made him nervous."

"Don't worry about Brian. He'll be thrilled to have a cop in the house. It'll give him something to talk about at school."

"I'll be lucky if he doesn't steal his gun to take to show-and-tell. Maybe Brian should stay at your place for a few days."

"Now that really would require some explaining, or do you want him to get the idea that his mother and the detective are having a passionate fling?"

"Brian is too young to know about passionate flings."

"I doubt that, but assuming he is, then he'll probably just feel abandoned and his psyche will be ruined forever. He's better off right here in his own bed . . . unless you would prefer to be alone with the detective," she said slyly. "Are you interested, Molly?"

"Go to hell, Liza."

"No time. I have a date. See you in the morning."

She breezed out, leaving Molly with a whole lot more to fear than the vague possibility that some unknown killer might decide to come after her. The biggest danger to her tonight was going to be having Detective O'Hara in her apartment, within a few skimpy yards of her raging and thoroughly irrational hormones.

10

Brian was watching a crash-bang rerun of *The Dukes of Hazzard* when Molly went to tell him that Detective O'Hara — Michael — was moving in temporarily.

"Okay," he said, barely sparing her a glance. The news clearly didn't faze him. It irritated her no end that Liza, who claimed to have absolutely no maternal instincts, seemed to know her son better than she did. She'd also been hoping that somehow his reaction would provide her with an excuse to keep the detective off her sofa.

"What's for dinner?" Brian asked instead.

Molly sighed, resignation washing over her along with an undeniable spark of anticipation. It was a spark she intended to ignore if she had to spend the entire night under an icy shower. "I don't know. He's taking us out."

"Okay." On the screen two cars playing bumper tag on some country road crashed into a fiery mess. "Yeah!" Brian said. "Did you see that, Mom?"

Molly cringed. "I saw it. Don't you have homework?"

"Just spelling stuff. I know the words."

"Are you sure?"

"Sure, I'm sure. Spelling's my best subject. You know that." During all of this his eyes never once left the television screen. He was saved from a motherly lecture about driving safely by a timely knock on the door. Since it was too soon for Michael to be back, she checked carefully before answering it. A week ago she wouldn't have bothered, trusting the guards to keep her safe from unwanted visitors.

Claire Bates stood on the threshold, still pale from her bout with the flu but looking every bit as glamorous as Liza had noted in their earlier conversation. Her chin-length hair had been streaked a soft ash blond. She was wearing linen slacks in a pale celadon green with a matching silk blouse and flat shoes just one shade darker. Chunky silver jewelry completed the fashionable ensemble. Her gray eyes were faintly troubled.

"I probably should have called first," she began apologetically.

"No, of course not. Come in. I've just made some Cuban coffee, or I could fix you a cup of tea."

"Nothing, thanks. My stomach's still pitching and rolling like a boat on the high seas. I had to come and see you to apologize for getting you mixed up in this awful business with Allan." She perched on the edge of a chair, her hands folded in her lap, her legs crossed demurely at the ankles. Only a former debutante who'd excelled at hiding her own nervousness would have picked up on the fact that her hands were anything but relaxed.

"Claire, please," Molly protested. "It's certainly not your fault. You could hardly know that Allan would be killed after that card game. You could help me figure out what might have gone on, though. There's a lot I just don't understand."

Alarm seemed to flare in the depths of those silvery eyes. "How could I do that? I wasn't there."

"But you know everyone who was there much better than I do. You could tell me how everyone usually interacts. Maybe then I could tell if anything was particularly off that night."

"Such as?"

"Is everyone in the group friendly?"

The calm facade slipped, replaced by unmistakable fear. "Dear God, you don't think that one of them did it, do you? That's not possible, surely. It had to be a stranger."

Molly shook her head. "I don't think so. I checked the logs that morning. No one came in or out of the building after midnight except residents. I double-checked the log at the gate just to be sure. There's no other access. Even if someone climbed the fence from the beach, the building doors are locked."

Claire shivered and turned paler still. "Maybe it was someone the guard knew well, but not a resident. Sometimes they get a little lax about enforcing the rules, especially with frequent visitors."

"No, this was a new guard. He wouldn't have recognized anyone. He even stopped me three nights ago, because I didn't have the new sticker on my windshield. I'm absolutely convinced that the murderer has to be from this building."

"Oh, God, how awful."

"But you can see why it's so important to think about any rifts, no matter how seemingly insignificant. The Winecrofts were arguing all during the game. Do they usually do that?"

Claire's face reflected her distaste. "I've never known them not to argue. I swear I can't see why she put up with him and that little nobody he installed down the hall. He'd been humiliating her like that for years. Ingrid is new, but she was hardly the first."

"Why on earth didn't Drucilla divorce him then?"

"He kept the business going and maintained all the right social contacts. He smoothed her way onto all the right boards. Besides, in some bizarre way I think it suited her purposes to stay married to a man like Allan. It gave her the freedom to do whatever she wanted to do."

Aha, Molly thought. Now they were getting somewhere. "You mean affairs?"

To her disappointment, Claire shook her head. "Not that I know of, though I've certainly heard the rumors that she was seeing this one or that one on the sly. I was thinking of all the social things she thrives on, the board of this, the luncheon committee for that. If she'd had to run the company herself, she wouldn't have had time left for the things she really enjoys. She likes playing lady bountiful. Drucilla goes to more balls and luncheons than any other five women I know. If she's not being honored herself, she's on the committee to honor someone else. It would drive me crazy. What could they possibly have had left to talk about after six or seven of those things in a row?"

A murder, perhaps? Molly resolved then and there to accept the invitation she'd just received to a benefit luncheon on Tuesday for some disease. She'd planned to send a check anyway, but the cause was suddenly far less important than the conversation. Drucilla had been listed as the event's honorary chairwoman.

"So Drucilla wouldn't be your number one suspect?" she said to Claire.

"Absolutely not. And Ingrid, for all her lack of morals, would be pretty far down the list too. Allan was her meal ticket."

"How did they meet?"

"I believe she did a commercial for one of his subsidiaries. It so happened he was meeting with the account executive in New York that day and the guy took him along to the shoot. Apparently it was her last job."

"If she was a model, she could certainly work down here. Agencies are shooting ads all over town."

"Allan didn't want her parading that body in front of anyone but him."

And all the residents of Ocean Manor, Molly thought, but didn't say. "Okay, so she gives up her career for him. What if she suddenly realized he was never going to get a divorce and marry her? Wouldn't that give her a motive?"

"Maybe, but she was probably better off with things just the way they were. She had his money and her freedom, especially during the summer when he and Drucilla went north."

"He didn't take Ingrid along?"

"Absolutely not. Their circle of friends up there would never have tolerated it. Drucilla comes from old money. They have their standards, even when it comes to affairs. Ingrid lacks class. Her presence would have been an embarrassment to Drucilla and Allan. And for all his flaws, he would never have subjected Ingrid to that sort of ridicule."

"Interesting that he seems more concerned with his girl friend's feelings than his wife's."

Claire shrugged. "I'm sure he felt Drucilla was well able to fend for herself. She may be able to portray the fragile feminine flower to the hilt, but underneath she has a will of iron."

Molly sighed. "If you eliminate Drucilla and Ingrid as suspects, who else is left? Tyler Jenkins? The Davisons? Roy Meeks? Any of the other couples there that night?"

Claire just shrugged helplessly. "I can't

imagine any of them being involved. Allan was Tyler's protégé, if it's possible for a sixty-eight-year-old man to have a sixty-two-year-old protégé. At any rate, he was counting on Allan to turn the management of the building around."

"What if he'd been disillusioned? Maybe Allan wasn't tough enough."

"You've got to be kidding. The man was leaving a trail of enemies because of his rules and regulations."

"There," Molly said, suddenly hopeful. "That's exactly what I need. What enemies?"

"Three fourths of the people in the building resented him for treating them like children. Maybe in their hearts, they knew he was after better management, but his whole focus seemed to be on such petty stuff. Getting rid of that cat, for instance. Have you talked to Mrs. Jenko?"

"Yes."

"What about the Firths? You heard about that incident over little Hettie's bare feet? Call them." Claire scribbled a number on a piece of paper. "There are a dozen more like them, who had run-ins with Allan over petty annoyances."

"Maybe some weren't so petty."

"Maybe not," Claire said, still looking

every bit as troubled as she had when she arrived. "I guess you always assume a murder is going to be over something big, something important. Not over whether or not some kid was barefooted in the lobby."

"And you're certain there were no deep-rooted feuds among the bridge players themselves?"

"The same people have been playing bridge on Tuesday nights since the building opened. Sure, there have been squabbles. Occasionally somebody gets especially worked up over a hand. Once Tyler accused Roy Meeks of cheating."

"What did Roy do?"

"He quietly folded his hand, stood up and said he'd be back when Tyler apologized. At the time Tyler swore that Roy would get an apology when hell froze over. He held out until the next Tuesday morning, then called Roy up. The game went on as usual Tuesday night."

Neither man's behavior was indicative of the kind of fury it had taken to drive that knife into Allan's back. "That's it?" Molly said.

"I'm sorry. I can't think of anything."

"How did you feel about Allan?"

Claire gazed unflinchingly into Molly's eyes. "I thought he was a nasty, abrasive ass, but I wouldn't have killed him. It takes too long to find a decent bridge player."

"Actually, Allan was pretty lousy the other night."

Claire seemed genuinely surprised by that. "Then his mind must have been on something else," she said with certainty. "He and Drucilla almost never lose."

Perhaps, Molly thought, his mind had been on those late-night threats or on some meeting he had scheduled for after the bridge game. Who was it Drucilla said had stopped by later? Juan Gonzalez? Molly didn't know him, but perhaps she should.

"Do you know anything about Juan Gonzalez?" she asked.

Claire shook her head. "Very little. I think he's a doctor, or maybe it's a lawyer. Anyway, he's very smooth, very polite. A bachelor."

"Were he and Allan friends?"

"I wouldn't think so. I don't recall ever seeing them together. If anything, I would have guessed he and Drucilla were friends."

"More than friends?"

Claire looked startled. "Why, no, I don't think so." She hesitated. "Now that you mention it, though, there was something . . ."

"What?"

"I can't put my finger on it — an intimacy, I guess you'd call it. It was the way they looked at each other when they thought no one was noticing. I never saw them alone, just at parties, occasionally at the pool, always with others around, including Allan. Why would you ask, though? Juan wasn't there that night. He doesn't play bridge as far as I know."

"Drucilla said he stopped by after I left. She said he'd come to see Allan, that he and several others were sitting around discussing business, when she left."

"Possible. The men often did that."

"Thanks, Claire," she said, walking her to the door. "You've been a big help. If you think of anything else, let me know."

"Perhaps she should let *me* know," Michael suggested, slowly removing his sunglasses so that Molly could get a good look at the storm brewing in his eyes. He was standing in the hallway, just close enough to have overheard yet more incriminating evidence that Molly hadn't mended her ways. She refused to feel guilty about it, not when she'd learned a couple of interesting tidbits to pass along.

"It's okay," she said soothingly, smiling brightly. "I'll share what I know with you."

"I do so love a witness who's willing to

cooperate with the police."

"Police?" Claire repeated weakly. "Oh, my."

Molly practically pushed her into the hall. "We'll talk again soon."

Claire was only too willing to take the hint. She virtually ran for the elevator.

Michael brought in a small canvas bag and a suit still in its dry cleaner plastic. He hung them neatly in the hall closet without asking directions or permission. Molly edged back into the living room, trying to figure out what she could put between her and the explosion she knew was coming. Since nothing looked suitably sturdy, she decided to rely on her wits.

"She dropped in. I didn't invite her."

"And who is she?"

"Claire Bates, the woman I substituted for on Tuesday night."

"And what did you and Mrs. Bates have to talk about?"

"This and that."

"Care to be more specific?"

"She gave me the Firths' phone number." She waved the paper for him to examine. "They're the people Allan harassed because their child was in the lobby without shoes."

"And?"

"I haven't called them yet."

"I meant, what else did you and Mrs. Bates talk about."

"Actually there is one thing that might interest you. I think I know who Drucilla might be involved with, and he was there Tuesday night."

For one lingering instant fury warred with curiosity. Michael was too good a cop to let the fury interfere with possible evidence. "Spill it."

"Juan Gonzalez."

"Any specifics?"

"Claire's gut instincts. I mean, she didn't think of that at first, but when I asked the question, she thought about it and said yes."

Michael groaned. "Well, that's certainly something we can take into court."

"Okay, so it's not exactly solid," she said, miffed at his reaction. "It's a lead, isn't it? Shouldn't you be grateful?"

"Oh, I am," he said. "Do you have a spare key for this place?"

Molly blinked and stared. "A key?"

"So I can get back in later."

"You actually want me to give you your own key?"

"Unless you'd rather wait up. Sounds cozy. I'd like that."

"I thought you were taking us to dinner."

"I was, until I got this hot new lead. Now

I'm going to spend the evening tracking down Juan Gonzalez and asking him about his current romantic entanglements."

"Not without me you're not. It's my lead."

"It *was* your lead. Now it's mine. I've got the badge that says so. Night, sweetheart. Never mind about the key. I'll just jimmy the lock."

Furious, she grabbed the closest heavy object to throw at his retreating back. Unfortunately, it was her key ring. It struck the target and clattered to the floor. He picked it up, jingled it cheerfully, and tucked it in his pocket. "Thanks. Sleep tight."

The only satisfactory projectile within reach now was a brass lamp with a marble base. It had cost over three hundred dollars. Even so, she had her hands around it when the door shut quietly behind him. She was tempted to sit up half the night if she had to, just for the satisfaction of heaving it at him when he finally came in.

Instead, she found her extra set of keys, told Brian to order a pizza for himself, and called Liza for the apartment number of the couple who'd monitored the comings and goings at Ingrid's apartment. Perhaps they'd seen Juan Gonzalez popping in on Drucilla at odd hours as well.

■ ■ ■ ■

Mr. and Mrs. Irv Loeffler were just about to go out for the evening when Molly knocked on their door. Mrs. Loeffler, Tess, was a tiny woman with keen, animated eyes. The minute Molly introduced herself as a friend of Liza's, those eyes sparked with lively curiosity.

"Irv, call the restaurant. Change the reservation."

"We'll miss the early bird special," he grumbled, but he took his plaid jacket off and hung it neatly in the closet. The instincts of a man who'd pressed too many rumpled coats in his day, no doubt.

"So we'll pay full price for a change," Mrs. Loeffler countered. "We can afford it. You cleaned enough suits to pay for dinner out once a week."

Despite his grumblings, Irv Loeffler had a twinkle in his eye when he went to phone the restaurant.

"Now, you come right on in, dear, and tell me why you've come."

Once she was seated, Molly hesitated. It wasn't exactly tactful to suggest that the couple was in the habit of spying on their neighbors. "Actually, it's about the Winecrofts. Did you see them often?"

"Socially? Oh, my, no. Irv and I mostly keep to ourselves. We both like to read. Probably a habit from living in Cleveland. In the winter about the only thing the place was fit for was curling up in front of a fire with a good book. Our children skied, but not Irv and me. What with one thing and another we were always too busy to learn. Besides, there's nothing I like better than a good mystery."

"Then you must be fascinated with Allan's murder?"

"Actually, that's a little too close to home for my taste," she said nervously. "A good puzzle in a book, that's the ticket."

"Have the police questioned you at all?"

"That nice detective with the Irish name came by, but I told him the same as I'm telling you. Irv and I didn't see the Winecrofts much, except at the elevator occasionally."

"But you knew about Ingrid?"

She shook her head. "Can you believe the nerve of the man? Parading that woman right in front of his wife. If Irv ever did something like that, I'd give him what-for, I can tell you that."

"Did Mrs. Winecroft have much company?"

"You mean men, of course. Well, I can't say for sure, not the way I could with Allan and Ingrid, but it did seem to me that she and that attractive Hispanic man were awfully chummy. My mother always told me that appearances are everything. You just don't have a man who's not your husband dropping by in the middle of the morning. Unless he's just there to fix the sink, it doesn't look proper."

"Do you know who he is?"

"José, maybe. Or Jesús. Is that it, Irv?"

"What's that, dear?"

She waved her hand impatiently. "The man who was always dropping by to see Drucilla. Is his name José?"

"That's gossip, Tess. You know how I feel about that."

"Irv," she said in that quiet, warning way that women for centuries had used to suggest dire consequences.

He heaved a sigh of resignation. "Juan," he said. "Juan Gonzalez. Lives upstairs in the penthouse. If you're going to talk about these things, I don't know why you can't keep the names straight. Now can we go to dinner before we miss the second reservation?"

Molly stood up. "Thank you both so much for taking the time to talk with me. I hope you enjoy your dinner."

Tess followed her into the hall. "Don't mind Irv. He's a regular old grouch whenever he has to pay full price for anything. Comes from living through the Depression, I suppose."

"It never hurts to be cautious when it comes to finances," Molly agreed. "How does he feel about the way these assessments keep going up?"

"Oh, please, don't even mention it. He gets apoplectic. Him and Ralph Keller down on two. To hear them tell it, there won't be a retiree able to afford this place if the board keeps on the way it has been."

"Did he ever talk to Allan about the way he felt?"

"He wrote him a letter, the same one he'd sent to Manny Mendoza the year before. The board doesn't pay a bit of attention to folks like us. They're a regular little clique. I'm surprised Allan was able to budge Manny Mendoza out in that last election. Of course, there's talk all the time that it was fixed."

"What about Mr. Keller? Did he complain?"

"Well," she began conspiratorially. "I wasn't there, but I hear he and Allan had quite a set-to out at the pool one day. If Irv hadn't grabbed Ralph's arm, he would have pushed Allan straight into the water."

"Did you mention that to Detective O'Hara?"

"Why, no. Oh, my, you don't think that Ralph . . . why, he would never kill anyone. Besides, he couldn't have done it."

"Why not?"

"The way I hear it, Allan was murdered late at night. Ralph is always in bed by ten, same as us."

As alibis went, it wasn't much. Molly decided she'd know more, once she'd had a chance to meet Ralph Keller herself.

"Thanks, again," she told Mrs. Loeffler. "Enjoy your evening."

She practically ran to the elevator and used the phone inside to call the front desk for Ralph Keller's apartment number. The elevator was already on the second floor by the time the guard had found it. She figured she had another ten minutes tops before the pizza arrived.

Outside Ralph Keller's door, she heard the television going full blast. She had to pound to be heard over the news. Finally the door was thrown open revealing a tall, barrel-chested man with a fierce expression.

"I ain't buying nothing," he said and nearly slammed the door. Molly wedged herself into the opening in the nick of time.

"I'm sorry, Mr. Keller. I'm not selling anything." She introduced herself. "I was just visiting with the Loefflers up on eight and they gave me your name. Could we talk for a minute?"

"What about?" His gaze narrowed suspiciously.

"The assessments. Mrs. Loeffler says you've been worried about the way they're going up."

"Damn right I am. There's no excuse for it." He hesitated for a minute, then opened the door wide. "Might as well come on in and have a seat."

"Thank you."

Though it was still daylight outside, the apartment was dark. The drapes had been drawn to block out the light and only a single lamp with maybe a sixty-watt bulb had been lighted. It created a circle of pale illumination that barely spread beyond the end table it was on. The place also reeked of pipe smoke. The cherry scent might have been appealing when fresh. Now it was stale, imbedded in every piece of overstuffed furniture.

"You must be from up north," she guessed, surveying the heavy fabrics and dark woods.

"Trenton. Lived there for sixty-five years. Would have stayed there till I died, but my wife wanted to move south. She came to Miami one February and never got over it being so warm. Insisted we move the day I retired. Don't you know, she passed away that first year. Never really had a chance to enjoy it."

"I'm sorry," Molly said. "I'm surprised you didn't move back."

"Guess I'd adjusted by then. Didn't seem to be much sense in it."

"If it's not too personal, are you on a pension? Social Security?"

He made a sound that might have been a snort of derision or maybe laughter. "No, ma'am. I did okay with my business up there. Had a restaurant, homestyle cooking, baked goods, that sort of thing. Opened a second one about ten years ago. The year I retired I sold out to some guy who started franchising 'em. They're all over Jersey now, a couple in New York and Connecticut. Got a nice payout and I'm still getting a little money in from selling him the name."

"So the assessments aren't going to really hurt you?"

"Lady, I'm not the sort to pinch a penny till it squeals, but I do believe in getting value for my money. This place is operated with a license to steal. No formal bids. No checks and balances."

"Doesn't Jack Kingsley have to get approvals from the board?"

That strange, rough hoot rumbled through him again. "You try telling him that. Talking to any of 'em is a waste of breath. If somebody's not getting kickbacks, I'll eat that old fedora hanging there on the hat rack."

"I heard you argued with Allan about all this."

"Tried to tell him plain and simple what was happening. He nodded, all polite like, but nothing changed. The next time we talked, I lost my temper. Probably would have shoved him in the pool, if Irv hadn't been there to stop me." He leaned toward her. "If you're thinking I was mad enough to kill him, you're right. I was."

Molly swallowed hard as the sound rumbled again in his chest. He stared her straight in the eye. "But I didn't."

Oddly enough, as creepy as the apartment was, Molly believed him. Which didn't mean, of course, that she wouldn't mention this conversation to Michael when he came in that night.

Once in her own apartment again, despite her solemn vow to wait up to divulge what she'd discovered, she fell asleep on the sofa.

She woke up in her own bed. How she got there didn't bear thinking about.

11

It was a great day for a funeral, at least if you were of the school that considered stormy skies and gloom to be redundant for an already depressing occasion. The Saturday skies over Miami had been washed clean by a brief predawn shower. A weak Canadian cold front, probably the last of the year, had whisked through, leaving behind bearable temperatures and a comfortable breeze.

Even without the good weather, mourners would probably jam the funeral home. Murder, money, and intrigue always drew. Molly did not plan to be among those at the service. Michael thought it best. Satisfied that she would stay put, he had left not five minutes before Liza arrived to convince her otherwise.

"It's our civic duty to go to the memorial," she said. "Allan was an important man on the island."

"When did you become so public-spirited? You're out of town half the time," Molly reminded her, weighing her own desire to go against Michael's probable fury if she did. Arguing with Liza made her feel noble. She had *tried* to reason with her, she could tell him.

"Which makes it all the more important that we catch the murderer. I won't rest a minute on my next trip if I have to worry that he's still loose in the condo."

"That *we* catch the murderer? That's the job of the police, as Michael reminds me at least once an hour."

"And I'm sure they're on top of it. But you have to admit there are angles they might overlook."

Michael O'Hara did not impress Molly as a man likely to overlook the least little detail. Look at the way he'd jumped on that Juan Gonzalez business last night. Whatever he'd found out, he hadn't deigned to share it with her. Feeling surly as a result and out of sorts because she'd missed the moment when Michael carried her to bed, she'd kept her own news to herself. As for her turning up at the funeral chapel, he was bound to be highly suspicious of her attendance at a memorial service for a man she claimed to have known only slightly. She tried explaining that to Liza. The words fell on deaf ears. Before she realized what was happening, she was in Liza's flashy little red car and on her way to the funeral. Fortunately, she'd been wearing black. Coincidence? Absolutely.

Okay, she had to admit to a certain curiosity. Would Allan Winecroft's lover show up? How would Drucilla react if she did? What about Juan Gonzalez? Would he be at the side of the mourning widow? Which of the Ocean Manor residents would appear? The bridge club participants? Molly scanned the crowd in search of answers.

Unfortunately, the first person she recognized was the homicide detective, who was making his way toward her at a clip that would have caught a running back at full speed. His expression wasn't exactly welcoming. She retreated instinctively to a safe spot behind Liza. Her neighbor's charms were considerable. She doubted that Michael would miss them.

To her astonishment he barely seemed to notice the dramatically attired redhead, whose only hint of black was a diagonal slash across a pristine white dress. His attention never once wavered from Molly's guilt-ridden face. Maybe he couldn't take the glare from Liza's dress.

"Why are you here?" He kept his sunglasses in place, but Molly could just imagine the flash of anger in his dark eyes.

"To pay my respects," she said. It came out sounding more like a question than a statement. Naturally, he caught the hesitation.

"Try again."

"That's my best shot."

Her refusal to be caught up in an argument over her motives seemed to surprise him. He finally nodded. "I suppose it's pointless to ask you to go home, since we discussed all the reasons earlier."

"Yes," Liza said for her. "We're here to help."

"Help who?"

He fastened his gaze on Liza. Well, to be more precise, he turned in her direction. Who could tell where he was looking the way those damned glasses reflected everything right back at you.

"Well?" he said.

"To help the police, of course. You can't possibly know everyone here."

"And you do?"

Liza scanned the crowd thoughtfully. "Yes, I think I do, as a matter of fact."

Michael blinked at the response. "You're joking."

Molly could have told him that Liza made it her business to know people. She'd been a highly successful public relations executive for a number of years, made a bundle, invested it wisely, then sold her business to gallivant around the globe. Occasionally, she guided tours just for the fun of it. At any rate, her PR instincts and her natural curiosity and friendliness kept her well informed on who was who in island life.

"No joke," Liza confirmed. "I get around." She pointed to a cluster of people standing near the doorway. "Mr. and Mrs. Lansing. He owns the shoe store on Miracle Mile in Coral Gables. You know the one, Molly. Designer shoes at discount prices, probably hot."

"Stolen?" Michael said weakly.

"Either that or knock-offs. He couldn't sell at those prices otherwise."

"And their connection with the deceased?"

"Their wives went to Sarah Lawrence together. They have dinner every Tuesday." She glanced at Molly. "Or is it Thursday?"

"Tuesday's bridge night."

"Right, Thursday then," Liza said. She pointed out half a dozen others, offering similar insights into their personalities, their business holdings, and their relationships with the Winecrofts. After an instant of open-mouthed astonishment, Michael took notes.

When she slowed, he glanced up. "How about the man standing by himself under the tree?"

Liza studied him for a minute. "He's one of yours."

"One of mine?"

"A cop."

"What makes you think that?"

"His eyes. He's watching the crowd. Nothing gets past him."

"Fascinating," Michael said.

"She's not that good," Molly grumbled. "She saw the two of you talking not five minutes ago."

Liza laughed, her expression unrepentant. "Well, that helped," she admitted. "So, do we get to stay?"

"Could you manage to keep your mouths shut and your eyes open?"

"A tricky skill," Molly retorted, "but I think we can manage it."

"Not me," Liza said. "I came here to ask questions. I'm leaving for China next week and I absolutely refuse to go off while there's a killer loose."

"Perhaps if I had a little more cooperation and a little less interference, I could wrap this up by next week," Michael said.

"I cooperate," Molly reminded him. "I shared that lead with you right away last night."

"Because I walked in and caught you discussing the murder with that Bates woman."

"What lead?" Liza demanded.

Molly pretended she hadn't heard either one of them. She glared at Michael. "On the other hand, you have shared diddly about what you found out." Her bargaining position would no doubt be seriously jeopardized if he found out how many other leads she'd developed last night. Right now he was on the defensive, and she liked it.

"Because you were asleep when I got in and I was in a hurry this morning," he said, his expression grim.

"Why didn't you just wake me?"

"*Madre de Dios,* woman, I picked you up, carried you to your room, and put the covers over you, and you never so much as blinked. Should I have set an alarm?" The brief explosion of Spanish was indicative of his irritation. It seemed to be a point of pride with him to restrict himself to using English. When he lost his temper, however, Spanish filled the air. Some of it, she suspected, would not be taught in class. "Okay, you're right," she said soothingly. "I don't even remember you picking me up."

Liza edged closer. "How is that possible?" she whispered. "How could you not know the man took you to bed? God, what a waste!"

"He didn't take me to bed," Molly protested, blushing furiously. She absolutely refused to look at Michael. "Not the way you mean. Let's get inside."

"But I want to hear more. . . ."

"I'm going inside," Molly announced firmly. She didn't wait to see if anyone was coming with her. She wedged herself into an aisle seat in an already packed pew. Even if Liza and Michael followed, they'd have to sit elsewhere. She was in no mood to deal with either of them. When they settled together two rows in front of her, she began to understand the kind of irritation that might lead someone to stab someone in the back. In her case, though, she wasn't sure which of the two she'd go after first.

After the minister intoned several somber prayers and half a dozen people delivered eloquent eulogies, Molly caught sight of the Ocean Manor accountant who had signed off on last year's budget. When he slipped out the back door, she followed.

"Mr. Rawlings, could I have a word with you?"

Stoop-shouldered from bending over a desk for thirty-five or forty years, Rawlings reminded her of a character from some dreary thirties movie, all black and white and gray. He hesitated at the edge of the lawn, squinting at her through thick glasses. "Do I know you?"

"Molly DeWitt. I live at Ocean Manor."

He jammed his hands into his pockets in a nervous search for his car keys. "Sorry, I'm in a rush. Tax season, you know."

"Could I make an appointment, then?" she suggested. At this rate, it was going to be a lost week again anyway. She'd already planned to go to the luncheon for Drucilla at the Intercontinental. She could squeeze Harley Rawlings in on her way to the luncheon if she couldn't persuade him to talk to her right now or she could see him Monday. Vince was going to be thrilled when she announced her schedule for the week.

The accountant's nervousness increased. His gaze darted this way and that, and he continued sidestepping toward the street, as if he could hardly wait to escape. "Did you want me to do your taxes?" he inquired.

"No, actually, I need your help understanding the building's budget. I'd be happy to pay you for your time."

"No, no, that isn't necessary. I'd be happy to explain it, but you see I'm no longer involved."

"You're not the accountant for Ocean Manor?"

"No, ma'am. Mr. Winecroft fired me."

"Fired you? Could he do that?"

He blinked several times. "Don't know if he could, but he did."

"When?"

"Last Tuesday, as a matter of fact. The day he was killed."

Before she could ask him another question, he scurried away.

"Well, I'll be," she murmured and tried to imagine the five-feet-six accountant jamming that knife into Allan's back in a fit of rage. The picture wouldn't come clear, but that didn't mean it hadn't happened just that way.

12

Molly was still staring after Harley Rawlings when the chapel doors opened and the crowd spilled out. Michael was the first one through the door, his gaze scanning the lawn until he found her. He reached her in five long strides, wrapped a hand around her elbow, and kept on moving. Molly had to take quick little running steps to keep up.

"We need to talk," they said simultaneously.

He stopped so fast, she bumped into him. He tilted his head. "Say that again."

"We need to talk."

He gazed at the sky in apparent disbelief. "Where's the lightning bolt," he muttered.

"You don't have to be sarcastic."

"Sarcastic? I'm flabbergasted. Why the turnaround?"

"Let's just say that a few things have come to my attention, and I thought I ought to share them with you."

"Praise be," he said, along with something in Spanish she had a hunch would blister her ears if she could translate it. "Let's go grab a cup of coffee at that shop across the street."

"Too crowded. There won't be enough privacy. Besides, I want to wait here a minute to see if everyone showed up."

"Everyone meaning?"

"All the suspects. Juan Gonzalez especially. Was he here? Once we got inside, it was so crowded I couldn't see."

"Yes, but you can scratch him from your list."

"Why? I found out for sure that he's been dropping in on Drucilla at all hours, whenever Allan wasn't around. They have to be involved."

Michael took off those blasted sunglasses and regarded her evenly. "You're sure now? This isn't just more wild speculation?"

"Absolutely not. After you left last night, I went to visit the couple across the hall, the Loefflers. I knew from Liza that they knew all about Ingrid and Allan. It stood to reason that they might have seen someone coming and going from Drucilla's."

"And they had seen Juan Gonzalez?"

"Yep. Often."

"Did they see him the night of the murder?"

Molly blinked. "I don't think so. At least they didn't mention it. Besides, they say they go to bed by ten. Why?"

"Because he claims that after he briefly chatted with Allan in the cardroom that night, he came up to see Drucilla and tell her that Allan had agreed to a divorce."

Molly stared at him. "A divorce? Drucilla wanted a divorce?"

"So it seems, at least according to Juan."

"If she wanted one and Allan wanted one to marry Ingrid, where was the need for persuasion?"

"As the story goes, Allan had been reluctant to give up his cut of the family fortune."

"Do you think Juan used that knife to persuade him?"

"He says it was Drucilla's settlement offer that did the trick. In retrospect, I have to wonder, though he did tell me there were half a dozen witnesses that Allan was alive when he left. I checked, and they all confirmed it."

"Maybe so, but would he have risked going to see Drucilla if Allan was likely to turn up at any moment?"

"What's the risk if Allan already knew all about them?"

"Which we can't prove or disprove now that he's dead."

"That is the dilemma," Michael confirmed. "The alternative theory is that Juan had his talk with Allan about whatever. Afterward, he hung around outside the cardroom until the others left. Then he went back and stabbed Allan. From there he headed to Drucilla's, knowing there was no chance they'd be interrupted by an irate husband."

Molly glanced toward the doors of the chapel just in time to see Drucilla exit with Juan at her side, solicitously holding her arm as she made her way to the waiting limo. They made a striking pair, he in his dark suit, she with a black mantilla over her red hair.

"So much for discretion," Molly muttered.

Michael steered her to his car. The Jeep, she noticed, had been washed for the occasion, but it still had a clutter of soccer equipment in the back. "Let's go to the grave site after all," he suggested. "See who else is weeping and wailing."

"Speaking of weeping, did Ingrid show? I didn't see her."

"She's over there by the steps."

Mourning became her. Dressed all in black, she looked glamorous and mysterious. She was standing alone, staring at the hearse bearing Allan's body. Occasionally she touched a handkerchief to her eyes. Molly glanced back as the procession drove off. Ingrid was still standing there, clutching one of the apricot roses Allan always sent.

On the way to the grave site, Molly filled Michael in on her conversations with Ralph Keller and with the fired accountant.

"My, my, for a woman who swore off investigating, you have been busy."

"Admit it. They're good leads."

"Yes," he said grudgingly. "I'll check them out myself this afternoon." He glanced over. "I haven't had a chance to ask before. Any calls last night?"

"None."

"Will you and Brian be okay alone in the apartment tonight?"

"Hot date, Detective?"

"It's Easter weekend. I have some family stuff. I could shake loose if you need me there, though."

"Staying in my apartment was your idea, not mine. I'll be fine."

He was quiet for several minutes. His fingers tapped a nervous beat against the steering wheel. "You and Brian could come along," he said, but without much enthusiasm.

"How would you explain that? Would you tell everyone you're holding us in protective custody?" She couldn't keep an edge out of her voice. Why bother to offer, when he knew what he was suggesting was bound to be awkward? No doubt that macho protective streak was surging again.

Challenged, he clenched his jaw. "There's no one to whom I owe an explanation."

"Oh? Bianca might not see it that way."

His smile was rueful. "Probably not."

Molly figured as long as the subject was finally out in the open, she might as well run with it, see how committed he was to the woman who answered his phone in the middle of the night. "So, what's the story with you two? Does she have some claim or not?"

The rhythm of his fingers against the steering wheel picked up. "Depends on whom you ask, I suppose."

"I'm asking you."

The drumming stopped. He glanced sideways for a beat. "Then the answer is no."

Molly held back a desire to whoop with delight. "She doesn't see it that way?"

"Let's just say I made the mistake of letting her think she had a hold on me. We're working it out."

"At the end of this process, do you expect her to go or stay?"

He studiously kept his eyes on the road. He switched on the radio. His fingers began to tap again, beats ahead of the salsa sounds that filled the car. "That's up to her," he said finally. "As long as she understands there's no future for the two of us."

"Then why not just tell her to go? You're copping out, Detective. Using her. Sounds pretty lousy to me."

"Look," he snapped. "I care about her. She's a good kid. She was there when I needed her. I don't want to see her hurt."

"How far will you go with that?" she asked, irritated by his apparent mastery of self-delusion. "Do you plan to marry her so she won't get her feelings hurt?"

He slammed his palm against the wheel. Apparently it was a thought that had crossed his mind before. He wasn't crazy about the question or about what his answer said about his lifestyle. "No, dammit. What the hell business is this of yours anyway?"

"Just trying to see what makes you tick."

"The same hormones that make any man tick."

"A cliché, then? How disappointing."

He glanced in her direction. Molly's own

sarcastic expression reflected back at her in the sunglasses. "I wonder something, Detective. I wonder if you're really as tough and controlled as you want everyone to think you are."

"Believe it," he said tersely.

Molly smiled as a reluctant sigh escaped him.

"You know," he said, "my life was moving along just fine before you jumped in and decided to examine it."

She held up her hands, all innocence. "Hey, I'm just passing through. Solve this murder and you never have to see me again."

"I can't wait," he muttered.

To her regret, it sounded suspiciously as if he meant it.

No mourners threw themselves on Allan Winecroft's casket at the grave site and confessed. Half the suspects weren't even there. Michael didn't even bother to leave the Jeep. He parked it where he could observe the proceedings, then sat there in stony silence. Molly walked over to the plot of newly turned earth and joined the throng listening to the minister's final prayers for Allan's eternal soul. When the graveside service ended, she murmured her condolences to Drucilla and, after casting a speculative glance at Juan, returned to the Jeep.

The ride home was as tense and subdued as any movie set during the filming of the climactic scene. When they reached Ocean Manor, Michael pulled up in front of the building and cut the engine.

"I'm sorry," he said, as if the words were unfamiliar and faintly troubling.

"For?"

"What I said back there. Sometimes you irritate the hell out of me. I've been telling myself it was professional anger. No cop wants an amateur screwing up an investigation. But . . ."

Molly waited. Finally he turned to face her. The sunglasses came off, revealing that vulnerability that was so appealing, and that he so rarely allowed anyone to get close enough to see. "Now I'm not so sure."

"And you don't like ambiguity."

"No."

She risked her own vulnerabilities. "Can I tell you something, without your making a federal case out of it?"

For an instant, he looked almost nervous. "You aren't going to confess or something, are you?"

She grinned. "Not to the murder. I was

just going to say that I'm not all that crazy about ambiguity myself. So if you happen to figure out just what it is you are feeling here, let me know."

His gaze locked with hers. He leaned toward her, then caught himself. Instead, his hand cupped her chin and the pad of his thumb caressed her bottom lip. "I'll do that."

Molly's knees were knocking so hard when she got out of the car, she could barely stand. She plastered a jaunty smile on her face and waved as he drove off to spend what was left of the weekend with another woman. Sometimes life sucked.

By Sunday morning Molly's mood had improved slightly, though not enough to convince her that an Easter egg hunt on the grounds would be terrific fun. Brian had his heart set on it, though. She mustered sufficient enthusiasm to drag on her clothes and go out to the pool where the dozens of children and visiting grandchildren were clustered in their holiday finery.

To her amazement, the first person she saw was Juan Gonzalez, surrounded by a trio of dark-haired girls dressed in frilly pink dresses. They were dancing around excitedly, pleading with him to help them hunt for the eggs. "*Niñas,* that would not be fair," he protested, laughing. "You must find the eggs on your own if you wish to win the prize. Now go and listen to the instructions."

"*Tío*, we need you," the littlest one said earnestly, turning her dimpled smile on him.

So he was their uncle, Molly thought as she walked over to join him. She grinned. "Looks like you have your hands full."

He lifted his soulful dark eyes to the heavens. "Yes. My niece brought the little ones by, then ran off to church. *Niñas*, this is Señora DeWitt." He pointed to the oldest, a plump child of maybe nine or ten. "This is Elena. That is Margarita. And the baby here is . . ."

"I am not a baby, *Tío*. I am 'cesca."

"Francesca," Juan corrected. "She is three and very precocious."

Molly called to Brian and his friends and introduced them. "Boys, why don't you take the girls with you to hunt the eggs. You'll find that many more, if you all work together."

From the disgusted expression on Brian's face, she had a feeling she would pay later for the suggestion, but he did as she asked. Juan looked relieved.

"Thank you. I was not looking forward to crawling around on my hands and knees at my age. Come, join me in the shade."

Molly followed him to two chairs under a striped umbrella. She took the opportunity to study him more closely, noting the distinguished streaks of gray in his coal-black hair, the expensive gold watch and ring, the silk-blend shirt and tailored slacks. Everything about him shouted understated wealth and classic taste. The sparkle of amused tolerance in his eyes when he'd spoken to his grandnieces seemed an unlikely response for a man who might have committed murder only days before.

"I saw how you watched me yesterday, señora. You know about Drucilla and me," he said, his voice quiet. "From the detective, I presume."

"And others."

He shook his head ruefully. "And we thought we had been so careful."

"Believe me, there were no rumors. I asked some of the most observant gossips about that. It was little things, an observation here, a comment there. They added up."

"I see."

Made bold by the crowd around them, Molly dared to ask, "Did you kill him?"

Laughing brown eyes met hers. "You are very brave."

"Not so brave. There are witnesses every-where."

"Foolhardy, perhaps."

She shook her head. "I don't think so. I can't deny you had the opportunity, probably even a motive."

"And what would that motive be?"

"You're in love with Drucilla. Allan might have proved troublesome, if you had aspirations to her and her money."

"I wanted Drucilla," he emphasized. "Not her money. I have more than enough of my own. I have businesses in Panama and throughout South America. They are not suffering. I would gladly share it all just for her love. She is a remarkable woman. At my age, after a lifetime of travel and experience, it is possible to recognize such value. I doubt that Allan ever appreciated her as he should have. He was a cold, crass man."

"You still haven't denied killing him."

He shrugged, a subtle lift of his shoulders. "Would my denial make so very much difference? You will reach your own conclusions, no matter what I say."

"Do you have any theories about who might have stabbed him? Was there an argument in the cardroom when you were there?"

"No. If anything, there was a rather dull

discussion of the upcoming baseball season. Allan was a Mets fan, I believe. Others preferred the Yankees. All rather tedious. Allan and I spoke in the corridor, and then I left. I presume he returned to defend his team."

A shadow fell across them just then. Molly looked up as Jack Kingsley pulled up a third chair. "Mind if I join you?" he asked, though he obviously wasn't waiting for the invitation. "God, it's hot out here." The freckles across his brow, where his sandy hair had receded, stood out even more prominently than usual. He blotted his face with a rumpled handkerchief.

"The kids look as though they're enjoying themselves," Molly observed, letting the conversation with Juan about the murder drop. "How long has Ocean Manor held the egg hunt?"

"I started it when I came," he said. "Used to do it at a condo up in Jacksonville when my own kids were small. There was some griping about the noise the first year, but after that everyone pitched in to help. Sometimes I think there are more grandkids here for this than come during the Christmas holidays."

"Are your own children here today?" Molly asked.

"No, they're too old for this. Both boys are in college now. One's studying law at Yale, as a matter of fact. The other one's in premed."

"You and your wife must be very proud of them."

"I'll tell you what I'm most proud of. They've never gotten into drugs. Raising kids these days is a crapshoot, with all that stuff around. You'll see for yourself, Mrs. DeWitt. Once Brian gets to high school, even junior high, you'll have to watch like a hawk to make sure he doesn't get mixed up in the wrong crowd. Hard to tell, too. They don't wear signs around their necks announcing it. In my day, you could pick out the tough kids, the ducktail haircuts and black leather jackets, cigarettes hanging out of their mouths. Today they look just like the kids next door."

Molly suddenly felt chilled, even though the temperature was already a humid eighty-five or higher. Only the reappearance of Brian, with Juan's grandnieces in tow, warmed her. With dirt and grass stains from head to toe, he looked wonderfully normal. Francesca and Margarita were equally disheveled. Only Elena's dress remained spotless, her patent leather shoes shiny, her long dark hair unmussed. She carried a basket filled to overflowing with brightly colored plastic eggs.

"*Tío,* we won," Francesca announced, twirling until she was breathless.

"And what did you win, *niña*?"

"Candy, of course," Kingsley said, smiling at them benevolently. "What would Easter be without lots of chocolate bunnies, right, girls? Come along and I'll see that you get your prizes."

Molly glanced at Brian. "Where are your eggs?"

He kept his eyes on the ground. "I gave them to Francesca," he mumbled. "She couldn't find any."

Molly exchanged a glance with Juan, whose lips were twitching with amusement.

"You are truly a gentleman," he said to Brian.

"Yeah, well, it's just a dumb game anyway."

Not so dumb, Molly thought, if it taught him such a valuable lesson about chivalry.

An interesting concept, chivalry. Juan Gonzalez, with his dignified, courtly ways, personified it. Would he have quietly provided Drucilla with an alibi for her own whereabouts at the time of the murder? In effect, that's what his own alibi had done. It had excluded him from suspicion, but it had also taken her out of the picture as well.

It was something a man deeply in love just might do.

13

The phone rang at one-hour intervals throughout the night. Each time Molly could hear breathing on the line, but while that was menacing enough, there were no verbal threats. She successfully resisted the urge to call Michael and ask him to come back, but by morning she was shaken and exhausted. It took every ounce of determination in her to drag herself to the office.

Jeannette took one look and began fussing over her. She poured a cup of strong, black coffee and brought it to Molly's desk. "It looks as if you need this, yes?"

Molly held her head up with effort. "Keep it coming and I might survive." She was too groggy to be sure why she wanted to, unless it was to figure out if Juan Gonzalez was trying to protect Drucilla because he was convinced of her guilt.

"What's on the agenda for the day?" she asked Jeannette.

"Larry Milsap called."

Molly groaned. "Don't tell me. Let me guess. He's lost the permits again."

"No, actually, he wants to stop by to discuss an ad he's doing next month. He was thinking maybe Brian would like to be in it."

Molly's flagging spirits revived ever so slightly. Brian would be thrilled. "What's the product?"

"He didn't say. He'll be here at eleven unless I call to cancel."

"I should be able to stay awake that long."

Jeannette looked troubled. "More calls?"

Molly nodded.

"You told the police?"

"Not yet. I made a note of the times. I doubt if they could have traced them. There wasn't time."

"Maybe you should get one of those call screeners from the phone company. That would tell you the number calling, yes?"

"Jeannette, you're a genius. Why didn't I think of that? I'd forgotten that they'd finally been approved." She dragged out the two volumes of the phone book — *A* to *K* and *L* to *Z* — muttering about the ongoing frustration of always picking the wrong tome to locate a listing. In one moment of absolute fury the previous year, she'd cut apart the white and yellow pages in each volume, then put all the white pages together in one functional book and all the yellow in another. This time, however, she actually found the phone company customer service number on the first try. Within minutes she had arranged for the caller-ID service. By the time she hung up, she was actually looking forward to the next middle-of-the-night call.

After that the day improved considerably. To her astonishment the meeting with Larry Milsap began on time. He breezed in wearing jeans and a flowered Hawaiian shirt, his brown hair pulled back in a ponytail. Despite his inattention to clothes and his maddening disregard for details, he was a genius at production. There was an unmistakable "look" to anything he did on screen. If his talented eye had spotted something special in Brian, Molly was too much the proud mother to disagree. They arranged for a screen test for Brian the following week.

"It's a formality, sweetie. He'll be perfect," Larry said, packing up his briefcase and heading for the door. "The kid already has a mouth on him. I could probably give him the product and let him ad-lib some of that sass, but the agency will provide a script. Thanks, hon. You're an angel."

Molly took the *sweetie, hon,* and *angel* in stride. He was the first person in days who hadn't asked about the murder. By the time he left, she actually thought the day was going pretty well. She ate lunch at her desk, read a script for a producer scheduled to begin shooting in July, and helped Jeannette catch up on the filing. It was nearly four when Vince buzzed her desk. Startled by the unexpected formality, she stuck her head into his office. "What's with you? You usually just shout."

The words were out before she took a good look at his expression. She had seen Vince look smug, sullen and superior, but this was the first time she'd seen him so somber. It somehow answered her question and made her very edgy. She stepped inside.

"What is it?" she asked, standing in front of his desk, her hands clenching the back of a chair. "Something's the matter, isn't it?"

"Sit down."

His mood was contagious. She suddenly felt very serious herself. "Maybe I ought to stand."

"Suit yourself. I just got off the phone with the county manager."

When he paused to let the significance of that sink in, she prodded, "And? Did he cut our budget? Eliminate the entire parks department? What?"

"He says you've been meddling in that murder investigation."

"So?"

"He wants it to stop."

Molly had a hard time accepting the notion that the county manager had nothing better to do in the midst of a near-catastrophic budget crisis than meddle in her private life. "Why does he care?"

"I'm not sure *why* matters. He's the boss."

"Not good enough. What the hell does he expect me to do? Somebody has to look out for my interests. First, I'm considered a suspect. Then somebody starts warning me that I'm in danger. Am I supposed to sit quietly and wait until I become the next victim or land in jail?"

Vince looked startled by that. "Do you honestly think someone might be after you?"

"Vince, I don't know. These calls shake me up. I had more last night that I haven't even told the police about yet. I actually considered tucking a butcher knife under my pillow. Then I thought about Allan Winecroft and decided against it. I figured it might end up in my back."

"Is the caller threatening you?"

"He didn't last night, but it's pretty obvious that someone thinks I know something about the murder."

"All the more reason to sit tight and let the police do their job. I assume they're taking the calls seriously. You want me to call the director?"

She shook her head. "Detective O'Hara was hanging around on an unofficial basis, but he can't be there all the time."

Vince's eyebrows rose. "Maybe he's just using the calls as an excuse to stick close. I've seen the way he looks at you."

"Trust me, the man is all business." There was no need for Vince to know that both she and Michael had recognized the potential for more intimate things developing. At the moment, though, the mysterious Bianca stood squarely between them.

"He's practically engaged," she added for good measure. It was a reminder to her as much as to Vince.

"The woman must love knowing he's hanging out with you."

"I doubt if she's thrilled," Molly admitted. Or maybe she was projecting her own jealousies onto the other woman. Perhaps Bianca was one of those saintly, understanding souls who had enough self-confidence to weather any competition without turning green with envy. Besides, no one had said Molly was any competition, least of all

Molly. She'd learned long ago to be careful what she prayed for. She'd once wanted Hal DeWitt and been granted that misguided prayer.

"Maybe she's making the calls," Vince suggested.

"The calls are the reason he's there. I doubt she'd give him an excuse to linger."

"No. No. Maybe she didn't start them, but maybe she's checking up on him now, calling to see if he's around. You know how these possessive chicks get."

"I wouldn't know," she said nobly. "But it doesn't surprise me that you do. Forget this fascination of yours with Michael O'Hara's girl friend for a minute. I'm more interested in figuring out who put a bug in the county manager's ear."

"From what you just said, maybe the girl did it. Benitez did suggest you take a little time off, get away for a while. That'd be a good way to get you out of the picture. He says you have leave coming."

Molly stared at him incredulously. "He checked my personnel records?"

"Apparently so."

Molly finally sat down. "Vince, don't you think that's a little odd? Doesn't the county manager have more important things to worry about than whether I have a few days of leave accumulated?"

"Frankly, I had the feeling he was less concerned about your vacation time than he was about my cutting you loose unless you got your nose out of police business."

"Cutting me loose?" Her voice rose to a shrill tone she didn't recognize. She forced it down. "Does that mean what I think it means?" That, more than a simple phone call, would certainly explain Vince's sober expression.

"You got it. He recommended that I fire you if you didn't cooperate. I told him it was a ridiculous request, that I couldn't let you go without cause, but he wasn't buying. He suggested I try insubordination for starters. I got the feeling more heads would roll if he wasn't satisfied."

"Meaning yours?" She could feel her hands turn to ice.

Vince shrugged. "There are only so many of us around over here, and he's been looking for an excuse to shake this place up again." He shook his head. "As if last year didn't turn us inside out."

Molly's temper, usually slow to rise, was rapidly reaching the boiling point. She leaped up and headed for the door.

"Where are you going?"

"To get to the bottom of this. I won't let

my career, or yours, for that matter, be jeopardized because some jerk downtown is getting pressured."

As she stormed out, she heard Vince's chair crash against the wall. He caught up with her in the parking lot. He was sweating profusely. "Come on, Molly," he coaxed. "You're going to back off, right?"

"That wasn't what I had in mind."

"Come on, you know blowing off steam won't solve anything. Think about it. Look, I'll even buy you and the kid a couple of tickets for California. You could make it a business trip, save the vacation time. Make some contacts, schmooze with the studio execs. Somebody needs to do it soon anyway."

Molly was beyond being cajoled or bribed. "Not on your life. I'm going to find out exactly who is responsible for having the county manager make that call. If I have to, I'll make so much noise the officials at the Metro Building will think they're in the middle of an LA earthquake."

"Oh, shit," Vince murmured, but he didn't try to stop her.

She used her cellular phone to call police headquarters in search of Michael. It was entirely possible, even after their improved rapport, that he'd decided to exert a little official pressure on her. She didn't think he'd have the gall to suggest that she be fired, but maybe the county manager had simply gotten carried away.

He picked up on the first ring. "O'Hara." His terse tone indicated his mood was about as pleasant as her own.

"I need to see you. I'm on my way."

"Molly?"

If she hadn't been so furious already, she might have considered his insulting failure to recognize her voice as a reason to snap. "Yes," she said tersely. "I'll be there in twenty minutes."

"I'm heading out the door in five. Can't it wait?"

"Unless you're going to investigate the murder of a top county official, no."

"You sound upset," he said cautiously.

"Bingo. No wonder you get so many commendations. Bye."

"Wait. Molly! Molly, are you listening?"

"Yes."

"I'll meet you at the soccer field. The kids have a game in an hour. We should have time to talk. Bring Brian and we'll have dinner after."

"This isn't a social visit," she snapped and hung up.

Molly turned the car toward Kendall.

When she reached the field, Michael was lugging soccer equipment from the Jeep to the playing field. He dropped an armload of shin guards and walked slowly back to meet her. When he reached out a hand to touch her, she jerked away. She didn't want the fireworks stirred by his caresses to confuse the issues.

"What's up?" he said, his expression guarded.

"For starters, why are you here instead of chasing down a murderer?"

"I'm pleased you're so concerned about how I spend my days. To answer your question, though, these kids don't have a lot of people they can count on. When I made the commitment, I wanted them to know I wouldn't let them down. Now, why are you here and in such a crappy mood?"

"I've been officially warned to stop meddling in police business."

He dared a smile. When she didn't lighten up, it died. "Okay, what's new about that? I've been begging you to steer clear of the investigation since the day of the murder. You don't pay any attention to me. Why should this be any different?"

"Because this warning carried the clout of the county manager. If I don't behave, I'm out."

"Out? As in fired? Are you sure?"

"Vince was very clear, and for all his flaws, he's loyal. He wouldn't pass along a message like that unless he knew that the county manager meant it and that there was no way out. Did you say something to the director?"

He shoved his hands into his pockets. "You should know me better than that. I don't need officials interfering in my job any more than I need amateurs. I certainly wouldn't say something that would jeopardize your career."

"Maybe you just said something casually, griped to another cop and it escalated, climbed up through the ranks."

"No."

"Have I stepped on some other cop's toes?"

"I'm in charge of the case."

"That doesn't mean someone else couldn't take offense."

"They would have complained to me, not my boss."

"Well, dammit, who's behind this, then?"

Michael looked thoughtful. "Off hand, I'd say the killer. Which leads me to wonder who at Ocean Manor has the ear of the county manager."

Molly stared at him. "Of course. Why

didn't I think of that?"

"Because I'm the more obvious choice, and you've probably been itching for a chance to yell at me ever since I left you on Saturday."

"Don't flatter yourself. I didn't give you a thought," she retorted, lying through her teeth, clinging to her pride. "It's true, though, that you were the more approachable choice. As furious as I am, I wasn't looking forward to dashing into the county manager's office for a confrontation without knowing exactly what I'm up against."

Michael's sudden grin was that of a kid just given an opportunity to dunk the principal in a tank of water. "On the other hand, I can hardly wait to butt heads with him," he said.

"Now?" she said enthusiastically.

"Can't do it now. First thing after the game, though. Are you going to stick around and cheer?"

"Why not?" she said agreeably. Michael's promise to take on the county manager was definitely something to cheer about, and she had every intention of being right in the vicinity when he did it. Whether inadvertently or intentionally, someone had first set her up as a murder suspect and now seemed intent on destroying her career. She wasn't going to rest until she'd discovered the culprit and strung him up by his toenails.

She was still trying to think of a fate vile enough for the guilty party when she heard raised voices on the field. More precisely, one raised voice. A woman's. She had her back to Molly, but it was evident from her stance that she was furious. Her hands were jammed in the back pockets of her tight-fitting jeans. Her shoulders were thrown back. Long, shiny dark hair swung with each shouted word directed at Michael. He listened in stoic silence as she ranted. From the tilt of his head, he was gazing at the sky in a *why me* posture.

"You promised that after the game the two of us would be alone for dinner for a change! What good are your promises to me? Why should I ever believe another word?" She waved a hand in the direction of the bleachers. "You bring her here to insult me."

Michael's response was so low, Molly couldn't hear it, but she'd guessed by now that the woman was Bianca and that she was more than upset over Molly's appearance on what she considered her turf. Molly watched with fascination as Michael's jaw tightened. She was surprised that Bianca seemed unconcerned that he was on the verge of exploding. Instead, the woman's clearly provocative words were coming faster now and in Spanish.

Michael shook his head and walked away. Bianca flew after him, stumbling a little as her high heels caught in the grass. A collection of bracelets clinked musically as she grabbed his arm and whirled him around. Molly waited for him to lash back, but if anything, his manner turned gentle. He leaned down and murmured something, soothing her as he might a skittish filly. Bianca suddenly laughed, the fireworks over. He walked her back toward her car, his hand sliding from her waist to her rear. The fond, intimate gesture was almost more than Molly could bear. Michael might say that Bianca had no hold on him, but his actions said otherwise. Suddenly she fully understood the possessive rage that must have surged through Bianca only moments before. Molly had to give her credit. She had given in more gracefully than Molly might have if their positions had been reversed. Then, again, what had Michael promised to soothe her fiery temper?

Michael came back and sat in the row below her on the bleachers, watching as the kids practiced. He kept his back squarely to her.

"Bianca?" she asked finally, staring at the back of his neck. The faint red beneath the tan hinted of tension or embarrassment.

He nodded, his eyes on the field.

"What'd you say to her to set her off?"

"I told her I had to work later."

"She must be used to that. Cops have crazy hours."

"I told her I wouldn't be home."

Molly's pulse bucked, then raced. "No wonder she was furious." Hallelujah!

"She'll live. I'm not so sure about you."

Lusty thoughts screeched to a halt. Molly swallowed hard as he turned an intense look on her. "I'm serious," he said. "I've got a feeling about this. I can always tell when a case is about to break wide open. I'm not letting you out of my sight until all the pieces fall into place and the right person is behind bars."

Molly couldn't tear her gaze away from the look in his eyes. The emotion was too raw. "You could have someone else stand guard."

"No," he said quietly as he stood up to go back to the game. "We're going to ride this out together."

If the rest of the night was any indication, it was going to be a hell of a ride.

Michael called all over until he finally

tracked down the county manager at his home. While Molly listened on the extension, he demanded to know to whom he'd been talking about the case. Roberto Benitez tried playing coy.

"I thought this was what you wanted, *amigo.* It came from the department that the DeWitt woman was getting in your way and on your nerves."

"I know better," Michael said. "My superiors and I haven't had a single conversation regarding Mrs. DeWitt's actions beyond the fact that she might be a witness."

"And a suspect," the manager added. "Is that not true?"

"Very low on the list."

"Then I think I am being generous in merely warning her. I could have suspended her for the duration of the investigation."

"I want to know exactly who involved you in this," Michael repeated. "You can tell me now or we can do it officially."

There was a long silence while Benitez considered the effect an official inquiry might have on his political fortunes. He served at the whim of some very fickle commissioners.

"I had several calls," he conceded finally.

"From?"

"The victim's wife spoke to my wife, as a

matter of fact."

"And? I don't believe for a minute that you'd take this kind of action based on some indirect comment from Mrs. Winecroft."

"Mr. Gonzalez also spoke to me, as well as Mr. Mendoza," he said with obvious reluctance. "It seems your witness has offended a number of important people."

"And now I'm offended," Michael retorted. "You know what happens when I get offended, don't you? I tend to start asking some very hard questions. I wonder why certain people find a need to come to you. I wonder if they're trying to protect their own asses. And I get really uptight that a county official might help them to do that."

"Detective, I have tolerated quite a lot from you in the past." The manager's voice was icy. "Do not step over the line."

"I might say the same to you. Good night," he said, then added as a pointedly derisive afterthought, *"sir."*

When he'd hung up, Molly walked back into the living room. "I guess it's a good thing I'm going to that luncheon tomorrow."

His thoughts clearly still on the call, Michael asked distractedly, "What luncheon is that?"

"It's honoring Drucilla."

He glanced up from his notes. "Exactly how is that supposed to help?"

"Mrs. Benitez, Mrs. Mendoza, and Drucilla all in the same room. Surely I can get a few clues about the men in their lives from that little scenario. Care to come along?"

He actually shuddered. "Not if they paid me."

"And I thought we were going to stick together like glue," she said, feigning disappointment. Actually, she was delighted she was going to have a chance at those three women all on her own. Having Michael breathing down her neck would have definitely cramped her style.

"I'm not sure I'm crazy about this," he said.

"I'll be fine," she said, filled with bravado from her previous investigative successes. "They're not likely to take me out at a charity luncheon. I promise, though, if any of them reach for the butter knife, I'll cut and run."

Michael looked more worried than ever. "Don't make light of this, Molly. We're not playing a game."

"Believe me, no one is taking this any more seriously than I am. My whole future seems to hinge on the outcome. Jailhouse gray would be lousy with my complexion."

"I'd be more worried about the alternative, if I were you."

14

Five hundred women, wearing vibrant spring colors and sipping mimosas, were wondering whether Drucilla Winecroft would dare to show up at the latest luncheon in her honor. If the committee members had been taking bets instead of selling raffle tickets, they would have scored a record haul.

Dozens of cocktail parties for film industry officials, plus more than her share of cotillions, had made Molly something of an expert at mingling at packed-to-the-walls occasions like this. As soon as she'd registered and paid for her ticket, she moved from cluster to cluster, smiling, listening, then slipping away without commenting on much more than the weather outside and the clothes in the room. The former was beastly, the latter stylish and expensive. She could have traveled to Europe on what a couple of the designer outfits must have cost. There was no need for a fashion show at this event. The spring collections of the country's top designers were represented right in the room.

According to Molly's unofficial tally, Drucilla was favored to appear, if only to prove that she wasn't behind bars.

Sympathy was also on the widow's side. There wasn't a woman in the room who didn't think that a satin-lined box was too good for the man who'd cheated on the ever-charming cultural benefactress. Feeding Allan to the sharks was the disposal method of choice. Since he was already in the ground, it was a belated thought.

During her first tour of the room, Molly had spotted the wives of several area mayors and chairwomen from at least ten other events she'd received invitations to during the course of the year. Drucilla had served on all the committees. It was payback time.

To her disappointment, though, Molly had yet to spot any of the women she'd hoped to see. Mrs. Benitez was short, so it was entirely possible that she was hidden from view in the center of the crush. Rosa Mendoza, however, was tall and a stately size sixteen. She tended to dominate a room, in the most positive sense of the word. Molly had watched her walk into a ballroom once.

Every head in the room had turned toward the force of her radiant smile, like flowers seeking sunshine. It had been an astonishing display. A woman like that would be an unmistakable asset to her husband. Molly wondered if Manny Mendoza deserved her. For Rosa's sake only, she hoped she was wrong about his possible involvement in some sort of cover-up attempt. His call to the county manager was suspicious, as far as Molly was concerned.

A chime sounded, signaling the start of the luncheon. Slowly, amid much laughter and the mingled scents of a dozen designer perfumes, the women began to enter the Intercontinental's waterfront ballroom with its spectacular view of the bay. Molly stayed by the center door, her eyes peeled on the crowd as the women passed by.

Finally, Mrs. Benitez, whom she'd met at several official county functions, appeared, all of her attention focused on the woman at her side. Molly stepped in front of her, smiled, and managed to inject a note of enthusiasm into her greeting. Startled, Mrs. Benitez faltered, then regained her aplomb. "Why, hello. Molly, isn't it?"

"Yes, it's so nice to see you again."

"Do you know Mrs. Jackson? This is Molly . . ." She hesitated.

"DeWitt," Molly supplied.

The county manager's wife suddenly appeared nervous. "Of course. I should have remembered."

"Yes, you and Drucilla were discussing me just the other day, I hear."

Mrs. Benitez tried subtly to scurry behind her guest, but Molly was able to get between them. "Why, yes," she said, glancing around with a desperate look in her eyes. "I believe she did mention you were neighbors."

"And that I'd found her husband's body?" Molly inquired politely. Mrs. Jackson gasped. Resigned that there was no escaping Molly's determination, Mrs. Benitez took the announcement with admirable calm.

"I suppose that might have come up. If you'll excuse us, we really should find our table."

Molly beamed again and stepped aside. "Certainly." She'd found out exactly what she'd been looking for. Drucilla had made that call to the county manager's wife. If she could just locate Rosa Mendoza now, she'd consider the day a success, even if she had to eat rubbery chicken for lunch.

With nearly everyone seated, there didn't seem to be much hope of spotting the developer's wife without weaving in and out among the fifty-five tables with their towering centerpieces of pink tulips reportedly imported from Amsterdam. With waiters already crowding the aisles, Molly resigned herself to going to her own table. Since she'd made her reservation late and alone, she'd been relegated to a table at the back of the room. The better to observe, she told herself, just as Rosa Mendoza swept down on her in a rustle of bright-red silk.

"Molly, I thought I saw you earlier, but in this mob, who can tell. I saw your name at the registration desk. You are alone, yes?"

"Yes. I didn't know until the last minute that I'd be able to make it. I didn't want to miss it. Drucilla's been through so much. She deserves this day of recognition."

Rosa nodded sympathetically. "You are right and it is a lovely party, isn't it? You will come to my table, *si*? I had a cancellation just this morning. There is a place. It has been a long time since we have had a chance to chat. It is so funny that now we are neighbors, I never seem to see you. We have much to catch up on."

"We do," Molly agreed. Perfect.

Rosa's table was crowded with women whose husbands did business with Manny. Many of them, in their own right, held important jobs or led major fund-raising efforts for various charities, but Molly was more fascinated by the connections to the developer. His name crept into the conversation at frequent intervals, always with the faintest edge of reverence.

Molly turned to the woman on her left, who was wearing a marquise diamond the size of a peach pit. "Your husband works with Manny?"

"Yes. They, how do you say, developed? Yes, developed many properties together. Hernando says Manny is a genius."

Rosa leaned over. "Don't let him hear you say that, please. I have much trouble carving his ego down to size as it is."

"He must be incredibly busy," Molly said.

"Always," Rosa lamented. "All he ever thinks of is work, work, work. Now that the children are grown, he is worse than ever."

"How did he find the time for the condominium association?" Molly wondered aloud.

"He said it was his duty. He created the property. It is where we live."

"Manny developed Ocean Manor?"

"*Sí*. It is, what is the expression, the jewel in his crown."

No wonder the man thought he would hold the throne indefinitely. Would his loss in the last election have made him so resentful that he would kill? Tonight's condominium association meeting would give Molly a chance to see the man in action. Maybe that would tell her if he was capable of murder.

Meantime, though, Drucilla had just been introduced to a standing ovation. The queen lived. Long live the queen!

Despite the thunder outside the rumble of discontent was evident long before Molly reached the meeting room. The emergency session of the Ocean Manor Board of Directors hadn't even started and already residents were sniping. If it weren't for her curiosity about who would emerge victorious in the latest quest for power, she'd have stayed home to watch *Jeopardy!* and then her favorite, the complex mystery puzzles of *Matlock.* She had a feeling tonight's live entertainment was going to be more akin to mud wrestling.

She slid into the back of the packed and already airless room and found the last vacant chair in the last row. Michael spotted her, inched his way through the crowd and leaned down to whisper, "Welcome to the Tuesday night fights."

Molly tried to ignore the way his hand rested on her shoulder, but she liked the sensation too much. "Already?" she said as

252

his fingers began a gentle massage. She felt her own tension begin to drain away. "The meeting hasn't even started."

"They've been battling over who gets to sit in the front row."

Actually, Molly decided after a few minutes' observation, the tense atmosphere was only slightly worse than last Tuesday night's battle between the Winecrofts. "Let's just hope this week's version doesn't culminate in another murder," she murmured. Michael's caress ended and she sighed.

As condo vice president Boris Yankovich gaveled the meeting to order, Tyler Jenkins wrested control of the floor microphone away from another speaker. "I'd like to say something."

He was immediately drowned out by catcalls from the audience. Boris moved ahead as if the older man hadn't spoken at all. "Ladies and gentlemen, we have to make a few decisions tonight."

It was evident that the ladies and gentlemen in question were seated at the head table, not in the audience. Not once did the vice president deign to glance in their direction.

He went on. "Due to the unfortunate death of our president, it is necessary that we move to fill that seat on the board. It has been recommended that we expedite that process by appointing a man whose vast experience more than qualifies him to step in, Mr. Manny Mendoza."

Molly's mouth dropped open in astonishment. "They can't do that."

Michael stared at her. "Why not?"

"The bylaws call for an election to fill any unexpired term with more than a year remaining. Allan was just elected to a two-year term a few months ago."

"They must know that."

"If not, Jack Kingsley should have told them. He's the one who told me."

Tyler was shaking his fist at the head table. "That's illegal," he shouted. His words were emphasized by another powerful clap of thunder.

"You're out of order, Mr. Jenkins," Boris said. He turned to the others. "Could I have a motion regarding Mr. Mendoza?"

Gerry Wilson waved a hand. "So moved."

"Second," Katie Winslow said.

"Discussion," Boris said, carrying on the mockery in an orderly fashion.

"Why do you bother paying an attorney?" Tyler shouted, not even bothering with the microphone. A few daring souls murmured agreement. None stood up. Jack Kingsley stood off to the side, rocking back on his heels and staring at the ceiling. Manny Mendoza was seated in the first row, briefcase in hand, the epitome of a man ready to get to work. Rosa had not come down to witness the coronation.

Molly kept waiting for someone to speak up and stop this charade. When no one budged, she started forward. Michael grabbed for her arm, but she shook him off. When she was halfway down the aisle, she caught sight of Liza's upturned face. With a subtle shake of her head, she gave Molly a warning, but Molly was too livid to be called off now. As the directors conferred in undertones, their hands discreetly over their own microphones, she tapped Tyler on the shoulder and gestured him aside. His ashen complexion alarmed her. "Sit for a minute," she whispered. "Let me try to get through to them."

Surprised by the unexpected backing, he nodded and sank onto one of the metal chairs.

"Excuse me," Molly said in a tone that carried to the back of the room. It was a skill she'd learned in elocution classes. At long last she'd found a use for it. The sound echoed as she waited. Slowly the room fell silent. The directors raised their heads and stared at her, obviously startled by her daring interruption.

"Why are you doing this?" she asked. "Each one of you has to know that the bylaws of this building require that there be an election process. Isn't that right, Mr. Kingsley? That is what you told me, isn't it?"

His slouched shoulders straightened. "Yes, ma'am. I believe I did. However, there are certain provisions, in an emergency, for bypassing that procedure. You can rest assured that we've checked all of this out with an attorney."

"Why would you want to, though? Why not give the residents the opportunity to speak out in the election they're entitled to?"

Even as she said it, she thought she knew the answer. For some reason this board wanted — possibly even needed — Manny Mendoza. They weren't willing to risk another election in which he might lose. Why? What had Allan discovered? What had he been on the verge of revealing when he was murdered?

Molly knew she couldn't very well stand up there and accuse the board, much less Mendoza himself, of doing something illegal. They'd have her in court charged with slander before the words were out of her mouth. Mendoza at least was powerful enough to make the charge stick, even if truth were on her side. That would also make him powerful enough to reach the county manager as well.

Caught up in her new theory, she murmured a few more wasted words and hurried to the back of the room where Michael waited, his dark eyes alternately surveying the crowd and watching her.

"Pretty gutsy stuff for a woman whose life already might be in danger," he said. His tone wasn't entirely complimentary. He took a closer look. "Are you okay?"

By way of an answer Molly dragged him outside the room.

"I think we've spent too much time worrying about the Winecrofts' marital problems," she said as they went back to her apartment. "From everything we've heard, those have been going on for a long time. There was no real reason for either one of them to turn violent all of a sudden. So what did change the last few months?"

Michael caught her train of thought at once. "Allan's election to the board."

"Right. I'm willing to bet that he stumbled onto some deep dark secret and that it has something to do with Mendoza."

"But if Mendoza's the one mixed up in

something shady, why would Drucilla and Gonzalez have called the county manager into this?"

"I think they're trying to protect each other. Neither of them is willing to admit the possibility that the other might be guilty of Allan's murder. If they'd just be honest and get everything out in the open about that night, I doubt they'd have any more worries on that score. Can't you just call Mendoza in for questioning?"

He shook his head. "I don't have the first real shred of evidence against the man. The most I could do would be to have an un-official chat. You can just imagine how fast news of that visit would reach the county manager's ear."

Seated in Molly's dining room, they were still debating the best course of action when they heard a knock at the door.

"I'll get it," Brian shouted, already running from his room. "It's probably Kevin. He was gonna come over to play video games." He threw open the door. "Oh, my gosh! Mom! Mom, there's a lady at the door and she's got a knife!"

15

Brian had sounded more fascinated than scared by the knife, but that wasn't Molly's reaction. She responded with a primal surge of terror, maternal instincts churning. She was on her feet and running, but even so it took only a half dozen of Michael's long-legged strides to beat her to the door. He had one hand under the lapel of his jacket and on the handle of his gun. His jaw was tensed, but other than that he appeared astonishingly cool and calm as he faced Drucilla Winecroft across the threshold.

"Back away, son," he said quietly. Molly wanted to scream. Then she saw Drucilla's expression. She was staring at Michael's gun in absolute terror.

"What is it?" she said, her voice quavering. "I haven't done anything."

"The knife," Michael said. "Hand it to me. Slowly."

"You're acting as if . . . Oh, my Lord, I

see. You thought . . . How terrible. Brian, sweetie, Molly, I'm so sorry if I scared you. I was just returning your things. With everything that's happened, I forgot I had them. I took them upstairs after the bridge game."

Understanding dawned in Michael's wary gaze. He nodded toward Molly. "These are yours?"

Finally Molly was able to drag her eyes away from her son long enough to take a good look at what Drucilla was carrying. Tucked under her arm was Molly's glass cake plate with the calla lily pattern. In her hand was the knife Molly had taken to the fateful bridge game. She knew it was hers because of the deep scratches in the handle. They had happened one night when the knife had slid, accidentally, handle first into the garbage disposal, creating the worst racket she'd ever heard. On the morning of the murder she'd never gotten close enough to actually see if the handle had similar scars.

"They're mine," she confirmed. "But I don't understand. I thought . . ." Her gaze rose to meet Michael's. "The murder weapon wasn't mine after all."

"Which explains why there was only one set of prints, the murderer's, not yours. Shit.

I'd better call the lab. We should have picked up on something like this that first day."

Molly invited Drucilla in and fixed her a cup of coffee, while they waited for Michael to get off the phone with the police lab. His terse orders crackled with impatience.

"They'll try to get back to me tonight."

"Why has it taken so long? Was the lab backed up?" Molly asked.

"Some nitwit didn't see the need to rush because somebody mentioned the prints were yours." He turned to Drucilla. "Mrs. Winecroft, have you given any more thought to what we discussed the other day? Did your husband have any enemies who might have made those anonymous calls?"

Drucilla sat at the table and leaned forward intently. "Detective, as you may have surmised by now, my husband was not a particularly kind or generous man. He was a perfectionist, and like all perfectionists he made his share of enemies. When he was running my father's company, he was despised by the workers because he wouldn't tolerate mistakes. The board, however, found no fault, because under his guidance the company was more profitable and respected than ever before."

"I'm not sure I understand what that

might have to do with the murder," Michael said.

Drucilla looked as if she didn't believe for a second that Michael's comprehension was the least bit slow. She answered anyway. "I'm afraid he ran this condominium the same way. He was putting pressure on everyone to make improvements in efficiency, to cut back the excess spending. Tyler knew how Allan was. Tyler held a seat on the company's board for years. He was a friend of my father's. We found our apartment while visiting him several years ago. At any rate, because he knew Allan's style so well, he encouraged him to run for the condo board. He was fed up with the lax business decisions being made around here."

"So while Allan was making improvements and cutting costs, he was doing it with a heavy hand?" Michael said.

"Absolutely. He was not the sort of businessman to care about making friends, as long as he improved the bottom line."

"You don't think he cared about the effect this had on people?" Molly said, trying to understand how anyone could totally separate the two issues. "What about Enrique, for instance? He'd worked here as a security guard since the building opened. He had a large family to support. Obviously, he'd been doing things the same way for years. Shouldn't Allan have given him a chance to change, or at least to explain?"

"If you're asking what I think, yes, he should have. Allan wouldn't see it that way. He saw things in terms of right and wrong, perfection and mistakes. He'd told the guards they were to log in every single nonresident car, and he wasn't beyond checking to see that they did. That's what happened with Enrique. One of Allan's cronies came over. Enrique recognized him and let him in and didn't write it down. Allan happened to check the log later that day. The visit wasn't there. He fired Enrique. For Allan, it was a simple matter. The man hadn't followed a direct order. I spoke with Enrique after that myself and offered to help him and his family in any way I could."

"You did?" Michael said.

"Of course. We had known the man for years. I occasionally hired him to tend bar at our parties. I told him I would help see that he got more of those jobs."

He ought to do very well, Molly thought. Drucilla's friends gave a lot of parties.

"What was his reaction?" Michael asked.

"He sounded very grateful. Enrique is a very gracious, polite man. That's why I've used him so often. He makes a lovely impression on the guests."

Molly had a sudden thought. "Do other residents hire him as well?"

"Certainly," Drucilla said. "I've recommended him very highly."

Michael nodded. "You're thinking that he might have had access to the knife, right?"

"It makes sense, doesn't it? We know the killer must have had a knife just like mine."

"But there's only one way the killer could have known to use the matching knife," Michael said slowly. "He had to have been in the cardroom that night. Was Enrique in the building? Would he have any reason to want to set you up? Is he even clever enough to try, or was it just an accident that the weapon matched your knife?"

"Are you speculating aloud or asking me?" Molly said. "If I knew all that, I'd ask for a transfer to the Metro police force."

Michael grinned. "Let's take it one at a time then. Was he here the night of the murder?"

"I didn't see him," Molly said. "Drucilla? Was anyone having a party that night? That's the only way he could have gotten on the grounds."

"Unless he told the man on duty he'd just come back to collect some of his things,"

Michael said. "If it was a guard he knew, he wouldn't have been questioned."

Molly shook her head. "The guard on the gate that night was new. He'd probably had all of the rules drilled into his head. In fact, he probably knew that letting an unauthorized person in was exactly what had gotten Enrique fired in the first place. It had to be a party. Was anyone having one that night, Drucilla?"

"None of our friends, but the log at the desk would indicate if anyone had a lot of guests in or if anyone held something in the party room."

"I'll call the desk," Molly offered, though she was certain she already knew the answer. The logs she'd seen had had no more than the usual number of drop-by visitors registered.

"Don't bother," Michael said. "I had all the logs taken to headquarters as evidence. I'll call over there in a minute. Let's get back to those other questions. How did you get along with Enrique, Molly? Was he holding any sort of grudge against you?"

"Absolutely not. In fact, he came by my office to talk after he got fired. I gave him the county job listings in case there was something he was qualified to do."

"Was he angry enough at Allan to kill him?"

"No."

"You sound certain."

"I am. If anything, he was hurt. He couldn't understand why anyone would do that to him after all those years."

Drucilla agreed. "He said as much when I talked to him, too."

"So, even if he had the motive and the opportunity, neither of you think he was capable of plotting Allan's murder, implicating Molly, and going through with it."

"Capable in the sense of being bright enough, maybe," Molly said. "He had some sort of graduate degree in Cuba, but it took him a long time in this country to learn the language. Whatever his field was, it required some sort of licensing, and I guess he never felt confident enough in his English to try for it."

"Even so, he's not your top suspect, right?"

"No," Molly agreed. Drucilla nodded.

Michael sat back and sighed heavily. "Which brings us right back where we were. We've got suspects all over the place, some with motive but no apparent opportunity, some with opportunity but no obvious motive."

"I'm sorry I wasn't more help," Drucilla said.

She looked as though she couldn't quite make up her mind whether to go or stay. Molly had the feeling she didn't really want to return to an empty apartment. "Why don't I pour you another cup of coffee," she suggested. "Maybe if we all put our heads together we can narrow things down a little."

"Good idea," Michael said.

"Are you sure?" Drucilla said.

"Absolutely," Molly said, going into the kitchen to make more coffee. Michael was right on her heels. He nudged her aside and took over the coffee-making duty.

"Yours is too weak," he said. "Sissy stuff. What did you think in there? For a woman who just lost her husband in a violent murder doesn't she seem oddly calm to you?"

"If the man was such a petty tyrant, plus a womanizer, she's probably relieved, especially if she wants to marry Juan Gonzalez."

"But you really don't think she's guilty, do you?"

Molly considered the possibility, trying to separate gut instinct from fact. "God knows she had the motive and the opportunity, but for some reason I just don't think so — for all those reasons we were discussing right before she came. I'm more convinced than ever we should check out Mendoza. Besides, if Drucilla had done it, I just can't imagine that she'd want to hang around with you any longer than absolutely necessary."

"Maybe it's my charm."

"You may be irresistible to most women, but . . ."

"Including you?" he interrupted.

"Don't fish for compliments."

"Interesting."

"What?"

"You're nervous."

"I am not."

"Then why are you pouring salt into the coffee?"

Molly's gaze jerked to the container in her hand. It was sugar. "You really are obnoxious, Detective."

"Because I was right?"

"You weren't right. It was sugar, not salt."

"Ah, but your reaction told me you weren't one bit certain of that. Only someone who's already rattled would have needed to look."

"Is that some strange police technique for determining guilt or innocence?"

"It has its uses."

She couldn't imagine that he would look

any more smug if he'd just solved the case. Molly decided right then against continuing an argument she couldn't win. The man did make her nervous. It always made her nervous being attracted to a man who was already spoken for, especially when he was sending out signals that weren't all that clear-cut. A devoted lover wouldn't be camping on her doorstep. He'd be home in his own bed with Bianca.

Or would he? Michael wouldn't be the first Latin male of her acquaintance to court one woman while living with or married to another. Something told Molly, though, that Michael had more scruples than that, probably because of his own irregular parental situation. And attraction aside, Michael was a damned good cop. He would never let his personal situation get between him and what he considered to be his duty.

Duty! The thought that he might classify her as no more than that depressed her.

"As I was saying," she said firmly, "I doubt murderers would risk revealing their guilt no matter how charming they might find you on a personal level. Drucilla's not budging, ergo she's innocent."

"I have to admit, my money's on someone else, too. Damn, I wish the lab would call back. I'd love to get a match on those fingerprints."

Just as they started back toward the dining room, where Drucilla was waiting, the front door burst open. Since she'd heard the key in the lock an instant before, Molly knew it was Liza, but Michael couldn't have guessed that. For the second time that night his body tensed. His hand was within inches of his gun.

Liza spotted the automatic gesture and skidded to a halt. "You don't need the damned gun," she said quietly, "but if you're any good at CPR, you'd better get out to the pool. There's a woman floating facedown. From my balcony it looks as though she's dead."

16

The woman found floating facedown in the clear turquoise pool, blond hair streaming, was Ingrid Nielsen. Although security guards had materialized instantly at Liza's frantic calls for help, by the time Molly and Michael reached the pool it was clearly too late for their energetic attempts at CPR. Michael checked to be sure, as did the doctor from the seventh floor. She was dead, sprawled on the rain-dampened concrete in a revealing bikini. The air was thick with humidity and hushed speculation. Molly kept thinking that someone ought to cover her up.

Michael tried to clear the scene of the crowd that had gathered, but it was impossible. Because of the condo meeting, more people than usual were out and about at this late hour. They moved back, but not inside. The sad part, Molly observed, was that no one seemed to be mourning Ingrid.

They were too busy wondering aloud about how she'd died, which one among them might be a murderer, and the effect this was likely to have on property values. Putting priorities in order and sensing panic, one of the island's top real estate agents was trying to reassure them that island condos would always bring top dollar. No one seemed to believe her.

"Mom." Brian's voice shook and his lower lip quivered. Molly had told him to stay upstairs. Naturally he hadn't. "Is she dead?"

"Yes." Worried about him, she steered him as far from the scene as she could, until the width of the pool and several people were between them and Ingrid's body.

"Did somebody kill her, too?"

"I'm not sure about that. We'll have to wait for the police to decide how she died."

"The police are lousy," he said, glaring at Michael on the other side of the pool, where he was organizing the crime scene investigators. "He promised to protect you. If he couldn't protect her, how can he take care of you?"

"Maybe he didn't know she needed protecting," Molly said slowly. Everyone had assumed that Allan's death was a single act of passion, that he'd been targeted because of his marital infidelities or his abrasive personality or the discovery of someone's dirty little secret.

Who, then, would have wanted Ingrid dead? Certainly at one time, Drucilla might have hated her enough to kill her, but now? With Allan dead, the affair was certainly over and Drucilla already had Juan anyway. For her, murdering Ingrid would be more or less redundant. Besides, Drucilla had been upstairs with them since before the storm ended. Surely that eliminated her as a suspect.

Molly tried to calculate the time of death to be sure. She hadn't seen Ingrid at the condo meeting. As a renter, she wouldn't have needed to be there. That sudden, intense storm had ended about an hour ago. Ingrid wouldn't have gone for a swim while it was still lightning and thundering. If she'd gone earlier, someone would have noticed the body much sooner. It made more sense that she'd been killed just minutes ago, right after the pool lights went off at ten. With the scudding clouds still overhead, it was unlikely anyone would have seen the murder, especially if she'd been knocked unconscious in the shadows, then tossed in the pool to drown. Liza had seen the body only because a distant flash of lightning had momentarily illuminated it.

If Molly was right about all that, Drucilla was out as a suspect. It was more likely that Ingrid had known something, the same something that had gotten Allan stabbed. Or she might have guessed the identity of the killer. Perhaps the two pieces of information went hand in hand. If Allan had known someone's secret, and if he had shared that information with Ingrid, then it was entirely likely that the killer had figured out that she was a danger to him too. Then, *bam,* there she was in the pool.

Not for one single second did Molly consider that it might be an accidental drowning. The odds that this was nothing more than coincidence were probably greater than those of being the only person to pick all six numbers in the Florida lottery. As for suicide, there were easier ways than trying to stay underwater long enough to die.

"Wait here," she told Brian. "I need to see Michael for a minute. I'll send Liza over here to wait with you. Okay?"

Brian put on a very brave face. "Sure, Mom."

She found Liza, then located Michael with the crime scene specialists. "Can I see you for a minute?"

"Now?"

"It has to do with the murders."

"Murders?"

"Don't be coy. You may not have the evidence yet, but you know as well as I do that she didn't throw herself in here because she was distraught over losing Allan. She thought she'd just struck it rich."

"Maybe she found out she wasn't mentioned in the will."

Molly hesitated. "Did she?"

"I don't know. I'm speculating, which is what you're doing."

"I like mine better. I think you ought to check her apartment."

"We'll get to it."

"Now," she said.

His gaze narrowed. "Why?"

"I think she knew something about Allan's death, either who killed him or the information he had that got him killed, which is pretty much the same thing."

He nodded slowly. "Okay. Could be. What is it you think we'll find in the apartment?"

"Okay, let's say Allan had told her something, late-night pillow talk and all that. Now, I'm still working on this part, but what if she said something to somebody at the pool, something overheard by the killer that let him know she'd figured it out. He couldn't very well let it go, could he?"

"No, but what's in the apartment?"

"A note, a name, I don't know. I just think you ought to check it out."

"We will."

"Now, dammit."

"Why the urgency? Shouldn't you be with Brian?"

"He's fine. Liza's with him. Now let's go. If I'm right, the killer's going to be up there looking for whatever she had too."

To her relief Michael nodded at last. It was a testament to the fact that he valued her opinion. He turned to one of the uniformed officers. "I'm going to check out her apartment." He motioned to Nestor. "I'll need a master key."

"*Sí, sí.*" The security chief pulled a ring with keys of every size and shape from his pocket as he hurried toward the building.

Upstairs, it took Nestor only two tries to find the right key for Ingrid's deadbolt lock. Seeing Molly's astonished expression, he said, "Is master key, *sí*? Must be on master or provide with copy for emergency. Pipes burst. Fire, maybe. You see?"

"I see," Molly agreed as Michael stepped into the apartment. She heard his muttered expletive before she got a good look inside.

"What?" she said.

He stepped aside. "See for yourself."

The apartment had been ransacked. If she hadn't seen the taut set of Michael's lips, she might have been tempted to gloat.

"Who else has a set of keys like yours?" Michael asked Nestor.

"The man in charge each shift, the chief engineer, the office."

"Michael, they wouldn't have needed a master key," Molly said. "She probably had her own keys with her at the pool when she was attacked. The killer could have taken those."

Michael radioed down to poolside. "Any sign of her apartment keys down there?"

"I'll check," the officer said. "No. Just a towel, sandals and some sort of T-shirt."

"What about pinned to her bathing suit? Sometimes swimmers do that, so they won't have to leave the key lying around."

"I'll check again, but I don't think so."

"Thanks, Marty. I'll be in the apartment awhile. When you guys finish down there, I need you up here."

"Ten-four."

Molly walked slowly around the apartment, paying particular attention to the places where the most damage had been done. It was hard to differentiate, actually. The whole place was a mess. Molly tried to put herself in Ingrid's shoes. Where would she have hidden something as important as a clue to Allan's murderer?

"Don't touch anything," Michael warned.

"I know. I just wish I knew exactly what I was looking for," she said as she went into the kitchen. By the phone she found a pad with several numbers scribbled on it, all with the island's 361 prefix. "Michael, do you have a notebook with you?"

He came to the door. "Sure. What did you find?"

"Just a bunch of phone numbers. Could be neighbors or stores."

"Or one of them could be the killer's." He copied the numbers down. "We'll call from downstairs."

Molly was ready to call right then, but didn't dare touch the phone. She used a corner of her blouse and one finger to pull open drawers and cabinets, but found absolutely nothing except the usual assortment of dishes, glassware, and pots and pans. There were no small kitchen appliances, not even a mixer. The refrigerator was nearly bare. A carton of milk, three containers of yogurt, and a chunk of cheese were on one shelf. Greasy residue from past groceries was on all the rest. There were two apples in the produce drawer. Apparently Ingrid had not been expected to cook for Allan. That made it all the more likely that at least some of those phone numbers were for local carry-out restaurants.

Molly moved on to the broom closet, which held a surprisingly complete stock of cleansers, polishers, brooms, and mops. Either Ingrid had preferred cleaning to cooking or she'd had a maid who insisted on being well equipped. Molly thought of the petite housekeeper she'd seen at the Winecroft apartment. Surely Allan hadn't been tacky enough to insist that the two women in his life share a maid. Of course, neither apartment was so outrageously large that one housekeeper couldn't have managed both as long as no meals were required. She already knew that the Winecrofts always ate out. She resolved to have another chat with Conchita as soon as she finished in here.

She wrapped a dishcloth around her hand and patted along the top shelf to make sure there was nothing there except dust cloths. Suddenly she felt something flat and hard underneath.

Uncertain what to do next, she called for Michael. He reappeared in the door at once. "What?"

"I think I found something. Can I take it out?"

"Use a cloth."

"I'll just wrap it in the dustcloths, okay?"

He nodded.

She folded the cloths around whatever Ingrid had hidden beneath them and pulled it out, then laid it on the counter. Michael used his pen to lift away the layers of cloth. A knife fell out. It was a large, lethal-looking carving knife.

"Why would she hide a carving knife in the broom closet?" Michael said, but Molly knew. Though the blade wasn't serrated, this knife came from the same set as the original murder weapon. She had one just like it in her kitchen.

"Don't you see," she said. "She knew the killer. This knife came from the same set. We already know there was a second set, because Drucilla just returned my knife. Ingrid figured it out, too. She must have been in someone's apartment and seen it."

"Or it was hers and she realized it could be incriminating."

"She wouldn't have a knife like this," Molly said with absolute certainty. "They're very expensive. She doesn't even cook."

"How can you tell?"

"I checked the refrigerator. The woman lived on dairy products. Her cholesterol was probably awful. Nope, I'm convinced she found the knife in the killer's apartment."

"There could be a dozen sets just like this in this building alone."

"Maybe, but only one of them is missing two knives."

"The killer could have had them replaced by now."

Molly shook her head. "He'd have to buy a complete set. Then he'd have extra knives he couldn't explain."

"So why not just throw out the set? Bingo, no incriminating knives at all."

"Because Ingrid already had this one. It probably has fingerprints on it, just like the murder weapon."

"Right," Michael said, looking impressed with her reasoning. Being taken seriously was heady stuff for a woman whose husband had belittled everything she said. "I'll send it to the lab. I don't get it, though. Why wouldn't she turn it over to us in the first place? She must have wanted Allan's killer caught."

"I have a theory about that," Molly admitted.

"I'm sure."

She scowled at him. "Do you want to hear this or not?"

"Please."

"Okay. What if she'd been left out of

Allan's will? Obviously she liked her life-style here. She had no source of income that we know of. She finds the knife, maybe some other evidence on the killer and decides to blackmail him. Chances are it's someone who has money, and clearly it's someone who doesn't want his or her secrets broadcast to the world."

"You've been reading too damned many scripts."

"Admit it," she said. "It's possible."

He grinned. "I didn't say they were bad scripts. Let's check her bank records."

They found her checkbook in her purse. Her balance was a scanty $24.87. Michael whistled as he discovered a deposit slip for $10,000.00 in cash. The money, however, was missing, taken, no doubt, by the killer.

"If I'd known blackmail could be that lucrative around here, even I might have been tempted into a life of crime," she said.

"So who on our list of suspects has the kind of cash to even fake a payoff like that?"

"Not me."

"You were at the bottom anyway."

"Thank you."

"You're welcome. Now who does?"

"Drucilla certainly. And Mendoza. Tyler Jenkins, I guess. Not the Davisons and probably not Roy Meeks. Certainly not the security guard. I like Mendoza. For some reason he really liked the power of the presidency."

"Or the kickbacks. If there was a lot of mismanagement going on, he'd probably been getting his cut to turn a blind eye to it."

"And his wife's a gourmet cook. I'd forgotten all about that until now. The paper did a big spread once on some of her recipes. She could very well have a set of knives just like these."

"Let's go pay them a visit, then."

"You'll let me tag along?" she said, surprised.

"If I don't, you'll probably try to climb onto the balcony so you can hear."

"I would never do that."

"Right."

Since his skepticism was working in her behalf, and since the Mendozas lived on the penthouse floor, Molly decided not to mention that she was terrified of heights. Even on her own lower balcony, she never went near the railing. Occasionally she tested herself by inching close to the edge. Each time she was struck by such an attack of vertigo she had to retreat immediately. As long as she stayed inside at the Mendozas', though, she ought to be just fine.

Unfortunately they weren't at home. They hadn't been at the pool either. No doubt they'd gone out to celebrate Manny's appointment to the Ocean Manor Board of Directors.

"What now?" she asked.

"We wait."

She glanced longingly at the door and thought of Nestor's ring of keys. "I don't suppose . . ."

"No, we cannot go in."

She sighed. "I know. It was just wishful thinking."

Just to be sure she didn't get any more dangerous and illegal ideas, Michael guided her to the elevator, his hand firmly in the middle of her back. The power of that totally innocent touch gave her plenty to think about. In the elevator he punched the buttons for her floor and the lobby.

"I've got to get back outside. Go on and get some sleep."

"Brian's out there."

"I'll have Liza bring him in."

Molly was suddenly too exhausted to argue. "You're probably right."

When the doors opened on five, Michael pressed the hold button and gazed down at her. Losing herself in the intensity of that look, Molly almost missed his words.

"In case I've forgotten to mention it, you've been a big help in this," he said.

Still dazed, she murmured, "Me? You think I've helped?"

He grinned at her astonishment.

Molly tucked her hands in her pockets to keep from throwing her arms around his neck. "Well, I'll be damned." That was all she needed to stiffen her resolve. She would discover the killer if she had to stay awake half the night to figure it out.

17

Michael hadn't returned by the time Molly left for work in the morning. Apparently, he wasn't having any better luck solving the two crimes than she was. He called, though, at midmorning.

"You okay?" he asked, his voice weary.

"About as tired as you sound," she admitted.

"Didn't you get any sleep?"

"Brian woke up twice with nightmares. I think seeing Ingrid's body made all of this real to him. He was pretty scared. He didn't want me to leave him at school today. It's the first time ever he hasn't been anxious to be rid of me."

"God, I'm sorry. I wish like hell I could wrap this up."

"Any new leads?"

"I've been running a paper chase on Mendoza all day. I want more than suspicions when I finally get to him."

"What have you found?"

"Zip. *Nada.* The guy's so clean, I'm surprised he's not up for sainthood."

"Too clean?"

"Let's just say I always find it a little odd when there's not so much as a traffic ticket on someone's record. Hell, I'd settle for an overtime parking violation. Otherwise I start wondering who's been taking care of them for him."

"The man builds parking lots. Maybe he's never needed to park at a meter."

"I'm too tired for cute, Molly."

"Sorry."

"Watch your step out there today. Don't wander around alone. Okay?"

She didn't need to ask why. She could sense Michael's conviction that the danger had magnified, that for the killer the stakes had gotten bigger than ever. "I'll be careful."

"I'll be by later unless something breaks. Have Liza or someone come by this evening so you and Brian aren't in that apartment alone."

Molly was quiet for several seconds before finally voicing something that had been on her mind. "Maybe I should send Brian to stay with his father for a few days," she said. She had considered that possibility with great reluctance when Brian lay trembling in her arms in the middle of the night. Then she'd thought about the last angry exchange she'd had with Hal DeWitt, the last of many times when he'd suggested she wasn't strong enough to have custody of their son.

"That's up to you," Michael said. "Could be, though, that he'd be more terrified if he couldn't see you and know you're okay."

She thought of Vince's offer to send both of them to California. If she mentioned it, Michael might very well insist she take Vince up on it. The truth of the matter was, though, that she wanted to stay near Michael. Since knowing him and feeling his respect for her grow, she'd felt herself getting stronger again, more in charge of her life. Foolhardy or not, she'd finally realized she really could take care of herself and Brian. With all that had happened, she hadn't cracked. She wasn't the inept woman Hal DeWitt had almost had her believing she was.

"We'll be there, when you get there," she said finally.

"Later, then."

Later, though, Molly had a brainstorm. It came to her as she was parking her car that night at the condo. They had never fully investigated the garage. She and Michael had both assumed that Allan's fury at Brian when he caught him playing there was linked to the fact that the kids were spraying the hose. What if that weren't the case? What if he'd just made a discovery and hadn't wanted the kids near it — whatever *it* was — until he'd had a chance to fully investigate?

With Brian upstairs waiting for her, she didn't dare take the time to explore now, but she vowed to get Liza to look after him so she could come back down. As soon as they'd had dinner, she called Liza.

"Can you come over and stay with Brian for a while?"

"Sure. What's up? You and the hunk heading out for the evening?"

"I don't think the *hunk* has time to date in the middle of a murder investigation. If he did, I'm not likely to be the companion of choice."

Liza gave an exaggerated sigh. "Priorities and timing are everything in life, aren't they? So what are you doing?"

"I just have to run an errand."

"Molly DeWitt," Liza said skeptically, "what are you up to?"

"An errand, that's it."

"Exactly what sort of errand are you running that isn't suitable for Brian? Do you have a fetish for X-rated movies you've never mentioned?"

Molly improvised. "He has homework."

"Which he probably finished hours ago."

Exasperated and guilty, Molly retorted, "Are you coming over or not?"

"I'll be right there."

Liza was there in two minutes carrying a baseball bat. Molly's eyes widened. "What on earth is that for?"

"Protection."

"I think you'll be safe enough in here."

"We're not going to be in here. We're coming with you."

"Liza, no. Not a chance."

"I'm not letting you go do whatever you're considering doing on your own. I'll use this on you, if I have to."

She actually sounded as if she meant it. Molly groaned and called Brian. "We're going down to check out the garage to see if we can figure out why Mr. Winecroft got so upset when he found you playing down there."

Brian's eyes grew as wide as Liza's had. "Mom, maybe this isn't such a good idea. Detective O'Hara really won't like it."

"And how do you know so much about what Detective O'Hara likes and doesn't like?"

"He called me this afternoon."

"He did? What did he want?"

"Just to talk and stuff. We made a deal."

"What kind of deal?"

"He said if I'd take care of you, he'd find the killer."

Quite a deal, Molly thought. Apparently, though, it had reassured Brian and that was all that mattered. "You can still keep your bargain. We'll all go to the garage together and we'll tell him everything we find."

Brian frowned. "Jeez, Mom, I don't think that's what he meant."

Molly's expression turned grim. "It's the best deal you're getting from me. We'll be just fine if we stick together. Liza has a bat."

Brian rolled his eyes. "Mom, have you ever seen her play ball? She'd miss an elephant."

Liza looked offended. "See if I ever play with you again, kid."

Molly left the apartment without waiting to see if they followed. She knew there wasn't a chance in hell that they wouldn't.

Ridiculously enough, they found themselves tiptoeing across the concrete in the garage. When they reached the well-lighted greenhouse area, Molly led the way inside. There was nothing spooky or frightening about the escapade so far. Nor was there anything especially revealing. A few pieces of rusted equipment had been abandoned in a plastic tray. Bags of fertilizer and potting soil were stacked in one corner. A hose lay coiled nearby. Other than that, the only things in the greenhouse were growing. A few palms, some more disgustingly healthy impatiens, a scraggly fern in dire need of misting.

Molly kicked at a bag of soil in disgust. "Well, this was certainly a waste of time."

"Maybe not," Liza said slowly.

Molly followed the direction of her gaze. She was staring at one of those portable sheds a few yards away. It was in an assigned parking place. Either an owner had put it there for additional storage or the space had been unsold and the shed belonged to the condominium.

"What's in here?" Liza said moving closer. Molly and Brian were right behind her.

"I'm not sure," Molly said. "I've never even noticed it before. I don't park on this side."

"I've seen it," Brian said. "It's open sometimes in the daytime."

"Have you seen the inside?"

"It's just boxes and stuff."

"Who's had it open?"

"Maintenance guys, people like that."

"Was it open the day you fought with Mr.

Winecroft?"

"I don't remember. I don't think so, unless Mr. Winecroft had just closed the door or something. Nobody else was here."

Molly tried the handle. It was locked. "So much for that."

"Wait a second," Liza said. She went back into the greenhouse and found a piece of wire that had been used to close one of the bags of fertilizer. She twisted it loose and brought it back. An expression of concentration on her face, she jiggled it in the lock for about fifteen seconds and the door swung open.

"How'd you do that?" Brian asked in awe.

"Don't you dare tell him," Molly warned. She scowled at her too curious son. "If I so much as see you within fifty yards of a locked door with a piece of wire in your hands, I'll ground you until you graduate from high school."

"Save the parental lectures," Liza said. "Let's check this out and get out of here."

They stepped inside. The shed was hot and stuffy, its single aisle narrow. Shelves lined both sides. The shelves were crammed with boxes, bottles, and jars of cleaning supplies. Whole drums of liquid carpet shampoo sat on the floor. In all, there was more than it would take to clean Ocean Manor from top to bottom for months on end.

"This hardly seems like the stuff over which murders are committed," Liza said. "I can't tell you the last time I got worked up over copper polish."

"A lot of copper polish," Molly pointed out.

Liza stared at her. "Meaning?"

"Do you know of any copper in our building? Maybe the pipes in the plumbing, but I doubt they spend a lot of time polishing those."

Liza grabbed up a bottle. "Maybe it can be used on brass. See, it says so right here. And there's brass in the elevators."

"Not enough to justify several hundred dollars' worth of polish."

"So maybe the order came in by mistake."

"Then why didn't someone send it back? How much of this was ordered because we need it and how much because somebody got a cut of the action?"

Liza was shaking her head. She gestured around the tiny shed. "The profit on this is peanuts."

"Maybe it's also just the tip of the iceberg. Come on. I want to call Michael and let him know. He can decide if it's important or not. I've got the budget figures upstairs, too. We can see how much all of this cost."

When they got back to the fifth floor, Molly's door was standing wide open. Liza stared down the hall indignantly. "Why, of all the nerve," she said and marched straight toward the apartment, bat upraised.

Molly caught her arm. "Are you out of your mind? Let's go into your place and call the police."

Before they could do that, though, she heard Michael's voice from inside her apartment. He was cussing someone out in a mix of English and Spanish. Molly caught the drift of his displeasure in both languages.

"*Madre de Dios*, are you *loco*? I told you not to let her out of your sight. I don't care if you followed her to the apartment and then sat out front to watch in case she decided to leave again. Didn't it occur to you that she could leave by foot or go someplace else in the building? The killer lives here, dammit!"

Molly touched his shoulder. Michael whirled around, his complexion an exhausted gray under the olive tone. He slammed the phone into the cradle and pulled her into his arms. "Jesus, I thought something had happened to you."

Molly could feel the slam of his heart in his chest, the tension in his muscles as his arms enfolded her. She might very well have stayed right where she was forever, but Michael let her go as a sigh of relief shuddered through him.

"Where have you three been? It took ten years off my life, when I came I here and you were missing. I knocked on every door in the hall. No one had seen you. You promised you'd stay here tonight until I got here."

"We went down to the garage," Molly said meekly, as Liza challenged Brian to a video game and left her alone with Michael.

"Why?"

"It occurred to me we might have missed something the last time."

"Did we?"

"Not in the greenhouse." She told him what they'd found in the storage shed and the significance she'd attributed to it.

"Could be," he admitted. "Where's the budget?"

She found the papers and handed them to him, then waited in silence as he went over the items under supplies. "Hell, I don't know what I'm looking for. I need cleanser, I buy one can of whatever's on sale. I have no idea what constitutes a good deal for a place like this."

"But Manny Mendoza would know."

Michael nodded. "It all keeps coming

back to him, doesn't it? I suppose it couldn't hurt to stop by for an unofficial chat."

He was halfway to the door before he realized that Molly was right where he'd left her. He grinned. "You, too. It'll look less official that way. Besides, then I'll know exactly where you are."

18

The Mendozas were having a party. At least fifty people were crowded into their penthouse apartment, sipping brandy, following what had apparently been a lavish dinner. The heavy scent of Cuban cigar smoke drifted into the room, even though the smokers had been sent to the balcony for their after-dinner indulgence.

"Molly, how lovely to see you again," Rosa said, looking surprised but delighted. "And Detective O'Hara, isn't it?"

Michael nodded. "Good evening, ma'am. I'm terribly sorry to intrude, but I need to speak with your husband for a moment. Alone, if that's possible."

"Why don't I show you into the den, then?"

As they crossed the living room, Michael greeted several of the Latin men whom Molly recognized as developers and bankers. As soon as Rosa had ushered them into the den and offered them something to drink, she said, "I think Manny's out on the balcony. I'll send him right in."

When Rosa had gone, Molly said, "There were enough power brokers in that room to buy and sell downtown Miami."

"That's probably exactly what they were doing. A lot of deals get made in social settings just like this."

Manny Mendoza came into the room just then, an unlit cigar firmly clamped between his teeth. He took it out and dropped it into an ashtray. "Rosa insisted I give them up. Can't break the habit, though," he muttered. He eyed the offending cigar as if it were responsible for his weakness. Then he smiled. Molly had seen expressions like that before on posters of benign dictators.

"Now, then," he said, taking a seat behind an oversize desk. Under other circumstances the desk's size might be functional. Tonight it was also intimidating, separating him from them, even though his words demonstrated a spirit of cooperation.

"What can I do for you?" he inquired. Shrewd brown eyes seemed to be assessing both Michael and Molly. He dismissed her and concentrated on the detective.

Michael leaned forward. "Mr. Mendoza, I'd like to ask you a few more questions about the night of Allan's murder. I believe you told me you had a meeting that night."

"Yes, a committee of the Latin Developers Association."

"In a Little Havana restaurant, is that right?"

"Versailles, yes."

"Do any of the other men who attended that meeting happen to be here tonight?"

Mendoza's eyes darkened with quick anger, but his voice remained impassive. "Quite a few of them, as a matter of fact."

"I'd appreciate it, if you would point them out to me in a moment."

"Friend," Mendoza began in a decidedly unfriendly tone, then, *"amigo."* With a glance at Molly he launched into a barrage of Spanish. He spoke too rapidly for her to follow what he was saying, but the increasingly furious expression on Michael's face suggested that Mendoza had made a very bad miscalculation.

"Mr. Mendoza, that is not how I conduct police business," Michael said. Since his own Spanish was flawless, Molly had the feeling he was deliberately using English as a slap in the man's face. "I don't intentionally set out to get Hispanics, nor will I accept a bribe to protect them, and I resent the hell out of the fact that you think I would. Maybe greasing palms is the way you got things done in Cuba. Maybe it still oils wheels for you in Miami. It doesn't cut shit with me."

Mendoza looked offended, though Molly wasn't sure whether it was by the accusation or the obscenity. He held up his hands in a placating gesture. "Detective, please. I meant no offense. I merely asked that you do nothing here tonight. Some critical business matters hang in the balance. I would hate to have them go the wrong way because of your ill-timed questions."

"If world peace hung in the balance, you might not be able to stop me from asking," Michael said, tension radiating from every indignant pore. "I will make every attempt not to upset anyone, but I'm trying to find a killer and some of your guests might be able to help."

"Only if you think that I am the killer, isn't that right? You wish to check my alibi?"

"Exactly."

"And can you not see that someone wishing to do business with me might have grave second thoughts if it were suggested that I might be involved in a murder investigation? Could you not call these people tomorrow? I will give you a list. It would be a favor to me, one I would not forget."

"I told you —"

"I know, and I apologize for any misunderstanding. I see now that you are a man of principle. That does not mean that at some time in the future I would not be able to pay you back for your kindness tonight, perhaps with a word in the right ear."

No matter how Mendoza tried to polish it up, it still sounded like bribery to Molly. She watched Michael's reaction. He continued to look as if he'd tasted water tainted with pond scum.

Sensing that he might be close to victory, despite Michael's expression of distaste, Mendoza said persuasively, "Perhaps you would like to stay, mingle a bit. You could observe, perhaps even ask a discreet question or two. I could trust you to be very discreet, could I not?"

"Fine," Michael said.

"That is wonderful," Mendoza said enthusiastically, beaming at his success. Molly doubted that he experienced losing often. "Come with me. I will have Enrique give you a drink."

At the mention of the guard's name Molly and Michael exchanged glances. Perhaps they would learn more tonight than they'd anticipated only moments earlier.

Michael hesitated at the door to the den.

"Where were you last night, Mr. Mendoza?"

"At the condo meeting. You were there, Detective. I'm quite sure you saw me."

"And after the meeting?"

"Rosa and I went to dinner, alone."

"Do you happen to have a credit card slip from the restaurant?"

"I always pay in cash, unless it is for business. However, you could ask. The waiters all know us. They would tell you we were there until nearly midnight. Now, please, follow me."

In the living room, he introduced them to several couples as if they were merely late-arriving guests, then pointed the way to the bar. "Enjoy yourselves. I am delighted you were able to stop by after all."

On their way to the bar, which had been set up near the balcony doors, Molly held Michael back. "Why did you agree to his terms?"

"For one thing, I spotted Enrique as we came in. I wanted a chance to speak with him. For another, it was clear we were getting nowhere with Mendoza. I didn't want his guests getting out of here tonight without my talking with them even if I have to do it discreetly and under Mendoza's watchful eye. You know some of these people, don't you?"

"Some."

"Then you might do a little mingling yourself. See what you can pick up."

"About Mendoza's alibi for the night of Allan's murder?"

"And last night."

Molly nodded. "Anybody in particular you'd like me to approach?"

"Take your pick," he said, handing her a snifter of brandy. He rolled his own expertly around the glass, then took a sip. "God, I hate this stuff. Enrique, I don't suppose you have any beer tucked behind there."

With that he turned his back on Molly and began a friendly conversation with the fired security guard. Left to her own devices, Molly mingled, listening to the flow of conversation around her, much of it in Spanish. Occasionally the sentences would drift from Spanish to English and back again, as if the speaker could express some things more clearly in one language than in another or was, perhaps, unaware of the switches entirely.

It was the head of the Latin Builders Association, a man with whom she'd often dealt when looking for special locations for various producers, who finally approached her. "Molly, you are looking lovely this evening," Xavier Nunez said, brushing his lips across her fingers in an old-world courtly gesture.

Despite the sincerity of the compliment, Molly suddenly realized how inappropriately she was dressed. The other women in the room wore fancy cocktail dresses, dangerously high heels, and enough gold jewelry to pay for a low-budget motion picture. Feeling the need to explain, she gestured at her slacks and blouse and picked up on Mendoza's earlier lead. "I was on a night shoot for a film and was able to get away at the last minute. Manny said to come by no matter how late it was."

"You would be beautiful no matter what you wore, señora. How is the movie business these days?"

"Picking up all the time."

"I have an interesting home you should visit. The architecture is very modern, very Miami. It is almost complete, but the owner will not take possession for a few months yet. I am sure he would be agreeable to having it used in a film. In fact I think he would find it most amusing. I could take you one day next week if you like."

Molly was only half listening by the time he finished. Distracted, she murmured her thanks and moved across the room in the direction in which she'd seen Jack Kingsley go with Manny Mendoza. Why would the manager of the condominium be at a party with the Mendozas and their high-powered friends? She went down the hallway after him, pausing outside the door to the den. It was closed, but she could hear the murmur of voices. If she recalled correctly, there was a bathroom connecting the den and the bedroom next door. Perhaps she could hear more clearly from in there.

Glancing down the hallway, she slipped into the bedroom and peered cautiously through the open doorway to the bath. The door to the den was closed. She went into the bathroom and checked to make sure both doors were locked. Then she listened.

"The board wasn't happy with that last supply," Kingsley said. "You'll have to increase the quality this time or I'll have trouble getting an approval."

"You forget that I am back. I will sign off. If I send you a higher grade material, that increases the cost to me. The increase will have to come out of your cut."

"No," Kingsley said. "It comes out of your share. You do what you have to do or I'll find a supplier who can come through for me."

"And who will sign the papers for you?" Mendoza countered. "You lost money those months when Allan was in charge. The college bills for your children did not stop, however, did they? Be sensible, my friend, or one of these days you're going to go too far. In many ways these penny-ante deals of yours are more trouble than they're worth."

Suddenly the picture came clear to Molly. It was the manager, not Mendoza, who'd been behind the purchasing decisions, obviously with Mendoza's cooperation. Mendoza's company was apparently getting its own share of the take.

With his business background and distaste for waste and mismanagement, Allan Winecroft had probably figured out the scam the first time he'd taken a good look at the books. Certainly he would have noticed the first time a major bid came in for supplies and was submitted from Mendoza's firm without competing bids. Even if he hadn't yet figured out who was responsible, if he'd objected strenuously, it would have threatened Kingsley's way of doing business. If he was raking in thousands of dollars a year in kickbacks, that was certainly motive enough for murder. Mendoza had a motive also. Had Allan exposed his role in the scheme, it would have damaged his reputation as a legitimate businessman.

But what about opportunity? Which man

had that? And how had either of them known about the matching knives? Was there a set in Kingsley's apartment? Or maybe even in this one? The two of them clearly worked together in everything else. What about the murder? Could they have plotted it together?

Molly slipped out of the bathroom and made her way to the kitchen, where the caterers were just cleaning up. She smiled brightly. "Excuse me, I just wanted to get a plain glass of water. Would you mind?"

One of the women nodded politely, got a glass from the cabinet and filled it with ice and bottled water. Molly sipped it slowly as she glanced around. "This is really quite a kitchen. Mrs. Mendoza has obviously done a lot in here. You must enjoy working for her."

"*Sí,*" the woman said. "She has only the best."

Molly's gaze focused on the butcher block table at the back of the room. A wooden knife holder sat on it. The handles sticking up looked exactly like her own. "Oh, are those those Swiss knives?" she said, already moving toward them. "I've been wanting to buy some, but they're outrageously expensive. Are they good?"

The caterer looked puzzled, but nodded.

"*Sí,* very good, very sharp."

Sharp enough to cut through human muscle anyway, Molly thought with a shudder. One by one she lifted them up, glancing at the blades. The paring knife was there, the utility knife, a bread knife, and a meat cleaver. The serrated knife and the carving knife were missing. Either Mendoza was behind the murders after all or Kingsley had had access to his kitchen on occasions other than tonight. Judging from the conversation she'd just heard between the two, it was likely that they met often. In fact, when Mendoza had been president of the board they would have had plenty of opportunities to plan and scheme together without anyone suspecting a thing.

Once he'd been voted off the board and was no longer able to protect Kingsley's unwise decisions, perhaps Mendoza had become a threat, too. She had just heard him suggest that he was about to cut the flow of money into the manager's hands by ending the sweetheart deals he'd been making. By implicating him in the murder of Allan, the manager would have rid himself of all interference so that his shady business could continue as usual. Or Mendoza could have decided to take matters into his own hands.

Her pulse racing with the excitement of her discovery, she went back into the living room and looked for Michael. Though the crowd was much thinner than when they'd arrived, she didn't spot him immediately. She was so busy looking, though, that she didn't see Kingsley coming up beside her. Before she realized he was there, his hand was under her elbow and he was wordlessly guiding her toward the balcony. Uneasy with his peremptory manner and filled with her own suspicions, she balked at the door.

"Please," he said then, smiling. "You look pale. A little air will be good for you. I'm sure you're distraught over seeing Ingrid like that last night."

"I've survived," she said, hanging back. He urged her forward. They were only twelve floors up, but for Molly that was several stories too many. She stayed as far from the metal railing as she could, her back pressed tight against the wall.

"No, my dear, you must see the view," Kingsley said, gesturing widely. "Because it's on a northwest corner, you can see the Coconut Grove skyline across the bay. It really is lovely from here, especially at night."

At Molly's failure to respond, a flicker of shrewd awareness sparked in his eyes. "Oh, that's right," he said with exaggerated innocence. "Heights make you nervous, don't they?"

Molly was trying to keep her teeth from chattering. She stared at the floor. Every time she dared a glance at Kingsley himself, she glimpsed beyond him and automatically calculated the drop to the ground. Dizziness swept over her.

"How do you know that?" she asked, her voice choked.

"I believe you mentioned it when you moved in. You said you could never live on a floor higher than the fire ladders could reach. That's why you picked the apartment on five, even though we had one available with a nicer view and a better deal."

Terrific, the sadist knew all about her fear of heights and had brought her out here anyway. She had to keep him talking. Sooner or later Michael would miss her and come looking. If she stayed calm and didn't look down, she'd be just fine. Maybe if she acted nonchalant, he would let her go, satisfied with having frightened her.

"Was there something you wanted to talk to me about?" she asked in the closest thing she could manage to a conversational tone. "If not, I'd like to go back inside. Detective O'Hara will be looking for me."

She took a step toward the door, but Kingsley's hand clamped around her elbow so tightly that she knew there'd be bruises by morning. He yanked her closer to the edge. Even though the railing was waist high and reasonably sturdy, Molly could feel bile rising in her throat. She tried to tell herself to remain calm, to keep talking, maybe get him to confirm some of her suppositions about what had happened. But that would mean telling him that she knew the truth and something warned her that would be the most dangerous thing she could do.

Or would it? Even if he was guilty, maybe she could bargain with him. Was it possible to bargain with a man who'd killed twice? Wasn't that what Ingrid had tried? Her attempt at blackmail had certainly backfired.

"You won't do it," she said with far more bravado than she was feeling.

His smile sent chills down her spine. "Do what? I am merely showing you the view." He backed away a step. "I am sorry if you were frightened."

He sounded very sincere. "Perhaps I should get you a drink. Wine? Brandy?"

The manager appeared so concerned Molly was caught off guard. She wondered if she'd been imagining the menace only seconds before. "No, thanks," she said hurriedly. "I was just getting ready to leave."

He nodded and stepped aside. "A pleasure seeing you as always."

Molly shivered. She had to force herself not to turn and run. Inside she spotted Michael, moved toward him and linked her arm through his. Though he kept talking, there was a quizzical expression in his eyes when he glanced at her. As soon as there was a lull in the conversation, she said, "I really want to get back to Brian. Are you about ready to leave?"

"Not quite yet," he said.

"Then I'll see you downstairs."

He regarded her worriedly. "Molly?"

"It's okay," she told him. "Really." Still shaken, she practically raced from the room. As soon as the door to the Mendoza apartment closed behind her, Molly released the breath she'd been holding. She was in such a hurry to get back to the relative sanctity of her own apartment, she almost took the stairs, then thought of being trapped in the stairwell with Kingsley or Mendoza after her. Again, a chill raced down her spine. She punched the button for the elevator again and again.

"Dammit, come on," she muttered, already regretting the impulse that had made her flee Michael's side. Too late now. She'd be fine, though, once she was home.

The elevator doors slid open and she stepped inside. They had begun to close all too slowly, when hands braced the two sides apart. The doors retracted and Kingsley stepped in. "If you don't mind," he said. "I'll just ride along with you."

Instinctively, Molly reached for the emergency button to set off an alarm, but the manager was quicker. Stepping neatly between her and the control panel, he pressed the button for the garage.

With every ounce of bravado she possessed, Molly said, "Hit five for me, please."

There was that slick, fake smile again as he said, "Not quite yet. There's something I'd like you to see first."

"What?"

"Don't be so impatient. We'll be there in just a minute."

In the garage he grabbed her elbow as roughly as he had earlier and guided her toward the greenhouse and toolshed. When they reached the shed, he opened the lock and shoved her inside. Molly knew she had to keep him talking, had to keep him from locking that door and leaving her in this metal box to die of the heat, if she didn't die of sheer terror first.

"Why are you doing this?" she demanded,

hoping for a confession she could pass along when she got out of this.

"Don't play games with me. I know you've figured everything out. I saw you try to slip away from the bathroom after my meeting with Mendoza upstairs. You went straight to the kitchen to check on the knives, didn't you?"

There was little point in denying it, she decided. "Did Mendoza kill Allan?" she asked, hoping that casting blame elsewhere would buy her a little time. Instead, Jack Kingsley looked insulted.

"Please," he said derisively.

Molly was startled by the too easy admission. Then, again, what could it matter? He was going to leave her here to die. Obviously he saw no reason not to tie up any loose ends for her satisfaction before he shut her in and locked the door.

"Okay, how did you know about the knives? It was very clever of you."

"Drucilla sliced a piece of cake for me when I dropped by the cardroom later that night. I didn't realize the knife was yours at the time, but the opportunity was too good to miss. When she'd taken it with her, I slipped upstairs, used the master key, and borrowed one from the Mendozas' kitchen. I figured I had two people in line in front of me as suspects. The owner of the first knife and Mendoza. Should have been the perfect crime. It would have been, too, if it hadn't been for that foolish girl. Ingrid had borrowed one of Rosa's knives one night and recognized that it and the murder weapon came from the same set. She had seen me coming from the Mendozas' apartment the night of the murder and put two and two together. She tried to blackmail me. I couldn't let her get away with it."

"So you killed her last night."

"I had no choice, just as I have none now."

Molly guessed his next move and tried to grab him as he backed out of the shed. She caught the edge of his sleeve and heard it rip as he shook her off, then slammed the door with a metallic crash. She threw herself against it, but it didn't give. She picked herself up and prepared to make one last desperate attempt, but she heard the ominous click as the door locked.

"Oh God," she muttered, sliding to the floor. "Oh, damn."

19

Twice during the endless, sweltering night Molly heard the distant sound of car doors closing. Each time she pounded on the walls of the shed and screamed at the top of her lungs. Each time she failed to attract any attention.

Morning would be better, she told herself repeatedly. More people would be coming and going. Perhaps someone from maintenance would even come to open the shed for supplies. Surely by then Michael would have launched a full-scale search as well. It would be okay.

But all the time she sought to reassure herself, she could feel the perspiration trickling down her back, feel the heat closing in and the air getting more and more stale and lifeless.

Inch by inch she searched the shed for some sort of tool that could be used as a lever on the door. Surely it couldn't take too much strength to pop the hinges on a temporary structure like this. The only thing she found was a supply of mop handles, and those couldn't be wedged into the tiny slit between the door and its frame.

She finally sank onto one of the boxes and tried to think. She needed to conserve her strength, too. Perspiring too freely would only speed the heat prostration she was facing if she wasn't found soon. It was too dark inside to see her watch, but from the way the heat was building, she could tell it was daylight. As the sun rose, so would the temperature in the shed. She had no idea how long a person could survive in that sort of intense heat, but it probably wasn't long. Hours, perhaps.

Bordering on panic, she began taking shallower and shallower breaths as perspiration dried and her skin burned feverishly. For something to do, she began counting supplies. Fifty ten-gallon drums of rug shampoo. Ten, no, twelve boxes of extra-large-size bottles of liquid soap. Five, no, eight — oh, God, how many cartons of paper towel rolls? They seemed to be swimming in front of her eyes. She licked her lips, surprised to find them already dry and cracked.

From what seemed to be very far away she heard voices. She had to signal them, had to make them hear her. She tried to scream, but her throat was dry, so very dry. With the last of her strength, she heaved a can of copper polish at the metal wall. It clattered noisily to the floor. She repeated the gesture again and again, for once grateful to Kingsley for the absurdly large order.

"Over here," someone shouted from nearby.

She heard footsteps, then Michael. *"Madre de Dios,"* he said, swearing impatiently. "Get it open. Molly, it's okay. We'll have you out in just a minute."

She could hear more curses, the jangle of keys, then finally the lock being tried. She struggled to her feet, but immediately sagged back down. The door was flung wide and Michael caught her just before she hit the floor.

She looked into his worried eyes and murmured, "What the hell took you so long?" And then she fainted.

When she came to, she was in a hospital bed, hooked up to an IV, a strange doctor hovering over her and Michael lurking watchfully in the background.

"It was Kingsley," she whispered, even though it hurt her parched throat to speak.

"I know. We got him. Mendoza finally confessed everything about the kickback scheme. While he was spilling his guts last night, one of the caterers came out and told him two of his knives were missing. I guess they didn't want to be blamed. They said you'd been snooping around in the kitchen. We looked for you, but both you and Kingsley had left the party. I swear to God the last eighteen hours have taken a dozen years off my life thinking he had you. We couldn't find Kingsley, even though we put out an all points bulletin. The Miami Beach police thought they spotted his car over there. Then we got a call from Bal Harbor. The Hollywood cops finally stopped him about forty minutes ago. When I realized you weren't with him, I nearly lost it. We tore the condo apart looking for you. It was Liza who suggested the shed because of what you all had found there earlier."

Because she couldn't deal with the emotions she thought she saw in his eyes, she said, "Brian?"

"He's right outside. I'll get him."

Barely a minute later, her son burst through the door and threw himself into her arms. His thin chest was heaving with sobs. Michael laid a hand on Brian's head, gently smoothing the light-brown hair that was damp with perspiration and tears.

Michael's gaze, though, was on Molly. "I

have things I have to take care of at head-quarters," he said quietly. "And you and Brian need some time alone."

Molly bit back her own cry of need and nodded.

He hesitated, his expression uncertain. "I could hang around if you need me."

She shook her head, not trusting herself to speak, not trusting herself not to beg him to stay now that his official duties were over.

"I'll be back when we have this all sorted out, okay?" The sunglasses went on then, but not before she caught the vulnerability that was all too evident in his eyes. He turned away.

Michael had taken several slow steps, when Molly called to him. "You are coming back?"

He nodded. "As soon as I can get here."

After he'd gone Liza took up his place beside Molly's bed. With Brian in her arms she fell asleep. When she awoke, Liza was still there and Brian was still sound asleep and clinging to Molly's hand.

For the first time since Molly had known her, Liza looked as if she were at a loss for words. "You want something to drink?" she asked finally.

"No, but you look as if you could use something." Molly touched her shoulder.

"Are you okay?"

Liza finally met her gaze, tears streaking down her face. "It's funny. You two are the closest thing to family I have. When we realized you were missing, I wanted to trade places with you. I was so terrified of what would happen." Her voice trailed off and she glanced at Brian.

Molly shuddered and stroked his hair. "I know. Me, too. It's the only thing that kept me going," she whispered, looking down at her son.

They sat quietly for several minutes before Liza murmured, "You're falling in love with the hunk, aren't you?"

Molly managed a grim smile. "If I had to put a label on what I'm feeling, I'd say I'm falling in love with the *possibility* of falling in love again. Michael possesses certain traits, a certain strength and sensitivity, that would make it easy to love him. He also has a few that drive me nuts."

"The man is hot, Molly. Why don't you sleep with him? That ought to clarify things."

"Or confuse them more than ever."

"How does he feel?"

"I don't know. Bianca's still in his life. I can't deny her existence. I can't wish her away."

"What does he say?"

"Not much, at least not on that subject."

The knock on the door startled them both. Liza grinned. "I think that's your answer now."

"Has it been that long?"

"I suspect he was in a hurry. I'll let him in and let myself out. Is there anything you need from home?"

Molly ran shaky fingers through her hair trying to sort out the tangles. She suddenly regretted not being able to take a shower, change into something besides this frumpy hospital gown, and put on makeup. How had she let the time slip away when she'd known Michael was coming back? Maybe she'd just been telling herself that this meeting wasn't significant, even though the thumping of her heart right now felt like a drum in a Sousa march.

"You look good," Michael said from across the room, when Liza had gone taking the still sleepy Brian with her.

A near-hysterical giggle climbed in Molly's throat, but she managed to swallow it.

"Your color's better."

"It usually is, when every drop of blood hasn't drained out of my face," she said wryly. "I've never been so terrified in my life."

He rocked back on his heels, hands in his pockets as if he wasn't sure what else to do with them. "Me, too."

"Because I was an innocent bystander who almost got killed? Afraid you'd slipped up in your duty, Detective?"

His lips twitched at her deliberate ploy. "No, Mrs. DeWitt, because you're you and for better or worse you've gotten under my skin."

"Sounds like an allergy."

He dared a step closer, looked around, and chose a chair about as far from her as he could get and still be in the same room. Molly shook her head, very much aware of his confusion. "You don't have to stay. I'm fine and you wouldn't be responsible even if I weren't."

"I feel responsible and . . ."

When he didn't go on, she prodded, "And?"

He shook his head. "I don't know what the hell to do about this. First of all, there's . . ."

Molly ignored the sting of tears and snapped, "Bianca. For crying out loud, you can say her name. I'm not that fragile."

He nodded slowly, his eyes troubled. "Yes, there is Bianca. On top of that, I'm not such a good bet when it comes to anything serious. I learned that being married. Being a cop and marriage just don't mix."

"You've taken an amazing leap of faith here. I thought we were talking about maybe having a date. You're worried about what happens after the wedding."

"Dates have a way of leading to marriage before you know what's happened."

"Not when you have two rational, thoughtful, very cautious people involved."

That drew a genuine smile that put sparks into his brown eyes. "Cautious, huh? You, too?"

"Damn right. I'm in no rush for any kind of commitment."

He nodded again. "So, you're willing to risk a date or two?"

"If anything happens to change your living arrangements, yes. But that's your decision, Detective. I'm not asking you to and I'm not making any promises after that."

"Fair enough." He stood up then and started toward the door. "I'll be in touch."

Molly clutched the flat hospital pillow so hard all the stuffing was squashed into one end. She managed a wobbly smile. "You do that."

"You'll be okay tonight?"

"Fine." *Just go! Go before I make an*

absolute fool of myself, she thought desperately.

Before she realized what he intended, though, he was across the room, apparently propelled by the same barrage of contradictory feelings that had her off-balance. He cupped her chin and tilted her head until their gazes clashed. He leaned down then until his lips brushed tenderly across hers. That faint, tentative whisper of a touch was filled with so much longing, so much purely sensual promise, that it left Molly weak.

"See you," he said.

"Yeah. See you." Her tone was so determinedly casual she could have been saying good-bye to the exterminator.

He was shaking his head. "No, no, sweetheart. When I say I'll see you, I mean it."

"Of course you will," she said jauntily. "If you're going to let Brian play soccer on your team, we're bound to run into each other."

"You talk way too much," he said, his mouth covering hers again. This time there was nothing sweet and tender about the kiss. This time the sensation was far more primal, filled with wicked heat and dangerous passion.

This time, when Michael walked away, Molly knew he'd be back. She believed in that much, at least.

HOT SECRET

1

Miami Beach, Florida
1992

Anyone who considered filmmaking glamorous had never been on a movie set at the end of a twelve-hour day. And at 10:00 p.m. on a hot and humid Saturday night, tempers tended to be frayed beyond repair. Veronica Weston's dressing room trailer, half a block long and complete with kitchen, practically reverberated with the echoes of an argument that had begun in mid-morning and gotten noisier and nastier with each passing hour. Anyone who knew the gist of the star's complaint wasn't sharing it with Molly De-Witt, who'd been assigned by the Miami/Dade film office to keep everyone happy. Judging from the shouts, she wasn't doing a wonderful job.

Hot, tired, and drained from the nonstop tension, Molly sat at the Cardoza's porch-front café in Miami Beach's rejuvenated Art

Deco district and sipped on her tenth iced tea since dinnertime. If she hadn't been working, she would have ordered something a lot more lethal. The thought of a piña colada or maybe a straight shot of Scotch held an almost irresistible appeal.

The door of Veronica's trailer crashed open and the star emerged in a dramatic swirl of hot pink chiffon that was more suited to a boudoir than to a public place. It was not a costume. Veronica dressed to suit her glamorous image.

The actress caught sight of Molly and made a beeline for her table. She flounced into a chair amid a cloud of pink. It was indicative of the neighborhood, a haven for trendy yuppies and high-fashion European models, that no one paid the slightest attention.

"That man," she said in apparent reference to the film's director, Gregory Kinsey, "has the talent of a toad. I will not listen to another word he says."

Since Veronica was making her comeback film after years of alcoholic decline, Molly thought it prudent to suggest a spirit of cooperation. "I'm sure he has your best interests at heart," she said.

"Ha!" Veronica gestured to a passing waiter and ordered a double vodka on the rocks. Apparently she wasn't worried about either slipping off the wagon or falling down drunk in her final shot of the night.

"After all, it's his reputation on the line as well," Molly ventured, feeling infinitely braver since her first observation hadn't drawn fire. She didn't dare suggest that Gregory Kinsey, whose last two pictures had been money-making Academy Award nominees, hadn't needed to take a risk on a woman who'd dragged her own last two films into overbudget box-office debacles.

Besides, she felt a certain amount of sympathy for the fifty-something actress, whose once-gorgeous face and career had been ravaged by alcohol. She admired the spunk it had taken to ignore all of the vicious tabloid gossip and return to the screen in a less than flattering role, a role Kinsey reportedly had fought to offer her. The fact that the two had been at loggerheads since the first day of production was no secret, and Molly wondered why the up-and-coming Gregory had bothered trying to salvage the woman's downsliding career.

Veronica gulped down the drink and ordered another. "You know, dear, you're really wasting your time in this town," she said, giving Molly a critical once-over. "You ought to move to L.A. That's where the industry is. Half the producers in that town would kill to have someone who could keep things organized the way you do. Does that boss of yours, Vince what's-his-name, appreciate you?"

The concept of self-absorbed Vincent Gates displaying gratitude was enough to make Molly smile. "No, but I happen to love Miami," she said. "And I'm not the issue, you are. What will it take to make you happy? Is there something I can do to make this shoot easier on you?"

Veronica seemed startled that anyone honestly cared what she wanted now that her stardom had crashed like a meteor plummeting to earth.

"Maybe you could go talk to Gregory," she said, slowly warming to the idea. "He'd listen to you. He's surrounded by all those sycophants. I haven't seen so much bowing and scraping since I met the queen. Did I ever tell you that story, dear? Well, never mind, now's not the time. You go speak to Gregory and then we'll talk about all that ancient history."

Molly was flattered by Veronica's faith in her persuasiveness, but she seriously doubted that the director was the least bit interested in her amateur opinions. From what she'd observed this past week on the set, Gregory Kinsey had a pretty good idea of exactly what he wanted in every shot. Barely into his thirties and riding an artistic high, he wasn't the type of director to encourage input. "What exactly is the problem between you two?" Molly asked.

"This godawful script is the problem. Have you read it? Does it make a bit of sense to you? No," she answered before Molly could comment. "Of course not. No woman my age is going to chase around after some worthless twerp like Rod Lukens. What kind of name is that anyway? It sounds like some cowboy drifter."

Since the entire plot of *Endless Tomorrows* was created around just such a chase and just such a drifter, Molly couldn't help inquiring, "Why did you take the role, if you hated it so much?"

Veronica directed one of her famous disbelieving glances at Molly. The subtle lift of one delicate brow spoke volumes on-screen and off. "Offers have not exactly been rolling in the last few years. Everybody wants young. Everybody wants sexy. They seem to forget there's an audience out there that's my age, that women my age can be sexy. I figured I owed it to my gender to prove that."

"And you needed the work," Molly dared

to guess.

Veronica laughed, a bawdy, raucous sound that carried on the ocean breeze. "Hell, yes, I needed the work. Do you have any idea how much a stay at that de-tox clinic costs?"

"Then I'm surprised you're so anxious to repeat it," Molly said with a pointed look at the second double vodka sitting in front of the actress.

Veronica didn't seem to take offense. "Don't worry about me, honey. I'm just getting my second wind. When Gregory calls for action, I'll be in front of the camera, hitting my mark and delivering my lines, no matter how absurd they are. The bottom line is I'm a professional and Gregory knows it. He's counting on it, in fact. He'll let me rant and rave all I want as long as I show up."

"So the tantrum's just for show?"

"Essentially," she admitted with a shrug. "Maybe he'll make a few little changes to pacify me, but he knows I can't afford to walk away from this project, no matter what I say."

"Then why bother? Doesn't all this arguing upset you? How can you possibly be creative in the midst of all this tension? I can't finish a grocery list if I'm under a lot of stress."

Veronica threw back her head, setting a shoulder-length wave of chestnut hair into sensuous motion. "Tension, honey? You call this tension? This is just a warm-up. You wait until we get to the love scene, and I refuse to get into bed with that sleazy character until he washes that gunk out of his hair."

Molly had to admit that Duke Lane's insistence on wearing a slicked-back hairstyle for the role of Miami Beach gigolo Rod Lukens was enough to make her own stomach churn. It might, however, be difficult to get him to step out of character in mid-production and wash his hair. "How do you plan on winning that one?" she asked.

"I've been thinking about insisting on a sexy shower scene which includes a bottle of shampoo. What do you think?" There was an impish gleam in Veronica's vivid green eyes as she contemplated the prospect.

Molly grinned back at her. "A stroke of genius."

"Yeah. Now if I could just figure out how to get him to try the mouthwash, too," she said wearily. She finished her drink and glanced at her watch. "What the hell is slowing things down now? God, I hate night shoots. They drag on forever. If the cameras don't roll soon, I'm going to have bags under my eyes the size of airline carryons. Honey, could you go check for me? If we're not starting soon, I'm going back inside to rest."

"No problem," Molly said. "I'll be right back. Any idea where Gregory is?"

"Probably in the production trailer trying to figure out how he got himself mixed up in this dud."

Molly cut through the Saturday night crowd milling along Ocean Drive past the string of hotels that had been painted the colors of dawn on the Atlantic — palest pink, mauve, turquoise, and sun-bleached white. Front porches that had once seen no more action than the squeaking of a rocking chair now served as swank outdoor cafés. Swimming pools had become the focal point of trendy sidewalk bars. On Thirteenth Street, which had been blocked off to accommodate the production, she passed Veronica's trailer and went on to the slightly smaller RV parked in front. A plastic sign declaring GK PRODUCTIONS, ENDLESS TOMORROWS was plastered on the side.

Molly tapped on the trailer door and opened it. A handful of exhausted-looking, jeans-clad men and women were collapsed into the chairs around a rectangular table along one side of the long, narrow room. Several were playing poker, while the others sipped sodas and watched in apparent boredom.

"Anybody in here seen Gregory?" she asked, stepping inside long enough to savor the Arctic temperature.

"He's with Veronica."

"No," Molly said. "She's been outside at one of the cafés with me for the past twenty minutes."

The legs of one tilted-back chair hit the floor with a thud. "Shit, man, not again," assistant director Hank Murdock muttered as he lumbered to his feet. "Come on, guys. Let's go find him."

"Find him?" Molly repeated. "You think he's taken off or something?"

"The street is crawling with broads and bars and bedrooms. Greg's not known for overlooking any of those opportunities, especially when they come in combination," Hank said in weary resignation.

"Does that mean you're going to have to shut down production for the night? Should I tell Veronica she can go back to her hotel?"

"Not yet. Tell her to hang loose. We may get this last shot in yet. Jerry, you check Veronica's trailer just to be sure he's not still in there. That's the last place any of us saw him. Maybe he stuck around to recuperate once Veronica got her claws out of him."

"Don't panic, man," Jerry Shaw said soothingly. "It could be he's with Daniel setting up the next shot."

"I'll check, but I'm not holding my breath."

Molly walked with Jerry as far as the star's trailer. "You all don't like Veronica much, do you?" she said to the young production assistant. He was only twenty-three and a recent UCLA film school grad, but this was his third film with Gregory Kinsey.

"She's making Greg crazy. That's not good for him and it's not good for the film. Other than that, I don't much think about her one way or the other." For his age he managed an incredible air of bored cynicism.

"Why do you suppose she gets to him? Surely, he's worked with other difficult actresses."

"Beats me. I'd have told her to take a hike the first day, but Greg wouldn't budge. He wanted her on this picture no matter what. Fought the studio and everyone else till he got his way." Jerry rapped on the trailer door and waited. When no one answered, he peered inside.

"Oh, hell," he muttered, the color draining out of his face. He leaned against the

338

side of the trailer and drew in a couple of deep breaths before shouting at the top of his lungs. "Hank, guys, get the hell over here."

"What is it?" Molly said, trying to peer past him. Jerry blocked her way. He wasn't quite big enough, though, to keep her from spotting one dungaree-clad leg at an awkward angle. She recognized Gregory Kinsey's well-worn cowboy boot. She swallowed hard and forced her eyes away. "Shouldn't you get inside and do something?"

"Sweetheart, there's not much you can do for a guy who's got a bullet wound in the middle of his head."

2

Chaos erupted as word of the shooting spread along Ocean Drive like news of free drinks. Crew members abandoned cameras, lights, and card games to join the shocked, tearful vigil outside Veronica's trailer. Despite Jerry's conviction that Gregory Kinsey was dead, Hank Murdock shoved the young production assistant aside and went into the trailer to check for himself. When he emerged, his own complexion was ashen.

"Greg's dead. He's been shot," he announced, his voice sandpaper rough and unsteady. He shoved his wide, workman's hands into the pockets of his well-worn jeans, but not before Molly saw how they trembled. She was every bit as shaken by Hank's obvious dismay as she had been by the sight of Greg's body sprawled on the floor.

From the first day on the set Hank Murdock had impressed her as the kind of solid, reliable man anyone would want around in an emergency, the kind of man who would be unfazed by any calamity. His calm, easygoing personality was the opposite of Greg's more volatile, creative frenzy. They'd made good partners. Now one of them was dead and the other obviously distraught.

Molly wondered if there was a prayer that the gunshot wound was self-inflicted. There was one school of thought around the set that Veronica could drive the most stable among them to consider ending it all. Molly thought, though, that the director would have aimed the gun at the actress.

"Shouldn't someone call the police?" she asked, since Hank seemed, for the moment at least, incapable of making decisions.

"Done," the off-duty police officer assigned to the production responded just as sirens began their nerve-racking whine a few blocks away. He was already trying to move people back from the door without letting them get too far out of sight. His partner was doing his best to establish a perimeter around an area meant to close in potential suspects and eliminate curiosity seekers.

With her own options quickly diminishing, Molly edged away from the two officers. She scanned the rapidly growing crowd, looking for Veronica, but there was no sign of the actress's glamorous attire amid the crew's denim and T-shirts. Surely the woman hadn't downed so many vodkas that she'd missed the sight of people streaming toward her trailer.

Torn between finding Veronica and calling her boss to report they were likely to be caught in the middle of a public relations nightmare, Molly prayed for a pay phone somewhere between the trailer and the outdoor café where she'd left Veronica. She could probably borrow a cellular phone from half the status-conscious people along the beachfront street, but that would mean having her conversation overheard by everyone who'd crowded around. There were also cellular phones galore in the production trailer, but the prospect of being inside that confined space with a murderer on the loose nearby made her stomach churn.

It hadn't been all that many months since she'd discovered a body in the card room of her own condominium. The murderer had later taken her hostage and left her to die in a sweltering storage shed. The claustrophobic memory was still spine-tinglingly fresh. She opted for a pay phone half a block away, searching in her purse for Vince's home number in her purse.

The call to Vince elicited a stream of obscenities. Since she'd barely said "Hello," she guessed she'd caught him in the middle of his Saturday night seduction ritual. No wonder he'd insisted the number be used only in dire emergencies. The flow of invective and the rustle of sheets stopped abruptly when she casually mentioned the murder. That, at least temporarily, cooled his ardor. She'd always wondered what it would take.

"Murder!" Vince repeated. "What the hell are you talking about? What murder?"

"Actually, there's a slim possibility that it might be suicide," she said demurely. "But I wouldn't count on it."

"Molly, who exactly is dead and precisely why do you think they've been murdered?"

The determinedly patient note in Vince's voice suggested that he'd finally recognized just how close she was to hysterics. Even her unobservant boss could tell that she was really not happy about being one of the two people to find Gregory Kinsey with a bullet through his head.

"Molly? Are you there? Molly!"

She sighed. "I'm here. Gregory Kinsey's been shot. He's dead. The police are on the way. That's all I know."

"Shit!"

"My sentiments exactly."

"Who did it?"

"Vince, I've already told you the sum total of everything I know. The murderer's name was not included. Don't you ever listen?"

They both knew the answer to that. Vince's attention span was only slightly lengthier than a toddler's in a toy store. Countless spurned women could attest to that.

"Stay there," he said. "Whatever you do, do not leave until you know exactly what's going on. If anyone from the media asks, issue some sort of statement. We regret, et cetera, et cetera. You know what to say."

She noticed that Vince did not offer to leave his comfortable bed to join her.

"I'll think of something," she said bleakly. She couldn't imagine what. The movie's publicist would probably have more than enough to say for all of them, and none of it was likely to improve the Miami area's image among production companies.

How did you put a positive PR spin on the murder of one of the nation's rising Hollywood talents while he was filming in your own backyard, so to speak? *Miami Vice* and countless movies had left the country with a slightly skewed impression of murder and mayhem in Miami-Dade County, but at least those deaths had been fictional. This one was distressingly real and likely to be splashed across the front page of every newspaper and tabloid around the globe. It would be a helluva blow to local tourism, and the Miami area film industry alike, unless the police could prove that the murderer was someone close to Greg, an import rather than one of the area's own criminals.

Once she'd listened to more advice and warnings from her boss, Molly dialed her neighbor, praying that Liza was home from whatever Third World country she was currently championing. She responded on the first ring with a breezy, cheerful greeting.

"Liza, it's Molly. I need a huge favor. You aren't going out tonight, are you?" The question wasn't absurd despite the lateness of the hour. Liza Hastings marched to her own particular social drummer. She thought nothing of joining friends at midnight to plan strategy for one of her causes or at dawn to tote a picket sign in front of some business they found offensive.

"Are you kidding?" Liza said. "I still have another five thousand save-the-rain-forest flyers to label and stamp. I'm surprised my tongue hasn't dried out. I wonder if all that glue has calories. I need to drop three pounds by next weekend, if I'm going to wear that slinky silver dress to that world hunger benefit performance."

"Liza!" If Molly didn't stop her now, Liza was likely to go off on some convoluted dissertation on world hunger. Her sharp tone apparently registered.

"Sorry," Liza said, immediately contrite. "What's the favor?"

"Brian is due home from his soccer game any minute and I can't get away from the film location. Can he stay at your place?"

"If he can lick stamps, he can stay. How's he getting home from soccer? Do I need to pick him up?"

"No. Michael or one of the parents is supposed to drop him off after they all go out for pizza."

"Michael, hmm?" Liza had taken an inordinate interest in Molly's relationship with the tall, dark, and handsome detective who'd investigated the murder in their Key Biscayne condo. The casual mention of his name had clearly placed her curiosity on full alert.

Hoping to forestall a lengthy interrogation, Molly warned, "Liza, I do not have time to discuss Michael O'Hara or my social life."

"Oh?" Liza said, all innocence. "I wasn't aware that you had a social life or that you could link such activity with Michael O'Hara in the same breath. Does that mean things have changed since I left for Guatemala last month?"

"It doesn't mean a damn thing, except that I am at my wits' end and I do not have time for this," Molly snapped, suspecting she was wasting her breath. Liza was not known for staying on track or taking a hint, no matter how directly or waspishly it was phrased.

"What's happening over there? Is it exciting? Maybe I should take a break from all this disgusting glue and bring Brian over to watch. I know it's late and all, but it's not a school night, right? Besides, I wouldn't mind getting a close look at Gregory Kinsey. From what I've seen he's quite a hunk."

"Not anymore," Molly mumbled.

"What?"

"He's dead."

There was an instant of stunned silence. Then, her tone suitably sober, Liza said, "Gregory Kinsey is dead? What happened? Molly, are you okay?"

Molly responded to the genuine note of caring in her friend's voice. "I'm as well as can be expected considering the fact that we are about to have police and reporters swarming all over the place, and I don't have answers for any of them. Not that the police are going to expect answers from me, but the reporters might, and if I don't have them, Vince will kill me."

"Molly, you're babbling."

"Don't you think I know that?" she retorted. "Liza, I've got to run. I have to get to Veronica. Greg's body was found in her trailer. I don't think she knows about it yet."

"Oh, my God. Do you suppose . . ."

Molly hung up without supposing a thing. She had to find the actress and warn her that all hell was about to break loose. Then she had to figure out how she could help to stem the tide of all the negative publicity.

Unfortunately, a survey of the outdoor café where she'd left the star less than twenty minutes earlier proved fruitless. Either Veronica was suspiciously aware of the fatal shooting in her trailer and had vamoosed to safer ground — Miami International Airport was a hub for all those tempting Latin American locations that didn't have extradition treaties. Or she'd gotten tired of waiting for her call and had simply gone back to her hotel in a snit. Either way, the police were not likely to be happy about the absence of a woman likely to be a prime suspect.

Rather than wasting time trying to guess

how Veronica's mind worked, Molly skirted the crowd outside the murder scene and went back to the production trailer. The same people were gathered inside. Now, though, a palpable tension had replaced the boredom.

Hank Murdock, his usually affable expression grim, tried to pop open a soda, only to drop the can and send a dark spray all over the pale green carpet. No one moved to wipe it up. Hank just reached for another can. Jerry Shaw sat at the table and drummed his fingers in a nervous rhythm. Molly sat down beside him.

"You okay?" she asked.

He shot her a disbelieving look. "Do I look okay? The country's greatest film director since Hitchcock has just been murdered by a conniving bitch and you ask if I'm okay? Are you nuts, lady?"

Hank glared at him. "Shut up, Jerry."

Jerry's face crumpled. "Jesus," he murmured over and over. "Jesus."

"Did you find Veronica?" Hank asked Molly.

She shook her head. "There was no sign of her at the café. I was hoping she'd come back here. I doubt she ventured back to her own trailer with all that commotion outside."

Jerry muttered a cynical remark under his breath, but Molly chose to ignore it. "Maybe I should call the hotel," she said. "If she's back there, she should be told what's happened."

"As if she didn't know already," Jerry muttered darkly.

"I thought I told you to shut up," Hank said. "Taking pot shots at each other won't help anybody right now. We need Veronica if we're going to bring this film in, so watch what the hell you say to the police."

Molly stared at him. "You intend to finish the picture?"

The assistant director met her gaze evenly. "There's a helluva lot at stake here. Besides, it's what Greg would have wanted. We all owe it to him to pull together and see that his last film is a fitting tribute to his genius."

The sound of distinct clapping came from the trailer's open doorway. "I couldn't have said it better," producer Laura Crain said as she stepped inside. Her brown eyes were red-rimmed, but her narrow face was utterly composed.

Molly couldn't tear her gaze away from Laura's performance. Gossip on the set and in the tabloids had linked Laura and her boss romantically from the first day of production. The chemistry between Greg and the older producer had been obvious to anyone observing them in the same room for more than a few seconds at a time. The long, soulful glances, the steamy stolen kisses, the briefest of touches that occurred too often to be accidental.

From what Molly knew, Greg Kinsey never made a film without making a conquest in the process. Forty-year-old Laura Crain, with her stylishly cut frosted hair and nearsighted squint, had apparently been chosen as beneficiary of his affections on this production. Had the thin, hyperactive producer known that the romance was doomed to end in the next couple of weeks? Or had she, like all the others in his past, assumed she would be the one who lasted?

Whatever her emotional turmoil over Greg's death, Laura Crain wasn't about to let it show. She was quite possibly the best actress of them all, Molly decided, watching her move to Hank's side. With her clipboard in hand, she methodically went over a dozen scheduling details as if the murder had been no more than a minor glitch in an otherwise routine day.

Hank listened for several minutes, then gently placed a hand over hers. "Stop," he commanded softly. "There's not a damn thing we can do tonight and you know it, so you might as well give it up. Go tell the crew to start breaking for the night. They can get the equipment loaded. They might as well get a decent night's sleep, once the cops are through."

Laura stared at him helplessly, tears shimmering in her eyes. "But . . ."

Hank's gaze locked with hers. "It's okay, babe. You hear me? Everything is going to be okay."

A fresh batch of tears finally spilled down Laura's cheeks. Hank stood up and awkwardly pulled her into his arms. As Molly watched, Laura's shoulders shook with silent sobs.

Of all the people affiliated with the production, Molly had worked with Laura most closely, but she didn't feel she really knew her. Laura was one of those women who never seemed to relax around other women, as if she viewed them all as competition, no matter how farfetched that idea might be. Even so, Molly felt she had to say something to her now, offer some sort of consoling words.

She crossed the trailer. "Laura, I just want you to know how very sorry I am about Greg. I'm here to help you in any way I can."

Laura whirled on her, her eyes flashing

furious sparks. "Help? It's because of you that this happened. Greg would be alive today, if you hadn't convinced him to bring this production to Miami. We could have shot it anywhere, but he told me how persuasive you were, how accommodating." Her voice turned even more spiteful as she added slyly, "I wonder exactly how accommodating you were."

"That's enough!" Hank said firmly to Laura, when Molly could only stand there gaping. He shot an apologetic look at her. "Molly, maybe you could go out and see what's happening. The sooner the police talk to all of us, the better. I need to call Duke Lane at the hotel and tell him what's happened. Then I'll go talk to the crew about the schedule."

Since there was nothing to be gained by standing there defending herself against Laura's ridiculous accusation, Molly left.

Outside, the temperature remained in the mid-eighties. The breeze off the Atlantic barely stirred the muggy air. It was still preferable to being inside the trailer where the temperature and the atmosphere were both icy.

Molly found the off-duty officer still standing outside Veronica's trailer and introduced herself. "Who's in charge of the investigation?" she asked him.

"Sergeant Jenkins. He's inside."

"Any chance you can find out what sort of timetable he has in mind for questioning everyone?"

The officer was past being anxious to please, but still too much a rookie to know how to dismiss her with the haughty glance his superiors had perfected. "I'm not supposed to leave here," he said, rather than refusing outright.

Molly glanced from him to the door and back again. "I'd say you can take two steps, open the door and poke your head in. If you'd rather not, I could do it myself."

He decided there was less to lose by asking himself than giving her permission to venture inside. Molly'd been right. It took him exactly two steps to reach the door. After one swift glance to make sure Molly hadn't followed, he opened the door a discreet crack and called to the sergeant.

A minute later a tall black officer who looked as if he'd played tackle for the Dolphins loomed in the doorway. He leaned down, listened intently, glanced at Molly, nodded, made a terse comment she couldn't hear, then shut the door. Firmly.

"He says he'll let you know when he's ready to take statements," the off-duty officer told her, an undeniable glint of satisfaction in his eyes. "Meantime, he says, don't go far."

"I wouldn't dream of it." She spotted an open table at the café across the street. "I'll be right over there, whenever he needs me." There wasn't a chance in hell that she'd go back to the trailer for another round with Laura Crain. She glanced back at the policeman. "If any reporters want a statement from my office, can you direct them across the street?"

He looked hesitant, but finally decided that wouldn't be breaking any of the rules drummed into him about crime-scene protocol. "I'll send 'em over. You might make out a list of everyone from the production company who was on the set tonight. It'll save Jenkins some time."

"I'll do what I can," she said, then walked back to the café and settled down to wait.

Apparently, Sergeant Otis Jenkins did not regard her as a primary witness. Nor did he seem all that interested in the list she had diligently prepared. Perhaps he'd merely decided to save the best for last. At any rate, by the time he finally got around to strolling across the street and joining Molly, she was awash in a sea of iced tea. It was a wonder she didn't slosh. Her nerves jangled from all the extra caffeine.

Sergeant Jenkins didn't waste a lot of time on preliminaries. Nor did he try to finesse any surprise answers from her. He merely announced that he'd already zeroed in on the killer. All he wanted were any of Molly's observations that might help him clinch the case.

Since catching a killer took time — unless he was foolhardy enough to stand around with a smoking gun still in his hand — Molly regarded the policeman skeptically.

"Was there an eyewitness?"

"Not to the shooting," he admitted.

"What, then? Fingerprints on the gun?"

"How about I ask the questions?"

"Ask away," Molly invited.

"Did you hear the argument between Gregory Kinsey and Veronica Weston?"

"I heard the noise, not the content," she said. With a sinking feeling in the pit of her stomach, Molly realized exactly where Otis Jenkins was heading — straight out on an obvious limb.

After the way he'd deliberately snubbed her earlier, she could hardly wait to saw it off.

3

"I don't think there's any question about who's responsible," Sergeant Jenkins told Molly with a certain amount of grim satisfaction written all over his face. He resettled his bulky frame in the cramped plastic chair, trying to find a comfortable position. He finally gave up and perched on the edge of it.

"Given the timing, the fact that Kinsey and Veronica Weston were overheard arguing all day long, and the fact that he's lying on the floor of her trailer, it all adds up to one thing," he concluded, snapping his little black notebook shut.

Before he could say what that one thing was Molly stepped in to question his addition.

"Where's the murder weapon?" Molly interrupted as casually as if she were inquiring about the location of the Atlantic Ocean across the street. "Was it in the trailer?"

Jenkins looked slightly miffed, a surefire indicator that she'd hit on something that was equally troubling to him. "Don't worry. We'll find it. And when we do, I'm sure we'll find Veronica Weston's prints on it."

Even though she couldn't dismiss the fact that Veronica was every bit as absent as the gun used to kill Greg, Molly shook her head. She was absolutely certain of Veronica's innocence.

"I don't think so," she told the disgustingly smug detective. "Besides, all the killer would have to do is toss it in the canal along the MacArthur Causeway or take a midnight ride into the Atlantic and toss it overboard. Odds are you'll never find that gun. So much for means."

Jenkins cast a pleading glance heavenward. "God, I hate people who think they know everything just because they watch reruns of *Perry Mason.*"

Molly scowled at him. "Forget Perry Mason. All it takes is a little common sense. It's pretty obvious you haven't got diddly beyond opportunity and, believe me, that's pretty shaky. What's Veronica's motive supposed to be? Gregory fought to give her this role. It was a break she badly needed. Why would she kill him in the middle of the production?"

His expression suggested he couldn't imagine why women did anything. He glossed over the problem. "Lady, by the time the night's over and we press charges, I guarantee we'll have means, motive, and opportunity pinned down."

To be sure she got the message, he ticked them off on his fingers. "If she came into town with a gun, we'll know it. If she bought one here, we'll find the record. There's your means. She was in that trailer. There's opportunity. The man was pushing her on the set, disregarding her opinions. I have half a dozen witnesses or more who'll swear in court that she hated the man's guts."

"Having a professional disagreement hardly translates into hating his guts," Molly shot back. "Besides, what about the fact that he was still alive when she left the trailer?"

The words were out of her mouth before she even realized consciously that she actually was able to provide Veronica with a nearly airtight alibi. Greg had been alive when Veronica crossed that street! Suddenly there wasn't a doubt in her mind about that.

Just as suddenly, the detective's gaze was riveted on her. "How do you know that?"

Molly considered her answer carefully, trying to determine exactly why she was so certain. It went beyond mere intuition, though she never dismissed that either.

"Because I was sitting right here listening to them arguing," she told him finally. "You could hear them blocks away probably."

Jenkins nodded. "That's what everyone's said. Like I said, the woman's guilty as sin."

"No. He was still shouting when the door of the trailer slammed."

As she described the moments before she and Jerry had discovered Greg's body, Molly tried to recapture the exact sequence of events. Even as she described what she remembered, she had the feeling that she was missing one crucial detail, but for the life of her she couldn't recall what it was.

"The next thing I knew, Veronica was walking across the street," she told Jenkins. "She was with me every second until four, maybe five minutes before we discovered the body. Besides that, she was the one who sent me looking for Greg. Would a woman who'd just killed a man do that? Where'd she hide the gun? She wasn't carrying a purse and I guarantee that flimsy chiffon number she was wearing didn't have pockets suitable for concealing a peashooter, much less a firearm."

Sergeant Jenkins did not give up easily. "It's hard to say what any of us would do given the right circumstances or how cleverly we might be able to conceal something. Now, let me see if I have this right. You're claiming that Veronica Weston couldn't possibly have shot Kinsey because you were with her up until a few minutes before you found the body, right?"

"Exactly," she said, pleased that he'd caught on so quickly. Before he could remind her how many seconds were required to pull a trigger, she added, "And during those minutes I was a lot closer to her trailer than she was. I would have noticed if she'd gone back."

The detective's gaze narrowed. "How well did you know the victim?"

Molly was shaking her head before the question was out of his mouth. "Oh, no, you don't. You're not going to pin it on me. My job depends on keeping people like Gregory happy, not shooting them in cold blood, no matter how often I might want to. And I happened to like Gregory Kinsey and his films."

"No motive?" he said, subtly mocking her.

"No motive," Molly concurred. "And for the record, no means. I don't own a gun and wouldn't have the foggiest idea how to shoot one."

"I'm so relieved. I don't suppose you have any inside knowledge about someone who, in your educated opinion, does have a motive?"

Molly wished with all her heart that she had an answer for him, if only to wipe the smirk off his face. Unfortunately, she didn't. "No," she murmured reluctantly.

"Excuse me? I couldn't quite hear that."

She glared at him. "No, I do not know who had a motive."

"Thank you. You may go home now. We'll be in touch about having you make a formal statement."

"Sorry. My boss has other ideas."

He stood up and loomed over her. "Unless your boss is the president of the United States or maybe the governor of this state, it might be best if you remember that I'm in charge around here now." He waved a finger under her nose. "I've read about you, DeWitt. You were up to your earlobes in that case over on Key Biscayne a few months back. Nabbed yourself a few headlines, so now you think you know it all. Well, I don't want you messing in my territory. Got it?"

Molly decided she did not like Sergeant Otis Jenkins. She did not like his superior, mocking attitude. It was obvious he intended to make her job as difficult as possible. Maybe he thought it was fair play, since she'd just shot a significant hole in his case against Veronica.

"Sergeant, believe me, if I had any choice in the matter, I would go home, pour myself a glass of wine, and forget all about the events of the last couple of hours. However, like you, I am paid to be here. I will try not to get in your way, but I will stay."

The masculine groan behind her registered about the same time that the Miami Beach detective deliberately turned his back on her. Since further conversation with Jenkins appeared likely to be unproductive, Molly turned and found herself face-to-face with yet another police detective, one with whom she'd become more or less intimately acquainted when he'd investigated the murder in her condo building.

As she met Michael O'Hara's resigned gaze, she mustered a cheery smile. She could guess with some accuracy what his reaction was likely to be to her declaration. Cops, to a man, were reasonably predictable when it came to having outsiders play amateur sleuth. Mix that with Michael's instinctive Latin machismo and mile-wide streak of protectiveness and she had a pretty good idea of what was on his mind.

"You heard?" she said, trying not to notice that he looked every bit as gorgeous as the last time she'd seen him. She'd had this wild hope that his appeal would fade with time. It hadn't.

When he nodded, she said, "How much?"

"Enough to know that you're up to your pretty neck in another murder investigation. Molly, take a little advice. Do what the detective suggested. Go home. I will be happy to take you, in fact."

She sighed. "Believe me, I wish I could, but I can't. The film office is going to have to do everything in its power to counteract the bad publicity from Greg's murder. Vince insists that I stick around for every little detail."

Michael grinned. "Exactly how many details are you expecting to get from Miami Beach's finest law enforcement officers?"

Molly glanced at the stiff, retreating back of Sergeant Jenkins. "Not many," she admitted. "What are you doing here anyway?"

He shrugged in a lousy attempt at innocence. "Hey, it's Saturday night. South Beach is hot. Even cops get a night off once in a while."

Molly glanced around for some sign of his live-in lover, the sexy and volatile Bianca. As far as she knew, they were still together, despite his vague promises to end the relationship. He seemed to be alone. He was wearing faded jeans that hugged narrow hips and a knit shirt, not the kind of classy attire a man with Michael's elegant taste would choose for a night on the town. It didn't add up, especially since no more than an hour or two ago he'd been coaching a gang of eight- to ten-year-old soccer players way down in Kendall. Judging from the grass stains on the knees of his jeans, he hadn't gone home to change. She probed for a more truthful explanation.

"So as long as you were in the neighborhood, you thought you'd check out the latest hot murder scene?" she said, her skepticism showing.

"You know how cops are," he said blandly. "We can't resist the lure of a dead body."

She shook her head. "Try again."

His grin was unrepentant. "Okay, you got me. I stopped by your apartment when I brought Brian home after the soccer game. Liza told me what had happened. She guessed you'd be in the thick of things. The three of us agreed that I'd come check things out and get you out of here."

"How democratic! Don't I get a vote?"

"It'd still be three to one. We win."

If she was prepared to be totally honest with herself, Molly had to admit that it had crossed her mind that Liza might tell Michael if the opportunity arose. She hadn't been at all certain what he would do with that information. As he was a Metro-Dade homicide detective, Miami Beach was not his jurisdiction. Nor was she his responsibility, for that matter.

Though she had seen Michael occasionally at Brian's soccer matches, more often than not Bianca was in the stands keeping a watchful eye on him. He'd been careful to maintain a polite distance from Molly in the months since he'd rescued her from that awful shed and solved the condo murder.

That hadn't stopped Molly from occasionally wanting to wrestle him to the floor and have her way with him. The man was sexy and elusive, a dangerous combination. Despite his past disclaimers, it was also clear to her that he was spoken for, which made him more dangerous yet. The fact that he was a memorable kisser added to the potential for fireworks. From her perspective the man represented nothing but trouble. Naturally, she was intrigued anyway.

Tonight, however, she was at least marginally more interested in his brain than in his body. He was a hotshot detective with an arrest-and-conviction record that was the envy of his peers and kept him on the good side of his superiors despite his troublesome tendency to question authority. Whatever his reasons for coming, Molly was very glad to see him. At times like these, it never hurt to have a staunch ally who knew the ins and outs of a murder investigation. She was not about to let him know that, though. A woman deserved to keep some secrets, after all.

Michael dropped into the chair just vacated by Sergeant Jenkins, waved her back into her own chair, and pinned her with that intense, brown-eyed gaze that had the ability to make the most reluctant witness spill his guts. It had an entirely different effect on her, but she was trying like the very dickens to ignore it.

"Fill me in," he suggested.

When he asked a question in that tone, she knew enough to cut to the bottom line. "Someone shot Gregory Kinsey in the head."

"Kinsey is?"

Molly regarded him incredulously. It frequently astonished her that not everyone followed the film industry as closely as she did. "He is . . ." She corrected herself: "He *was* one of the most talented new directors in Hollywood."

She listed his string of smash box-office hits. No sign of recognition flickered in Michael's eyes. She had a hunch if she added

Greg's list of female conquests, he might have better recall.

"How long's he been in town?" he asked.

"Production started the beginning of June. He was here a week or so before that. He made one or two trips prior to that to set things up."

"Not long enough to make any enemies, then?"

"None I'm aware of. He was a perfectionist, which could set some people off, I suppose, but generally he was pretty easy to get along with."

"Into drugs?"

"Careful, Detective. You're guilty of stereotyping. All those Hollywood badasses do cocaine, right?"

"Just covering all the bases. Drug deals gone wrong account for a lot of untimely deaths around here."

"Believe me, I'm no expert, but from what I saw Greg was as straight as they come. The only things that made him high were great lighting and a perfectly delivered line."

"Anybody blow their lines today?"

Molly scowled.

"Okay," he said without the faintest hint of regret, "let's assume for the sake of argument that the killer is most likely someone connected with the film. Has Kinsey been coming down hard on anyone in particular?"

Molly was amazed at how quickly they fell into their old routine of tossing around ideas and evidence. "I've gone over and over Greg's interaction with every crew and cast member since the minute they arrived on location. I haven't been on the set every minute, but I think I have a pretty good idea of the dynamics."

"And?"

"On the surface, every single person involved seemed to regard Greg with a certain amount of awe. When people had legitimate gripes, he listened. Once he made a decision, though, it was final and everyone knew it. Only Veronica dared to argue with him. Believe me, though, she could hold her own without resorting to shooting someone. Everyone connected with GK Productions had a vested interest in keeping Greg alive. As for Veronica, she had more to lose than anyone else if Greg didn't finish this picture."

"Then why is this Veronica the one Jenkins is zeroing in on?"

"I don't think he is anymore, at least not exclusively. I tried to set him straight. Veronica was with me at the time Greg was shot. He was still alive when she left that trailer. I

369

heard him shouting after she'd slammed the door and started across the street."

"Then why'd she skip?"

"How do you know that?"

"They put out an APB on her while I was driving over here. Innocent people don't usually run."

"Maybe she figured they'd blame her and got scared. Maybe she just got fed up with waiting and left before she even realized anything had happened. There's only one way to find out."

Michael was shaking his head before she'd finished the sentence. "Oh, no."

Molly was already on her feet. "Oh, yes. I'm going after Veronica. I have to warn her that the police are looking for her to question her."

"If she's the killer, don't you think she'll have guessed that?"

"She is not the killer. How many times do I have to tell you that?"

"Until you can suggest a viable alternative," Michael retorted. "Until then everyone connected with this production is a suspect. Including, I might add, you."

"Oh, please."

"Just stating the facts as Sergeant Jenkins is likely to view them. Despite whatever he said about presuming Veronica to be guilty,

I'm sure he'll do a thorough investigation to rule out all the other candidates. In the meantime, don't you think you ought to get home to your worried son and distraught friend?"

Molly glowered at him. "Brian will want all the gory details. As for Liza, the only thing she's distraught over this week is the decimation of the rain forest. If I get home too soon, she'll have me licking envelopes. You, too."

"I'd rather lick a few envelopes than watch you get entangled in another murder investigation. Didn't you learn anything last time?"

Molly had to admit that Michael looked genuinely troubled by the prospect of her involvement. "I didn't ask to be involved with this one. It happened. I'm here. I can't very well pretend everything's hunky-dory, can I?"

"You could," he said — a little wistfully, it seemed to Molly.

"But I won't." She could be every bit as bull-headed as Michael O'Hara. "I don't suppose you'd like to have a little chat with Sergeant Jenkins before we leave?"

"We?" he repeated, ignoring the rest. He, at least, knew better than to interfere in someone else's case.

"I can't imagine that you actually intend to let me go in search of Veronica on my own. I mean, I could sneak away when you're not looking, but being the outstanding detective that you are, you'd figure out in no time where I'd gone. Then you'd feel morally compelled to chase after me. Ergo, we might as well go together and save on mileage for the county."

A familiar, irksome expression of tolerant amusement spread across his face. "Since you're the only one on the clock, we'll take your car."

Once they were in her snappy white LeBaron convertible with the top down, Molly regarded him slyly. "What exactly would it take to get you officially involved in this case?"

"An act of God," he said. "Don't even think about it."

"Just curious," she said blithely. If she couldn't get him on the case officially, she'd just have to see that his curiosity was aroused. Veronica ought to be able to accomplish that without batting so much as an eyelash at him. At heart Michael was a man who just loved rescuing damsels in distress.

4

The hotel housing the cast and crew from the *Endless Tomorrows* production was one of the larger Art Deco structures facing the ocean. Its exterior was a brilliant white, trimmed in shades of turquoise and yellow. Elaborate bas-relief designs edged the doorway. A stucco railing, trimmed in the same pastel shades, curved around the porch that embraced two sides of the building.

At the moment that porch was crammed with enough reporters, photographers, and television cameras to intimidate anyone less determined than Molly was to enter the building. A harried hotel night manager, his balding head bathed in perspiration, was attempting to placate the hungry newshounds.

"Sorry," he said. "I cannot allow you inside. I must protect the privacy of our guests. You understand."

They obviously didn't understand anything except their own need for information. They pushed forward, backing him
into the glass door. Another few minutes
and he was likely to be as squashed as some
bug on a windshield.

"Is Veronica Weston hiding out inside?"
one aggressive TV reporter demanded, shov-
ing a microphone toward the man.

"I really cannot answer your questions."

Molly pushed her way through the crowd
until she reached the door. Michael was one
step behind her. He leaned down and spoke
quietly to the manager. Relief spread across
the man's face. "Yes, yes, at once," he said,
turning a key in the door.

Before they could enter, a reporter from
the morning paper tugged Molly to one
side. Though he looked as if he'd been
awakened from a sound sleep and had
grabbed the nearest rumpled shirt from the
laundry basket, she recognized him from
the mug shot that always ran with his
Sunday column.

"You're with the film office, right?" Ted
Ryan said. "Mrs. DeWitt?"

Molly nodded.

"Can you get me inside?"

"And have the rest of these guys accuse
me of playing favorites? I don't think so. I'll

try to get all of you whatever statements you need from anyone connected with the film. I can give you one myself on behalf of the film office."

"Fine. I'll take that at this point. I've got another twenty minutes to file. After that, anything I get will have to wait for the Monday paper. I'm ready to try climbing up the fire escape. I think my photographer's already halfway up to Veronica Weston's floor. Is she in there?"

"As far as I know."

"Are the police going to arrest her?"

At a warning glance from Michael, Molly modified her response to a politically correct "You'll have to ask the police that."

"What about you? What did you see at the scene? I hear she and Kinsey have been at each other's throats ever since shooting started. Any idea why?"

Molly shook her head. "Look, the only thing I can comment on for the record is that the film office will do everything in its power to cooperate with the authorities to see that the killer is identified and brought to justice."

"Come on," Ryan cajoled. "You can do better than that."

"Not and keep my job. Let me get inside and see if I can get someone from GK

Productions down here to make a statement, okay?"

He motioned toward Michael. "What's he doing here? He's from Metro homicide. Is he on the case?"

Molly could just imagine the headlines: METRO CALLED IN TO BAIL OUT BEACH POLICE.

"No," she said hurriedly. "Absolutely not. Sergeant Jenkins is in charge."

"Then what's O'Hara doing here? It's his kind of case, isn't it? High profile. Politically sensitive."

Michael overheard the question and apparently guessed the direction of Ted Ryan's thoughts. "Can't a guy go out with a pretty lady without you trying to make something of it?" he inquired lightly.

He stepped closer and slid an arm around Molly's waist to lend credence to his comment. Molly shot an incredulous look in his direction. She did not, however, pull away the way any sensible liberated woman might have under the circumstances.

Ryan looked skeptical, but he stepped aside to let them get into the hotel. "Make it snappy," he pleaded, glancing at his watch. "I'm desperate."

"Aren't we all," Molly muttered under her breath as she considered why she had permitted Michael to get away with such a sly innuendo about their relationship. Fortunately, she didn't have long to consider the implications. The elevator ride to Veronica's floor was mercifully short, allowing minimal time for introspection.

Veronica, wearing ice blue satin lounging pajamas with a plunging neckline, opened the door of her suite. She was clutching a tall tumbler of vodka. Molly could fully understand now exactly why Greg had cast her. She would fascinate any man old enough to distinguish between sexy glamour and the mere physical attractiveness of youth. It was pretty much like comparing rare vintage wine to grape juice. The source might be essentially the same, but only a fool thought they tasted alike.

The dazed expression on Michael's face told Molly he could fully appreciate the difference. Hooking him was going to be even easier than she had anticipated. What she hadn't counted on was this nearly uncontrollable urge she had to kick him.

"Veronica Weston, this is Michael O'Hara," Molly said.

At the mention of Michael's name, Veronica shot a disbelieving look at Molly. It was the same reaction most people had when trying to reconcile his dark-eyed, distinctly

Hispanic appearance and faint accent with his Irish name.

As Molly understood it, the contradiction had to do with a vanished American father who left Cuba before discovering that his lover was pregnant. Michael's sentimental mother had given her son an Irish name in the man's honor. No one seemed quite sure if the father's name had actually been O'Hara, and no one, least of all Molly, knew with any certainty the impact this casual naming had had on shaping Michael's personality. Lord knew, he had the capacity for typically Latin machismo. The Irish influence was less easy to detect.

Right now, however, he was displaying a gentlemanly courtliness toward Veronica, who was suddenly radiating charm in sufficient kilowatts to light downtown Miami. The pair of them made Molly sick. Had everyone but her suddenly forgotten about the murder?

"Don't you think we should be concentrating on Greg?" she blurted finally, interrupting the flow of compliments Michael was directing toward the actress. Apparently he'd seen plenty of old movies, even if he was sorely behind the times on current filmmakers.

Both of them turned to look at Molly. Michael appeared slightly startled by her presence. Veronica looked irritated.

"Why on earth would I wish to discuss that imbecile?" she said, indicating a certain lack of respect for the dead or complete ignorance regarding his recent fate. Molly was so certain of the latter that she turned a look of triumph in Michael's direction. He was too much a cop not to take the hint.

"When did you leave the location?" he asked, slipping automatically into the interrogator's role he'd sworn not to take in this case.

Veronica answered without the slightest hint that she thought there was anything odd about the question or Michael's interest in the answer. "It must have been shortly after ten o'clock, wouldn't you say, Molly?"

"Later. It was nearly ten-thirty when you sent me to look for Greg."

Veronica nodded, sending her shoulder-length sweep of chestnut hair into sensuous motion. "Of course. I waited for some time and when neither you nor Greg came for me, I decided to call it a night."

"Was that before or after the police arrived?" Michael wanted to know.

"Police?"

Veronica managed a totally blank expression. It convinced Molly, but then she had to concede that they were dealing with a superb actress.

"You didn't hear the sirens?" Molly said.

"Who pays attention?" she said with an indifferent lift of one shoulder. "I spent months in New York, when I was doing that dreadful play on Broadway. Sirens blared all night long. I learned then to tune them out. What's this all about? Did something happen after I left?"

"Gregory Kinsey is dead," Molly said.

Veronica's eyes widened, and she took a long, slow drink of vodka, finishing off the last of it. She set the leaded crystal glass very carefully on the coffee table. Finally she swallowed hard, then looked directly into Molly's eyes.

"I don't believe it," she said convincingly. "How did it happen? I wasn't crazy about the man, but dead? He was so young." Without the glass to steady her hands, they fluttered nervously before she finally clasped them in her lap.

"Someone shot him," Michael said, his gaze pinned on her, obviously watching for signs of guilt.

"In your trailer," Molly added, so the actress would know exactly what she was up against.

Astonishment filled Veronica's eyes. "You

don't think . . . Surely, you can't possibly . . ." She glanced from Molly to Michael and back again. "You do, don't you? You think I did it."

"I don't," Molly said stoutly. "I'm convinced it had to have happened while you were with me."

Veronica watched Michael, then asked, "Do you believe her?"

"It's not my case," Michael replied. "I'd have to say, though, that Molly does have pretty decent instincts when it comes to people. I think I know her well enough to say that I doubt she'd lie just to protect you. Unfortunately, her word may not be enough. From what I understand, there are a few minutes unaccounted for when Molly left you to go look for Greg."

"But I could see the trailer," Molly argued.

"The whole time? You told me you went inside the production trailer to ask for Kinsey."

She hadn't considered that as a flaw in her defense of Veronica, but she could see now that it might be. "That took thirty seconds, a minute tops," she argued. "That's hardly enough time for Veronica to leave the café, shoot Greg, and escape without me or anyone else seeing her. He had to have been killed before that, during the fifteen or so minutes Veronica and I were together. What I can't figure out is why no one heard a shot."

"With all that music blaring from every café on Ocean, I doubt you could hear a bomb drop over it," Michael reminded her.

"But . . ."

Veronica held up one perfectly manicured hand. "Molly, dear, if you will slow down for just one minute, I believe I can end all this absurd speculation about my role in Greg's death. I know for a fact that I was not the last person to see him alive, at least if we assume that your theory about the time period in which he was shot is accurate."

"What?" Michael and Molly said in unison.

"It's true. Just as I left the trailer Greg's latest conquest arrived. Surely you've seen her around the set, Molly. The tall, angular brunette with the kind of bone structure the camera loves. She doesn't speak much English, but I doubt Greg was interested in her conversational skills."

"Of course, that's it," Molly said as the elusive detail clicked into place. She had heard raised *voices* — plural, not just Greg's — even after she'd spotted Veronica crossing the street. She hadn't readily linked the exchange to Greg because the shouts hadn't been in English. "She's Cuban, isn't she?"

"No. She's European," Veronica said with certainty.

"Italian, then?" To Molly's ear most of the Romance languages sounded pretty much the same at top volume. She understood Spanish only if someone spoke it very slowly and gestured at the same time. She'd taken French in school, which came in handy in Miami only when she had to deal with the occasional Canadian tourist or the Haitian immigrants whose Creole language owed its roots to French.

Veronica beamed. "Yes, of course. I remember now. She is a fashion model. She is here for a photo shoot for some European magazine. Greg met her at one of the cafés along Ocean Drive, two, maybe three days ago. You know how he falls in love with a gorgeous face. They've been inseparable ever since."

"I thought he was romancing Laura Crain," Molly said.

"Who's that?" Michael asked.

"The producer for the film. Greg was executive producer and director. Laura was the line producer. She handled the details with the studio in L.A. that's backing the film, saw to it that the budget was in line. She came here even before Greg to negotiate some of the contracts with the local unions, finalize housing for the cast and crew, that sort of thing. I worked with her quite a bit."

Michael nodded and turned back to Veronica. "Had Kinsey dumped her for this model?"

"I doubt it. The model was here only through tomorrow, according to what I heard. Greg probably intended to go right back to Laura the minute she'd gone. Besides, he was a very practical man. He wouldn't want his producer to take off before the movie wraps."

"Nice guy," Michael said. "Any idea what he and the Italian bombshell were arguing about?"

"No," Veronica said. "I was too furious with him myself to listen to the details of some contretemps between lovers."

Michael nodded slowly. "Okay. So he's got these two women on the hook. One of them we know had a fight with him tonight. The other might have discovered his fling and gone after him in a jealous rage. When Sergeant Jenkins gets here, I suggest you tell him everything you know about these two women. I don't suppose either of you knows the model's name?"

Molly and Veronica both shook their heads.

"Who's this Jenkins person?" Veronica asked, just as someone started pounding on the door of her suite.

"Police, Ms. Weston. Open up."

"That's Sergeant Jenkins," Molly said ruefully. "I don't suppose there's another way out of here."

Michael grinned at her as he went to the door. "Feeling guilty all of a sudden?"

"Something like that," Molly admitted, wishing he weren't opening the door quite so eagerly to admit the Miami Beach detective. "I did promise to stay out of his investigation."

"We all know what *that* promise is worth," Michael said.

Judging from the infuriated expression on Sergeant Jenkins's face when he realized who was in the room, she regretted she hadn't risked diving through a window.

Sergeant Jenkins looked more and more depressed as Molly and Veronica combined to shoot holes in his theory about the murder.

"So, you see, you ought to be out looking for that model," Molly concluded. "She was probably the last one to see Greg alive."

"Terrific. That's just great. I'm supposed to send people up and down Ocean Drive, maybe even along Collins Avenue, asking for an Italian model whose name we don't know. Do you know how many of these fashion things are going on over here at any one time?"

"Six last week," Molly retorted.

When he gaped at her certainty, she reminded him. "It's my job to keep track."

"And every one of those six shoots had dozens of models, right? Any other helpful suggestions?"

Molly shrugged. "Sorry. That's the best I can do."

The detective glanced over his notes. "What about this Duke Lane? He seems to be the only member of the cast who wasn't around tonight. How come?"

"He wasn't on call tonight," Veronica said.

"But he is your costar, right?"

"He has second-lead billing," Molly said quickly before Veronica could deliver one of her scathing comments about Duke Lane. "He should be around here, if you want to speak to him. Everyone was booked into this hotel."

Jenkins nodded. "I'll check before I leave. I assume I can count on all of you to come to me if you think of anything else that will help move this case along."

Molly nodded dutifully. Veronica and Michael were slightly more convincing with their replies. At least, the sergeant appeared satisfied.

As he opened the door to leave, a distinguished-looking man with a salt-and-pepper crewcut and clothes that looked as if they'd been bought on London's Savile Row hurried down the corridor. He spotted Veronica and held open his arms.

"Veronica, my dear, what is this terrible thing that's happened? They tell me Greg is dead. You must be devastated."

Before he could embrace the actress, Jenkins stepped into his path. "Who are you?" he inquired.

"Jeffrey Meyerson, Ms. Weston's fiancé."

Veronica appeared slightly nonplussed by the assertion, but she didn't deny the relationship. She merely looked the man in the eye and asked, "What are you doing here, Jeffrey? I thought you were flying to Rome this weekend."

"I intended to, but I thought I'd stop off and surprise you. Then when I saw Laura in the lobby and heard what had happened, I was doubly glad I did. Are you okay, my dear?"

"I'm fine," Veronica said, sounding incredibly sober and convincing for a woman who'd downed several double vodkas over the past few hours.

Despite Veronica's reassurances, Jeff Meyerson surveyed the trio of onlookers and suggested, "Perhaps, if you could leave us alone."

Jenkins looked disgruntled by the dismissal, despite the fact that he'd been on his way out the door not two minutes earlier. Michael nudged Molly toward the door as well.

"What's your hurry?" she grumbled as he tugged her along to the elevator.

"I want to get to a phone," he replied.

"Why didn't you just use the one in Veronica's room?"

"I didn't want Jeffrey Meyerson listening in."

"Why not?"

"Because the last flight from L.A. should have gotten in about three hours ago. Unless that flight was very late, it should have put him in town just in time to have murdered Greg Kinsey."

5

Molly tried not to gloat. She really did. But even though she knew she should leave well enough alone, the first words out of her mouth were, "I knew you couldn't resist."

Michael turned, his expression puzzled. "Resist what?" he asked. He didn't seem nearly as pleased as she was by the observation.

"Getting involved."

"I am not involved," he said emphatically. He jammed his hands into his pockets as if that would keep them from reaching for the phone again.

"Then why are you calling to check on flight schedules?"

He lowered the receiver of the pay phone back into place. "Instinct," he admitted. "But you're right. This is not my case. I'll find Jenkins and tell him what I suspect. Wait here."

Before Molly could protest, he'd stalked

off across the black-and-white hotel lobby that looked like a set from some thirties musical with Ginger Rogers and Fred Astaire.

"Well, damn," Molly muttered as she watched him disappear into the meeting room off the lobby where the police had apparently set up a temporary headquarters. This was not what she'd had in mind at all. Obviously, the hook hadn't sunk in deep enough. Michael had wriggled loose.

Thoroughly disgruntled, she walked over to the front door of the hotel, expecting to find the throng of reporters still lurking like seagulls awaiting a tasty catch. Instead, they had vanished, either satisfied by statements from the police or in search of more cooperative sources.

More likely, like Ryan's photographer, they'd headed for the fire escapes.

At any rate, outside it looked like any other Saturday night. Molly watched the endless parade of couples in attire that ranged from the downright eccentric to the most stylish available. As their conversation and laughter filtered through the glass, she tried again to sort through the various relationships she'd observed among the cast and crew on Greg's production.

Twenty-nine-year-old Duke Lane, of the

slicked-back hair and bad breath, had been Laura's choice for leading man, from what Molly had read in the trades. His box-office following climbed with each new project. While Veronica's scathing assessment of the way he'd chosen to play the character of Rod Lukens was right on track in Molly's opinion, there was no arguing that he was giving a compelling, realistic performance. It was no doubt based on his own experiences. The man had an enthusiastically reported history of charming older women who could advance his career.

Still, if he hadn't been the director's first choice and if Veronica's complaining was beginning to get through to Greg, was it possible that Duke might have felt he had to kill the director? Molly dismissed the idea almost before it was fully formed. In that scenario, he'd probably have gone for Veronica. Besides, the picture was nearly complete. Greg would not have recast the role at this late date, no matter how he felt about Duke.

As for assistant director Hank Murdock, he'd get a directing break now that Greg was dead, but again, at this late date, how much good would it do him? *Endless Tomorrows* would always be regarded as Gregory Kinsey's last picture no matter who directed the final few scenes.

Production assistant Jerry Shaw didn't stand to gain anything from the director's death. To the contrary, he was barely out of the UCLA film program. He was riding quite happily on Greg's coattails.

Cinematographer Daniel Ortiz, who'd allegedly been busy setting up for the next scene at the time of the killing, owned a piece of GK Productions. The company's fate rested with the rise or fall of Greg's star. Molly would have to find out what would happen to GK Productions now that its primary owner was dead, but odds were it had a better future with him than without him. If so, the temperamental but talented Ortiz wouldn't want him dead.

All of which brought Molly right back to the women in the case. Again she dismissed Veronica as the least likely of the suspects. Laura Crain was Molly's first choice, if only because the producer had blindsided her earlier with that attack suggesting that Molly had used sex to lure Greg to Miami. There was also the jealousy motive to substantiate the choice. Laura might have sought revenge against the man who was publicly humiliating her.

As much as she wanted to pin it on Laura, however, Molly couldn't entirely dismiss the possibility that the mysterious model had ended her argument with Greg with a gunshot. Oh, how she'd like to find her before the police discovered her identity.

Just then she heard a commotion at the registration desk in the lobby. When she turned, she spotted a dark-haired, khaki-clad photographer, laden down with camera equipment, who was arguing with the clerk behind the counter. He hadn't come through the door since she'd been standing there, so she had to assume the man was checking out.

She listened to the exchange for several minutes before realizing that the two were arguing in a mix of English, Spanish, and a third language.

Italian! Of course! This had to be the photographer on location with Greg's model friend. As she had told Sergeant Jenkins, there were six crews currently shooting fashion layouts all over town, but only one that she knew of had an Italian photographer.

She inched closer to the desk, trying to detect the man's name in the barrage of words being flung back and forth. She finally gave that up as a lost cause. They were talking so rapidly she couldn't even distinguish one word from the next.

When tempers seemed to have cooled a bit, she tapped the photographer on the shoulder. "Excuse me."

He turned his still-stormy, intense gaze on her. "Yes?" he said, immediately studying her with a photographer's critical eye. Boredom followed rapidly. Molly didn't delude herself that she was model material, but his relatively quick dismissal hurt.

She pulled one of her business cards from her purse and handed it to him. "You are here from Italy, aren't you?"

"Yes."

"Are you working with a particular model? Dark hair. Dark eyes." Admittedly, it was a weak description given the likelihood that it applied to half the models on location.

"I work with many models," he said carefully. "Why do you ask this?" He studied her card more closely. "You have work for one of my models?"

She considered a blatant lie, but settled for a half-truth. "It's possible," she said. "Someone told me this one is very beautiful. I'm in touch with a number of casting directors who might be interested."

"Casting directors? These are from pictures?"

"Yes. We have a crew filming here now, GK Productions. Perhaps you've heard of them? Gregory Kinsey? He's very famous."

His expression immediately closed down. He handed the card back to her with a disdainful glance.

"She would not be interested," he said, confirming her guesswork. She had the right photographer, and with any luck he could be persuaded to lead her to the right model.

"Perhaps I could ask her myself. What's her name?"

"She would not be interested," he repeated, then turned his back on her.

The reaction removed any lingering doubts that she had the right man. He clearly knew which model she meant, knew of her connection to Greg. And he was clearly protecting her, which must mean that he knew about the murder.

She moved to a more unobtrusive part of the lobby and watched as the photographer made a hurried call on one of the house phones. Then he gathered up his luggage and equipment and went outside, where a taxi was already waiting.

Molly nabbed a passing bellman. "Is there another way out of here besides that elevator?"

"The fire stairs. They come out on the alley in back."

"Damn," she muttered, racing through the

door just in time to see the taxi turn into the alley.

She ran after it, cutting into the alley just as the taxi door slammed shut. It sped off in the opposite direction before she could get halfway down the alley. Cursing under her breath, she turned around and ran smack into Michael.

"What the hell do you think you're doing?" he demanded.

"Trying to stop Greg's model friend from skipping town before we find out what she knows about the murder."

He regarded her incredulously. "You found her?"

"I found the photographer she's been working for. Unfortunately, he figured out what I was up to and had her sneak down the stairs and come out of the hotel back here. I never even got a glimpse of her."

"Then what makes you so certain it was the right one?"

"Couldn't you, just for once, trust me? If I explain all that, they'll be halfway to Rome."

He ignored the sarcasm. "Any idea where they were headed?"

"Offhand, I'd say the airport. Isn't that where you'd go, if you wanted to leave town in a hurry?"

"Not at this hour. There are too few flights to choose from. I'd find some out-of-the-way hotel, hide out for a day or two, and then leave from Fort Lauderdale or West Palm Beach on a flight going somewhere other than Italy. I'd be a lot less conspicuous that way."

Molly shook her head. "Will I ever be able to think deviously enough to keep up with you?"

He grinned. "Is that a compliment?"

"Given the context, I'd have to say 'Yes.' Under ordinary conditions, however, it's not a particularly attractive trait."

"I'll try to use it judiciously."

She scowled at his teasing tone. "At any rate, the cab company ought to be able to tell us who's right."

"I don't suppose you got a glimpse of the taxi number or the license tag?"

"Actually, I did," she said. She repeated the digits, along with the name of the taxi company, which had its headquarters only a few blocks away.

"Then let's get back inside and give it to Sergeant Jenkins."

Molly tried to hide her disappointment and failed. "We're not going to track it down ourselves?"

"Not a chance, sweetheart. You've done

enough amateur sleuthing for one night. We are going home."

"It would only take one little phone call. We'd turn the information over to the sergeant."

"The taxi company is not going to give that kind of information to anyone other than someone on official police business."

"You have a badge number, credentials, the whole nine yards," she reminded him. "You probably even have a contact there who'd like to do you a favor."

"But I am not the officer in charge of this case," he said with the pious tone of an altar boy wrongly accused of snitching a taste of wine. "I'm off duty, out of my jurisdiction. Are you getting the picture yet?"

"Yes," she said with a sigh. "What am I supposed to tell Vince? He expects me to handle things here."

"Tell him that the police have everything under control. Tell him that they hope to have the case wrapped up very quickly."

"Is that the truth? Or is that just meant to pacify him?"

"What do you think?"

"I think you've spent too much time around stonewalling public information officers. By the way, did Jenkins check on that flight from L.A.?"

"Better a little stonewalling, than a lot of wild speculation." He ignored the question about Jeffrey Meyerson's flight.

Molly gave up on that and tried to explain that facts tended to put a lid on speculation. She was so busy making her argument convincing that she barely noticed that Michael had steered her down the block and into her car.

"Give me five minutes," he said. "Then I'll take you home."

Obviously he had no idea what she could accomplish in five minutes if she put her mind to it. As soon as he'd left, she raced for the pay phone on the corner, dropped in a quarter, and called the taxi company.

"I'm calling from the hotel. One of our guests left something behind and I'm wondering if you could tell me where your driver dropped him off. The pickup was about five minutes ago, a couple. Italian. Giovanni, yes. That's it."

The dispatcher named an address in Little Havana. "That's a motel, I think," he added. Molly could visualize him leering as he said it. She was familiar with the name. Not far from the airport, the motel wasn't a stop-off for international travelers. Its usual clientele tended to rent by the hour.

Molly was back in her car, looking as innocent as it was possible for a guilty person to look, by the time Michael returned. He regarded her suspiciously.

"What's up?"

"Actually, I'm starving," she said. "I was hoping maybe we could stop for something to eat."

"We could just walk to the News Café. It's only a few blocks down."

"Actually, what I'd really like is a *medianoche* or a Cuban sandwich. Could we go to Versailles or someplace else over on Calle Ocho?"

"This sudden craving for Cuban food wouldn't have anything to do with a certain motel, would it?"

Molly felt her cheeks turning pink. "How did you know?"

"When Sergeant Jenkins called the taxi dispatcher, the man said he'd just had another call about the exact same couple. He said he'd told the woman they'd been dropped off at a motel in Little Havana."

"Oh," she said meekly. "I don't suppose . . ."

"No."

"But . . ."

"No." He glanced across at her. "Still hungry?"

"No," she muttered. "I'll drop you at your

400

car on my way home."

He actually laughed out loud at that. "Not a chance. I won't rest easy until I know you're home and safely tucked in for the night."

"You planning to stick around for that?" she inquired testily.

His gaze caught hers and held. "Don't tempt me, Molly DeWitt," he warned softly. "Don't tempt me."

Awareness slammed through her and left her downright shaky. "How's Bianca?" she said in a desperate rush.

His eyes never left hers. "Fine," he said. "Last time I talked to her."

"You're not living together anymore?"

"No."

"I see," she said. "Whose choice?"

"It was mutual."

"I see."

His lips curved just slightly. "Do you really?"

Actually, what she saw with a flash of vivid insight was a night of pure, unadulterated lust and a morning filled with regrets. She toyed with the tantalizing prospect of ignoring her common sense, indulging in some hot, steamy sex, and simply dealing with the regrets when the time came.

Then she decided regretfully that she and

Michael had skirted enough danger for one night. There were too many questions she wanted answered before she slept with a man who fascinated her the way Michael O'Hara did. Tonight she was too exhausted to ask a single one of them.

Since she feared that she'd murmur something incriminating if she opened her mouth at all, she remained silent for the rest of the drive back to Key Biscayne.

"You going to invite me up?" Michael inquired as they pulled into the driveway at the Ocean Manor condominium. His tone was casual, but the look in his eyes was anything but.

"Not tonight," she said finally.

"Too bad," he said, still keeping it light. "I was going to tell you what Sergeant Jenkins found when he checked the airlines about flights from L.A."

Molly chuckled at the deliberately devious ploy. "You can tell me that right here."

He shook his head. "I think I'll save it for breakfast."

"Breakfast?"

"I'll pick you up at ten."

"That's not breakfast. That's brunch, especially with an eight-year-old boy in the house."

"Give Brian a bowl of cereal to tide him

over until I get here. I usually refuse to budge before nine thirty on my day off. I'm making an exception for you."

"Oh, in that case, I suppose I should be suitably grateful."

He leaned over and pressed a quick kiss against her lips. He was there and gone before the gesture had time to set off sparks. "Don't tax yourself. Just try to stay out of trouble until I see you again."

"I'll do my best," she promised. She had a feeling she'd already dodged the worst of it. A seductive Michael O'Hara — an apparently available Michael O'Hara — represented trouble with a capital *T* to most any woman past puberty. To one who'd clung to celibacy as fervently as Molly had ever since her divorce, he lured like those sirens who beckoned ships to their doom.

Even so, she couldn't help wondering what it would be like to court disaster.

6

It wasn't until she was upstairs that Molly realized how cleverly Michael had stranded her right where he wanted her — far from the scene of the crime. If she hadn't been quite so exhausted, she might have dragged Liza out to chase after the sneaky detective who'd left her with nothing to drive. She wondered what would happen if she called the police to report that he'd made off with *her* car.

So much for the chance to race back to Miami Beach to do a little more sleuthing. There were plenty of people she hadn't really talked to after the discovery of Greg's body, beginning with the film's somewhat enigmatic director of photography, Daniel Ortiz.

Sternly reminding herself what curiosity did to that ill-fated cat, she checked her answering machine for messages instead. There were half a dozen from Vince, all self-described as urgent, and one from Liza telling her that Brian was sound asleep in her guest room and that he might as well stay the night.

"I, however, am waiting up for you," Liza's taped message reported. "I want to hear everything the minute you get home and I do mean *everything,* including how you're getting along with the hunk. Whoops! Probably shouldn't have said that. He could be there listening. Sorry. See you."

Molly chuckled at Liza's belated sense of discretion. She started for the door, only to hear the key turning in the lock. Obviously, Liza had heard her come in and hadn't trusted her to stop by and fill her in.

"Hey, there. It's me," Liza called from the doorway. "You alone?"

"What if I weren't?" Molly said. "It'd be too late now."

"True, but nothing shocks me anymore, and I'm a specialist at hasty exits."

"Right. Like the time you got out of Spain one step ahead of that bullfighter who took a fancy to your . . ."

"Never mind what he took a fancy to," Liza said, curling up on a corner of the sofa and tucking her bare feet under her. Her moussed, flattop hairstyle gave her the look of an innocent pixie, but the expression in her eyes was every bit as intent as Michael's in mid-interrogation.

"Okay, tell me what happened," she demanded. "Who killed Greg Kinsey?"

"About the only thing I can say with certainty is that it wasn't me," Molly told her from the kitchen. She poured them each a glass of wine before joining Liza.

"Is Michael working on the case?"

"Officially, no, but he can't resist checking out clues any more than I can. Thanks for sending him over, by the way."

"*Sending him?* Are you kidding? I mentioned murder and the man flew out of here. I barely had time to tell him where you were. God, I love all that macho protectiveness."

"I told you, he can't resist a good homicide investigation. It doesn't have anything to do with me," Molly said, deciding Liza did not need to know just yet that Michael had all but invited himself into her bed tonight.

"Right. The man decided to spend his one night off chasing a killer who's not even in his jurisdiction. I'm telling you, Michael O'Hara would not have gone anywhere near Miami Beach tonight if you hadn't been involved."

Molly couldn't stop a wistful, unliberated

sigh. "I have to admit I was glad to see him. It's as if whichever side of my brain is supposed to do deductive reasoning goes into high gear the minute he's around."

"To say nothing of your hormones."

"Okay. That, too."

Liza drank the last of her wine and stood up. "You look beat. Since you can't offer me anything juicier than speculation, I'm going home. I'll send Brian over in the morning."

"Just make sure he's back here before ten. Michael's picking us up for brunch."

"Oh, really? Maybe I'm getting out too soon after all. Isn't there some other little detail you'd like to share with your best friend?"

"Wipe that smirk off your face. There are no details," Molly retorted. "I'm going to bed. Let yourself out."

As it turned out, going to bed was achieved far more easily than getting to sleep. She kept remembering the sight of Greg Kinsey lying dead and the sound of the heated argument that had preceded it by what must have been no more than minutes.

"Tell me about Kinsey," Michael suggested midway through brunch the next morning,

407

after he and Brian had filled Molly in on every detail of the soccer game she'd missed. Her son beamed as Michael lavished praise on a shot he'd made. She knew how he felt. She wouldn't mind basking in a little of Michael's admiration.

Michael had arrived precisely at ten, wearing perfectly pressed navy blue slacks, a pale blue dress shirt with the sleeves rolled up to his elbows, and an expensive gold watch no thicker than the very masculine hairs that subtly shadowed his arms. Lord, the man was sexy, Molly had thought then and thought again now. What had possessed her to send him away the night before?

At the sound of Michael's chuckle, she blinked and stared. "What?" she said blankly. Regretfully, she forced her gaze away from his hands and her attention away from the decidedly wayward thoughts about what those hands could have been doing to her during her long, sleepless night if she hadn't had an attack of conscience. Or cowardice. Probably the latter, she decided with a sigh.

A knowing twinkle sparked in his dark brown eyes. "Kinsey," he reminded her. "Tell me what he was like."

"You mean when she found his body with the bullet hole in the middle of his forehead?" Brian asked hopefully. At eight he was fascinated with anything that made Molly squeamish. The more gore, the better.

"No, I mean when he was alive," Michael told him, barely hiding a grin. "I pretty much know what dead guys are like."

Brian looked disgusted. "If you guys are gonna talk about all that boring stuff, can I go play on the beach?" he asked. "I finished eating a long time ago."

"Go," Molly said. "You know the rules. Stay within sight and don't go in the water."

"And be careful crossing the street," Michael added, glancing toward Ocean Drive's parade of convertibles and open Jeeps filled with teens and practically shaking with the sounds of rock. "The traffic's bumper-to-bumper."

When Brian had successfully navigated the street in front of the outdoor café, Molly considered Michael's question about Greg.

"He was driven," she said finally. "I've never met anyone so totally absorbed in what he was doing. He seemed to have this vision of what a scene should look like on screen, how it should be played. More important, he knew how to communicate that vision to those around him. I think everyone on the picture was really psyched about working with him."

"Had all of them worked with him before?"

"I think most of the crew had. I'm not so sure about the actors. I know this was the first time he'd worked with Duke Lane. Laura had insisted on casting him, and Greg respected her judgment when it came to box-office decisions."

"Why was she so anxious to get this Lane in the picture? Isn't he one of those hunk-of-the-month types?"

"Pretty much," Molly agreed. "But unlike some of the others, he can act. That was critical to Greg. He would never have agreed otherwise, I'm sure."

"Was this Laura more interested in his acting or his body?"

"Duke and Laura?" She tried to envision it and shook her head. "I don't think so."

"Okay, what about the others? Was Veronica someone Greg had used in other movies?"

"No, and that's what was so odd about him choosing her for this role. No one, from Laura to Hank to the production assistant, thought he should take a chance on her."

"Why? She has an incredible track record."

"*Had* an incredible track record," Molly

corrected. "Her last couple of films were disasters, primarily because of her drinking. Supposedly she's gotten herself straightened out, but until Greg came along no one wanted to risk another overbudget debacle. She delayed her last film by nearly a month while she sobered up enough to shoot the final scenes."

Michael regarded her doubtfully. "Wasn't that vodka she was swilling down like water last night?"

"It was."

"Looks to me like she not only fell off the wagon, but is headed for a crash landing."

"I know. I don't think she was drinking when production started, though. In fact, I'd swear she was stone-cold sober every time I was on the set."

"When did that start to change?"

Molly thought back to the first time she realized Veronica had started substituting vodka for her bottled mineral water. "A week ago, maybe less."

"When did the fights with Kinsey start? About the same time?"

"Oh, no. She and Greg started battling on the first day of production. I've never seen two people go at it the way they have, especially two people with no past history."

"You're sure there's no past history there?"

"Not according to anyone I've talked to, and that includes Greg and Veronica. The tension on the set was beginning to take its toll. Yesterday, between that and the heat, everyone was snapping."

"What were the fights about?"

"The script and Duke Lane. Veronica wasn't wild about either one of them, and she was not shy about expressing her opinion. The writer, a newcomer named Jonathan Fine, has hidden out in his hotel room since the first day of production. She humiliated him in front of everyone. Greg had to talk him into staying around to make any script changes he needed."

"And Duke?"

"Duke steered clear of the set whenever he could. I have to give him credit. He never let her attitude get to him, at least not in public." She looked up just then and caught sight of the actor waiting for a table. "Speak of the devil."

Michael followed her gaze. With his eyes hidden by sunglasses, Molly couldn't see his reaction, but his surprised tone said it all. "That's Lane?"

"Yes."

"I thought he'd be . . ." Apparently words

failed him.

"Taller? Sexier?"

"More imposing," Michael countered, which was a nice way of saying that Duke Lane wasn't exactly ready to do health club ads. Molly had had the same initial reaction. On-screen he had a larger-than-life presence. In person, with his slight frame and five-feet-seven-inch height, he was unimpressive, as ordinary as the boy next door.

Until he smiled. Then any woman would be able to say exactly what all the excitement was about. That smile combined a boyish eagerness to please and sleepy sensuality in a way that invited thoughts of wild sexual adventures. The glint in his eyes promised intelligence and fun. Molly had discovered that the expression didn't lie. Duke Lane was both smart and witty, facts too often lost in the Hollywood hype. She wanted Michael to see that side of him.

"Think we should ask him to join us?"

Michael gave her a wry look. "Could I stop you?"

"Admit it," she said. "You're every bit as curious as I am."

He leaned back in his chair. "True. Bring him on."

Molly stood up and walked over to the young actor, who was wearing faded jeans, a T-shirt, and cowboy boots. It was the same laid-back clothing style affected by his character Rod Lukens, the dressed-up boy-toy of the film. Either he liked to stay in character or he didn't waste his millions on wardrobe.

"Duke?"

He turned toward her and the famous Duke Lane grin spread across his face. "Molly! What a relief! I hate going out by myself. Some chick spots me and the next thing I know I'm mobbed. If I'd had one more hamburger from room service, though, I think I would have thrown up."

A pleasant image, Molly thought. "I'm with a friend. Come join us."

She led the way back to the table and made the introductions. She neglected to mention that Michael was a cop. Since he wasn't here in any official capacity, she figured it wasn't relevant. Interestingly enough, he didn't offer the information himself.

With a slight wave of his hand, Duke was able to get the attention of a waitress who'd been ignoring them since the instant she realized Michael wasn't interested. She sashayed over so fast she stirred a breeze that sent napkins from half a dozen tables fluttering to the ground.

Despite his claim that he craved anonymity, Duke removed his sunglasses and directed his baby blue eyes straight at the waitress, practically commanding her to recognize him. She didn't fail him. Her own eyes widened and her pencil dropped to the ground. Michael retrieved it since she seemed too busy staring in openmouthed adoration.

"You're Duke Lane," she said finally. "Ohmigosh. Wait'll I tell the others. Oh, wow!"

"What's good, honey?" His tone suggested he was interested in more than what was on the menu.

"Salads," she said in a breathy voice that indicated she had fallen victim to his sexy innuendoes. "We have *really* good salads."

Duke seemed to tire of the game. "Then bring me one," he said abruptly. "Dressing on the side. A bottle of mineral water." He winked at her. "We'll talk about dessert later."

Molly noticed that Michael was watching the entire act as if he ought to be taking notes. She felt like reassuring him that his own technique was considerably more effective, at least on any female over twenty-one.

"Terrible about Greg," Duke said when

the waitress had left. "I had the car radio on and I heard it on a newsbreak. I almost crashed into a guard rail."

"What time was it on?" Molly asked, relieved that Duke had brought the subject up himself. "I didn't even think to see what time the story broke on the news."

"Midnight, maybe later. I was coming back to the hotel from having drinks with a friend down in Coconut Grove, some yuppie bar. Man, you ever go there on a Saturday night? That place is overrun with kids. I've never seen so many convertibles and boom boxes in one place before, except maybe Santa Monica beach in the summer."

"Any thoughts about who might have shot Kinsey?" Michael asked.

Duke frowned. "Who shot him? You mean it wasn't some kind of mugging or something? They didn't give any details on the radio. They just said he was dead."

Molly shook her head. "We were still on location. His body was found in Veronica's trailer."

The actor looked genuinely shocked. "Oh, man, you're kidding me. I know those two fought like jealous ex-lovers or something, but I didn't think she'd pull a gun and shoot him."

"So you think she did it?" Michael said,

pouncing on Duke's comment.

Duke looked confused. "But you-all just said . . . He was in her trailer. I just assumed."

"Veronica has an alibi," Molly said staunchly. Michael looked unconvinced. So did Duke.

"You checked it out?" Duke said.

"I didn't have to. I'm her alibi, at least for all but a minute or two."

"No kidding. Then your guess is as good as mine. Everyone else loved Greg."

"Including you?" Michael inquired mildly, managing to sound as if his interest was only that of a casual bystander.

Duke turned his most sincere gaze on Michael. "Including me," he said emphatically. "I know he didn't want me on this picture. Hell, I know what half the serious directors in Hollywood think of me. They think I'm a no-talent hotshot who's trying to capitalize on my looks."

He leaned forward, his expression intent. "Well, you ask any director who's actually worked with me and you'll get a different story. I know what the hell I'm doing in front of a camera. That's why the audiences want to see me, not because I've got some killer smile and a decent body. Those don't mean shit if you can't deliver your lines.

Too bad Greg's not alive to tell you what I'm saying is true. We talked plenty over the last couple of weeks and the man respected me. I turned his attitude around and, believe me, it didn't happen because I could smile."

Duke leaned back in his chair, his arms crossed over his chest. His belligerent expression dared them to challenge him.

Michael met his gaze evenly, then finally nodded. "Okay, so you and Kinsey got along in the end. Somebody on the set didn't get along with him quite as well. Did you ever hear anything, see anything that looked like maybe somebody might not be as enchanted?"

"Besides Veronica, nobody. I flat-out don't believe there's a person involved with this production who could have killed him."

"You know anything about his personal life?" Michael asked.

To Molly's amazement, Duke didn't seem thrown by Michael's persistence. He answered readily.

"Nope. What the man did on his own time was none of my business. I was too busy keeping my own squeeze happy to worry about his."

"Is your *squeeze* involved with the production?" Michael seemed to stumble over the description a bit.

"What difference does that make?"

"If she's been around, maybe she noticed something."

Duke hesitated for a split second before responding. "She's been around town, not around the set. Moviemaking bores her to tears."

Molly regarded him oddly. She tried to recall seeing Duke with a woman at any time since he'd arrived. She honestly couldn't remember a single occasion. He showed up, played his scenes, then retreated to the privacy of his trailer or went back to the hotel.

"Has she been here all along?" she asked cautiously. Apparently something in her tone alerted Michael that she wasn't entirely buying Duke's story. He turned his most penetrating gaze on Duke.

"From day one," the actor assured them both.

"Where is she now?"

"Asleep. Daylight's not her gig."

"Did you talk with the police last night?"

"I got a message they were looking for me, but we crashed when we got back to the room. I'll check in this morning."

Just then a car cruised to a stop right in front of them and Sergeant Jenkins emerged. He scowled at Molly and Michael. "You two are a long way from home, aren't you?"

"Just out for a pleasant brunch," Molly said cheerfully. "Care to join us?"

He looked at Duke Lane for several seconds before recognition sparked in his eyes. "Maybe I will at that." He waved his driver on, then stepped on the curb. He grabbed a chair from the next table, and wedged it between Molly and Duke.

"Duke Lane, right?"

"Yes."

"Sergeant Jenkins, homicide. Didn't you get my messages?"

"We were just talking about that. I figured I'd check in as soon as I got back to the hotel."

Jenkins glared at him. "Some police officers might view that attitude as uncooperative."

Duke shrugged. "Everybody's got hang-ups. Me, I'm the most cooperative guy you'll ever want to meet, once I've had my morning coffee. Before that, I can be real mean."

Jenkins glanced pointedly at the coffee cup. "Drink up. Then you and I are going down to headquarters for a friendly little chat."

Molly tried to hide her disappointment. She'd been hoping he'd go over Duke's story right here and now. Maybe he'd get an answer to the question uppermost in her mind.

Why the hell would Duke be lying about some woman when everyone on the set and in Hollywood knew he was gay?

7

"What was that all about?" Michael asked Molly the instant Otis Jenkins and Duke Lane left for the police station.

"What was what all about?"

"Don't you dare play dumb with me," he chided. "Your eyes will give you away every time. You picked up on something. What was it?"

When he was regarding her with that intent, dare-you-to-lie cop look, Molly found it virtually impossible to skimp on the truth, even when she wanted to. "All that talk about Duke's squeeze," she admitted. "I've never once seen him with a woman."

"So he's discreet. So what?"

"He's not only discreet. He's gay."

Michael looked as if she'd just announced that cows flew. "Him? No way. Didn't you see the way that waitress reacted to him? I think she slipped him her phone number on one of those little napkins she dropped in his lap."

Molly shook her head. "You saw what you expected to see when some heartthrob is out in public. Forget the way *she* reacted to him. Think about the way he reacted to her. He played the role to get her attention, but he never once looked her over."

Michael nodded as comprehension slowly dawned. "Okay, say you're right."

"I am right."

"*Say* you're right," he repeated with careful patience. "What possible difference does it make as far as Greg's murder is concerned?"

That stymied Molly as well, which was why she hadn't particularly wanted to bring it up. "If he'd lie about one thing, why not another?" she ventured.

"Maybe. Or just maybe he had a crush on the director."

"If he did, it was definitely unrequited. Greg's list of conquests, *female conquests,* was endless. To hear some of the guys tell it, he couldn't keep his pants zipped."

Michael's brows rose. "Exactly what do you and the boys discuss in your spare time?"

"They don't necessarily say things like that to me. They just say 'em when I'm

423

around."

"Fascinating," he said, sounding oddly disgruntled. "If Greg wasn't gay, then Duke Lane's sexual preferences probably don't matter."

"Unless he propositioned Greg anyway and Greg shot him down."

"That's a stretch. You couldn't build a case around something as speculative as that, not without witnesses."

"At this point, I don't see much we can build a case around. I'm grasping at straws here. Help me out. You're the hotshot detective."

Michael opened his mouth, but Molly cut him off. "And if you dare tell me to leave it to the Miami Beach police, I'll scream."

"I wouldn't dream of it."

"Good."

"There is something I would like to know, though." At her nod, he said, "Why is it that you are constitutionally unable to leave well enough alone? I could understand it when it was your condo president and we thought the murder weapon belonged to you. But this time? I don't get it. This kind of idle curiosity can get you killed."

"It's hardly idle curiosity. I was assigned to keep things running smoothly for this production. Instead, the director winds up dead. You've met Vince. If you were me, would you want to go to work tomorrow morning without some answers?"

"Molly, the man can't hold you accountable if some lunatic pulls a gun and shoots someone."

"Vince can and, believe me, he will. Especially if he happens to get half a dozen calls from county officials wanting to know how the hell he could have allowed this to happen? He is more than willing to throw the burden of answering that question off on me. Surely you've dealt with the occasional boss who survives by passing the buck."

From Michael's expression, she could tell that he had.

"True," he said. "Okay, let's make a deal, then. If you have a theory about what happened, you'll tell me about it and let me do some unofficial snooping. If you find something concrete, you'll tell Sergeant Jenkins at once and let him check it out. You will not stick your own neck out. Deal?"

With those brown eyes pinning her in place, Molly would have made a deal to sell her soul. "Yes," she said finally. "I promise."

Even as she said the words, she had a feeling they were likely to have about as much substance as her wedding vows. She'd meant them heart and soul at the time, but after a while they had lost their meaning.

The apt comparison came up again an hour later, when she and Michael left the elevator in her condo just in time to run smack into her ex-husband, who was prowling the hallway outside her apartment. Hal DeWitt ruined his good looks by glaring at her. He was obviously in a foul temper.

"Where's Brian? I'm taking him home with me," he announced without so much as a by-your-leave.

"He's outside and no, you are not taking him anywhere," she retorted, glaring right back at him. The man always brought out the worst in her. Since he often chose to ignore his son unless he could use Brian to gall her, she had no doubt about his motive in showing up today. He'd read about the murder and decided she was once again endangering his child.

"I won't allow him to live with a woman who's a damned jinx."

"Jinx," she repeated incredulously, her voice climbing.

"Two men are dead," he reminded her, a stubborn, accusing set to his jaw.

"Not because of me, they're not."

Since he couldn't win that argument, he directed a scathing glance at Michael.

"Who's he?"

She made the introductions warily, watching as Michael seemed to sum Hal up with a quick once-over. Hal was still a very good-looking man, obsessive about staying trim and keeping a year-round tan despite the well-publicized risk of skin cancer. Unfortunately, he was well aware of his attractiveness. He'd skated through life on little more than his charm and his easy smile. Both were wearing thin, along with his carefully styled dark hair, which no longer quite covered his receding hairline.

Given a little time and vastly improved objectivity, Molly had finally come to see Hal DeWitt for what he was — a shallow, vain man who took delight in belittling everyone around him. His cutting remarks no longer had the power to hurt her. That didn't stop him from making them, however.

He waved the local section of the Sunday paper in front of her. "Just look at this! There you are, smack in the middle of another murder, your picture on page one. Don't you give a damn what your son thinks of you?"

Molly could practically feel Michael tense beside her. He took a protective step closer.

"Brian seems to think his mother is a very

special woman. I'd say he's got it nailed," he said to Hal. His voice was deceptively mild.

Hal's face reddened. "This is none of your business. We're talking about my son."

Michael stepped toward her ex-husband, but Molly put her hand on his arm to stop him from defending her. She was getting better all the time at standing up for herself. Lord knew, Hal gave her enough practice.

"He's my son, too, and don't you ever forget it!" she reminded Hal coldly. "If you want to come inside and discuss this rationally, fine. If not, you can leave."

"If I leave, I'm taking Brian with me."

"No," she said with icy calm. "He will spend next weekend with you as scheduled, but he will not leave here with you today. I will not have his life disrupted because of your whims. If you so much as think of violating our custody agreement, I'll have you arrested and charged with kidnapping."

"And I will be only too happy to make the arrest," Michael offered.

Hal's expression turned mean. "This is between my wife and me."

"Your ex-wife," Molly corrected. "And as far as Michael's willingness to haul you off to jail, I will be only too thrilled to accept his help —" she regarded Hal meaningfully

— "if it comes to that."

Few people ever talked to Hal DeWitt that way, and up until recently Molly had been no exception. He seemed stunned by the change in her. Sometimes, she thought wryly as she waited for his decision, she was every bit as startled as he was. Sparring with Michael had sharpened not only her wits but her self-esteem. *He* took her opinions seriously, something her husband had never done.

Whatever cockiness Hal had been feeling visibly drained right out of him. He salvaged some tiny measure of dignity by stalking off to the elevator without another word.

When he'd gone, Michael looked as if he were sorry he hadn't had the chance to throw a punch. Hal often made Molly feel that way as well.

"Do you think we ought to go down and make sure he leaves without taking Brian?" he said.

Molly shook her head. "The last thing he wants is to be labeled a kidnapper. He'd rather act the martyr. He'll get a lot of mileage out of that."

"How long did you stay married to the guy?"

"About six years too long. I should have left when Brian was a baby, but I thought he ought to have a father, even if I had to put up with a lousy husband. I figured I only got what I deserved. Then one day, not all that long ago, I might add, I woke up to the fact that I was a pretty decent, capable woman and I stopped doing mea culpas over robbing my son of a dad. I don't do anything to stand in the way of Hal and Brian having a relationship. I've never said one harsh word to Brian about his father and I hope I never will."

"Staying quiet must test your willpower."

"Oh, there are days," she admitted. "It's funny, though. I think Brian's figured Hal's shortcomings out for himself. No doubt one of these days Hal will blame me for that too."

"Maybe he'll just wake up eventually and realize he ought to be damned proud of having such a savvy kid."

Molly chuckled. "I'm afraid you're crediting Hal with the ability to handle more introspection than he's capable of. The man doesn't mind gazing in the mirror, but he doesn't waste a second trying to understand what's in his heart."

He studied her with obvious concern. "You okay with what went on just now?"

"I'll survive."

"I could stay."

As tempting as the idea sounded, Molly shook her head. She wasn't going to turn to Michael out of loneliness and need. Whenever they finally got around to changing the nature of their relationship into something more intimate, it would be because the timing and the motives were right for both of them.

Michael took a step closer and Molly found herself backing up against the wall. Her breath snagged in her throat as he braced one arm on each side of her. "We have some unfinished business between us," he said, brushing a stray strand of hair away from her face. His fingertips skimmed her cheek. "One of these days we're going to have to take care of it."

Molly's mouth seemed to go dry. As she moistened her lips with her tongue, Michael's gaze never left her mouth. Finally, when the tension between them was tightrope taut, he bent his head and slanted his mouth over hers. Instead of taking, though, as Hal had always done, Michael seemed to be giving her strength, filling her with something unfamiliar. It felt tantalizingly like joy, bursting inside with the radiance of sunbeams.

On the other hand, it might have been pure, unadulterated lust. It was impossible to think straight with all that hard, male sexiness and heat pressed against her. One more dizzying second and she was likely to forget all those commonsense warnings.

"Whoa," she said, ducking under his arm and frantically trying to get the key to go into the suddenly impossible-to-find lock.

Michael stilled her trembling hand, took the key, and had the door open in a heartbeat, no small feat considering exactly how fast her heart was pounding.

He rubbed his thumb across her bottom lip. "I gather that's my cue to leave."

Molly summoned up the last remnants of her common sense. "Yes," she agreed.

A man of less conscience would have heard *maybe* in her breathless voice. Michael merely winked. "Soon, sweetheart. Soon."

Molly watched him stroll down the corridor. As soon as the elevator doors closed behind him, she collapsed against the wall. If she'd had a hankie, she'd have waved it to cool her overheated flesh. If she'd lived at Tara a century or so ago, she'd simply have swooned and been done with it. She would have blamed it on her corset, though. Self-deception had its merits, especially when she didn't care to deal with the alternative emotions.

The door across the hall inched open. Liza poked her head out. "Coast clear?"

Molly nodded.

Liza stepped into the hall. "Lordy, lordy," she murmured. "I do believe I felt the earth move clear in there."

"You were watching?" Molly said indignantly. "Everything?"

"Your ex and I had just finished having a depressing tête-à-tête when you arrived. Considering his lousy mood, I couldn't very well abandon you."

Molly grinned. "I don't suppose you ever considered actually announcing your nearby presence or maybe even joining us out here for the festivities?"

"Actually, I saw my role as backup. Not that you needed it with the hunk prepared to rush to your rescue."

"Weren't you satisfied then that I was in good hands?"

"Absolutely."

"And?"

"You wouldn't have wanted me to miss the end, would you? This was definitely R-rated stuff. Maybe X-rated. To be perfectly honest, I was ready to come out here and invite the man in myself if you turned him down."

"I'm glad you controlled yourself."

"Yes, well, with murder uppermost on everyone's mind these days, I figured it was best not to risk it."

"Good thinking."

"Did you-all figure out the killer over quiche?"

"Afraid not. Speaking of which, I'd better get inside and work up a new statement for the media."

Liza shook her head. "I doubt you're going to need one. Vince is on the air as we speak telling the world that he will personally see that the killer of the great Greg Kinsey is brought to justice."

Molly gaped at her. "How does he intend to do that?"

"Beats me. I think it came as a surprise to that Sergeant Jenkins, too. He looked as if he wanted to stuff his beefy hand straight down your boss's throat and rip out his tongue."

"I know the feeling," Molly told her. "It comes over me at least once a day."

Inside her apartment, the phone was ringing. With Liza trailing along behind, she went inside and snatched it up before the answering machine could kick in.

"Molly, it's Veronica Weston. I'm terribly sorry to bother you on your day off, dear, but I have a bit of a problem. You did say you wouldn't mind helping me."

"Of course, Veronica. What can I do?"

"Actually, it's Jeffrey." She lowered her voice to a discreet whisper. "Something's not quite right about this visit. If I didn't know better, I'd say he knows something about the murder."

Molly's breath caught. "You think he did it?"

"Oh, no, of course not," Veronica said in an unconvincing rush. "I just think he knows something he's not telling me."

"Have you asked him if he's keeping something from you?"

"Well, of course I've asked. He simply looks at me with this odd little look in his eyes, then he goes off somewhere. I'm telling you it's giving me the shivers."

"I can understand why that might be disconcerting, but what can I do to help?"

"I thought perhaps we could meet for drinks. You could ask a few pointed questions."

"I think we probably should leave the pointed questions to the police," Molly said nobly. Liza silently applauded, though her expression was disbelieving. Molly scowled at her.

"Besides, if he won't talk to you, why on earth would he talk to me?" she added.

"Actually, since you were here when he arrived and you were with those two policemen, I may have given him the idea that you were here in an official capacity as well."

"You told the man I was a cop!"

"Not specifically," Veronica said offhandedly. "I just sort of left him with that impression. It's not the same thing as lying. You can see that, can't you?"

Actually, Molly thought the distinction was pretty slim. Michael would absolutely love to hear that she was running around town impersonating a police officer. Then, again, perhaps she owed it to Greg to do whatever she could to find out what had happened to him and why. She was only going over to have drinks with the man. What was so terrible about that? The answer to that probably depended a great deal on whom you asked. She decided not to ask anyone.

"I'll be there in half an hour as soon as I make arrangements for my son. Your suite?"

"No, dear. We'll meet you in the lounge in the lobby."

If she hadn't been so busy trying to squash her own guilt, Molly just might have paid more attention to the note of satisfaction in Veronica's silken voice.

■ ■ ■ ■

Jeffrey Meyerson looked like a character from a Noel Coward drawing room comedy. Elegant and precise, with a dapper red silk handkerchief tucked in the breast pocket of his white linen jacket, he was armed for his interrogation with a martini in one hand and his rapier wit. Molly might have been charmed if she hadn't been so certain it was all an act.

Veronica sat stiffly by his side, her eyes hidden by her trademark rhinestone-trimmed sunglasses, her brow furrowed with concern. If she'd been aware of the lines the worry sketched on her face, she would have been horrified. She gulped down a double vodka and waved the empty glass imperiously in the direction of the waiter.

"Veronica, dear," Jeffrey scolded mildly. "One's your limit."

She ignored him and reached for the second drink the instant the waiter set it on the table.

"Mr. Meyerson," Molly began.

"Jeffrey."

"Jeffrey, then." She smiled at him. "I'm a little confused about your sudden arrival yesterday. Veronica never mentioned that she was expecting you."

"I told you, my dear, it was to be a surprise. I simply couldn't bear being away from her another minute. Since I had this trip to Rome, I impulsively decided to route myself through Miami."

"From Los Angeles?"

His expression grew puzzled. "Of course."

"Then I must admit, I'm more confused than ever. It was well after midnight when you arrived at the hotel. The last flight from L.A. arrived in Miami hours before that on Saturday."

"I went by the location before coming to the hotel," he said without missing a beat. "That's how I knew about what had happened to Greg. The news was being discussed by everyone. There were policemen all over the place at Veronica's trailer. Naturally, I wanted to learn all I could before coming to the hotel. I knew she would want to hear the latest news."

"You never once considered that she might be a suspect herself? He was found in her trailer, after all."

He regarded her indignantly. "Absolutely not. Veronica is not capable of murder. Besides, what reason would she have? Gregory Kinsey idolized her."

Veronica and Molly both gaped at that,

though the actress recovered more quickly than Molly.

"That's a very strong word," Molly suggested.

"Strong, but accurate. Everyone knew how badly he wanted her for this film."

"Did you know Greg yourself?"

"No. I'm sorry to say I never met him."

"Then you have no idea why he fought so hard on Veronica's behalf?"

Molly watched him closely and caught the faint uneasiness that passed over his face before he shook his head. "No," he said quietly. "I have no idea at all."

The denial was firm, but there wasn't a doubt in Molly's mind that it was also a lie. Veronica was right. There was some secret her fiancé was keeping, and it almost definitely had something to do with the murder.

Her promise to Michael to pass along her theories before she acted on them crossed her mind. She would keep the promise . . . as soon as she knew just a little bit more about what made Jeffrey Meyerson tick.

8

Even though she was exhausted, even though she'd promised Brian that she'd spend some time helping him with his summer school science project from hell, even though Michael was likely to be furious, Molly found she couldn't resist temptation. The exit for Southwest Seventh Street was right on her way home. One-way heading west, the street ran parallel to Calle Ocho — Southwest Eighth Street, in the heart of Miami's Little Havana neighborhood.

She drove west as far as Le Jeune, then circled around to come east on Calle Ocho. She passed a park where old men sat playing dominoes. Occasionally the games erupted into violent arguments, but today, in the hot, late afternoon sun, it looked peaceful enough.

Store signs in this section of town were no longer in English. Along with cafés with walk-up windows selling *café cubano* and made-in-the-USA Havana cigars, *bodegas,* restaurants, *farmacias,* and stores selling statues of the saints, there were also several discreet motels where Latin men took their mistresses for afternoons or evenings of lovemaking.

Hidden behind a line of palm trees, Molly spotted the one where the Italian model and her quick-thinking photographer had reportedly fled the night before. She pulled into the parking lot of the one-story, pale blue stucco motel. Almost all of the spaces were empty. Apparently most of the men who frequented motels such as this did so during the week. Sundays were, no doubt, reserved for families and the sanctity of marriage. Amen.

As she contemplated her next step, second thoughts began sprouting like weeds. She couldn't very well start banging on doors. Nor was she thrilled about walking into the lobby and demanding to see the guest register. She doubted one existed anyway. Her only hope was to find a greedy desk clerk and hand over sufficient cash to loosen his tongue. It all seemed a little tawdry and melodramatic, but she was too curious about the model to back out now.

She clutched twenty bucks and one of her business cards and marched into the tiny reception area, noting that the tiled floor had been swept clean and the furniture polished to a gleam. A bored, overweight clerk glanced up from his racing form, took one look at her, and hurriedly dropped the paper. His smirk was the dirtiest thing in the place.

"English?" Molly inquired hopefully.

"*Sí*," he said, still leering. "You need room? One hour? All evening?"

Molly laid the twenty-dollar bill on the counter. "I need information."

He regarded the money with interest at first, then with great sorrow. He shook his head. "Sorry, senora. No information."

She hadn't really expected him to be forthcoming. After all, the people who frequented this place expected total anonymity. A clerk who blabbed about the clientele wouldn't last long. At the same time, the Italian was hardly likely to be a regular customer and this man was equally likely to know that.

She placed her business card with its county logo where he could see it. Her thumb just happened to cover the name of her department, leaving her level of official authority open to speculation. For the first time, he began to look uneasy.

"I'm looking for a man, a photographer.

He'd have lots of camera equipment with him. Also a beautiful model. Italian. They came here last night, very late."

He listened intently, but she couldn't tell from the blank expression in his eyes if what she was saying didn't register or if such a couple simply hadn't checked in. He glanced around warily, then put his hand over the twenty.

"I not tell you this, *sí?*" he said urgently.

"*Sí,*" Molly agreed.

"*Numero ocho.*"

"They are still there?" she said, and realized she was startled that Officer Jenkins hadn't been here and scared them away.

"*Sí, sí.*" He hurriedly nabbed the money and shoved it into his pocket. He glanced at his racing form and reached for the phone.

"*Gracias,*" Molly said to his T-shirt-clad back.

Outside she had the creepy feeling that the clerk's lecherous eyes were still on her as she walked along the side of the motel hidden away from the street. A bed of bright red geraniums ran along the wall, the last blossoms wilting in the summer sun. Number eight was at the end, its door freshly painted in pristine white. The drapes were drawn tightly.

Taking a deep breath, Molly knocked hurriedly before she could lose her nerve. She could hear the faint sounds of people scurrying around inside, then sensed someone's gaze on her through the peephole. She knocked again.

She could hear the hushed sounds of what could have been an argument, then the door opened a crack. The face that peered out at her had the calm tranquility of a Madonna. Only the eyes, dark brown and round as saucers, gave away any hint of fear.

Molly poked her card through the opening in the doorway. The door closed while the chain was removed, then opened again.

Greg's model, if that was indeed who she was, was wearing a skimpy bandeau top and shorts, a revealing outfit Molly wouldn't have dared ten years and ten pounds ago. Thick black hair fell in exotic waves to her shoulders. Her face, with its angles, full pouting lips, and soulful eyes, was a photographer's dream and any man's fantasy. There was an earthy sensuality about the model that was all the more astonishing because she couldn't have been much older than seventeen or eighteen.

Molly glanced into the dimly lit interior beyond her and recognized the photographer she'd met the night before — Giovanni if the taxi dispatcher had gotten it right. He was angrily puffing on a cigarette held between thumb and forefinger in European fashion. He didn't seem pleased by her ingenuity in finding them.

"Why have you come?" he demanded over the sound of Spanish announcers describing a soccer match on TV.

"To speak with your model," Molly said.

"She speaks little English."

Molly didn't take his word for it. She turned to the girl and smiled. She received a tentative smile in return. "You speak English?" Molly asked.

"Yes, I speak some," she said.

"What's your name?"

"Francesca."

"You knew Greg Kinsey?"

Tears shimmered in the girl's eyes. Her words spilled out in a torrent of English and Italian, all mixed together in a way that was beyond Molly's comprehension. The tears tracked down her lovely face and splashed onto her bare shoulders. The photographer lifted his hands in a gesture of helplessness and glared at Molly as if the girl's distress were all her fault.

She led the girl to the bed, murmuring soothingly until she began to calm down.

"Tell me why you and Greg argued," she urged.

Huge brown eyes, still filled with tears, stared back at her in obvious confusion.

"Argued," Molly repeated. "Why did you fight?"

"I'll tell you why they fought," the photographer snapped, taking impatient strides across the room. "He was no good. He made promises."

"What sort of promises?"

He shrugged. "A role in his picture, fame. Who can say what it would take to turn a young girl's head? He made good on none of these promises."

Molly began to see why her pretense of having work for Francesca at the hotel the previous night had met with such disdain. "They fought about this last night?"

The photographer began another tirade, only to be interrupted by Francesca. "No," she said softly. "It was not that way."

Molly held the girl's trembling, ice cold hands. "What way was it then? You tell me."

"I loved him. I wished to stay with him. Here, in Miami. He told me to go home."

The photographer suddenly looked defeated. "He was a fool," he murmured in a way that told Molly that he himself was enchanted by this child-woman. Had he been furious that the director had rejected her? Or that he had dared to take her as his lover in the first place? Had he been angry enough to kill Greg?

"Were you there when they argued?" Molly inquired.

"No," he said at once. "I came after . . ."

"After what?" she said.

"After they argued," he said swiftly. Too swiftly?

As if he'd guessed her thoughts, he said, "He was alive when we left."

Francesca was nodding as well. "He was alive." Her voice broke as she added softly, "It was the last time I saw him so."

"And you left together?"

The photographer glanced at Francesca as if trying to communicate with her silently. To Molly he said simply, "We left together."

Molly gazed into Francesca's troubled eyes and knew that the photographer was lying. But why? Was he protecting the woman he loved with the fabricated alibi? Or himself?

It was beginning to seem that there must have been a steady stream of people in and out of that trailer, all in a scant matter of minutes — Veronica, Francesca, Giovanni, and, if those three were to be believed, the killer.

Although she didn't entirely dismiss the girl and the photographer as suspects, she asked, "Did you see anyone else near the trailer?"

Francesca shook her head. "No one."

"The policemen were at the end of the block," Giovanni said. "Otherwise, no one."

Molly recalled where the off-duty officers had been stationed to keep out curiosity seekers. The side street where Veronica's trailer had been was cordoned off at both ends of the block with guards at each end. Others stood guard along the stretch of Ocean Drive where the actual filming was taking place in front of a Deco hotel.

"How did you get past the policemen in the first place?" she asked.

"Gregory had introduced me to them," Francesca said. "He had given me a pass." She reached into her huge purse and rummaged around, finally extracting a slip of bright yellow paper. "You see? It gave me permission to enter."

GK Productions had issued permanent passes to all those connected with the film. Guests of the cast and crew were given similar slips with specific dates filled in and initialed by Laura Crain. No one was allowed on location without one of those slips.

Molly studied Francesca's slip and noted that it had been signed by Greg himself, not Laura, and that it was open-ended. It was unlikely that either of the guards would have argued with the director's authority, despite whatever instructions Laura had given them.

"You have one of these as well?" she asked Giovanni.

He shook his head. "I came onto the street through an alley. They did not see me."

Which meant that anyone could have done the same, Molly deduced. So much for the sanctity of the set. The list of suspects did not have to be limited to those connected with the film, after all. Anyone determined enough and familiar with that alley access could have slipped onto the street and away again without ever being seen by one of the guards.

Molly sighed. Instead of filling in gaps of what she knew, it seemed she was only raising more questions.

"Thank you for seeing me," she told them. "Will you stay on here?"

"The police have told us to stay, yes," Giovanni said. "We wish to cooperate. I did not like this man Gregory Kinsey, but I have respect for his work. I did not wish to see him die."

"Then the police know you are here?"

"They know, yes."

"Will you stay here or move back to

Miami Beach?"

"Here is best. There are no memories for her. Hopefully it won't be for long."

Molly noticed that Francesca was twisting a rosary in her hands. If the strand of beads was wound much tighter, it would snap. Francesca's eyes were filled with sadness, and suddenly Molly realized that she was perhaps the only one who truly mourned Greg Kinsey.

She placed her hand over the girl's. "If you would like to talk, call me," she said impulsively. "I'll leave my card on the dresser."

Francesca bit her lower lip to stop the trembling. She nodded. Giovanni stepped closer and laid a hand on her shoulder. He murmured something in Italian that drew her gaze up to meet his. She smiled tremulously.

"That is better, *cara mia,*" he said. He glanced at Molly as she went to the door. "Francesca will be fine. I will see to that."

Feeling more exhausted than ever, Molly quietly shut the door and walked to her car. As she pulled out of the lot and headed east on Eighth Street, she caught a glimpse of the driver of a car just turning into the motel. Unless she was very much mistaken, the driver was Otis Jenkins. She doubted the detective was there to rent a room. If Francesca and Giovanni blabbed about her visit, she was going to be in even deeper hot water with the Miami Beach Police Department.

So what else was new? She didn't regret tracking down the model and the photographer one bit. It gave her more pieces of the puzzle to use when she tried to explain things to Vince in the morning. Unfortunately, the only piece of information her boss was likely to be interested in was the name of the killer, and she was no closer to knowing that than she had been before.

At home Brian and Liza were in the dining room with some sort of contraption rigged up on the dining room table. Water was everywhere. Molly eyed the mess warily. "What is it?"

"A desal . . . a desal something," Brian said, regarding it proudly. "Pretty awesome, huh, Mom?"

"A desalinization device," Liza corrected. "It's a winner, if I do say so myself."

"It's awesome," Molly agreed, trying to sound enthusiastic, rather than thunderstruck. "I don't suppose either of you considered putting some plastic under it, so the water wouldn't destroy the finish on the dining room table."

Liza and Brian glanced guiltily at the spotted surface. "Think of it this way," Liza said. "He'll probably be able to sell this thing to the government and make a fortune. You can buy a new table."

"Is it finished?" she inquired cautiously.

"Yeah. It's great. Want to see it work?" Brian asked.

She sat down. "Go to it," she said more enthusiastically. If sacrificing the dining room table meant her son never had to know how little she understood science, it was a small price to pay. Last year's project, which had gotten a paltry C-minus, had nearly robbed her of her sanity. This one looked like an A to her.

Later, with the science project safely in its box and Brian tucked into bed, she fell gratefully into her own bed. But instead of getting some much needed sleep, she spent another restless night pondering the intricate web of lies being spun around Greg Kinsey's death.

Love — or some of its darker permutations — had made suspects of a wide variety of people connected with the director. Even though she was convinced if they could unravel the lies they would identify the killer, she had no idea which thread to tug on first.

Sitting in the Metro/Dade film office in the old Vizcaya estate gatehouse with Molly and Jeannette, Vince waved a handful of newspaper clippings in their faces on Monday morning. It was the first time Vince had been in the office before nine in all the years Molly had worked for him.

Vince explained to anyone who asked that he had to stay later in the evening for all of the office's West Coast contacts. Those who didn't ask already knew that he tried to fit at least nine holes of golf into the early morning hours. When nothing was on his calendar, he went ahead and played the full eighteen. It took a crisis of major proportions for him to schedule anything before noon. Molly supposed the murder qualified.

As the clippings fluttered, Molly managed to catch mastheads from half the major papers in the U.S., plus a couple from overseas. The headlines in English were not encouraging.

"It's a disaster," he said, confirming her own quick analysis. His expression was accusing. "How could you let this happen? The reason I sent you over there to baby-sit this production was to keep everybody happy. I assumed you knew that also meant they should stay alive."

Jeannette shot Molly a sympathetic look as Vince's tirade went on. "I've had calls from the county manager, half a dozen different local mayors, to say nothing of tourism officials and the film liaison in Orlando who can't wait to snatch victory out of the jaws of our defeat," he said. "Are you trying to destroy this office?"

"Excuse me?" Molly said incredulously.

Jeannette muttered under her breath in Creole. Molly had a feeling that if she'd known exactly what the Haitian clerk was saying, she would have echoed it. Their boss had a way of viewing all calamities in relation to the safety of his own neck.

"I did not kill Gregory Kinsey," Molly reminded him slowly and emphatically. "I could hardly cover up the man's death. Did you want me to dump the body in the Everglades and hope that nobody noticed the man was missing? Maybe I should have finished directing the picture myself."

Vince gaped at her sarcasm. Finally his shoulders sagged, and he dropped the clippings on his cluttered desk. "No, of course not. How are we going to handle this, though? Do you realize that I had half a dozen calls at home over the weekend from producers we've been trying to lure to south Florida? They're all very nervous."

"I think you can safely reassure them that we do not have a serial killer on the loose who's targeting Hollywood directors," Molly said dryly.

"You don't know that."

Molly rolled her gaze heavenward and prayed for patience. "Okay, Vince, what would you like me to do?"

"We have to solve this thing as quickly as possible if we're going to minimize the damage. Talk to that cop friend of yours, the one who worked on the murder in your building."

"I have talked to him. It's not in his jurisdiction. He's with Metro, not Miami Beach."

"But he's good, right?"

"He's good."

"Then I'll take care of it."

Molly didn't like the sound of that. She had a strong hunch Michael would like it even less. "What are you going to do?" she asked cautiously.

"Don't give it another thought," Vince said, looking more cheerful. "Just get the hell over to GK Productions and do whatever you can to keep them from packing up and fleeing to L.A. to finish this in the studio. Take Jeannette with you," he added magnanimously. "She can answer phones, take dictation, whatever they need."

Molly cast a look at the thirty-year-old Haitian woman with the close-cropped hair and regal bearing. She was the bane of Vince's existence. Her round mahogany face was totally devoid of expression, but Molly could detect the twinkle in her eyes. Jeannette loved to mutter darkly in Creole whenever Vince irritated her. He was convinced she was putting a curse on him. Because she was damn good at her job, he couldn't fire her, but he grabbed at any opportunity to send her on whatever assignments he could justify out of the office.

Molly hid a grin. Vince and Jeannette must have really been going at it this morning, if he was ready to loan her out to a production company. Since Molly was anxious to get to GK Productions herself, she didn't waste time arguing that the county might look askance at paying a clerk's salary so she could answer someone else's phones.

"Come on, Jeannette, let's get going. I'm sure they'll be thrilled with the extra help."

GK Productions had taken up an entire floor of one of the most recently renovated Ocean Drive Art Decohotels. Since it was off-season for Miami Beach, Molly had been able to help them get fantastic rates for the offices and for the cast's housing. They'd even redecorated their best suite for Veronica.

Laura Crain, Hank Murdock, and production assistant Jerry Shaw were huddled around a table in Crain's third-floor hotel suite when Molly and Jeannette arrived just after nine thirty. She'd hoped for a few minutes alone with the normally late rising producer, but obviously the current production crisis had changed everyone's sleep schedule.

Or possibly, Molly thought, judging from the overall appearance of exhaustion, the trio had been up all night. An ashtray overflowed with cigarette butts and a room service cart was littered with the remains of some unidentifiable meal. Dinner? Midnight snack? Breakfast? It was impossible to tell from the congealed leftovers. Jerry was clutching the receivers of two phones, speaking alternately into each of them. He looked desperate.

She introduced Jeannette to everyone and explained that Vince had sent her along to help out in any way they needed her to. Laura Crain started to say something, but Hank stopped her with a look.

"Great," he said. "These phones have been ringing off the hook. Jerry can't keep up with the calls. Another hour of this and he'll be back in his room having a nervous breakdown."

"Just tell me what you'd like me to say," Jeannette said, "and I'll get to work."

While Hank gave her instructions and Jerry gratefully relinquished the phones, Molly asked for a cup of coffee. "Is there any left?" she said, moving automatically toward the room service serving cart.

"I've just ordered up another pot," Laura said. "Should be here any minute."

"It looks as if you all have been at this for a while," Molly observed.

"Since last night," Hank said. "I'm getting too damned old to miss this many hours of sleep."

"We had to make some decisions," Laura retorted sharply. She looked every bit as brittle as she sounded. Her makeup had long since worn off, leaving her pale. Her green eyes glittered too brightly. Her hair was mussed and she twisted one strand around a finger. Molly doubted it would take much for her to snap. Oddly, though, today there was little obvious evidence of grief for a just-murdered lover.

"Every day we're shut down costs us thousands," Laura said. "We were already over budget. I spent all day yesterday on the phone with the head of the studio trying to convince him not to scrap the project and eat the losses. Fortunately, half of his key executives were away from L.A. for the weekend, so they couldn't get together and compare notes until today. When they call here around noon, we'd better have a plan or we'll be on the next plane home with an unfinished picture that will never see the light of day."

Molly already knew how Vince would take that news. She'd be lucky if he didn't fire her. Come to think of it, they'd all be lucky if Dade County didn't simply drop the department from its budget. There were already some who considered a film office frivolous. They seemed to think production companies would swarm to Miami whether anyone smoothed the way for them or not.

"What do you expect to happen?" she asked Laura.

"They'll moan and groan and threaten a little. Then they'll agree to giving us another two weeks," she said confidently. "If Hank takes over now and we don't lose another minute of production time, we have a chance of bringing this in close enough to budget to keep everyone reasonably happy."

Molly watched for Hank's reaction. If he was eager to direct the rest of the picture and hoped to negotiate an on-screen credit with Greg for bailing them out, he hid it well. If anything, he looked resigned rather than elated.

Even so, Molly had a hard time imagining anyone's not being thrilled at the amount of attention this picture was likely to generate, no matter how the reviews turned out. The simple fact that it was Greg Kinsey's last picture would draw curiosity seekers to the theaters in droves.

"This could be quite a break for you, couldn't it?" she said to Hank.

Rather than reacting with outrage or deliberate innocence, Hank regarded her with amusement. "Playing detective, Molly?"

She felt heat steal into her cheeks. "You have to admit that taking over as director on a Greg Kinsey film could be construed as a motive for murder."

"It could," he said agreeably. "But I was in the production trailer with half a dozen other people at the time Greg was murdered. You found me there yourself."

Molly tried to recall the scene in that trailer when she'd gone in search of Greg. Hank had been seated at the table, a cup of coffee in hand. Jerry and several others had been playing poker at that same table, but there had been no cards in front of Hank. Because he'd just returned from murdering Greg?

"Why weren't you in on the poker game?" she asked.

"I don't gamble. Haven't in years. Lost too much of my pay at the tables in Vegas."

"Why are we wasting time discussing this?" Laura demanded. "The cops have questioned all of us. We don't need to be answering her questions as well."

"I'm just trying to help," Molly countered.

"How? By pointing a finger at one of us to get some local psycho off the hook?"

"Where were you?" Molly retorted before she could stop herself. "You weren't in the production trailer."

Molly wouldn't have been surprised if Laura ignored the blunt question, but the producer actually seemed anxious to share her alibi.

"No, I wasn't in the trailer," she said. "I was back here taking care of business. That's what Greg hired me to do. He hated the paperwork, hated dealing with all the numbers guys at the studio."

Molly knew that was true enough. Laura did have the organizational and logistical skills of an army general. She'd moved the cast and crew around town with a minimum of fuss. She could identify every one of the locals hired, practically right down to their Social Security numbers. Unfortunately, she didn't waste a lot of time on charm. Other than Greg, and possibly Hank, Molly wasn't sure anyone got along with her.

Before she could ask Laura if anyone had actually seen her at the hotel at the time of the murder, an argument broke out in the adjoining room. The connecting door burst open and Daniel Ortiz stormed in.

A Dodgers baseball cap covered his prematurely graying dark hair. A religious medallion dangled from a chain around his neck, providing an interesting contrast to the bloodred logo of some heavy metal rock group that adorned his black T-shirt. He was trailed by two men Molly recognized as key technical experts on *Endless Tomorrows*. As she recalled, one had something to do with sound, the other with lighting.

"We've got a problem," Ortiz told Laura, dropping a handful of pages on the table in front of her. "There's no way to do all these scenes in the same day. No way. What the hell were you thinking of?"

"I was thinking of trying to make up some of the time we lost. Hank said we could do it."

Ortiz did not spare the new director a glance. He kept his attention on Laura. "I do not do schlock. If we push like this, there will be mistakes. Paul and Ken agree."

"Do Paul and Ken also agree they'd rather shut down production now?" Laura inquired.

The director of photography finally looked at Hank. "Is that the choice?"

Hank nodded, looking fairly miserable. "I hate it, too, but Laura's right. We're going to have to make some compromises. Work with me on this and maybe we can pull it off."

The director of photography took off his cap and shoved his hand through his thick hair. He stared out the window for several minutes, then nodded abruptly. "If this is what we have to do, then it's what we'll do. Come on, Hank. Let's see what we can figure out."

When Hank had left the room with the

others, Molly sat down next to Laura. "Daniel owns part of GK Productions, doesn't he?"

Laura regarded her warily. "Still playing amateur sleuth, Molly? It's a dangerous game," she warned.

"Come on," Molly pleaded. "Help me out here. You must want to see Greg's killer caught as much as anyone."

After a momentary hesitation, her gaze challenging, Laura finally rubbed her eyes with the back of her hand and sighed.

"Okay, yes," she said. "Of course, I want to see Greg's killer caught, but I can't start thinking about all that now. If I do, I'll come unglued. Greg placed a lot of faith in me when he gave me this job. I can't let him down."

"He was your mentor?"

"Yes."

"How does Daniel Ortiz fit in?"

"He and Greg went to film school together. They did their student project together. It was a natural fit. He may not have liked it, but Greg knew how to talk with the money guys, how to get the most out of an actor. Daniel knows how to capture it on film."

"What happens to GK Productions with Greg dead?"

Laura shook her head. "I don't know. The company's not worth much with Greg gone, unless Hank can prove himself on this picture. Frankly, he's a decent director, maybe even better than Greg, but he's too low-key, too content to be second-in-command. It takes ambition to make it in this business, and Hank's not driven enough to really scramble for the top spot. It was a good match. He bailed Greg out whenever Greg started drinking or womanizing. He did it too damned much. Greg never had to grow up."

The last was said with an edge of bitterness. Molly recognized that it was as close as Laura was likely to come to an admission that she recognized Greg's flaws and hated him for them.

"Are you so sure Hank wasn't tired of bailing Greg out? Maybe he'd had to do it one time too many," Molly suggested.

Laura's eyes glinted angrily. "No, dammit. Hank did not kill Greg. For all I know you did it yourself. You had the hots for him. I saw that the first day you showed up on the set. You were hanging around all the time, ready to do any little thing he asked of you."

"Usurping your role," Molly shot back. "Were you jealous, Laura? Maybe not of me, but how about the model Greg discovered a few days ago? Did his affair with her make you furious enough to kill him?"

Laura looked as if Molly had pierced her heart with a knife. "What Greg and I had was special, damn you. Don't try to take that away from me. Don't," she said softly, brushing fiercely at the tears that ran down her cheeks.

Before Molly could apologize, Laura jumped up and ran into the bathroom, locking the door behind her. Molly heard the water start to run and looked helplessly at Jeannette, who shook her head as she listened to someone at the other end of the phone line. She held the phone out. "It's for you."

Molly was still trying to figure out if Laura's outburst stemmed from despair or guilt. She reluctantly walked over to take the phone. "Who is it?" she asked Jeannette.

"He didn't give his name. His tone didn't encourage questions."

"Molly DeWitt."

"Mrs. DeWitt, this is Sergeant Jenkins. I want you at the Miami Beach Police Station."

"When?"

"Now," he said tersely and slammed the phone down.

Molly didn't have any trouble guessing

what the detective wanted. No doubt he had a few questions about her presence at the motel the previous afternoon.

10

The area around the Miami Beach Police Department on Washington Avenue was in a state of evolution. Two blocks west of Ocean Drive, Washington was a hybrid of old-style open-air fruit markets, trendy restaurants, discount pharmacies, and souvenir shops. Nightclubs appealing to the young bumped right into shops supplying wheelchairs and canes for the elderly. Garish china flamingos and gaudy T-shirts were sold next to yuppie fashions. The old Fifth Street Gym, where top boxers had trained for decades, was only a few blocks away. Parking was at a premium.

Molly found a metered spot two blocks over and made her way to the fancy new police headquarters. The made-over building was at least three or four times the size of the cramped old structure that had been an easy stroll from the famed Joe's, where chilled stone crabs had become a world-class delicacy.

Molly walked into the brightly lit police station lobby and immediately felt like a criminal. No doubt, after the meddling she'd done the previous day, she deserved to.

Reporter Ted Ryan, his shirttail pulled loose, his tie askew, came rushing down the hall after her. "Molly, wait. I really need to talk to you."

"Not now." She wanted to get her meeting with Jenkins and its likely lecture over with. With production scheduled to begin again in the morning, she had plenty to do to help smooth the way.

"At least tell me what you're doing here," Ted pleaded. "Has there been a break in the case?"

Molly stopped reluctantly and shook her head. "Not that I'm aware of."

"Then what? You didn't come all the way over here just to chat."

"Maybe I did," she replied. "Some of my best friends are policemen."

Ted looked desperate. "Come on, Molly. How about we trade information?"

Molly studied him thoughtfully. It wouldn't hurt to know what the word on the street was about the murder. Ted would have heard all the latest rumors by now.

"What information do you have?"

He shook his head. "You first."

"Oh, no. You want anything out of me, you cough up what you have first. I can always wait to read it in the morning paper."

Reluctantly, Ted opened his notebook and flipped through a few pages. "Okay, here it is. According to my sources, they've assigned someone new to take over the case. My guess is it's that hotshot friend of yours, Michael O'Hara."

"Oh, my God," Molly murmured under her breath. She saw a bench up ahead and sank onto it. Ted sat beside her. She looked him straight in the eye. "Are you sure?"

Ted nodded. "The guy who told me is pretty reliable. O'Hara was on the scene the other night. It all hangs together."

"But he's Metro. And he just happened to drop by Saturday night. He wasn't working. I can swear to that." As she caught Ted scribbling, she added, "Off the record, of course."

"Molly!"

"You want to cost me my job? All I can say on the record is that the Metro/Dade film office deeply regrets the death of Gregory Kinsey, while on location here. Period. End of statement."

Ted rolled his eyes in disgust.

"I know, but that's all I'm allowed to say for attribution," she said. "Anything else I say is just background. You'll have to get it officially from someone else. Now why do you think a Metro cop has been assigned to take over the case?"

"The way I hear it someone demanded he be brought in to try and solve this thing before the publicity gets out of hand." He regarded her slyly. "You wouldn't know anything about that, would you?"

"No," Molly said weakly. She tried to inject a note of conviction into her voice. "No. Absolutely not."

Ted grinned. "Methinks . . ."

"Don't think, Ted. Isn't that one of the first tenets of sound journalism? Stick strictly to the facts. No suppositions. No guesswork. No thinking."

"Then it's true," he gloated. "I knew it."

Before he could take any more wild leaps of logic and wind up with confirmation of some other theory he'd developed over the past forty-eight hours, Molly raced down the hall. She had no idea exactly where Sergeant Jenkins's office was, but from the argument that was echoing off the walls she had a pretty good idea. At least one of the voices sounded all too familiar. So did the tone.

Molly skidded to a halt and looked through a window into a cramped office that looked as if a hurricane had recently passed through. She stopped just in time to see the Miami Beach detective slam his phone back into the cradle. He glowered at Michael, who was fiddling with a pair of sunglasses. Michael jammed the glasses back on his face and scowled, then took them off again.

"Well?" he said.

"Dammit, you know what the chief said," Jenkins retorted. "He confirmed it. You're on the Kinsey case. Of all the jackass moves, you son of a bitch. Don't you have enough to worry about on your own turf?"

"Dammit, Jenkins, I don't like this any better than you do, but we're stuck with it. Let's try to make it work."

"Hell, no," Jenkins said with exaggerated generosity. "You want the case this bad, it's yours."

"I do not want the case," Michael retorted, biting off each word.

"Yeah, sure. I'm supposed to believe that."

"It's the truth."

Molly felt as if she were trying to watch a tennis match from the vantage point of the net. Sergeant Jenkins served up another sly dig about Michael walking off in the middle of his own investigation.

472

"Couldn't break that case, so now you're over here messing in mine."

"I'm here because somebody in the county wants it that way. I'm beginning to see why," Michael shot back, jamming his sunglasses into place.

That was a sure sign that he was losing his temper. Molly had observed that he used those sunglasses to shut out the world when he'd lost patience with it nearly as often as he did to shade his eyes.

Sergeant Jenkins still wasn't content to let it rest. "I can see the press hasn't labeled you an ambitious hotshot for nothing. With an ego that size, I'm surprised you bother with us lowly mortals at all," he said, and stalked from the office.

He was so angry he didn't even notice Molly as he stormed by. Just her luck. Considering the furious expression on Michael's face, she might have been better off with Jenkins.

When Michael finally glanced Molly's way, she stepped into the office and inquired innocently, "All done being territorial?"

Michael lifted his hands in the air in a gesture of total frustration. "The man's a jerk. I didn't ask to be assigned to this case. The way I've got it figured, your boss whined to my boss, who whined to the

County Commission, and the next thing I know I'm meddling in a case that belongs to the Miami Beach Police Department."

He came over until they were toe to toe. She forced herself not to retreat. He removed his glasses so Molly could get a glimpse of his cold, hard stare. "Now how do you suppose that happened?"

Molly winced. "You sound as if you're blaming me."

"If the shoe fits."

"It doesn't. Vince whined, not me."

"But who put the notion into his head? You're not suggesting that someone just drew my name out of a hat, are you?"

Molly tried to recall her exact conversation with her boss. Unfortunately there might have been the tiniest hint that Michael O'Hara could get to the bottom of Gregory's murder and end this public relations nightmare for the film office. Whether it was Vince's conclusion or hers hardly seemed to matter. Michael was here and she had a pretty good idea why.

"No," she said meekly. "I might have mentioned your name when Vince asked who solved that murder in my building."

"I'm delighted the two of you hold me in such high regard, but the next time you get yourself tangled up in a murder, make sure it's in my jurisdiction if you want me to be involved. I don't like butting heads with other cops, especially when they're perfectly competent."

Hoping to get herself off the hook, Molly reminded him, "You just called Otis Jenkins a jerk."

"It's his general attitude I'm not crazy about. There's nothing wrong with his intelligence or his credentials. I don't even blame him for being mad as hell. I'm mad as hell. I was in the middle of another case, not as flashy maybe, but the guy was just as dead and his family is justifiably concerned with catching the killer."

Molly winced. "You were pulled off that case?"

"Practically in the middle of an interrogation."

"Someone took over for you, though, right?"

"Sure. Some other overloaded detective got another case dumped in his lap, so I could come over here and baby-sit this investigation."

"I've got a motive worked out for Hank Murdock," Molly said, hoping to distract him.

He responded in terse Spanish. She knew the word for "thank you." The phrase he'd uttered hadn't sounded much like that. Neither had the tone.

"Don't you want to hear it?"

He sat down in Jenkins's chair. "Sure. Why not. Start by telling me again who this Murdock is."

Neither his tone nor his expression was exactly inviting, but she told him anyway. "Assistant director. My impression is that he's always stayed in the background. You know the kind, competent but not ambitious. In fact, that's exactly how Laura Crain described him. Now *Endless Tomorrows* is practically dumped in his lap. A lot of people will be watching to see if he can sustain Greg's level of creativity."

"How old's this guy?"

"Forty-five. Maybe fifty, but I don't think so."

"Let me see if I'm following you here. You think this guy who is forty-five, maybe fifty, and has never displayed any sign of burning ambition decides to off the director of this particular film so he can finally have his big break? Is that right?"

Molly felt her cheeks burn. "It doesn't sound so logical when you say it."

"It isn't," he said flatly. "Not unless the man is having a mid-life crisis of gargantuan proportions."

She glared at him. "There's no need to be so sarcastic. I'm just trying to help."

The reminder didn't seem to placate him. "What are you doing here anyway?" he inquired. "Shouldn't you be on location holding Veronica Weston's hand or offering assistance to that barracuda who's in charge of production?"

"Sergeant Jenkins summoned me here. I'm not sure exactly why," she said, figuring Michael was in no mood to hear the specifics. Naturally, though, he couldn't leave well enough alone.

He regarded her suspiciously. "Now why would Jenkins want to talk to you?"

"I can't imagine."

"Molly?"

"Really, you'll have to ask him. I guess since he's gone, I might as well take off, too." She backed to the door. "You want a lift over to the location?"

He shook his head. "No, thanks. I'll be going with Jenkins."

"I don't think so."

"Why not?"

"He just pulled out of the parking lot. If anyone else had pulled into traffic the way he just did, the chief himself would have gone out to ticket him."

"Damn," Michael muttered. He was on

his feet and across the office before she could blink. He yanked open the door, then glanced back at her. "Well, come on. There's no point in trying to find two parking places on Ocean Drive."

"You're welcome," Molly grumbled.

If he caught the remark, he chose to ignore it. When they reached her convertible, he held out his hand for the keys. "I'll drive."

"Hoping to strand me without a car again?"

"It's a thought."

"You really are in a nasty mood. Don't take it out on me."

He drummed his fingers on the steering wheel as they waited for an old lady pushing a shopping cart filled with groceries to cross the street. From the set of his jaw, she guessed he was struggling between fury over the circumstances in which he'd found himself and his normal decent manners.

"Sorry," he said as if the word were one with which he was slightly unfamiliar.

She nodded. It was nice that she'd been able to wrench an apology out of him. She had a hunch, though, that the tentative peace they'd reached was likely to give way to another round of verbal warfare once she admitted the real reason Jenkins had probably called her to the station. She figured she might as well get the confession out of the way.

"Remember that model? The one Greg was supposedly involved with?"

Michael turned toward her. "Yes," he said very slowly. "What about her?"

Before she could say a word, he apparently read the answer on her face. "You didn't talk to her?"

"Actually, I did," she said in a rush. "The photographer, too."

Michael slammed his hand on the steering wheel. "I don't suppose you just happened to run into them sunning themselves on the beach?"

She shook her head. "I went to the motel. I bribed the desk clerk to tell me which room they were in."

"Are you out of your mind?"

"Do you want to hear this or not?"

"Fine. Of course. Tell me what you discovered on this little adventure."

"Her name's Francesca. She admits she and Greg fought. She was furious because Greg didn't want her to stay behind with him. The photographer was furious because he's in love with her and he resented the way Greg used her and dumped her. They both had motives and opportunity, but they both swear he was alive when they left him in Veronica's trailer Saturday night."

"And you believed them?"

"I believed her. Him, I'm not so sure about."

"Why?"

"I told you, he was jealous. Besides, he all but warned her right in front of me to keep something a secret."

"Like what?"

"He said they left together. Then he looked at Francesca as if he was trying to tell her not to contradict him."

"That's one possibility. The other is that he's protecting her."

"Yeah, I know. What are you going to do next?"

He pulled the car into a tight space at the oceanfront curb, then removed his sunglasses long enough to look her straight in the eye. "I'm surprised you intend to leave the next step up to me."

"You are the detective," she said dutifully.

"Try to remember that."

"By the way, I almost forgot. Jeffrey Meyerson has an excuse for the delay between the arrival of his flight and the time he showed up at Veronica's hotel room. He stopped by the location first."

Michael groaned. "Don't tell me. Let me

guess. You've talked to him, too."

"Well, Veronica did call me and ask me to come by," she said defensively. "She was worried that he might know something about the murder."

"And did he?"

"Not that I could discover."

"Any other little tidbits I should know about? Things perhaps the police haven't stumbled on yet?"

Molly smiled brightly. "Nope. None that I can think of."

"I'm sure you'll let me know if you just happen across some evidence."

"Absolutely."

Michael put a hand on her elbow and turned her to face him. "Molly, I'm serious about this. Can I trust you to pass on whatever you discover, however insignificant it may seem to you?"

"Of course you can trust me," she said indignantly.

"Can I?" he said. "You made me the same promise just yesterday."

"And just look at all the information I gave you today."

He shook his head. "There's no arguing with you, is there? You have an answer for everything."

"I try," she said, purposely ignoring his

exasperated tone. "You may not believe this, but I really do appreciate the fact that you listen to me. You take what I tell you seriously . . . even when you are furious with me."

For an instant he looked taken aback. Then a faint smile touched his lips and was gone. "Yeah, well, don't ever tell anyone I said this, but you've got good instincts when it comes to people."

"Just think what I could do if I had access to an evidence lab and a few crackerjack technicians," she said, winking at him as she went off to take the elevator back to Laura Crain's suite.

"Don't even think about it," he warned as the doors of the elevator slid shut. They didn't close quite fast enough, though. She still heard the unmistakable sound of his laughter.

11

Molly figured she'd escaped the worst of Michael's wrath. Despite his anger and his protests, she felt much better knowing that he was on the case. In fact, she was downright cheerful as she went back into the production office.

Jeannette looked far more harried than she ever did in the film office, even on the worst days with Vince on her case. She glanced up from the phones and waved Molly over. When she'd put the caller on hold, she asked, "You have anyplace else you can be for the next couple of hours?"

Molly shook her head. "Why?"

"You might want to stay out of Laura Crain's path. She's convinced you carried some tale off to the police that explains why both Daniel and Hank were called in for questioning. They just left in the middle of one of her production meetings and went downstairs."

Molly glanced around the room. Jerry Shaw was the only other person in here, and he was busy scribbling all over one of the scripts. "Where's Laura now?" Molly asked.

"The bathroom." The normally unflappable Jeannette looked genuinely distressed. "You sure you don't have urgent business back at the office? She is a crazy one."

Molly shook her head. "I can't run off and have her accuse me of abandoning her in her hour of need. You can imagine how Vince would love that. I'll stay here and take my chances. Thanks for warning me, though."

She crossed the room and stopped by the production assistant. "Hi, Jerry. Anything I can do to help?"

He looked up at her and shook his head.

Molly persisted. "Has tomorrow's schedule been worked out? I can start coordinating with the Beach authorities as soon as I know what locations you need."

"You'll have to ask Laura. She keeps changing her mind. It's driving everyone crazy."

"Why isn't Hank making the decisions?"

Jerry blinked at her. "Well, he is. Sort of. Laura keeps countermanding him. She's better at logistics and stuff. She wants Jonathan to make some adjustments to the script that'll speed things along. Daniel and Hank agreed, but no one can find him."

"Maybe he got tired of everyone ignoring his suggestions," Molly said.

"Not everyone. Just Veronica. She made the guy's life a living hell. If I were him, I'd be back in L.A. by now. Laura made sure that wouldn't happen. She's holding all the tickets."

"Has he checked out?"

"No. He's just laying low."

"Then maybe he's on the beach or having lunch at one of the cafes."

"Could be, but I don't have time to go look for him. I have to finish these script notes. Could you try to track him down?"

Since looking for the writer beat waiting for Laura to throw one of her tantrums, Molly agreed.

She found thirty-year-old Jonathan Fine some fifteen minutes later on the porch of a hotel five blocks south. He was sipping what looked like a double shot of Scotch and staring at the ocean, his expression bleak. Molly slid into the seat across from him, wondering how he stood the glare and scorching heat of the direct midsummer sun. She was drenched in perspiration just from walking a few blocks in the humid, 88-degree weather. It probably helped that each time the hotel door opened a rush of cool air breezed past.

"Hi," she said, taking in the rumpled shirt with its exotic and colorful flowers and the khaki shorts. The clothes contrasted sharply with his bookish horn-rimmed glasses. He looked like a writer's idea of what a screenwriter in Florida ought to look like. He also looked as if he'd feel more comfortable in a three-piece suit with his blond hair trimmed to executive neatness, instead of scraping his collar as it was now.

"You looking for me?" he asked, barely sparing her a glance. He sounded as miserable as he looked.

Molly nodded. "Laura wants some changes in the script."

"So what else is new?" he said. If anything, he looked even more woebegone. He turned his gaze on Molly. "Maybe you can explain why they bought it in the first place. About the only thing left from the original is the title, and I understand some marketing guy at the studio hates that."

"It must be frustrating. This is your first feature film, isn't it?"

He nodded. "Yeah. I used to be in a business that made sense."

"What was that?"

"Banking."

No wonder he looked as if he ought to be wearing a suit. "From what I've seen of banks collapsing, you may have gotten out of that just in the nick of time. How did you sell the script to Greg?"

"He banked at my branch in Santa Monica. One day there was a problem with his account and we got to talking. I told him I'd been working on this script. I'm sure people said that to him all the time, but he asked to see it. After he read it, he called me. He actually said then that he liked it."

Jonathan finished off his drink. "Greg helped me find an agent, took out an option, and then started trying to put the financing together. Everybody told me it was a fluke, that I shouldn't quit my day job, but would I listen? No. I was so sure this was it, my ticket to fame and fortune. Jesus, was I naïve."

"What you accomplished is pretty incredible," Molly said. "I've seen the statistics. The odds are against a beginner breaking in with a first script."

"But how am I supposed to reconcile what's on the screen with what I put on paper? Duke likes to ad lib and Greg let him. He said Duke's an instinctive actor."

"You don't agree?"

"It's bull. He just can't memorize his

damn lines. As for Veronica, she wants to play the role like she's still twenty-seven. If the script had called for a woman that age, Greg wouldn't have cast her. She blames me for making her seem old."

"What'll happen now that Greg's dead?"

"God knows. Hank can't control the cast and Laura's more interested in the bottom line."

He sighed heavily and blinked several times behind his thick-lensed glasses. "Sorry. You didn't come chasing after me to listen to my gripes. What do you need?"

Molly winced. "Actually, Laura . . ."

"Has a few changes. You said that. I guess I blocked it. Well, come on. I might as well get it over with."

He staggered a little as he stood up, then squared his shoulders. Molly wondered if perhaps she should have insisted on coffee before dragging him back to the hotel.

"Are you working on another script?" she asked.

For the first time he gave her a rueful grin. "Yeah, this one. Maybe once it's done, I'll be able to write something that a director and the stars will actually love as it is. I'm not holding my breath, though."

Molly wondered idly if Jonathan Fine was disturbed enough over what had happened to his script to murder the man responsible. She dismissed the thought immediately. He seemed too mild-mannered to shoot someone in cold blood. If he was anything like other writers she had known, though, he probably had a keen eye for human frailties.

"Tell me something," Molly said. "You know everyone connected with the film. Have you had any thoughts on who might have shot Greg?"

Jonathan stared at her, his eyes blinking even more rapidly. "Me? Why would you ask?"

"Because you're an astute observer of people. You've probably taken traits from everyone involved in GK Productions and created new characters, in your mind, if not on paper."

A dull red crept up the back of his neck. Since his back hadn't been to the sun, Molly had to assume she'd guessed correctly and that he was embarrassed by her observation. "Maybe a little."

"Well, then? Anyone capable of murder?"

He considered the question thoughtfully. "Daniel has the temper for it," he said finally. "Laura's probably calculating enough. Duke might do it to protect himself. I don't know about the others."

"Veronica?"

"Not a chance," he said without hesitation. "She vents all her anger with words. She'd cut a man to ribbons with that sharp tongue of hers, but then she's ready to kiss and make up. She even sent a bottle of champagne to me after she publicly shredded a scene of mine day before yesterday."

Satisfied that his observations jibed with her own, Molly picked up the pace. Maybe the heat would sweat some of the alcohol out of the writer's system.

Minutes later, she delivered a reasonably sober Jonathan Fine to Laura. She felt almost guilty for doing it when Laura promptly began berating him. Jonathan pulled himself together sufficiently to defend the pages of script she wanted cut.

"Do you want this movie to make a bit of sense?" he finally snapped in exasperation.

"Of course, but we can handle some of this in cover shots, second unit stuff. We don't need dialogue."

"Maybe we should have hired a cast of mimes," Jonathan retorted.

From her place beside Jeannette, Molly cheered the return of his fighting spirit.

"You look pleased with yourself," Michael noted, coming up behind her.

"Just watching a shift in the balance of power."

"Laura Crain?"

"Yep."

"Who's that with her?"

"Jonathan Fine, the screenwriter. She's been giving him fits from the beginning, but today she seems even more tense than usual. Want me to introduce you, or would you rather wait for one of her better days?"

Michael watched Laura's tirade with evident fascination for several minutes. The look on his face might not have been so worrisome if Molly hadn't known how attracted he was to volatile women. During one unforgettable scene at the soccer field, she'd seen for herself how quickly Bianca's temper flared and how Michael had seemed to enjoy the passionate bout.

"Michael?"

"No, thanks. I'll introduce myself," he said and crossed the room.

Laura listened, her expression wary, as he showed her his badge. "I don't have time for this," she snapped.

"Make time," Michael countered in a friendly but adamant tone. He pulled up a chair.

Molly was prepared to gloat, but unfortunately Sergeant Jenkins arrived just in time to take the wind out of her sails.

"You and me," he said, gesturing toward

the door. "Out there."

"We could talk here," Molly said hopefully. She wanted witnesses. Jenkins looked capable of a little police intimidation. He'd probably stop short of outright brutality.

He shook his head. "Now."

Molly followed him into the hallway. "I came straight down to the station when you called," she said hurriedly, hoping to forestall some of his anger. "You were just leaving."

"I know. I know. I saw you lurking around out there in the hall. Don't think I don't know who's responsible for getting O'Hara over here. Don't expect him to bail you out."

"I don't expect anything from him."

"Then maybe you'll explain to me what the hell you were doing at that motel on Eighth Street yesterday. Unless you're having an affair you're trying to keep secret, my guess is you were paying a call on one of my prime suspects. Why'd you go chasing after Francesca after I'd specifically told you to keep your nose out of this investigation?"

"You seem to know it all. Why bother asking me?"

"Because I want to make a point. I get very irritated when amateurs mess with my case. My ulcer starts acting up. There's not enough antacid on the face of the earth to make it quit, and that makes me cranky. When I get cranky, I start making calls. Official calls. Are you catching my drift here?"

"You'd like me to stay out of your way or you'll call my boss."

"You're mighty quick for a white girl."

"Could I ask one question before I go?"

"Certainly," he said magnanimously.

"Why is it that only one person in that motel room is on your list of suspects? The way I've got it figured, both of them have motive and opportunity."

His gaze narrowed. "Meaning?"

"Meaning Giovanni has an obsession with his star model and he was at the scene of the crime," she said. "I'm sure you'll follow up."

She left him with his mouth gaping and a murderous look in his weary, bloodshot eyes. He slammed his fist into the wall and took off for the stairwell. She had a hunch he was worried that he'd break her neck — to say nothing of several sections of the Florida criminal code — if he waited for the elevator.

"How are you and Sergeant Jenkins getting along?" Molly asked Michael that night. He had wrangled a dinner invitation out of her late that afternoon. He'd brought along all the files on the case, probably just to remind her how much work she'd been responsible for having dumped in his lap. He'd also suggested she stop by the film office for her own file on Greg Kinsey and GK Productions. The file was crammed with publicity about the director and the film, along with copies of their shooting permits and schedules.

"Better than the two of you," he said. "He seems to find you worrisome."

"I'm sure you were able to commiserate with him on that score."

"I tried giving him some tips on handling you."

"Oh, really? How fascinating. Just when did you come up with these helpful hints?"

"About three days into that last case. I decided if I was going to survive with my sanity intact, I was going to have to find a way to work with you, instead of butting heads with you all the time."

"Which no doubt explains tonight's dinner invitation," she said wryly.

He smiled. "Exactly. You and I are going to discuss every single person involved in this case. You will offer your wisdom and insights. Then you will leave the rest to me."

"Happily."

His eyebrows lifted a fraction, but he refrained from comment.

Fortunately, Brian chose that moment to come barreling through the front door with two of his friends. His blond hair was damp from a recent swim and his bare feet were covered with sand. "Hey, Mom, what's for dinner?"

"No 'Hello'? No 'How was your day, Mother?' " Molly inquired with a grin.

"Sorry, Mom. Did you catch any bad guys?"

Michael chuckled. "Maybe you ought to have a chat with your son about the exact nature of your job description."

She shot him a rueful look, then turned back to Brian. "You forgot the sun tan lotion again, didn't you?"

He blinked and stared at her. "How'd you know?"

"Mothers know everything."

"Come on, really."

"Because you've got more freckles on your nose than you did when I saw you this morning. Now go out on the balcony and brush off the sand."

Brian glanced down as if the fine coating of sand had mysteriously appeared. He brushed at it.

"Brian, not in here!"

"Sorry." Brian poked Michael in the arm, then gazed at him hopefully. "You gonna stay for dinner?"

"That's the plan," Michael told him. "You guys been practicing your soccer?"

"Yeah. We'll be ready by Friday. Kevin's got an awesome move to show you."

"Awesome, huh? I can hardly wait."

Brian and his friends detoured to the balcony, swiped at the sand, then went on to his room. Michael gazed after them. "You know how lucky you are?"

"Brian?"

"Yes. He's a great kid."

"I know it. Some days he's the only thing that gets me through." She regarded Michael oddly. "The way you feel about kids, I'm surprised you haven't gotten married and had a few of your own."

He shrugged. "It takes a lot to put up with the kind of lifestyle a cop has. I've never been willing to put any woman through that."

"I'm sure Bianca would have been more than willing."

"Maybe. It never came up," he said in a way that put an end to the conversation.

Since Molly was inclined to keep probing, it was probably just as well the phone rang.

"Mrs. DeWitt?"

"Yes."

"It's Jeffrey Meyerson."

His breathless tone immediately grabbed Molly's attention. "What's wrong, Mr. Meyerson?" she asked.

At her deliberate mention of Jeffrey's name, Michael glanced up from his stack of papers.

"It's Veronica," he said, sounding rattled. "She's been hurt."

"Hurt how? Was she in an accident?"

"She fell. They're taking her to the emergency room at Mount Sinai now. Can you meet us there?"

"Certainly. How badly is she hurt?"

"I think she's more shaken up than anything. It's not the fall I'm worried about."

"Oh?"

"I'm almost one hundred percent certain that she fell because someone shot at her."

12

"Someone fired a shot at Veronica?" Molly repeated, dismay spreading through her. "Where? What happened? She wasn't hit, was she?"

Before Meyerson could provide any details, Michael had snatched the phone from her hands. She glared at him but retreated. This was his job, after all. At least the police angle belonged to him. Her job, in Vince's eyes anyway, probably included preventing incidents such as this.

With the incisiveness of an outstanding detective, Michael asked several terse questions. Unfortunately, Molly couldn't hear the replies, and Michael wasn't nearly as generous about repeating them aloud as she had been. Curiosity was killing her.

Five minutes later he hung up the phone, his expression grim. "Let's go."

Molly responded at once to the sense of urgency in his tone. "Just let me see if Brian can go over to Kevin's for a while."

She made a quick call, then went through the apartment to get the boys from Brian's room. "I have to go out for a while. Kevin's mom said you can stay at their apartment until I get back. You'll have dinner there. Okay?"

"What's going on?" Brian said, looking from her to Michael and back again. "Another dead guy?"

He was clearly fascinated. The other two boys looked equally hopeful. They were at an age when the more gruesome something was, the better they liked it. She'd worried for a while that her precocious son's fascination with blood and gore was abnormal. After getting to know a few of his friends, however, she'd realized all eight-year-old boys were exactly alike.

Molly shook her head. "No, there is not another dead guy. There was an accident. Veronica Weston was hurt. We're going to the hospital to see her."

All three boys looked disappointed. They were only too ready to go to Kevin's.

As soon as she and Michael were on their way in his car, a mud-splattered wagon with soccer gear jumbled in the back, he said, "I'll drop you at the hospital. Then I want to swing back to the hotel and take a look at the scene."

Molly wasn't about to be left out of the search. She offered a more appealing alternative. "We could reverse that. I could look with you, then we could both go to the hospital."

"I thought Veronica would be your primary concern."

"She's okay. Meyerson said so. I'll do her more good if I can help find the person who fired the shot."

"If there was a shot."

Molly recognized the set to Michael's jaw. "You didn't believe him, did you?"

"I'm not sure. I believe she fell. I believe she probably even heard something. A shot? I don't know."

"Why would she say something like that, if it weren't true?"

"Publicity. Sympathy. Maybe to divert suspicion."

"Meaning?"

"If she could convince police that someone shot at her, then we'd have to accept the possibility that she's a potential victim, not a suspect. Carry that one step further and maybe the shot that killed Greg was actually meant for her. It would divert our attention from Kinsey's background."

Molly stared at him blankly. "Where'd

that farfetched idea come from?"

"It's not so farfetched. It happened in her trailer. It was late at night. The shot was fired from some distance. Maybe all the killer saw was someone moving and fired before he or she realized it wasn't Veronica."

Molly considered Michael's unexpected theory. She turned to stare out at Biscayne Bay as they sped west across the Rickenbacker Causeway. The splashy setting sun had cast pink shadows on the water.

It had never occurred to her that Greg's death might have been accidental, that he might simply have been in the wrong place at the wrong time. Though Michael was right that it was possible, something about the theory didn't ring true.

"You say the shot was fired from a distance, right?"

"From outside the trailer anyway. Not from the steps or inside."

"So it would take a real marksman?"

He glanced over at her. "Probably. What's your point?"

"The bullet hit Greg in the middle of his forehead, didn't it?"

"Yes."

"Okay, say I'm a sharpshooter and I'm essentially firing at a shadowy figure. Wouldn't

I be able to see that it was a man or a woman, or at least guess that from the height? Veronica's barely five feet three. Greg was six feet, maybe even an inch or two taller. Besides, wasn't the door open? No glass was broken. And the bullet was from a small-caliber gun. It wouldn't be accurate from any great distance, right?"

Michael grinned. "Exactly. You're starting to think like a cop."

Molly didn't waste time basking in the rare compliment. More concerned with the implication, she immediately asked, "Then we can rule out any kind of mistake in Greg's death?"

He shook his head. "You can't rule it out, but you can assume it's pretty damned unlikely."

Minutes later they had traveled back across Biscayne Bay on the MacArthur Causeway, then straight east to Ocean Drive. Michael pulled into a parking space a block from the hotel.

"Where was Veronica when she heard the shot and fell?"

"From what Meyerson said, they'd been for a walk along the ocean. They had crossed the street and were about to go into the hotel."

"Did the shot come from behind them, in

front of them, or from the side?"

"That's the problem. He has no idea."

"Then you can't actually expect to find a bullet out here."

Michael shrugged as he slammed the car door and locked it. "We can always try." He held out his hand. "Let's go."

Though the sun was rapidly sinking in the west, the summer night was still light enough for them to see clearly. Molly was all set to start searching the sidewalk on her hands and knees, but Michael headed straight into the hotel lobby and looked for the bell captain.

"I understand Ms. Weston took a fall outside the hotel tonight," he said. "Did you see it by any chance?"

The older Hispanic man — Rolando, according to his nametag — nodded. "*Sí!* I saw her."

"Can you show us?"

"*Sí!*" He hurried through the front door and led them to a spot in the middle of the sidewalk, just to the left of the entrance.

"Who called for an ambulance?" Molly asked.

The old man shook his head. "No ambulance. I go inside to call right away, but the gentleman, he tells me 'No.' He say they will take a taxi to the hospital. Does this make sense? No. *Muy loco.*"

Molly shot a puzzled glance at Michael. "Why would he do that? I know he said she wasn't seriously injured, but wouldn't he want to be certain?"

"I guess that's something else we'll have to ask him," Michael replied. He turned back to the bellman. "Did you see anything else? Someone running away, perhaps? Someone who looked suspicious?"

"No, senor. Nothing. It is very quiet tonight. Very hot. People don't come so much, not until later."

"Any police around?"

The old man shook his head.

"Okay. *Gracias, amigo.*" When they were alone, Michael said, "Let's take a look around. It'll be like hunting for a needle in a haystack, but maybe we'll get lucky, if there really was a bullet."

They combed the sidewalk across the street, the paved roadway, the sidewalk in front of the hotel, even the front porch and the side of the building. There was no trace of a bullet or any mark that might have been left by one.

Michael finally gave up. "Let's get over to the hospital. When we get there, though, you go in and talk to Veronica, while I take Meyerson aside. I don't want them hearing what the other one's saying. We'll compare notes later."

Molly regarded him intently. "You still think Meyerson's mixed up in Greg's death, don't you? You think he invented this as some sort of smoke screen."

"Let's just say I've never been entirely satisfied with his explanation about his arrival in Miami and the length of time it took him to get to the hotel."

They drove into the parking lot at Mount Sinai, where the best view of Biscayne Bay was wasted on empty cars. In the emergency room Michael flashed his badge around and the triage nurse sent them back to the cubicle where Veronica was being treated.

The actress lay on a stretcher, looking a little wan, but otherwise fit. Not one hair was out of place. She took one look at Molly and demanded, "Can you spring me from this place? Jeffrey has this crazy notion that they should keep me overnight for observation. I absolutely refuse to spend one minute in one of those tacky, indecent hospital gowns."

"I think it makes sense, dear," Meyerson said, his tone placating. "You've had a terrible fright."

"Oh, for heaven's sakes, it's not as if anything dreadful happened," she said

505

impatiently. "I fell. People stumble all the time."

Before Meyerson could respond, Michael took his arm and steered him out of the treatment area. "Why don't you explain what happened?" he suggested as he led the man away.

Molly stepped closer to the stretcher and took Veronica's hand. It was ice cold. She felt surprisingly frail. The actress's personality was so forceful, Molly had never really noticed until now just how petite she really was.

"How do you feel, really?" she asked when they were alone.

"I'm perfectly fine. Being thrown to the ground like that was something of a shock, but aside from a couple of bruises, there's no damage done."

"Thrown to the ground," Molly repeated slowly. "I thought you fell."

"Jeffrey thought he heard a shot. He grabbed me and pushed me down, then fell on top of me. It was all terribly dramatic and dear of him, but to be perfectly honest, I think he was imagining things. Perhaps he felt guilty for not being here on Saturday and thought a rescue would salvage his pride."

"Then you didn't hear a shot?"

"I don't believe so. Of course, Jeffrey was awfully certain." Her brow creased with worried lines. "You don't suppose there really was a shot? Who on earth would want to kill me?"

Molly pulled a chair up beside her. "Let's think about that for a minute. Is there someone you don't get along with?"

"I suppose any number of people find me overbearing and demanding, but I don't think any of them would see that as grounds for murder. Even that Jonathan Fine person knows there's nothing personal in the things I say about his script. Everything I say is for the good of the film. I've had more experience than the whole bunch of them put together. Not that anyone asks my opinion."

She gave Molly a cheerful grin. "I suppose it's just as well that I'm not the kind of woman to wait to be asked, isn't it?"

Molly couldn't help laughing with her. Veronica had a certain indomitable spirit that she had to admire. No doubt that spirit had stood her in good stead as she'd battled her drinking problem.

Thinking of that, Molly reluctantly asked, "You hadn't been drinking or anything when you fell, had you?"

Veronica's expression turned sad. "I'm not surprised that you should ask about that, but no, I hadn't been drinking. Believe it or not, I do know my limits."

"Limits?"

Veronica sighed wearily. "Please, don't lecture. I've heard it all. No, I shouldn't touch a drop, but I seem to go for long periods when one or two drinks is plenty. Then something happens and, I don't know, I get crazy. One, two, ten drinks aren't enough. Do you know anything about alcoholics?"

Molly shook her head. "Not really, except some people should never take that first drink."

"And yet some of us have to, some of us need the booze to dull the pain."

As she spoke, a single tear tracked down her cheek. Molly had no doubt at all that it was genuine. Veronica's hand trembled in hers.

"Do you want to talk about it?"

With her free hand, Veronica reached for a tissue and wiped away the tear. She shook her head. "No. It's not something I can discuss. Not ever."

"Surely you talked about it with counselors when you were in that de-tox program."

"No. I couldn't even trust them with this. If it ever came out . . ." She sighed. "It simply can't and that's that."

Molly considered arguing with her, but she could see from Veronica's intractable expression that it would do little good. Whatever secret she had been hiding, for however long, was going to remain just that: her secret.

And her torment.

In the end, it was Michael who persuaded Veronica to remain hospitalized for the night. Molly wanted desperately to find out why he was so determined, but all she could do was to stand silently by as he cajoled until the actress finally said "Yes."

They stayed with her while she was taken to a VIP suite and settled in, then drove Jeffrey Meyerson back to the hotel.

"I suppose I must tell Ms. Crain what's happened," Meyerson said.

"Absolutely," Molly said. "It could affect tomorrow's shooting schedule, especially if she expected Veronica to be ready for an early makeup call. Would you like me to speak with her and explain that Veronica won't be available at least until midday?"

"Would you, my dear? That would be so helpful. This entire ordeal has exhausted me. And I must call Rome and explain that my arrival has been delayed."

"It must be the middle of the night there,"

Molly protested.

"My friends tend to party until the wee hours. I'm sure they will be awake. Even if they are not, they will forgive me when they hear what has happened to Veronica. She absolutely enchanted them when they visited Hollywood last winter."

"I'm not surprised," Michael said. "She's a charming woman. Have you known her long?"

"We met several years ago, under less than ideal circumstances. We knew immediately that we were kindred spirits."

"What were the circumstances?" Molly asked.

"It was one of those addiction treatment programs. She was trying to get off booze and I was having a little problem with some pain-killers my doctor had prescribed for a back problem."

"Then you didn't know Veronica from her film work?"

"I knew who she was, of course, but no, that was not a circle in which I traveled."

Molly promptly jumped to all sorts of conclusions that were based on Jeffrey Meyerson's explanation and her own growing distrust of the man. He was too polished, too slippery. And for some reason he had lied about Veronica's hearing the shot. It might have been a minor discrepancy in their stories, but it also might be an indication that there had been no shot at all.

Why, though? What did Jeffrey Meyerson have to gain by setting up some fake rescue attempt? Molly's best guess wasn't particularly flattering. Chances were he was a man who'd seen Veronica as a meal ticket and latched on for the ride. He certainly seemed to make more of their relationship than the actress had actually admitted to. Veronica had never confirmed that there was any engagement.

"What about Greg Kinsey?" Michael asked. "Did you know him?"

Meyerson shook his head. "Never met the man. I wish I had. From everything I've heard, he was a great talent. What a shame to lose him before he could do his greatest work."

He sounded sincere enough. Molly wondered, though, if the extraordinarily protective Meyerson had found Greg's treatment of Veronica too demeaning. Would he have seen that as grounds for murder?

At the hotel, he hurried off to his room and Molly made a quick call to Laura's room. The producer wasn't in, so she left a message with Jerry Shaw.

"Is that going to foul up the morning

schedule too badly?" she asked.

"I don't think so. We can juggle a couple of scenes. Shoot around Veronica, then do her pickups when she gets here."

"Terrific. Thanks, Jerry. I'll see you in the morning."

When she'd hung up, she found Michael on a pay phone across the lobby. "Yeah, that's right. Meyerson, Jeffrey, and Weston, Veronica. Do what you can for me and fax it, okay? Thanks."

"Who were you calling?" Molly asked.

"An investigator I know in L.A. He owes me a favor. He'll dig around a little and see what he can come up with."

"Is he checking on anyone else?"

"Not yet. He's been working on Kinsey a couple of days, but he hasn't come up with anything much beyond his official bio. The guy wasn't mixed up in anything illegal or, if he was, his record had been wiped clean."

"How about GK Productions? Can he take a look at how the company was set up?"

"Why?"

"I'm just curious about what happens now that Greg's dead. I know Daniel owns a piece of the company, but I'm not sure about Hank and Laura. They may have been employees or they could be co-owners. It would make a difference when it comes to motive."

Michael nodded and reached for the phone. "Les, it's me again. Check into a film company for me, while you're at it. GK Productions. I need to know the setup. Who gets it with Greg dead? Who owns a piece? Yeah, a GK Productions without GK doesn't make much sense to me either, but who knows. There's a Daniel Ortiz, who reportedly owns a chunk. He's the director of photography on this picture, probably on all Kinsey's other films as well. Listen, if you come up with anything tonight, I'll be at this number."

He reeled off Molly's home number, then hung up.

"You're coming to my place? Am I cooking?" Molly asked.

"No. It's ten o'clock at night. Let's go for Cuban."

Molly tried to hide her surprise at the offer to take her onto his turf. She was even more surprised when she realized the tiny Little Havana restaurant was owned by an uncle, who greeted Michael boisterously, seated them with a flourish at a formica-topped counter, then brought them huge platters of *palomilla* steak smothered in onions, along with black beans and rice and sweet, fried plantains.

Tio Pedro, his pristine white apron stretched taut over an impressive belly, his black hair shot through with gray, and his black eyes alive with laughter, stood over them as they ate. He nodded approvingly as Michael finished every bite on his plate, then polished off her leftovers.

"Where you been?" he demanded of Michael when he was satisfied that his nephew would not starve to death. "Elena and me, we not see you for two, maybe three weeks now."

"Working, Tio. You know how it goes."

"Not working too hard to have dinner with a pretty woman, I see. Your mama has met the senorita?"

Michael chuckled. "You ask too many questions, Tio. You are embarrassing Molly."

Tio Pedro didn't look the least bit contrite. "You bring her for Sunday dinner. I invite the whole family."

Molly held her breath, waiting for Michael's reply. She had no doubt that Sunday dinner was a major event in his large Cuban family. To be asked was probably significant, something reserved for a girl friend of some importance.

Michael looked at her. "What about it? You feel like braving the inquisition? You can bring Brian."

Trying to match his casual note, she nodded. "Sure. Sounds like fun."

Michael chuckled at that. "Fun is not the way I would describe one of the family get-togethers, especially when you are on display."

"Display?"

"To see if you are suitable for the most eligible bachelor in the family."

"I don't suppose you'd like to give me odds on getting a satisfactory approval rating."

He winked. "I wouldn't worry about it. My opinion is the only one that counts."

13

Less than seventy-two hours after the death of Greg Kinsey, the entire cast and crew, with the exception of the still-hospitalized Veronica, assembled at the same oceanfront location where the murder had taken place. The production trailer was parked on the same side street. Veronica's impounded trailer had been replaced by one slightly smaller awaiting her arrival. Duke Lane's trailer with its special dark-tinted windows had been parked around the corner. Despite the brilliant glare of the sun on sand and sea, the vibes were very dark.

Molly found Laura Crain and Hank Murdock in the production trailer just after 8:00 a.m. They were already immersed in a stack of script pages with little yellow flags marking key sections scheduled for filming that morning.

"We'll finish up here by one o'clock and break for lunch," Laura was saying. "Then I want everything set up in that fake fishing village over on Virginia Key no later than two."

Hank was already shaking his head. "It won't work, not unless Veronica gets here before noon. I can't get her shots done in an hour. She has three pages of dialogue in that scene with Duke. You know damn well she'll never get it in one or two takes. She'll probably spend that long arguing with Jonathan about her lines. Is he on the set, by the way? We can't waste time chasing him down every time she complains. I want him in here all day."

Laura nodded. "I'll take care of it." She glanced at Molly. "Think you could get him for me?"

Molly reached for a cellular phone.

"I said *get him,* not call him," Laura snapped.

Molly considered reminding the producer that she was not her errand girl, but decided it wouldn't accomplish a thing. Laura seemed to consider everyone connected with the film, with the possible exception of Hank, and before him Greg, as her personal lackey. After listening to Laura tell Hank what to do just now, Molly wasn't sure the hapless director didn't fall into the same category.

"Stress," she mumbled under her breath as she shut the trailer door behind her. Everyone on the set was bound to be under incredible stress this morning. Between the murder itself and anxiety over Hank's ability to fill Greg's shoes, it was no wonder everyone was edgy. By afternoon, she hoped, things would settle down or there could well be another murder on the set.

Molly was halfway back to the hotel when to her absolute astonishment she spotted Vince coming toward her. The last time her boss had actually bothered dropping by a film on location in south Florida, the star had been the previous month's *Playboy* centerfold. They couldn't have ejected him from that set with dynamite. Usually he preferred golfing with the studio execs or ogling the starlets at the lively wrap parties that concluded the film company's stay in south Florida.

"What brings you by?" she inquired warily. He was actually wearing a jacket, formal attire for a man who preferred lime-green golfing pants and knit shirts in a rainbow of pastels.

"Politics," he said in a rare display of total honesty. "I figured I'd better try to smooth things over, offer my condolences, et cetera. Where are you headed?"

"Laura just sent me in search of the screenwriter. They want him on standby."

"She's in the production trailer?"

"With Hank. She should be trying to bolster his self-confidence. Instead, she seems intent on making him panic over the shooting schedule. If I were Hank, I'd tell her to get the hell back to the hotel and stay there. He won't do it though. Maybe you can get her out of there."

Vince regarded her blankly. "How?"

"I'm not suggesting you use your usual technique. You don't need to seduce her. Just ask to meet everyone. Play the role of local dignitary to the hilt. You can ooze charm when you want to."

Her boss seemed to consider that a compliment. He waved distractedly as he marched off to impress Laura Crain. He was obviously completely confident he could do it.

Molly found Jonathan Fine in his room, still half asleep. To answer her knock he'd dragged on a pair of pants for decency's sake, but wore no shirt. He was so thin she could practically count his ribs.

"Hank needs you on the set," she told him.

Without his glasses, the writer squinted at her. "Molly?"

"Yes."

"I was up most of the night making the changes Laura wanted. Does he need me now?"

"He says he does."

Jonathan sighed heavily. "Wait a sec. I'll come with you. See if room service can bring up a pot of very strong coffee on the double."

Molly nodded and made the call while Jonathan retreated to the bathroom to shower. He emerged in minutes, wearing shorts and yet another brilliantly flowered shirt. His glasses were in place, but his eyes still looked vague. He hadn't shaved and a faint stubble shadowed his jaw.

"Coffee?" he murmured desperately, blinking at her.

"On its way."

"Thank God." He sank down on the side of the bed to wait.

"You worked all night?"

"Until five this morning. What time is it?"

"Eight twenty."

"Shit."

"Was it just last night's hours or are you not a morning person?"

"Mornings are fine. I just prefer six or seven hours of sleep before they arrive."

A tap on the door announced the arrival of the coffee. Jonathan gratefully drank down an entire cup, poured a second cup and said, "Let's do it. I should live."

They got back to the location just in time to hear Laura scream, "I want you off of this set. Now! Am I making myself clear?"

Molly was about to run to Vince's rescue, but it seemed the person Laura was dismissing so summarily was Michael. It didn't seem like the best approach to take with the policeman in charge of investigating Greg's murder. Michael, however, actually looked amused.

"Sorry. I'm here for the duration," he told her. "I have statements I need to go over with some of your people."

"Not in the middle of production, you don't," Laura shouted. "Do I need to call the mayor of this goddamn town to get you out of here?"

"You can call anyone you want. I'm staying. Maybe we should start with your statement," he suggested pleasantly. "That way your crew can get to work."

It was the best suggestion Molly had heard all morning, but Laura apparently didn't see it that way. She was still making noises about reporting Michael to every official from the mayor to the governor. Molly was surprised she left out the President of the United States.

"That does my heart good," Jonathan said as they watched Michael depart with his reluctant witness. "It almost makes getting up worthwhile."

"I know what you mean," Molly said, wondering where Vince had gone since he obviously wasn't with Laura.

He turned up just as she found a place behind the cables where she could watch Duke Lane shoot his first scene of the day.

"Thanks a lot," he muttered in her ear.

"For what?"

"Sending me in to see that woman without a rabies shot. She's a viper."

"Your charm failed you?"

"A dozen bottles of champagne couldn't mellow her out. Why'd Kinsey put up with her?"

"Word was he was sleeping with her."

Vince shook his head in bemusement. "He was a braver man than I."

Considering Vince's enthusiastic pursuit of a wide range of women, Molly considered that high praise for Kinsey or a damning indictment of Laura. Probably a little of each.

"Quiet on the set," Hank finally shouted. He glanced at Daniel Ortiz, who nodded. "Roll film." He gestured toward Duke Lane. "And action."

The scene required a highly emotional delivery, one of the toughest to begin cold, especially with a stand-in substituting for the missing Veronica. Duke never faltered. A tense three minutes later, when Hank said, "Cut and print," the crew burst into applause.

"He's good," Vince said, sounding astonished.

"To be perfectly honest, he was better this morning than I've ever seen him. I have a hunch Veronica and her tantrums make him nervous."

"He actually said his lines the way I wrote them," Jonathan said, his tone suggesting amazement.

While he waited for Hank and Daniel to set up for his next shot, Duke made his way over to Molly, Vince, and Jonathan.

"Good changes," he told Jonathan.

"You were really on this morning," the writer told him. "Too bad Veronica missed it."

"She would have hated it," Duke said ruefully. "She likes to step all over my lines. Watch when we shoot her angles later. She'll be all over the place."

"Didn't Greg try to control her?"

"Greg thought she walked on water," Duke said. "Don't ask me why. She treated him the way Laura treats all the rest of us, like dirt."

"Taking my name in vain?" Veronica inquired, strolling up in the middle of his comment. Jeffrey Meyerson, looking distressed, was at her side.

"Now, dear," he said soothingly. "Don't get upset."

"Oh, shut up, Jeffrey," she said.

Duke met Veronica's gaze evenly and didn't waste his breath offering an apology. After a beat, she actually winked at him and the tension snapped.

Molly studied her closely. "You're okay?"

"Fine," the actress said. "Jeff, go find the makeup girl and tell her I'm here. Molly, could you be a dear and let Hank know?" She gestured to Jonathan. "Bring along the new pages. We can go over them while they're working on my hair and makeup."

"Certainly," the writer said, looking miserable.

Hank came over just in time to hear the exchange. "No changes, Veronica. We're shooting this the way Jonathan wrote it. Duke's already done his angle."

Veronica responded to the challenge in Hank's tone with a terse "We'll see."

"I told you," Duke mumbled, following Hank back to the set.

Hank draped an arm over Duke's shoulder and leaned close. Whatever he was telling the actor so intensely seemed to relax him. Duke was smiling when he stepped back in front of the camera. Daniel shot him a thumbs-up as Hank called for action to begin again.

"How's Hank doing?" Michael whispered to Molly as he joined her.

She raised her finger to her lips. Michael waited impatiently for the next break in filming when she was finally able to speak. "He's in control so far. Better than I expected, in fact. If Veronica's on good behavior, this may go smoothly."

"You idiot!" Veronica's shout couldn't have been timed more perfectly if Jonathan himself had scripted it. "Are you trying to ruin me?"

Hank and Molly started for Veronica's trailer just in time to see a furious Jonathan Fine storm through the door. "Keep her away from me," he said to Hank. "If you need me, I'll be back at the hotel."

"I need you here," Hank pleaded. "Wait in the production trailer."

Jonathan ran his hand through his hair but finally nodded. "One word from her, though, and I'm on the next plane out of here. I don't care if I never sell another script."

Molly rushed up the steps to Veronica's trailer. Inside she found the actress surrounded by a hair stylist, a makeup artist, and a frantic Jeffrey Meyerson. She was looking rather pleased with herself.

"What on earth did you say to Jonathan?" Molly asked her.

"I told him this was my film, not Duke Lane's, and that he'd better not forget it." She picked up the new script pages from her dressing table and dumped them into the trash for emphasis. Molly winced.

"They're just tightening up a few scenes to speed up production. They were probably making a few adjustments just in case you couldn't get here today."

"Bullshit. Now that Laura's in charge, she wants to turn this into Duke's film. If I have to call my agent and get him involved, then that's what I'll do."

Hank sighed heavily. "Okay, everyone out of here," he said. "Veronica and I need to talk."

When Jeffrey stayed where he was, Hank said, "You, too, Meyerson. Molly, I'd like you to stay."

The only reason Molly could think of for being included was Hank's belief that she had a soothing effect on his temperamental star. Personally, she would have rather been in Siberia. She thought Veronica was behaving like a spoiled brat and wasn't sure she wouldn't tell her as much given another display of her lousy temper.

When everyone else had left, Hank sat across from Veronica.

"You know we have a problem here," he said.

She nodded. "I'll say."

"You're not helping," he said flatly. "You can make or break this film. It's your choice. Now, me, I think this can be the best thing you've ever done, but you have to trust me."

Some of Veronica's defensiveness faded. "Explain," she said imperiously.

"You dominate every scene in which you appear. What does it matter if Duke has a few more lines? He's playing to you. There will never be a question of who this picture belongs to. You have star billing. This is not some cameo appearance. You carry it. It would make life a lot easier if you'd give Duke and Jonathan a break. You have them so terrified the only time I get any decent work out of either of them is when you're not around."

Veronica looked stunned by Hank's frank assessment of her effect on the others. "I just want this to be a great film."

"That's what we all want. If you'd spend half as much energy in front of the camera as you do off-screen, there wouldn't be a star in Hollywood who could hold a candle to you."

Veronica blossomed visibly under Hank's deft praise. Molly silently applauded. He seemed to know exactly how to appeal to her sense of vanity. Veronica would not want it known around Hollywood that she and she alone had turned yet another film into a disaster.

"You're quite a flatterer, Mr. Murdock," Veronica said, bestowing one of her most brilliant smiles on him. "I think I could learn to adore you. Now let's get this show under way."

Hank grinned back at her. "Thank you. I'll send Jerry for you when we're ready."

Molly wondered if Veronica noticed his sigh of relief as he exited the trailer.

"You old fraud," Molly said, when they were alone. "You knew from the minute he walked in here you were going to do as he asked, didn't you?"

"It never hurts to remind everyone of who I am," Veronica said, fluffing her chestnut hair until it fell into its usual sensuous waves. "Of course, I still think Duke Lane is an impertinent twit who's trying to steal this picture."

"The better he looks, the better you look," Molly reminded her. "If the audience doesn't love him, they're going to think you're the twit for chasing after him."

Veronica's brow knit as she considered Molly's analysis. "You have a point, my dear. Tell Duke I'd like to see him. Perhaps we can put this rivalry to rest."

Molly wasn't so sure that was the best idea she'd heard all day, but she left to follow the actress's instructions. She ran into Michael just outside the door.

"I thought maybe she'd taken you apart in there," he said.

"I notice you didn't rush in to my rescue."

"Last I heard, you preferred to stand up for yourself."

Molly didn't bother to respond to that. "She wants to see Duke. Think I dare send him in?"

"You know her mood better than I do. I can always stand guard."

"Probably not a bad idea."

Molly found Duke hiding out in his own trailer. "Veronica wants to see you."

He drew his sunglasses down just low enough to peer at her over the top rim. "You're kidding me."

"Nope. She wants to make amends."

He looked even more disbelieving, but he settled his glasses back into place and followed Molly back to Veronica's trailer. He rapped on the door and stepped inside.

Molly and Michael lingered just outside. Just when Molly was convinced that things had to be going smoothly, she heard Veronica's voice climb.

"Don't you threaten me," Duke countered just as loudly. "Push me too hard and I'll tell everyone what I know about you and Greg Kinsey."

"You bastard," Veronica said in a low tone that Molly and Michael heard only because Michael had yanked open the door about two seconds before.

He stepped inside and looked from Duke's angry face to the flaming pink in Veronica's cheeks. "Maybe you'd better tell me what you know," he said quietly to Duke.

Veronica looked shaken. She stared at Duke intently, her expression pleading. He muttered an oath under his breath, then met Michael's gaze evenly.

"I don't know a thing," he said flatly. "I was just blowing off steam."

"That's not the way it sounded."

Duke shrugged. "I'm a hell of an actor."

Molly and Michael both looked from

Duke to Veronica and back again. There wasn't a doubt in Molly's mind that Duke was lying through his teeth, but short of hooking him up to a lie detector and questioning him from now till dusk, she couldn't see any way of getting him to say anymore.

Veronica, on the other hand, looked as if she'd crack if they asked her anything more consequential than her name. Molly couldn't help wondering why.

14

Hank saved Veronica from having to say another incriminating word at that moment. He called for both the actress and Duke Lane to shoot their critical farewell scene. Given the high emotions off the set, they should radiate tension on screen.

"The minute you've finished, you and I are going to have a little chat," Michael told the actress as she practically bolted from the trailer.

She glanced toward Molly with a look of pure desperation, but Molly could only shrug. When Michael wanted to question a murder suspect, she could hardly intervene. As much as she didn't want to believe that Veronica had anything at all to do with Greg's death, she had no evidence to prove it. As far as she knew, Michael had no evidence to prove otherwise, but then that was exactly what he was hoping to discover in that interrogation.

In front of the camera Veronica's nervousness was unmistakable, even worse than it had been on the first day of shooting when everyone knew how much was at stake for her in this film.

She blew her first, simple line half a dozen times. Hank spoke to her with incredible patience. Even Duke himself sought to soothe her nerves by taking her aside and whispering to her. She smiled shakily at him, but couldn't hide the worried, distrustful look in her eyes.

Even so, on the next take, she delivered the lines — all three pages' worth — flawlessly. It was a bravura performance under the tense conditions. This time, when Hank called "Cut," the crowd gathered around the perimeter applauded. Duke took Veronica's hand and kissed it with a dramatic flourish. Clearly flustered by the gesture, she met his gaze. Whatever she saw there must have reassured her because she walked toward Molly and Michael with a renewed spring in her step and a confident set to her shoulders.

"Come along," she said to them. "You can ride over to Virginia Key with me. Jeffrey should have luncheon waiting in the trailer."

Indeed the small, damask-covered table was set with expensive silver, crystal, and china. Champagne cooled in a bucket and a colorful fruit salad rested on iced plates. Jeffrey welcomed them as if the luncheon were being served in some elegant dining room rather than in a made-over recreational trailer that had been hurriedly spruced up for Veronica's temporary use. He'd even added a bouquet of yellow roses, reportedly the actress's favorite. Veronica said nothing about his efforts. She seemed to take them as her due.

As the trailer left Miami Beach to go to the Virginia Key location, Michael asked Veronica what Duke had been talking about when he'd threatened her earlier.

"After lunch," she said insistently. "We shouldn't let all this lovely food go to waste."

"And after lunch, you'll use the next scene as an excuse," Michael said. "Why don't you just tell me whatever you know now? Get it over with so you don't ruin your digestion."

Since no one was eating the beautifully displayed meal, Molly thought worrying about the star's enjoyment of it was wasted effort.

Veronica finally lifted her gaze until she was staring straight into Michael's eyes. "I don't know anything," she said, her voice steady.

"You're saying Duke was lying earlier, that his threat meant nothing?"

"That's what I'm telling you."

Despite Veronica's sincere delivery, not even Molly believed her. Michael tried another tack. "Tell me about your relationship with Kinsey."

"He had a reputation as a hot director. We didn't always agree. We argued quite a bit, in fact. I'm sure everyone has told you that already."

"When did you meet?"

"When he contacted me about starring in this movie. Our agents arranged a breakfast meeting at the Beverly Hills Hotel." She glanced at Molly. "You must let me take you there the next time you fly out to L.A. The place raises the concept of power breakfasts to new heights."

"Did you and Kinsey get along then?" Michael persisted.

"It was a pleasant breakfast. I believe I had fresh strawberries."

Molly seriously doubted Michael was interested in the menu. Even so, he inquired pleasantly, "And Mr. Kinsey?"

"Melon, as I recall. Eggs Benedict. I told him he was probably killing himself with all that cholesterol."

"I'm sure he appreciated your concern,"

Michael retorted dryly, just as his beeper went off. He glanced at the calling number, then reached for the cellular phone he'd been carrying around on location.

"O'Hara," he said tersely once the call went through. He listened intently. The rest of them sat around watching him. Jeffrey tried to break the silence, but Veronica cut him off with a look.

"Okay, got it," Michael said. "You'll fax the rest to the office? Right. I'll call if I need anything else. Thanks."

All three of them watched him expectantly. He foiled them all by returning at once to that long-ago breakfast at the Polo Lounge of the Beverly Hills Hotel.

"What was your impression of Greg when you met him?"

"He was a pleasant young man," Veronica said. "What more can I say? You can't tell how talented someone is just by talking with them. I screened several of his films later that same day. Those told the story. This was someone I knew I should work with. The clippings my agent gave me about his background and successes intrigued me."

"Did he explain to you why he was so intent on casting you in this picture?"

She hesitated, then said, "No. I assumed he simply thought I was right for the role."

"Surely other actresses would have been equally right. Good roles for women your age are tough to come by. Competition must have been fierce."

"It may have been. I can't really say. To my knowledge I was the only one Greg ever considered."

"Why?" Michael repeated.

"Greg is the only one who could answer that."

"Unfortunately, he's dead."

Veronica blinked rapidly at Michael's harsh tone. "I think we're all very much aware of that, Detective."

"But you don't seem nearly as concerned about finding his killer as I am. Why won't you tell me what Duke was talking about?"

"I can't," she said, her eyes suddenly welling with unshed tears. If it was a deliberate play for sympathy, it didn't work.

"Can't or won't?" he asked, hammering at her. No one had touched a bite of the food on the table. If Molly's was any example, their stomachs were all tied in knots.

"I don't know," Veronica swore. "I'm telling you the truth, Detective. I don't know what Duke Lane knows or thinks he knows."

Michael muttered an oath and sat back. "Okay. We'll save it for later."

Jeffrey Meyerson scowled at him. "Really,

I must protest. Can't you see how your questions are upsetting her?"

"I'm trying to conduct a murder investigation. People tend to get upset now and then. If Ms. Weston has nothing to hide, then my questions shouldn't distress her."

"Your tone would distress Attila the Hun," Molly mumbled just loud enough for him to hear her clearly. He reached over and circled her wrist with his hand. He applied just enough pressure to warn her to keep her smart remarks to herself.

The minute the trailer pulled into the road to Virginia Key and the quaint, colorful fishing village that had been constructed for use as a working film set, Veronica practically ran in search of Hank. It was the first time she'd ever been on the set before her call.

Michael stood in the doorway and watched her go.

"Are you satisfied?" Molly demanded. "You were actually cruel in there."

"I was doing my job," he retorted, lifting his sunglasses so she couldn't miss the banked fury in his eyes. "And the next time you decide to interfere, I'll charge you with obstruction of justice."

Molly gaped at him. "You're serious, aren't you?"

"You're damned right. I wanted to put the fear of God into her in there. She knows something and I want to know what. With you and Meyerson rushing to her defense, she squirmed off the hook."

"She's a human being, dammit. Not some fish you're trying to reel in."

"She is a murder suspect," he said flatly. "Maybe the best one we've got."

"She didn't do it," Molly countered.

"Thank you for your unbiased, fact-based opinion," he snapped. "Now, if you'll excuse me, I'll get over to headquarters so I can take a look at the reports Les just faxed to me."

"How are you going to get back?"

"Unless I miss my guess, Otis Jenkins followed us over here in his car. He'll take me. I think he'll be very interested in what Les has to say about your innocent star."

Before Molly could demand to know what he meant by that, he'd crossed the street and climbed into Jenkins's unmarked car, which was indeed waiting.

Molly stared after them as the car's tires spun on the dirt shoulder before making a U-turn and heading out at a speed a good twenty miles an hour over the limit. Molly hoped they bounced over a speed bump at that pace and had some sense knocked into their hard heads.

If Veronica Weston refused to answer Michael's questions, there was one other person who had the same information, Molly realized as she brushed away yet another mosquito. After days of rain and weeks of still, hot, humid air, the pesky insects had multiplied into irritating swarms. The production assistant with the can of bug spray was the most popular man on the set.

Duke Lane had raised the issue of some secret he and Greg Kinsey had shared involving Veronica. Molly had no doubt that his quick denial had been a lie. She walked down the dirt path from the set until she located his trailer parked in the scant shade offered by a row of Australian pines.

Duke's terse "Yes" was all she got in response to her knock. She opened the trailer door and stepped inside, savoring the dark interior and chill air. A flute sonata that Molly recognized as Mozart's played softly.

The actor was lounging back in a padded swivel chair, his feet propped on an ice chest. His hands were folded in his lap. A dog-eared, open book lay on his chest. Thoreau's *Walden.* She would have considered it an odd choice had she not read that he was among those fighting to save the lovely, historic pond and its serene surrounding forest from developers.

Molly couldn't tell if Duke's eyes were open or not. Despite the dim lighting, he was wearing his sunglasses.

"We need to talk," she said, taking the chair opposite him.

"About cabbages and kings?"

"About Greg Kinsey and Veronica Weston."

"Sorry. No can do."

"Why not? You obviously know something. Veronica's terrified."

Duke whipped off his glasses, lowered his feet to the floor and leaned forward, his expression intent. "You know the hell of it? I really did throw that comment out just to see what happened. I really don't know a damned thing. I just picked up on some weird vibes about those two over the last few weeks. I took a chance that my observation would shake Veronica enough to get her to cooperate in that last scene. I was as stunned as anybody when she reacted the way she did."

"I don't believe you."

"It's the truth."

"Okay, let's talk about those vibes, then. What did you see or think you saw?"

"You want a beer?"

Molly shook her head. He opened the cooler, withdrew a light beer in a glass bottle, and popped off the cap. After he'd taken a long, slow swallow, he sat back in his chair.

"I guess it started with the way Greg watched her. I mean the woman's a beauty, especially for someone her age, but Greg always had this slightly awestruck look on his face. You know what I mean?"

"Not really," Molly admitted. "Maybe he'd always admired her films and was thrilled to be working with her."

Duke considered the explanation. "Oh, there was some of that. No doubt about it. But this was something else, something personal."

"Are you saying he was attracted to her? It wouldn't be the first time an older woman appealed to a younger man."

"Hell, no. Greg had a type. Dark-haired, thin to the point of emaciation. Like Laura and that Italian model he fell for. He also liked to play the role of mentor, liked the adoration. Veronica doesn't fit into that mold at all. She seemed to appreciate his talent, but she certainly wasn't in awe of him."

"Are you saying this feeling, whatever it was, was more on Greg's side than on Veronica's?"

He hesitated before answering. "Yeah. I think it was."

"How well did you know Greg?"

"Professionally. We didn't socialize, either before production started or since. We have different agendas."

"Meaning he chases women and you don't," Molly suggested with as much subtlety as she could manage.

Duke grinned ruefully. "You can say it, Molly. I'm gay. It's not something I bother to hide. People can accept me or not. My agent says I'm nuts to go public. He thinks it'll hurt me in the long run, but so far I've done okay. I don't regret being so straight-forward about my sexuality."

"You tried to hide it when we were with Michael the other day. You referred to your squeeze several times in a way that implied it was a woman."

He shrugged. "Cops make me nervous."

"You guessed he was a cop? He hadn't even been assigned to the case at that point."

"Observing people is what makes a good actor. I know all the signs. Besides, he had too many questions for some casual acquaintance of yours. I figured I'd play out the scene and see what happened."

"Okay, since you know, then you probably also know he wondered if you had a thing for Greg."

"So he said. I didn't. Why waste energy on something that can't be?"

"But there is someone here with you? A man?"

Duke nodded. "Don't bother trying to speculate. He's not on the film, not even in the business."

"But he is your alibi for Saturday night when Greg was shot. Have you told Michael about him?"

"O'Hara has all the information he needs to conclude that I wasn't anywhere near Miami Beach at the time Greg died. I'm sure he's checked it out. He strikes me as a pretty thorough guy."

Molly nodded. "Which means if you are lying about what you know about Veronica and Greg, he'll find out. He won't be happy that you've withheld information."

"Do you believe me?"

She gazed into his guileless eyes and decided that whatever else Duke Lane might skirt the truth about, he wasn't lying about this. On some things she simply had to go with her instincts, and he had convinced her.

"Yes," she told him finally. "I believe you. But if you think of anything else, anything that might explain these feelings of yours about the two of them, will you pass it along?"

"To you or the cop?"

"I have a hunch the cop would prefer it if you gave the information to him firsthand." She grinned. "I wouldn't mind hearing it second, though."

Duke nodded. "That's a promise, then."

She glanced at the table and spotted a cellular phone. "Mind if I make a call?"

"Be my guest."

She dialed Liza. "I need another favor," she said, when she got her. "I'm stranded out here on Virginia Key and I need to get over to the Beach. Can you pick me up and give me a lift to the police station over there?"

"A break in the case?"

"Could be. Michael's friend in L.A. picked up on something and he's checking it out now. He wouldn't tell me before he left here."

"What'd you do to tick him off? Meddle in his investigation?"

"Something like that."

"And you're on your way to do more med-dling?"

"Only if you'll come get me. Otherwise I'll be stuck over here dying of curiosity."

"Where are you exactly?"

Molly described the location and Duke's trailer.

"Can I meet him?" Liza asked. "We've crossed paths at a couple of these big environmental fundraisers, but we've never met. I'd like to tell him how much I admire his idealism."

"If you get here before Hank calls him to the set, I'm sure Duke would be happy to hear he has yet another fan."

"On my way."

Duke's gaze had narrowed at Molly's end of the conversation. "Not some teenybop-per? You wouldn't do that to me."

"Actually this fan admires your mind. She's tackling the rain forest this month."

Duke sank back in his chair and replaced his sunglasses. "Call me when she gets here. I'm gonna meditate."

The hum of the air-conditioner had almost lulled Molly to sleep in the couple of minutes it took Liza to arrive. She and Duke compared notes on the environment, mutual friends, and the ozone layer while Molly stared longingly at Liza's car.

"Why doesn't your friend just hang out here with me?" Duke finally suggested. "If she doesn't mind lending you her car, that is. I'll give her a lift home later."

Liza tossed the keys to Molly in mid-sentence. "I guess that's a 'Yes,' " Molly concluded. "I don't suppose either of you has a theory about how I should get my own car back to Key Biscayne later?"

"Have the hunk drive it," Liza said.

"The hunk?" Duke repeated with evident fascination.

"Never mind," Molly said hurriedly. "I'll work it out."

If the look on Michael's face when he and Jenkins tore away an hour before was any indication, she doubted she could count on *the hunk* for much of anything at the moment.

15

Before heading back to Miami Beach, Molly decided to make a quick run home to check on Brian. Although Kevin's mom looked after both boys during the summer, she worried about his becoming in essence a latch-key kid. Fortunately, Brian had become a favorite of Nestor, the condo's head of security. He was a former Nicaraguan Freedom Fighter, and she knew no harm would come to her son as long as Nestor was on duty.

She pulled up in the circular drive in front of the building and parked the car. Nestor greeted her with a worried look and a barrage of Spanish. The only word she understood clearly was *esposo*.

"Whose husband?" she demanded of the obviously distressed guard. "Not mine? Here?"

"*Sí, sí,*" Nestor said. "Senor DeWitt. *Aquí.*"

548

"Oh, dear Lord," Molly said and took off at a run. What was Hal up to now?

Upstairs she found her son planted on the sofa. A stubborn, sullen expression on his face exactly matched that on his father's. Hal was pacing, his long angry strides taking him from living room to dining room, from the front door to the balcony's sliding glass doors.

"Brian, go to your room, please," Molly said, every muscle in her body tied in knots.

He didn't waste a second complying, which told her just how tense things had been before her arrival.

"What are you doing here, Hal?" she said quietly, determined to fight the urge to scream at him at the top of her lungs.

He glared at her belligerently. "I came to see my son."

"Why were the two of you arguing if it was as simple as that?"

"He wanted me to leave with him," Brian said from the hallway. Obviously he'd never made it all the way to his room.

"Okay, Brian, leave us alone now, will you?"

He looked undecided.

"It's okay," she told him. "I promise."

As soon as she was certain he had finally gone, she whirled on Hal. "Don't you ever,

ever do something like this again. If I have to I'll go to court, have our custody agreement invalidated, and get a restraining order against you."

"You weren't here. What the hell difference does it make to you if I spend a few extra hours with my son?"

Molly took a deep breath and tried to calm down. "If I thought for one minute that was all you'd intended, I would be delighted. Brian would be thrilled."

"What makes you think it was anything more?" he said sullenly.

"The fact that you came roaring in here on Sunday threatening to take him away. The fact that you usually cancel half the days you're supposed to spend with him. The fact that you haven't called him once except on Friday nights to let him know when you'll pick him up. Should I go on?"

Hal remained stonily silent.

"You don't want a son," she said in a low voice. "You want a weapon to hold over my head, and I can assure you, Hal, that I will never, ever allow you to use Brian that way. He's a great kid and he still loves you. Don't do anything to cost yourself that love."

Hal sighed and sank down on the sofa. He ran his hand through his thinning hair. "All this stuff you get yourself mixed up in, it makes me crazy. What's happened to you?"

Molly regarded him sadly. "I've grown up."

"You consider it grown-up to get yourself involved in two murder investigations within six months?"

"Dammit, Hal, I don't go out searching for dead bodies. But when something like these murders happens, I'm going to do whatever I can to see that the killer is caught."

"That's why we have police, or hadn't you heard? Maybe that's the real truth. You've got the hots for that Cuban cop who was hanging around here on Sunday."

"Whether I do or don't is none of your concern. Now, if you don't mind, I need to spend a few minutes with Brian before I go back to work. You can let yourself out."

With that she left him where he was sitting and went to Brian's room. She found him staring at a video game on the TV screen. Some kind of ooze was swallowing up the good guys and her son was doing nothing to stop it. She sat down beside him.

"You okay?"

"I guess." He looked at her solemnly. "He wanted me to go home with him. I told him I couldn't, not without asking you." Tears welled up in his eyes. "I don't have to go, do I?"

"Of course you don't have to go. Not today. But your father does love you. Sometimes he just doesn't see how to let you know that. Can you try to remember that and give him a chance?"

"I love him, too, but not when he acts all crazy the way he did today."

"He did that because he was worried about you and mad at me."

"Why?"

"He thinks because Greg Kinsey was killed that you might be in danger too."

"That's dumb."

"I know that and you know that, but your dad worries. Remember how you used to be scared of the dark until he showed you that there was nothing hiding in the closets or under the bed? We need to show him that the things he's scared about aren't there either. Okay? Can you help me do that?"

He swiped his tears away with the back of his hand. "Has he gone?"

"I think so."

"Can I go to Kevin's now?"

She ruffled his hair, which was about as much affection as he would allow these days without squirming. "You bet," she told him.

"I'll try to get home early. We'll order a pizza."

"Neato," he said, his grin back in place. "See you, Mom."

"Yeah, see you." *I love you,* she said to herself.

A half hour later Molly stood outside Jenkins's office and tried to work up the courage to knock on the door. Not only did Michael look busy, he looked angry. Either the papers in front of him didn't contain the information he'd hoped for or it was worse than he'd expected. She figured it was a toss-up as to which it was. The only way to find out was to go inside.

She opened the door and stepped into the cramped room. "Should I go or stay?" she asked when he finally looked up.

"Stay," he said grimly. He waved in the general direction of a chair buried under layers of files.

"Wasn't the report what you'd hoped it would be?"

"It's interesting," he said, tossing it over. "Take a look."

Surprised, Molly took the faxes and began to read through them. They were the investigator's reports on Jeffrey Meyerson. While they didn't offer anything concrete to prove that he hadn't sneaked into town, shot Kinsey, and then feigned a much later arrival, they also shot the hell out of the theory that he'd latched on to Veronica for her money.

Jeffrey Meyerson owned enough property in Beverly Hills, Santa Monica, and Malibu to support a hundred households in lavish style. He'd inherited some, parlayed his investments into a level of wealth that few men even imagined, and shared his bounty with half the charities in Los Angeles. He had an apartment in Rome, another in Paris, one in London, and an entire floor in a co-op facing Central Park in New York.

According to half a dozen bankers, real estate experts, and civic leaders, the only tarnish on Meyerson's glittering record was a brief bout with an addiction to pain-killers prescribed following a particularly nasty bumpy landing of his private plane. He'd considered that a warning and had sold the jet thereafter and booked himself into first class on commercial flights. His most recent had been on Saturday night into Miami.

He had never dabbled in Hollywood's riskiest business, films, until this past year when he'd taken a gamble on a small studio that reportedly insisted on a high level of artistic integrity.

Molly glanced up. "Let me guess. That studio was financing this picture for GK Productions."

"Bingo."

"Is that how Veronica got the part?"

"Les says everyone at the studio is very tight-lipped about which came first, the financing or Greg's casting of Veronica."

"It would devastate her to discover that he only hired her to please Jeffrey."

"And we don't know that's what happened. Care to make a few calls to your contacts and see what the scuttlebutt is?" he asked.

"Vince won't like it."

"Blame it on me. Besides, he'll like it even less if we don't solve this case in the next day or two."

Molly tried to determine who might know more about how the financing for *Endless Tomorrows* was arranged. Laura Crain would doubtlessly know. So would Daniel Ortiz. Unfortunately, they were both on hand and still considered suspects. She doubted they'd want to chat about Meyerson's role in GK Productions.

Unofficially, though, one person in L.A. might talk. Greg's agent, the man who'd put the deal together. Alan Nivens had the hottest agency in town at the moment. He liked to boast of the deals he made, and Greg had been one of his most shining success stories. Molly had met him once on a trip to the Coast and knew he had been influential in convincing Greg to film in Miami.

She flipped open the thick address book she kept in her purse and dialed his number. His secretary put her right through.

"Alan, I'm so sorry about what happened to Greg," she said.

"I know you are, babe. I'm devastated. Everyone out here's in mourning. Do the cops know any more?"

"They're working on it. You could help them out, though."

"Anything, babe. Name it. I won't rest until I know Greg's killer is in jail."

"What do you know about a man named Jeffrey Meyerson?"

"Social bigwig, charities, real estate," he said without an instant's hesitation. Then more cautiously, he asked, "How'd his name crop up?"

"I hear he bankrolled this picture."

Now Alan did pause. "Where'd you hear it?"

"It doesn't matter. Is it true?"

"He put some money in it, yes."

"Before or after Greg cast Veronica Weston?"

Alan chuckled. "I knew I liked you, babe. You are one very smart cookie."

"Come on, Alan. Quit the flattery and tell me."

"Meyerson and Weston are an item. Everyone out here knows that."

"Is that why Greg cast her?" she repeated.

She heard Alan's fingers drumming on his desk.

"Absolutely not," he said finally, a little too emphatically. "He liked her work, or at least that's what he told me. I couldn't shake him on it. Meyerson got into the act later. Much later, as a matter of fact. Greg didn't want to go to him at all, but Veronica insisted when she realized the picture might not get made."

"Thanks," she said. "I'll keep you posted on the investigation."

"They gonna release Greg's body soon? We want to schedule a memorial."

"I'm sure his family will be contacted as soon as the police say it's okay."

"He has no family. They should call me. The kid was like a son to me. I'll take care of the arrangements."

Since Alan Nivens wasn't much more than ten years older than Greg, Molly doubted the sentiment, but she didn't call him on it. "I'll see that the police are told," she said.

"Told what?" Michael wanted to know as soon as she'd hung up.

"That Alan wants to be notified when Greg's body can be released. He wants to schedule a memorial service."

"Should be in a day or two. What else did he have to say? I gathered from what you said he knew about Meyerson's involvement with the film."

"He swears the appeal to Meyerson was a last-ditch attempt to salvage the film. Veronica insisted on asking him, reportedly against Greg's wishes. No one else wanted to play, probably because of Veronica's reputation for drinking, although Alan didn't come out and say that."

"So Jeffrey didn't demand the casting as part of his agreement to finance?"

"Alan swears hiring Veronica was Greg's decision and that it came prior to the contact with Meyerson. He doesn't know why Greg insisted on it so stubbornly."

While they both tried to figure out the implications of the report and what Molly had learned earlier from Duke, the phone rang. As Michael listened to the caller, only a slight widening of his eyes gave any indication that he found what was being said to be fascinating.

"Well?" Molly demanded the minute he'd hung up.

"Just wait."

"For what?"

Before he could respond, the fax began spewing out pages. Michael picked them up and started to read. His blank expression didn't give away anything. It was driving Molly nuts.

"Are you going to share or am I going to have to rip those pages away from you?"

Michael stared at the report for another full minute before tossing it over to Molly. "See what you make of this."

"What?"

"Just read it."

The investigator had faxed a report from a private hospital about a hundred miles north of Los Angeles. It was dated slightly more than thirty-one years earlier. The name on the top meant nothing to her.

"Who on earth is Francine Weatherly?"

"According to Les's sources in L.A., that was the name of a character from a movie."

"A movie? When?"

"Thirty, thirty-one years ago. The role was played by Veronica Weston. It earned her an Academy Award nomination for best supporting actress."

Molly gaped. "You're suggesting that Veronica entered some hospital using her character's name as a pseudonym nearly thirty-one years ago? Why bother? She certainly didn't hide the fact that she went into that alcohol treatment program last year."

"Maybe she felt that was a whole lot more socially acceptable than having a child out of wedlock and giving the baby away."

Molly regarded him with astonishment. "She had a baby? That's never been reported. Never."

"Obviously that was the point."

Molly didn't believe it. Beyond the bouts of drinking, there had never been the slightest hint of scandal surrounding Veronica Weston. Granted, she didn't strike Molly as the maternal type, but would she have given up a baby for adoption and kept the secret all these years? She studied the hospital record and the attached birth certificate trying to imagine some other conclusion. She couldn't come up with one.

"There's something more, isn't there?" she said, studying Michael's disgustingly smug expression. She'd seen that expression on his face before, always when he was this close to wrapping up a case.

"Haven't you figured it out yet?" he said

with an infuriating, teasing glint in his eyes.

"Stop playing guessing games with me and spit it out."

"Look at the birthdate," he urged patiently. "Look familiar?"

June 15, 1961. It was familiar because the cast had celebrated a birthday on that date. Greg Kinsey's birthday.

"Oh, dear God," Molly murmured as she finally made the connection. "You're suggesting that Veronica was Gregory's mother, aren't you?" She stared at Michael. "Is that really possible? Are you sure?"

"I'm not sure of anything, but it would certainly explain why Gregory was so determined to give her a break. It would explain those vibes Duke said he felt whenever he was around the two of them."

"You think Greg knew she was his mother?"

"It's the only thing that makes sense. Les is still checking out whether he could have found out. I expect another call in a few minutes. He has some sources with those groups that help adoptees track down their natural parents. Besides, I'm not that fond of coincidences, at least not whoppers like this."

"What about Veronica, though? Does she know?"

"That's the big question, isn't it? What do you think?"

"I don't think so." She hesitated. "On the other hand, maybe that would explain some of the tension between the two of them. If she was feeling guilty, she'd probably be very short-tempered."

She stared at Michael, her eyes stinging with tears at the implication. "My God, can you imagine what she must be going through, if she does know? How could anyone hide that kind of grief?" She shook her head. "She can't know. As much as I respect her acting abilities, I don't think even she is talented enough to cover up all the sorrow and guilt a mother would feel at the death of a son, especially a son she'd never acknowledged."

Michael stood up. "There's only one way to find out. As soon as Les calls back, we'll go talk to Veronica."

16

Molly checked the production schedule and saw that shooting was to end by dusk. It was nearly eight thirty now. In no more than an hour Veronica would be back at the hotel having dinner and studying her lines for the next day.

The film's already rigorous shooting schedule had become even tighter with the necessity of making up for the delays due to Greg's death and earlier snafus in production. Violent thunderstorms had postponed one day of outdoor shots. Another day had stalled when three key people had gotten food poisoning from food left too long without refrigeration on location.

"I think we should wait and go to the hotel," she told Michael. "Veronica shouldn't hear something like this on location, not with everyone around."

"You're right. Let's grab a sandwich or

something and then get over to the hotel to wait."

"Just let me call Brian. I promised him pizza tonight."

Michael regarded her evenly. "Maybe that's not a promise you should break." Years of childhood separation from his own mother had made him ultra sensitive to parent-child relationships.

Molly was torn herself. Michael was right, especially after what had happened earlier with Hal. But Veronica was likely to need her, too. Least important but certainly a factor was her own curiosity.

If what Michael was surmising about the relationship between Greg and Veronica was true, then everything hinged on whether the actress knew about it. If she hadn't known, then she could still reasonably be considered a strong suspect. If she had known — or even guessed without actual confirmation — then Molly couldn't believe that Veronica could have fired the shot that killed her son.

"If Liza's home, maybe she'll order pizza tonight. Then I'll make it up to Brian tomorrow."

"I thought you left Liza on location with Duke Lane."

"I did, but he promised to drive her home. I think he wrapped up earlier today than

Veronica. It only takes about five minutes to get to the condo from Virginia Key."

Liza picked up on the second ring. She was at home with Duke Lane. Molly knew better than to think it was anything more than mutual love of the environment, so she didn't hesitate to ask if Brian could join them.

"I think there's been a break in the case. I'd like to stay here and see how it plays out."

"What's happened?" Liza asked.

"I can't say yet. Not until we know more."

"We?"

"The police," Molly corrected over the sound of Liza's disbelieving laughter. She added defensively, "I'm involved, too, you know."

"You're nosy," Liza countered. "So am I. Stop in the minute you get home. Brian will be fine here with us. Should I call down to Kevin's or will you?"

"I'll call. I need to explain to him why I'm breaking a promise."

Brian took the news with stoic good humor. "You always want squishy mushrooms on the pizza, anyway. Liza doesn't like those."

Molly teased him right back. "Liza also won't let you eat meat, kiddo, so forget the sausage and pepperoni."

"Who says? She always lets me order anything I want. She just picks it off of her part and I get extra."

"Sounds like a deal to me."

"You gonna catch the killer tonight?"

"I don't know," Molly said honestly. "But we may be getting close to figuring it out."

"Is Michael with you?" he asked, a worried note creeping into his voice.

"Yes."

She heard his tiny sigh of satisfaction. "Then he'll take care of you."

Molly glanced across the desk and met Michael's gaze. "You bet," she said.

"Can I talk to him?"

"Sure." She handed the phone across the desk, then listened to Michael's solemn conversation with her son.

"I promise," he vowed, his gaze still holding hers. "I will take very good care of your mother. Later, sport."

When he'd hung up, a smile played about his lips. "I guess I have my job cut out for me."

"Oh?" she said, her cheeks flaming. There was no telling what instructions Brian had given on her behalf.

"I am not to keep you out too late. I am not to let you get anywhere near a gun. And

I am not to let you get kidnapped by the killer again." He smiled ruefully. "He reminded me that I fell down on the job last time."

"He still thinks you walk on water."

"And you?"

"I think I'll plead the Fifth on that one."

"Worried about incriminating yourself, huh?"

"Never mind. Can we get out of here now? I feel Otis Jenkins's hostility practically bouncing off these walls."

"I know what you mean. Fortunately, I talked the brass into letting him be the one to fly out to L.A. to dig around for things like the incorporation papers on GK Productions and Greg's will. He was more than happy to be out of this head-to-head rivalry. He should be there soon. Hopefully, he can dig up something concrete by tomorrow. Les said he'd help him with contacts."

They were nearly out the door when Francesca and her photographer came up the steps of the police station.

"What brings you two over this way?" Michael inquired. "Not thinking of flying back to Italy, are you?"

"We would like to go, yes," Giovanni replied. "Can you not release us, if we promise to fly back any time we are needed?"

Michael shook his head. "Sorry. I just need you to stick around a few days more." He still held their passports to assure their compliance.

Francesca muttered a torrent of Italian. The photographer retorted with one terse word, which silenced her for a moment. She appealed to Molly with a look. "I wish to say good-bye to Gregory. Is possible?"

Molly gaped at her. "You want to go to the morgue?"

Giovanni threw up his hands in a gesture of frustration. "She is crazy. I cannot talk her out of this. She says she needs, how can I say in English, to closing the door."

Even with the slight mangling of the phrase, Molly understood what he meant. Naturally the young girl felt she needed closure, but Molly shook her head. "I don't think this would be a good idea," she told her. "His wound is very bad. You would not like to remember him like this."

Michael put a hand on the model's shoulder. "She's right. Let it go."

Francesca uttered a tremulous sigh, her expression defeated. "I cannot do this?"

"You could," Michael said gently. "But I would advise against it."

She looked from him to Molly, then to

Giovanni. "I will not go, then."

The photographer put his arm around her and led her away.

"She's not really on your list of suspects anymore, is she?"

"The long list, not the short list," Michael replied, watching the girl leave. "That photographer could make the short list, though. He's obsessed with her."

"That's what I thought, too. And he admits coming to Veronica's trailer after her."

"Where would he get a gun, though? It always comes back to that. He didn't bring one into the country. I checked on that."

"This is Miami," she reminded him. "Guns aren't exactly impossible to lay your hands on."

"If you know where to look, who to ask. You think he knows the right people?"

"Probably not," she admitted. "But neither does Veronica."

"We'll see," he said. "We'll see."

An hour later, after they'd sampled several appetizers at an upscale Middle Eastern restaurant, Molly and Michael took the elevator up to Veronica's suite. Jeffrey Meyerson greeted them at the door, his expression unwelcoming.

"We need to have a talk with Ms. Weston," Michael told him.

"Now's not a good time," Jeffrey said. "Couldn't you come back later? Maybe tomorrow."

"No," Michael said. "We need to see her now."

"It's okay, darling," Veronica called from the bedroom. "Let them in."

Jeffrey looked unhappy, but he stepped out of their way and gestured toward the living room. A room service tray held coffee, cups, and half-eaten chicken salad sandwiches on croissants. A pale pink rosebud — a lover's gesture or a hotel nicety — provided a festive note to the skimpy meal. An empty vodka bottle had been upended in the trash can and a fresh bottle, its cap still off, sat on the wet bar. Obviously Veronica had given up any pretense of being on the wagon.

Jeffrey rinsed out the cups, dried them, and offered coffee. His hand shook as he poured the still-steaming liquid into two cups. Either he was hung over from the luncheon champagne he'd finished off or very nervous. Molly wondered again what Jeffrey Meyerson had to be nervous about. His gaze kept darting to the manila folder Michael had placed on the credenza.

It was fifteen minutes before Veronica joined them. During that time Jeffrey kept up a constant barrage of inconsequential chatter, like a host making small talk with strangers at a dinner party arranged by his wife for her friends.

Veronica swept into the room at last, her trademark chiffon billowing behind, this time in a shade of pale yellow that erupted into brilliant orange at the hem.

"I'm so sorry to have kept you waiting," she said as she waved in the general direction of the bottle of vodka. Jeffrey took the hint and poured a double shot over ice. He handed the heavy crystal glass to her and served up a warning look at the same time.

"What can I do for you?" Veronica asked. Nothing in her tone or her manner betrayed any hint of nervousness.

"I'd like you to take a look at this, see if it means anything to you," Michael said, handing her the folder. Jeffrey looked as if he wanted to snatch it away from her.

Veronica took one look at the hospital record and birth certificate made out in the name of Francine Weatherly and turned the shade of library paste. She crumpled into an armchair, the swirls of chiffon settling around her.

"Are you okay?" Molly asked, concerned

by her lack of color.

"No," Veronica said flatly. She stared at Michael. "What does this have to do with anything? Why would you dredge up something like this after all these years? It can't possibly have any bearing on the case."

Before Michael could respond, Molly stepped in. She sat beside Veronica and held the woman's hand as she said gently, "Look at the birth certificate again, the date. Remember when we celebrated Greg's birthday?"

"What are you saying?" Veronica whispered, her eyes wide with shock.

"I'm asking you if there is any chance, any chance at all, that Gregory could have been your son."

"Oh, my God," Veronica said, tears spilling down her cheeks. "Oh, my God."

Jeffrey looked as if he wanted to murder the pair of them. "Why did you have to blurt it out like that? Leave us alone," he demanded. "Just leave us alone."

Michael regarded him apologetically. "I'm afraid we can't do that. If it's true, this could have a material bearing on this case." He turned a compassionate gaze on Veronica. "Is there any chance?"

Her hands covering her face, Veronica nodded. "It's possible, but I didn't know. I swear to you I didn't know."

"We think that Greg did know."

"He did," Jeffrey said, defeat in his voice. "I spoke to him on the day he died. I had always thought there was something a little odd about the way he fought so hard to keep Veronica on this film. At first I thought it was simply that he liked her work, wanted to give her a chance to redeem herself, but as time went on, I saw that it was much more than that. I did a little investigating of my own."

Veronica regarded him incredulously. "You knew? You knew and you never said a word to me? How could you, Jeff? How could you do that to me?"

"I had to, my dear. Can't you see that? I didn't want to tell you until I knew for certain. When I found out, I asked Greg about it. He admitted it. We both agreed that I should be here when he told you. That's why I flew in on Saturday, to be with you when you found out that he was your son. When I got here and discovered that he'd been murdered, I didn't know what to do. I wasn't sure what the implications were."

"So you never said a word to anyone?" Molly asked.

"Not one word," he confirmed.

"Did anyone else know?"

"To my knowledge, no."

"But someone must have," Molly said. "Someone who would have benefited from Greg's will, but only if he had no living relatives."

"Exactly," Michael concurred. "I hope to hell Jenkins can get his hands on that will tonight."

Molly's gaze was fixed on Veronica. She looked shattered, as if nothing in the world made sense to her anymore. Molly guessed she needed to talk, to say out loud what she had hidden for all these years.

"It just can't be," she said over and over. "It would be too bizarre, too awful."

Michael said, "It's probably not necessary now that we know he admitted the truth to Jeffrey, but I'm trying to get Gregory's adoption records unsealed. What I have so far indicates that he was adopted by a wealthy Santa Barbara family. The birth date matches."

Veronica kept shaking her head. "I never knew," she said sorrowfully. "I never understood why he wanted so much to work with me, why he fought the studio. You think it was because he knew even then, months ago?"

"Friends of his adoptive parents told

police in Santa Barbara that he'd been looking for his natural mother for several years.
They said he knew it upset his parents, so
he'd never told them whether he'd traced
her. They both died not knowing if he'd suc-
ceeded."

"Why did you give him up?" Molly asked,
hoping that she was doing the right thing in
trying to get the actress to open up. "In the
sixties no one would have condemned you
for having a child without being married."

Veronica shook her head. "You're wrong
about that. My son wasn't illegitimate. I was
married when he was conceived, but my
husband was a real bastard. I didn't want
him near my child."

Molly was shocked. "There's never been
any mention of a marriage in any of the bios
I've read, not back then."

"The studio kept it hushed up. I was
barely eighteen when we got married and
just getting a reputation as some sort of sex
goddess. The studio and my husband, who'd
directed my first two films, agreed it would
spoil the image if the marriage were made
public. Everyone was very paternalistic
about it, and I was too naïve to argue."

"Then what happened?" Molly prodded,
when Veronica seemed uninclined to go on.
"Why did you give up your baby?"

Veronica took a deep breath. She kept her gaze fastened on Molly as if she couldn't bear to face anyone else in the room.

"When things fell apart, I tried to get a divorce, but by then my husband was convinced his fate was linked to mine. It was hard enough battling that without telling him about a baby. He would never have let me go."

"But he did let you go," Molly said.

"In a way. I told everyone I needed to get away, to get my head together. Then I went into hiding for the last few months of the pregnancy. I arranged for a private adoption so there would be fewer official questions. I couldn't risk anything leaking out in the press. It was best all the way around to give up my son, but I never forgot about him. Never. I regretted it more than I can say, but it was the only way I could think of for both of us to survive."

Again tears welled in her eyes. "Do you know the real tragedy of all this? I saw that Greg cared for me. Underneath all the fighting, all the screaming over the script, I could see that he really cared what happened to me on-screen. I didn't understand why it mattered so much to him, but it was there, always. The caring. The demand for every shot to be perfect. I thought it was simply that he was a perfectionist. He knew I was his mother and he loved me, but he never knew, *never,* how much I really loved the son I gave away."

As Veronica wept over the loss of that son, over the harsh words they'd exchanged in the brief time they'd had together, Molly and Michael slipped out of the suite. In the elevator, Molly saw the haunting pain shadowing Michael's eyes and realized that memories of his own childhood must have been stirred by Greg and Veronica's tragedy. The years he had been alone in the U.S., his mother still in Cuba.

She silently slid her hand into his. At first he resisted. She could feel his muscles tense. Then he relaxed and curled his fingers around hers. He said nothing as they walked away from the hotel. He didn't need to. Even without words, she had never felt closer to him.

17

"I still can't figure out how we're any better off now than we were before we found out about the connection between Veronica and Gregory," Molly grumbled, trying to speak loudly enough to be heard over the sidewalk café's reggae band. "Knowing about the relationship, it would make more sense if he'd been furious over her abandonment and had killed her."

"Think about motive," Michael said patiently as his gaze automatically scanned the crowd. "Who has the best motive?"

Watching him, Molly wondered if he ever fully relaxed or if his cop instincts were always at work. She had a hunch that if she asked an hour from now he would be able to describe to the last detail what the patrons around them looked like, their mannerisms, and any visible idiosyncrasies they had.

"Are you listening to me?" he asked, when

she'd gone a full five minutes saying nothing.

"Hmm?" Molly blinked, then wondered
exactly why it was that they were possibly
the only two people sitting here on a moonlit
night with something other than romance
on their minds. Maybe because murder had
a dampening effect on the libido. She
dragged her thoughts back to the gist of his
question.

"I'm listening," she said.

"Okay, then. Would the relationship between the star and the director have given
someone else a motive to kill him?"

Michael sounded like an instructor trying
to make a point to a rather dull, dim-witted
student. Oddly enough, she didn't resent it.
At least he was sharing information with
her, treating her insights with respect, forc-
ing her to be analytical rather than emotional. Personally, she thought a good blend
of gut instinct and a keen eye for the facts
were exactly what made him such a good
detective. He, however, seemed unwilling to
admit to the conclusions he reached intui-
tively. She slowly sipped her wine and gave
the question the consideration he obviously
expected.

"Yesterday, before we found out about his
background, I would have said Jeff Meyer-

son," she admitted. "He's engaged to Veronica. Or so he says. She doesn't seem all that committed. At any rate, if he's planning to marry her, maybe he didn't want a son in line as an heir to her estate. I should have known it would be too tidy and too obvious."

"Don't beat yourself up over it. You had the right idea, just the wrong person, at least on that basis. From everything you told me, Veronica doesn't have much of an estate. She needed this job just to survive, right?"

"Yes. She told me as much."

"And he has a fortune."

"So we discovered. Then we can scratch Meyerson off the list?"

Michael shook his head. "Not so fast. What if he thought Greg was likely to ruin his relationship with Veronica, that she'd become so caught up in her newfound son that she would no longer spare any time for him? If he's obsessed with her, that could drive him to murder the competition."

Molly was shaking her head before he'd finished. "No way. If he truly loves her, he'd never rob her of the chance to know her son."

"I mentioned obsession, not love."

"If you're going for that angle, then I like our Italian photographer better. He's obsessed with the gorgeous, nubile Francesca."

"You just don't want it to be anyone you know."

"Maybe," she conceded. "It's no fun considering the possibility that someone you know is capable of pulling a gun and shooting down a friend, or at least someone who probably considered him or her a friend."

"Who's your choice, then? You know all of the players better than I do. Hank Murdock benefits from Kinsey's death because he'll get a shot at finishing the movie. Spice that with a professional rivalry and you have a decent motive."

"But he was in the production trailer with witnesses."

"All right, then, Duke Lane. What's his stake in this?"

"None I can imagine. Laura Crain might have pressured Greg into hiring Duke in the first place because of his box-office status, but he and Greg got along. He doesn't need all the publicity the murder has generated. Every female in America already knows who he is. Besides, from what I hear, he wants this picture wrapped in a hurry so he can get on with the next one. I wouldn't have given the man a lot of credit for brains a few days ago, but since then we've talked a couple of times. He's smart.

He has to know that a murder at the least will delay production." She shook her head. "I think we can eliminate Duke."

"Too bad," Michael grumbled.

Molly grinned. "You just hate having a suspect who gets more press attention than you do."

He regarded her indignantly. "You're treading on thin ice, sweetheart. I can get you back on that suspect list faster than you can say 'Lights, camera, action.' "

Molly shook her head confidently. "I don't think so. You want to be out of Miami Beach and back on your own turf too badly to waste time trying to make a case against me."

"Maybe so," he said, sliding his sunglasses down a fraction to level a look at her. "But Otis Jenkins is just itching to take you on."

Molly decided this would be an excellent time to divert Michael's attention in another direction. "How about Daniel Ortiz?"

"If he gets a bigger stake in GK Productions, maybe. Besides, witnesses place him on the set at the time of the shooting. He was setting up for the next shot."

Playing devil's advocate, Molly countered with, "He could have slipped away. Things are so chaotic between scenes, no one would have noticed if he'd left for a minute or two.

Face it, that's all it would have taken to slip over to Veronica's trailer, wait for her to leave, then shoot Greg and count on Veronica's being blamed."

"If that's the scenario, then it had to be someone who didn't know she was his mother. No one would expect a mother to be blamed for shooting her son. How about Laura Crain? What do you think of her as a suspect?"

"Opportunity? Probably. She claims she was back at the hotel, but no one else was there with her."

"No one saw her on the set either."

"Which doesn't mean she wasn't there," Molly argued. "Again, everyone who's actually working has a lot going on between takes. Maybe they'd notice a stranger, but not someone connected with the film, someone they're used to seeing around all the time."

Something was troubling her, but she couldn't quite put her finger on it. She tried to envision the way events that night had unfolded, at least as they knew them.

Greg and Veronica had been inside her trailer, arguing over the script. Then, as she'd been leaving, Francesca had barged in, furious because Greg didn't want her to stay in America with him. Giovanni had come after her, and the two of them had left together, or so he had said. With all that happening and only a limited time period between their departures and the discovery of the body, surely one of them should have spotted the killer, even if they weren't aware of it. Especially if the gunman had stood outside the trailer and fired.

Good Lord, that was it! No one in his right mind would have stood on the side-walk and fired a gun, not with off-duty policemen at each end of the block and other members of the cast and crew all too likely to come along at any second. Greg's killer had to have been inside. She tried to recall the angle of his body in relation to the door, but her memory failed her. She hadn't wanted to remember the way he had looked.

Her excitement began to fade. What difference did it make? They already knew that in all likelihood Greg had been killed by someone who knew him. Anyone in the cast or crew could have traced him to Veronica's trailer, waited for him to be alone, and then gone in on some pretext or another.

"What are you thinking?" Michael asked.

Molly's head was reeling and it wasn't from the wine. "How do you do this? From what I can see there are still a solid half-dozen people with either motive or opportunity."

"You just keep narrowing things down, until there's only one possible conclusion. Then you pray you can come up with enough solid physical evidence to cinch the case."

"Let's talk about the physical evidence a minute. Was there anything odd inside the trailer?"

"Odd in what way?"

"I'm not sure. It just occurs to me that anyone who tracked Greg down in Veronica's trailer, then went in to shoot him may have had some sort of cover story, maybe script notes he needed to see, checks he needed to sign. I don't know. Was there anything in that trailer that shouldn't have been there?"

"Nothing that seemed particularly odd or out of place to me, but let's go check it out. The trailer's been impounded and sealed. I have bags of evidence at the station. Take your pick."

"The bags of evidence, I think."

"Let's go."

When Greg's personal effects were brought out, a shiver sped down Molly's spine. She felt as if she were invading his privacy as she looked through his wallet, then sorted through the rental car keys, some loose change, and a dozen or so scraps of paper. Most of them were little pink message slips with names written in Laura's careful, schoolgirl printing. A couple were scrawled by a masculine hand. Probably Jerry's.

Molly studied the slips. She recognized most of the callers. Alan Nivens had placed three separate calls that night. Jeffrey Meyerson had called once, much earlier in the day. A reporter for *Variety* had called wanting to confirm a rumor. The message didn't note what the rumor was, but apparently Greg had guessed. He had crumpled that message into a tiny ball. Francesca had called twice. And several men whom Molly knew to be connected with the studio had called within minutes of each other.

Those last messages were written in a cramped, angry script. Apparently Laura had been furious about something, perhaps at them, perhaps at having just been forced to convey a message from her competition for Greg's affections. Her pencil had actually poked a hole in the paper on one of the messages.

"Look at this," she said, handing Michael the messages. "Look at the way Laura was bearing down. There's a hole. She must have been irate."

"Over what, though?"

"Being pestered by Francesca and taking it out on the calls that followed?"

"Why didn't she just ignore Francesca's calls, not tell him about them at all? She wrote those messages in a nice, precise hand."

"It would go against the grain for a woman like Laura to fail in her duties, though I'm sure she was tempted to do just that. Besides, Francesca would probably ask Greg why he hadn't returned her calls. He'd guess what had happened and Laura couldn't risk that. She certainly didn't want him to fire her."

Suddenly Molly recalled the way Laura had looked when she'd finally walked into the production trailer after Greg's body had been found. She'd looked tearful, but controlled. Not grief stricken. Molly remembered thinking at the time that it was quite a performance for a woman whose lover had just been shot.

She glanced over the messages again and noted the times they were taken. The last call from Francesca had come barely an hour before she and Jerry had found Greg's body. The calls from the studio came in right after that.

"I think maybe we need to have a talk with Laura," Molly said.

"About?"

"What exactly went on the last time she saw Greg. Judging from these messages, it had to have been in that time span between the time Veronica left Greg in her trailer and the time he was killed."

Michael took the messages back and studied them. "The time's on here, but not the date. He could have been carrying these around for days."

Molly shook her head. "Greg was methodical about messages, in part because of the time difference between here and L.A. He made it a point to go back to pick up his messages about eight every night. That meant it was only five on the Coast and he could return any calls before people left for the day."

"This was Saturday. Would he have worried about business calls on the weekend?"

"Look at the messages. He was getting calls at all hours, every day. Every one of these messages came in between six o'clock and ten p.m."

"But what day?"

"It had to have been Saturday. Otherwise, he would have returned the calls and tossed the messages."

Michael nodded. "If you're sure of that, then let's go have a talk with Laura. If we can place her in that trailer at the critical time, we definitely have a liar."

"More important, we may have a killer." Considering the way she felt about Laura Crain, nothing would have pleased Molly more.

18

They were in the creaking hotel elevator on their way to the production office when Michael's beeper went off. When he saw the calling number, he promptly punched the button to take them straight back down to the first floor.

"Who is it?" Molly wanted to know. It had to be important to keep him from going after the probable killer.

"Jenkins. He could have found something. We ought to know that before we go in to see Laura."

"I could go ahead," Molly suggested, counting on the statistics that indicated a single crime of passion was not indicative of a penchant for shooting down everyone in sight. Maybe she could wrench an admission from Laura by giving her a shoulder to cry on.

"I don't think so," Michael said.

"But I could tell her I needed to check

the production schedule. She'd never know what I was really there for. Maybe she'd open up, if I sounded sympathetic. She doesn't really have a woman around to talk to."

"I thought your impression was that she didn't much like women. Besides, exactly how much snooping around do you figure you could accomplish before she caught on?"

"I'm counting on you to arrive before we get to that point."

"And if I'm delayed?"

"I'll beat a hasty retreat. I promise."

"I need only ask your son about tonight to have a pretty good idea what your promises are worth."

Because the barb struck home, Molly glared at him. "Was that reminder entirely necessary?"

He nodded, his expression grim. "I thought so."

Since his impression of her was so low anyway, Molly didn't feel the least bit guilty for the last-second dash she made back into the elevator as the doors slid closed. She felt an instant's satisfaction as she caught Michael's stunned expression. Or maybe that had been fury.

Okay, so what she was doing was rash and

impulsive and foolhardy. She wasn't actually going to accuse Laura of anything, though. She'd just snoop around a little, sound her out. Maybe she'd even stumble across a gun. Laura might not know Miami well enough to have taken the murder weapon and pitched it into some nearby body of water. There were plenty to choose from, of course, but maybe the producer hadn't been thinking clearly enough to dispose of the gun right away. Hell, it could have been in the bottom of that voluminous purse she carried with her everywhere.

To her surprise, the door to the production office was closed and locked. She knocked, but no one answered. All the better, she thought, as she used the key she'd been issued on the first day of production.

Inside, one lamp burned dimly, casting eerie shadows around the room. The heavy drapes had been drawn, blocking out the silvery moonlight that shimmered on the ocean and at least some of the noise from the street. Suddenly the room seemed spookier than she remembered, perhaps because she'd never been in it alone and at night before. Perhaps because its usual occupant might very well be a murderer.

She wondered if Michael would take the next elevator up after her or if she had time to do some genuine sleuthing. As much as she wanted to poke freely around in drawers, she was forced to admit that she wished he'd hurry up. The closed, dreary atmosphere was giving her the creeps.

So get busy, she told herself. She moved deliberately to the desk and began opening drawers. They were every bit as organized as Laura herself. Files were neatly labeled and in alphabetical order. Bills had been sorted and stamped according to date received. Payment check numbers had been noted. Payroll records were in their own orderly drawer. It all seemed a little compulsive, even to someone used to keeping her own files relatively organized.

Still, so far it was pretty boring stuff, Molly noted as she came upon a file of contracts. Most were standard, according to what she knew of the industry. Duke got a hefty bonus at various stages of the film's success. Veronica's deal guaranteed her specific perks suitable to a legendary glamour queen. The cost was insignificant for most, but they underlined her status as being one step above everyone in the cast except Duke.

A quick scan of the remaining contracts revealed deals with everyone in the cast and crew with the exception of Hank, Daniel, and Laura herself. Molly guessed that was because all of them owned a piece of GK Productions and had their own separate salary arrangements because of it.

The bottom drawer in the desk was locked. Molly found a paper clip, bent it until it was nearly straight, then tried to jimmy the lock. As she was working at it, she noticed scratches in the surrounding wood. They had been there before she'd started her amateur attempt at lock picking. Someone else had wanted access to this very same drawer. Since the desk had been brought in especially for the production office, she knew with absolute certainty that those marks were recent. Presumably, though, Laura would have had a key. Who else would be interested in whatever was locked away?

To know that, she had to get inside. She knelt down to get a better view of the lock. She was still in that incriminating position when the connecting door to Laura's room swung open, filling the office with a bright stream of light.

"What the hell do you think you're doing?" Laura demanded, closing the door carefully behind her before crossing the room.

Molly was reasonably good at thinking on

her feet. Unfortunately she wasn't on her feet. She was on her knees with a paper clip stuck in a locked drawer. She considered lying through her teeth and saying she needed the production schedule, but she knew only too well it was posted quite visibly on the bulletin board beside the door.

Recalling that there had been no file marked PERMITS, she said, "I was hunting for the permits you'll need for tomorrow's shooting schedule. I wanted to be sure you had them all and that they were up-to-date, now that we're running behind by a couple of days."

Laura continued to look skeptical, but she came over, nudged Molly aside and retrieved a file from the top of the desk, the one place Molly hadn't searched. She'd saved the obvious for last, figuring nothing incriminating would be in plain sight.

She stood up and took the file. "Thanks."

"It's awfully late," Laura noted, with a deliberate glance at her watch.

"I know, but I just thought of this and I wanted to be sure it was taken care of."

"You came all the way back from Key Biscayne? Why didn't you just call?"

"Actually, I was still in the neighborhood. I had a meeting with Veronica and it ran late. I stopped for a glass of wine after that."

"With that cop friend of yours?"

Molly nodded.

"Where is he, then?"

"He was beeped. He needed to make a call."

"He could have made it from up here."

"True. I guess he just wanted to be sure it was billed properly since it was long distance."

"Police business, then?"

Molly shrugged. "I assume so." She studied Laura. "I'm surprised you weren't in here working. You usually burn the midnight oil."

"Actually I was exhausted. I thought I'd get a decent night's sleep for a change. I haven't slept well at all since Greg was killed."

"I can imagine," Molly said, wondering why the producer would say she'd gone to bed early, when she was obviously still dressed in her street clothes. Of course, they were slightly disheveled. Maybe she'd fallen asleep with them on.

Laura had carefully put herself between Molly and the desk. Her expression perfectly bland, she said, "If there's nothing else, I think I'll lock up as soon as you've gone. I want to get back to bed."

Just then the phone rang, startling them

both. Laura made no move to pick it up.

"Aren't you going to answer it?"

"No, it's late. The desk will take a message."

"Right," Molly said and started for the door. She stopped and turned back. "One last thing," she said, careful to keep her voice casual. "On the night Greg died he had a message from a reporter that seemed to upset him. Any idea what that was all about?"

Laura shot her an uneasy look. "I don't know what you're talking about."

"But you did take the message, didn't you?"

"Yes, but I didn't cross-examine the man. Now if that's all," she said pointedly.

Defeated, Molly backed toward the door. "I'll see you in the morning," she said as she carefully shut the office door behind her.

In the corridor she lingered outside Laura's door, not the least bit certain why she was doing it. She heard the faint click of the connecting door shutting, then the muffled squeak of mattress springs. Nothing suspicious in that. Laura was doing exactly what she'd said she was going to do. She was going back to bed.

And then Molly heard, plain as day, Hank

Murdock saying, "What took you so long? Who was in there?"

Molly couldn't hear Laura's reply, which didn't much matter since she knew the answer.

"What the devil did she want?" Hank said.

Laura's voice rose slightly. "She said she was looking for the permits for tomorrow's shoot," she said defensively.

Silence followed, then Hank's voice. There was a new, unfamiliar tension to it. "Did you believe her?"

"No, but there's nothing in there that would be worth anything to her. Let her play amateur sleuth if she wants to. For God's sakes, Hank, the sooner they arrest someone for Greg's murder, the better off we'll all be."

Hank muttered a curse, but then the bedsprings squeaked again. Molly got the distinct impression from the subsequent silence that Laura had found a way to ease his mind. She had also given her a whole new angle to consider. She could hardly wait to get downstairs and tell Michael that Hank Murdock had apparently taken up where Greg Kinsey had left off with Laura Crain.

Molly waited nearly ten anxious minutes for the elevator to come before finally deciding it was stuck on another floor. She headed for the stairwell, recalling that Francesca had taken these same steps down on the night of Greg's murder to avoid bumping into Molly or the police.

Molly was halfway down to the street level when she heard running footsteps on the stairs. This wasn't someone who was stealthily sneaking up on her. It was someone in a hurry. Of course, with the elevator not functioning, it could be anyone. She reassured herself that there was no reason for the cold chill that swept over her or the suddenly quickened pumping of her heart.

She hurried her own steps, but the person was clearly gaining on her. She could practically hear whoever it was hitting three steps to every one of her own. The sound reverberated off the walls. She had only one more floor to go when a hand closed over her shoulder, scant inches from her neck where her pulse skittered wildly. A scream began deep inside but choked in her throat.

"Just listen to me, Molly," Laura said in a low voice. "If you do exactly as I say, you'll be just fine. My car is half a block down, right at the end of the alley. We're going to get in it. Understand?"

Since Molly figured Laura's gun was probably aimed about level with her heart, she had no delusions about disagreeing with the producer's plan. The only thing she could do was stall for time, then pray that the side street was still so crowded with passersby that Laura would be able to do nothing if she made a break for it.

"Why, Laura? Why did you kill Greg?"

"I didn't," she said so convincingly that Molly stopped in her tracks.

She whirled around to stare at the producer. "You didn't?" she repeated, unable to keep the astonishment and disbelief out of her voice.

"No, you little fool. But I know who did. I'm trying to save your neck. Now will you hurry up and move before we both get our heads blown off."

This was probably no time for indulging in idle curiosity, but Molly couldn't help herself. "If you didn't do it, who did?"

"Three guesses and the first two don't count."

Suddenly Molly realized that only one person could have sent Laura plunging down this staircase after her. "Hank?" she breathed softly. "When did you know?"

Just then a door somewhere above them opened. "Laura?" Hank called. The plaintive tone of his voice sent a chill down Molly's spine.

Laura motioned toward the door and this time Molly didn't hesitate before racing down the remaining steps. She hit the bar across the door at full force, but it didn't budge.

"What's wrong?" Laura demanded, her gaze directed up the stairwell.

"It's jammed or locked."

"It can't be locked. It's a fire exit. Hit it harder."

Molly threw her full weight against the door just as Hank rounded the final turn in the stairwell. The door burst open just as he aimed his gun at the pair of them.

"I think we'll all leave together," he said softly, gesturing for them to precede him.

Molly was certain her legs would never move again. She froze where she was at the sight of the gun aimed directly at her.

"Move it," Hank said, nudging her with the gun. The cold press of metal sent acid pitching in her stomach.

"Why, Hank?" she said quietly. "Why did you kill him?"

He didn't answer. The only indication she had that he'd even heard her was the increased pressure of that gun against her ribs. He urged them relentlessly down that dark alley. There were no windows looking out on the alley at ground level, so it was unlikely anyone would see them from inside the hotel. Nor were there any cans or bottles she or Laura could kick, creating enough noise to draw attention. Their only chance would come when they reached the street. She tried to concentrate all of her attention on planning for that.

Perspiration beaded on her forehead and the nape of her neck. It ran in icy rivulets down her spine. Hank's silence was the worst of it, worse even than the terrifying press of the gun. If he would just talk to her, she could better sense his mood, better guess the exact moment she ought to run for it. She glanced at Laura and saw that she looked more resigned and weary than terrified.

When had her instincts deserted her? Until tonight she would have bet her life that Hank Murdock was incapable of murder. Now there was every indication that he had killed not only once, but intended to again. What could have driven this quiet, dedicated man to murder?

If he was involved with Laura, would he have been so incensed by Greg's moves on her that he finally shot him in a jealous rage? But why wait until almost the end of the picture? Could the timing have been a last desperate attempt to gain recognition as a director by completing the film in Greg's stead? The motives raced through her mind like film on fast forward, leaving impressions but no conclusions. Obviously Laura possessed some incriminating piece of information that she hadn't shared with anyone else. Did it have to do with those messages?

"Did you hate Greg?" she asked. "I thought the two of you were best of friends."

"We were," he said softly, an unexpected catch in his voice.

Molly seized on that faint hint of emotion. "Then he must have done something to make you very angry that night. What did he do?"

They were almost to the street. She could hear the laughter of a passing couple, the grinding start of a motorcycle. But there was still no response from Hank. The barrel of the gun seemed to tremble against her back. Because he was losing his nerve? Because something she'd said had reminded him that the man who'd died was, in fact, his best friend?

"Did I ever tell you how often Greg spoke of you when we were making plans for this production?" she said. "He respected your work. Maybe even more than you did, he said. He was anxious to see that you got the break you deserved."

"Bullshit," he said succinctly. "He was going to force me out."

"Force you out," Molly repeated slowly. "Could he do that?"

"Yes," Laura said with a sigh. "He had the power to do it. You might as well tell her everything, Hank."

"A few years ago I had some heavy gambling debts," he said, reminding Molly of his claim that he hadn't been in the poker game that night because he no longer gambled.

"Greg loaned me the money to pay them off with my share of the company as collateral."

"But why would he force you out now?"

It was Laura who answered. "The studio had been on him for weeks about cutting overhead. With the picture close to done, they wanted Hank off the payroll. They waved a deal for additional films under his nose if he could streamline the company. That reporter had gotten wind of the studio's offer. He called Greg."

"And me," Hank added. "The son of a bitch called me. That's how I heard about it. Not from Greg. From some stupid reporter."

"You confronted him and he confirmed

it," Molly said.

She dared to turn her head to catch a glimpse of him. His face was an expressionless mask, but his eyes were filled with some dark agony. As if he'd guessed what she could read in his eyes, he looked away. At the same time, they reached the street.

Molly used the tiny fraction of a second while Hank's attention was diverted to wrench free from his grasp and run. She lurched, nearly stumbled, then raced toward Ocean Drive, where she knew there would be more people and safety.

At the corner she ran headlong into Michael. His arms came around her, steel bands of comfort and courage. His gaze locked on hers. "You're okay?"

"Yes," she said shakily. "Go or Hank will get away. Laura's car is at the end of the alley. She's still with him."

Instead, he pulled her tight against him, so she could feel the thundering beat of his heart. "So help me God, if you ever, ever do anything that stupid again, I will break every single bone in your body myself," he swore fervently, adding an impassioned speech in Spanish that she suspected was better left untranslated.

"I'm okay. I swear it. Please, go after Hank."

"He's not going anywhere. He's waiting with Laura right by his car."

Molly's head snapped up. She glanced down the block and saw Hank leaning against the front fender, his shoulders slumped. Laura was holding the gun as if it were something distasteful.

"He's giving up?" she said incredulously.

Michael nodded. "Looks that way," he said as two other officers went down the block to take Hank into custody. As they passed by on their way back to the police cruisers on Ocean Drive, Molly stopped Laura. "Thank you for coming after me."

"I didn't do it for you," Laura said bluntly. "I couldn't let Hank get in any more trouble than he's already in. It was partly my fault in the first place. If only I'd told him what I suspected, he might have been prepared. I might have been able to make him see that it was purely a business decision, that it had nothing to do with his worth as a director. Instead, when that reporter hit him with it, he felt betrayed, by Greg, by me. Add to that the rumors he had to contend with all the time about Greg and me . . ." She shrugged. "It's no wonder he snapped."

"But the gun," Molly said. "Where did he get the gun?"

"I had it. Since I had to deal with large

amounts of money occasionally, I got it for protection. He knew where I kept it."

"But you didn't know he'd taken it?"

"No. Not until tonight when everything started to add up." She glanced at Michael. "You knew, didn't you?"

At Michael's nod, Molly regarded them both with surprise. "When?" she said to Michael.

"Otis Jenkins had a talk with the studio. They told him about cutting Hank loose. He also found out that Laura had a permit for the gun. I tried to call you in the suite twice to warn you to be careful if he was around."

"I only heard the phone ring once," Molly said.

"Hank took the second call," Laura said. "I heard enough to guess what was happening. That's when I came after you."

"Thank you again."

"Can I go to the police station with Hank?" Laura asked Michael.

"No, but I'll give you a lift over there. I have to get over to headquarters and wrap this up. Just give me a couple of minutes with Molly."

Laura nodded and walked away.

"Can you get home okay?" he said, his fingers splayed against her cheek.

"Sure," she said. She'd finally stopped shaking at least five minutes back. "There's one more thing I don't understand."

"What's that?"

"On the night Jeffrey pushed Veronica, was there really a shot?"

"Yes. Hank thought she'd seen him coming out of Greg's trailer that night."

"But when the first shot missed, he never tried to kill her again."

"Probably because he knew by then that Veronica hadn't seen him."

"I wonder how she's doing?"

"Why don't you go up and see her? She'd probably be glad to have a friend around, now that her son's killer has been caught."

Molly touched his cheek. "That's what I love about you. For a tough cop, you're a real softie."

He grinned. "Don't let it get around. It'll ruin me on the streets."

She had started into the hotel, when he said, "Molly."

She turned back.

"I'll give you a call about Sunday."

When Molly regarded him blankly, he said, "The dinner at Tio Pedro's. You aren't going to chicken out on me, are you?"

"Not a chance," she said bravely. After

tonight meeting Michael's family would have to be a piece of cake.

ABOUT THE AUTHOR

Sherryl Woods was born in Arlington, Virginia on July 23, 1944. She graduated from Ohio State University with a degree in journalism. She spent more than ten years working as a journalist, most of them as a television critic for newspapers in Ohio and Florida. For several years, she also coordinated a motivational program for the more than 8,000 employees at the University of Miami-Jackson Memorial Medical Center.

Her first novel, *Restoring Love,* was released in 1982 under the pseudonym of Suzanne Sherrill. Her second book, *Sand Castles,* was published the same year under the pseudonym of Alexandra Kirk. In 1985, she started writing under her real name and by 1986, she was writing full-time. She has written over 100 romance and mystery novels including *Not at Eight, Darling; An*

O'Brien Family Christmas; Sweet Magnolias; the Chesapeake Shores series; The Molly Dewitt Mysteries series; and *The Christmas Bouquet.*

The employees of Thorndike Press hope you have enjoyed this Large Print book. All our Thorndike, Wheeler, and Kennebec Large Print titles are designed for easy reading, and all our books are made to last. Other Thorndike Press Large Print books are available at your library, through selected bookstores, or directly from us.

For information about titles, please call:
    (800) 223-1244

or visit our website at:
    gale.com/thorndike

To share your comments, please write:
    Publisher
    Thorndike Press
    10 Water St., Suite 310
    Waterville, ME 04901